A BRIDE'S STORY

9

Kaoru
Mori

TABLE OF CONTENTS

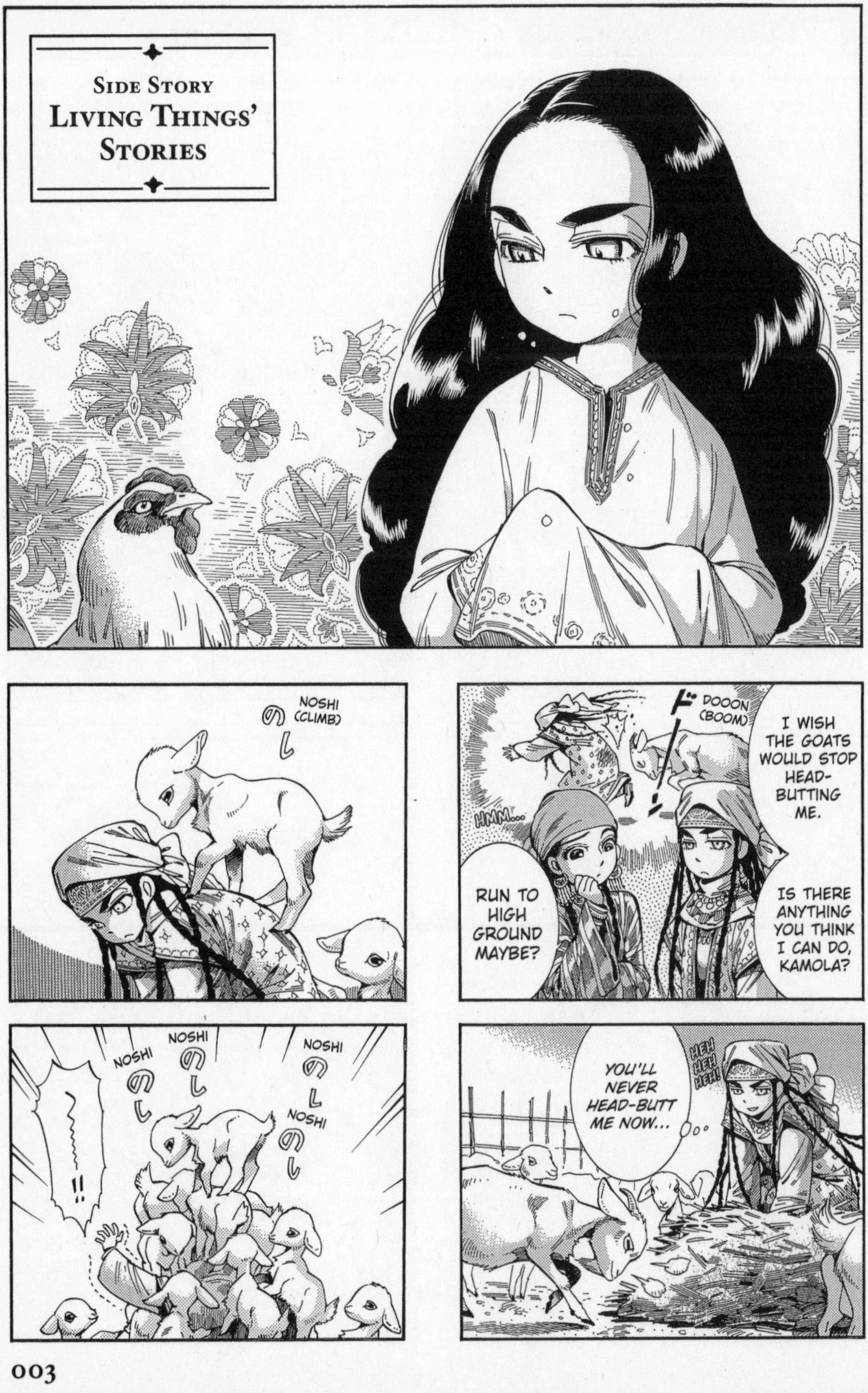
Side Story
Living Things' Stories
DOOON (BOOM)
I WISH THE GOATS WOULD STOP HEAD-BUTTING ME.
HMM...
IS THERE ANYTHING YOU THINK I CAN DO, KAMOLA?
RUN TO HIGH GROUND MAYBE?
NOSHI (CLIMB)
HEH HEH HEH!
YOU'LL NEVER HEAD-BUTT ME NOW...
NOSHI
NOSHI
NOSHI
NOSHI
!!

STORK

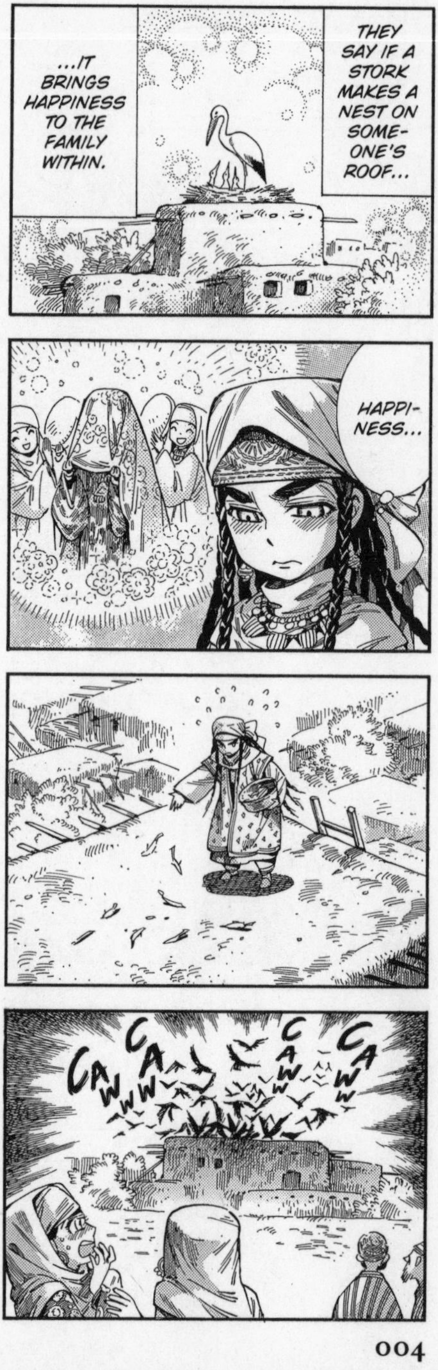
THEY SAY IF A STORK MAKES A NEST ON SOME-ONE'S ROOF...
...IT BRINGS HAPPINESS TO THE FAMILY WITHIN.
HAPPI-NESS...
CAWW
CAWW
CAWW
CAWW

RUNAWAY CHICKENS

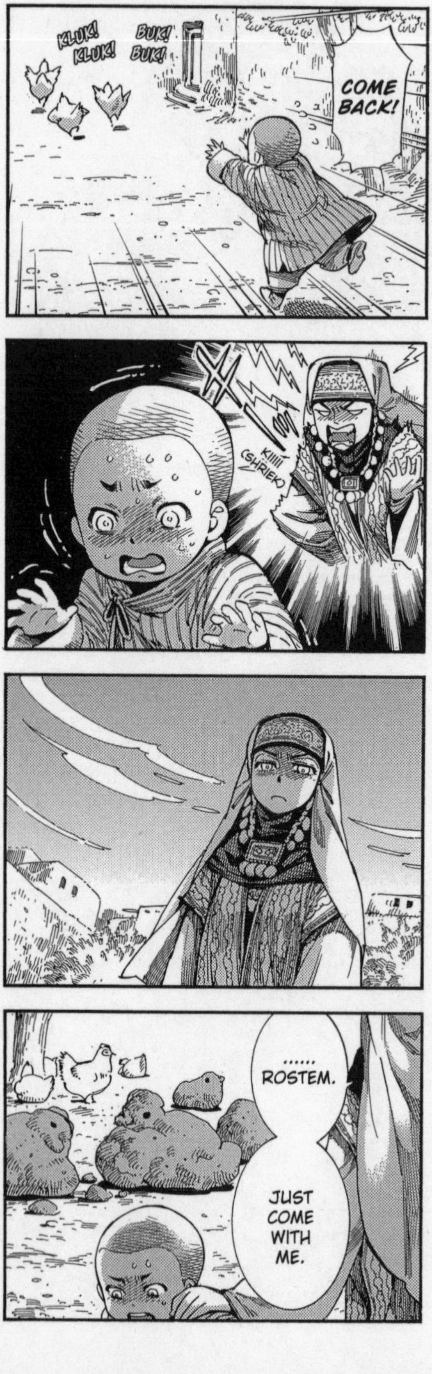
COME BACK!
BUK! BUK!
KLUK! KLUK!
KIIIII (SHRIEK)
...... ROSTEM.
JUST COME WITH ME.

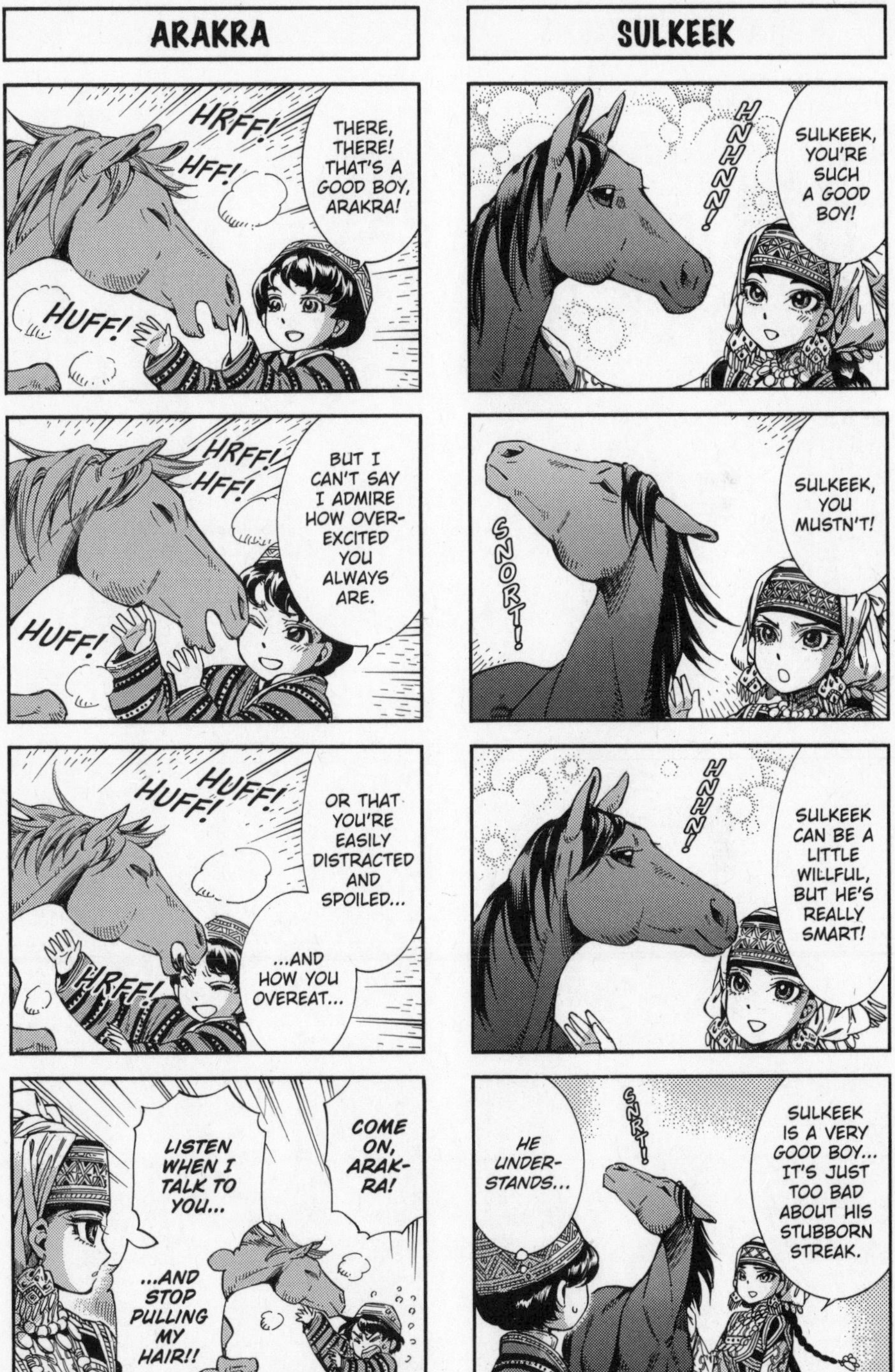
SULKEEK
SULKEEK, YOU'RE SUCH A GOOD BOY!
HNHNN!
SULKEEK, YOU MUSTN'T!
SNORT!
SULKEEK CAN BE A LITTLE WILLFUL, BUT HE'S REALLY SMART!
HNHN!
SULKEEK IS A VERY GOOD BOY... IT'S JUST TOO BAD ABOUT HIS STUBBORN STREAK.
SNRT!
HE UNDERSTANDS...
ARAKRA
THERE, THERE! THAT'S A GOOD BOY, ARAKRA!
HRFF!
HFF!
HUFF!
BUT I CAN'T SAY I ADMIRE HOW OVER-EXCITED YOU ALWAYS ARE.
HRFF!
HFF!
HUFF!
OR THAT YOU'RE EASILY DISTRACTED AND SPOILED...
HUFF!
HUFF!
...AND HOW YOU OVEREAT...
HRFF!
COME ON, ARAKRA!
LISTEN WHEN I TALK TO YOU...
...AND STOP PULLING MY HAIR!!

LIGHT HUMOR

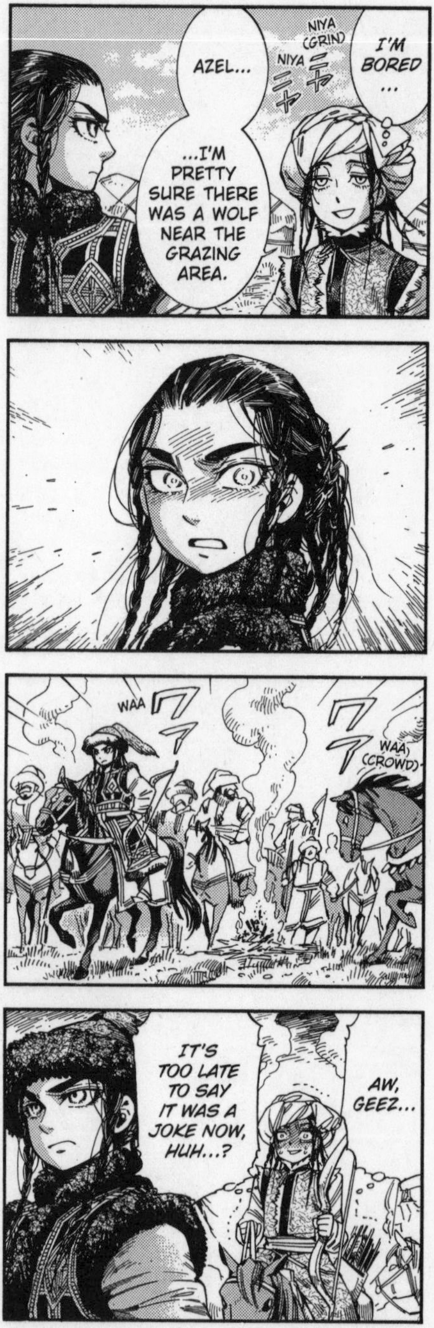
I'M BORED ...
NIYA NIYA (GRIN)
AZEL...
...I'M PRETTY SURE THERE WAS A WOLF NEAR THE GRAZING AREA.
WAA (CROWD)
WAA
AW, GEEZ...
IT'S TOO LATE TO SAY IT WAS A JOKE NOW, HUH...?

WOLF!

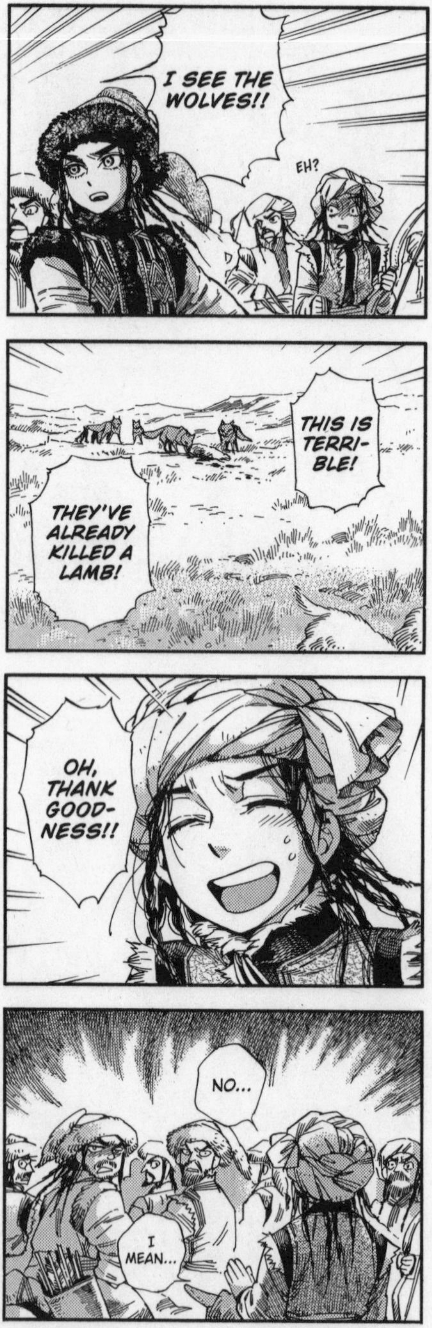
I SEE THE WOLVES!!
EH?
THIS IS TERRI-BLE!
THEY'VE ALREADY KILLED A LAMB!
OH, THANK GOOD-NESS!!
NO...
I MEAN...

BAIMAT, IT'S UP TO YOU

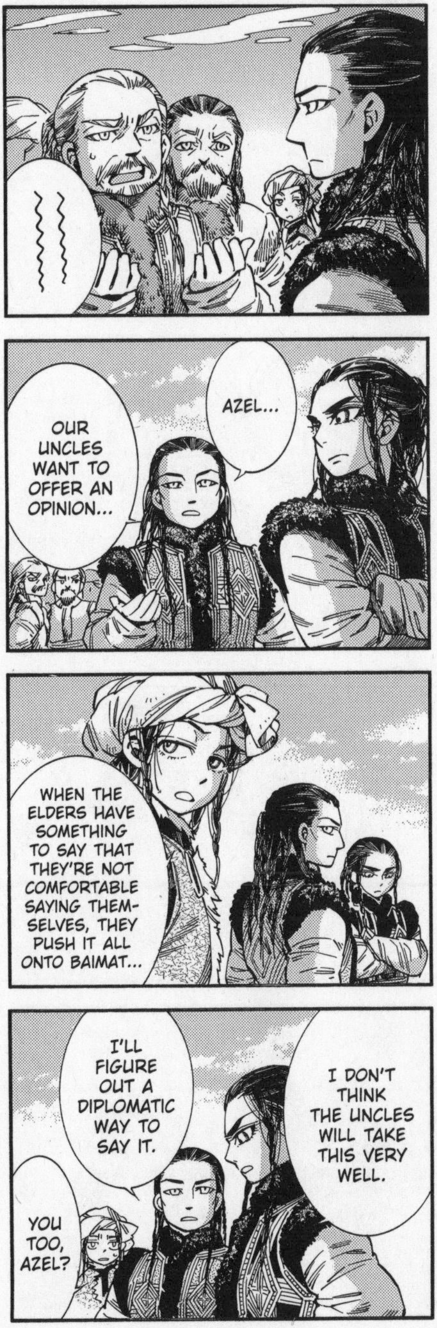
AZEL...
OUR UNCLES WANT TO OFFER AN OPINION...
WHEN THE ELDERS HAVE SOMETHING TO SAY THAT THEY'RE NOT COMFORTABLE SAYING THEM-SELVES, THEY PUSH IT ALL ONTO BAIMAT...
I DON'T THINK THE UNCLES WILL TAKE THIS VERY WELL.
I'LL FIGURE OUT A DIPLOMATIC WAY TO SAY IT.
YOU TOO, AZEL?

YES

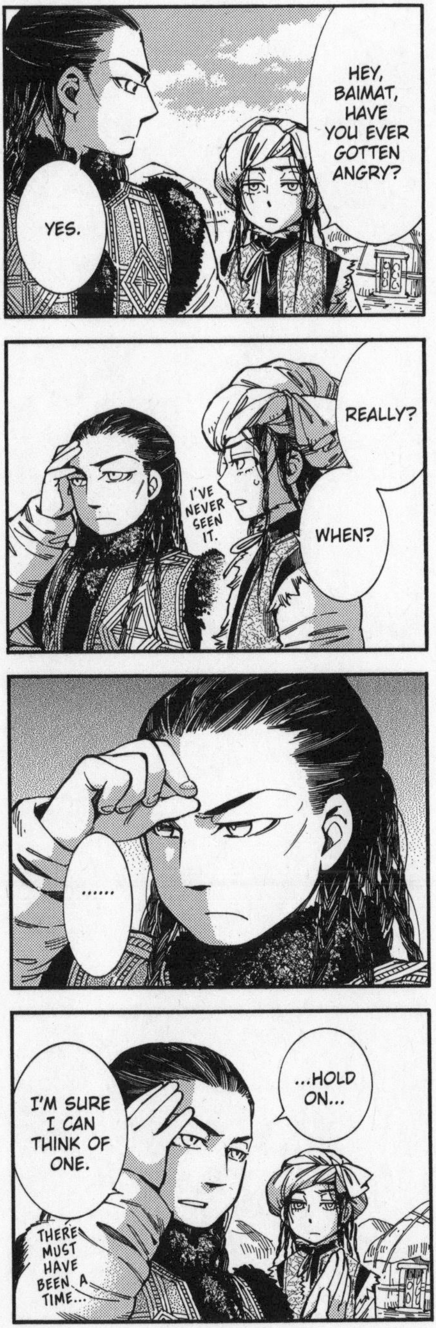
HEY, BAIMAT, HAVE YOU EVER GOTTEN ANGRY?
YES.
REALLY?
WHEN?
I'VE NEVER SEEN IT.
......
...HOLD ON...
I'M SURE I CAN THINK OF ONE.
THERE MUST HAVE BEEN A TIME...

IN LOVE

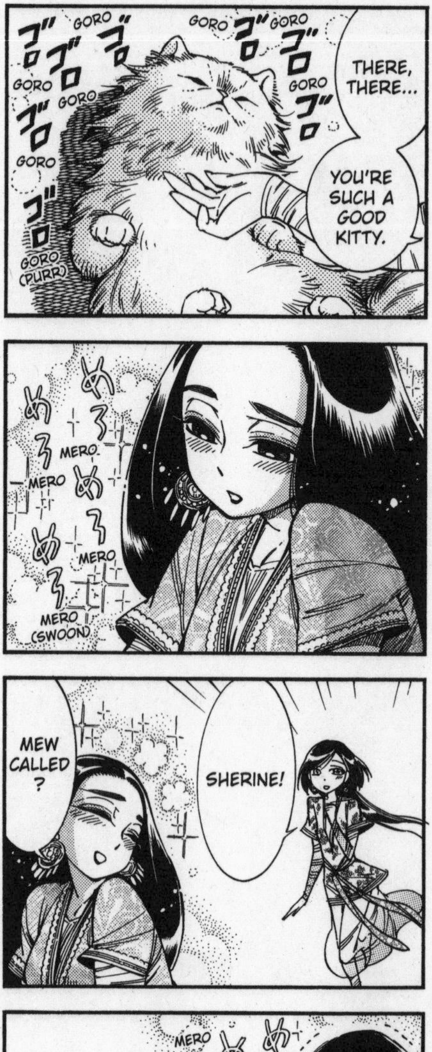

THERE, THERE...
YOU'RE SUCH A GOOD KITTY.
ゴロ GORO
ゴロ GORO
ゴロ GORO
ゴロ GORO (PURR)
めろ MERO
めろ MERO
めろ MERO
めろ MERO (SWOON)
SHERINE!
MEW CALLED ?
めろ MERO
めろ MERO
めろ MERO
めろ MERO

SNORES AND SLEEP-TALKING

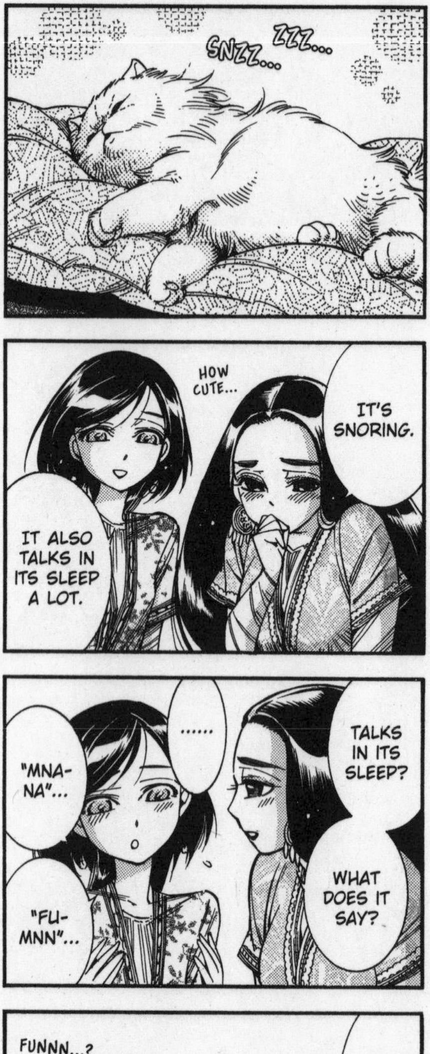

ZZZ...
SNZZ...
IT'S SNORING.
HOW CUTE...
IT ALSO TALKS IN ITS SLEEP A LOT.
TALKS IN ITS SLEEP?
......
WHAT DOES IT SAY?
"MNA-NA"...
"FU-MNN"...
HOW CUTE...!
MRRN...?
FUNNN...?

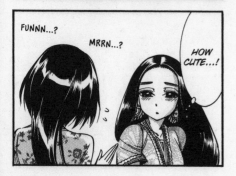

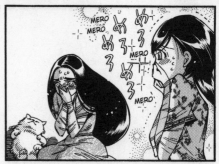

WHICH ONE

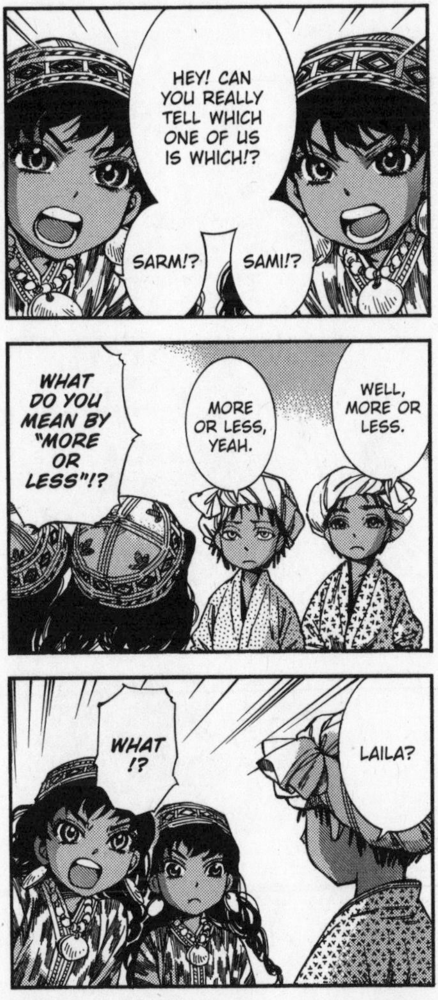
HEY! CAN YOU REALLY TELL WHICH ONE OF US IS WHICH!?
SAMI!?
SARM!?
WELL, MORE OR LESS.
MORE OR LESS, YEAH.
WHAT DO YOU MEAN BY "MORE OR LESS"!?
LAILA?
WHAT!?
LAILA.
AH!

ONE-ON-ONE

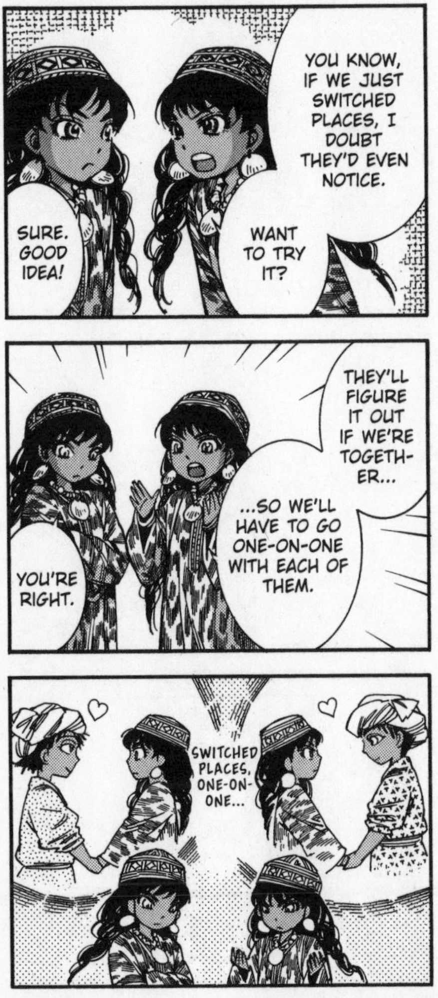
YOU KNOW, IF WE JUST SWITCHED PLACES, I DOUBT THEY'D EVEN NOTICE.
WANT TO TRY IT?
SURE. GOOD IDEA!
THEY'LL FIGURE IT OUT IF WE'RE TOGETH-ER...
...SO WE'LL HAVE TO GO ONE-ON-ONE WITH EACH OF THEM.
YOU'RE RIGHT.
SWITCHED PLACES, ONE-ON-ONE...
THAT'S NO GOOD!!
NO GOOD, NO GOOD!!

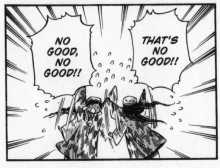

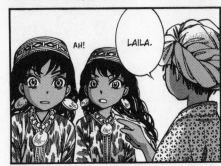

JUST FINE

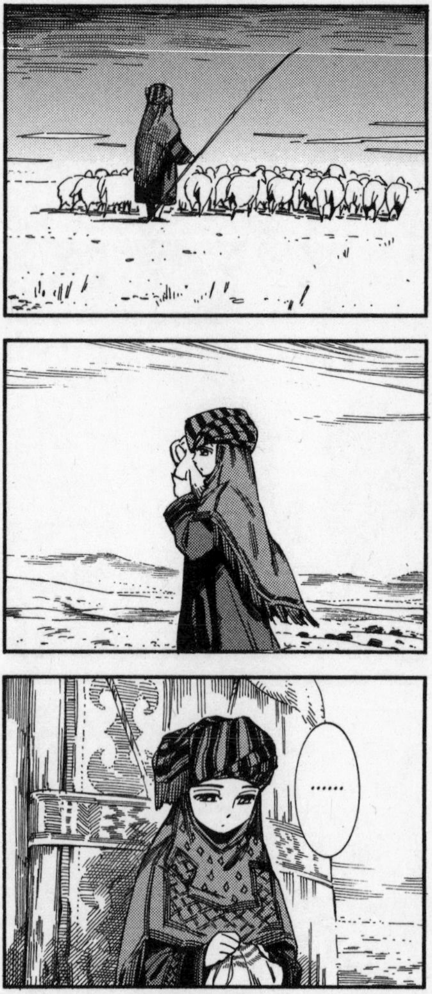
......
......I'M JUST FINE, CHUBAR.

WHEREVER

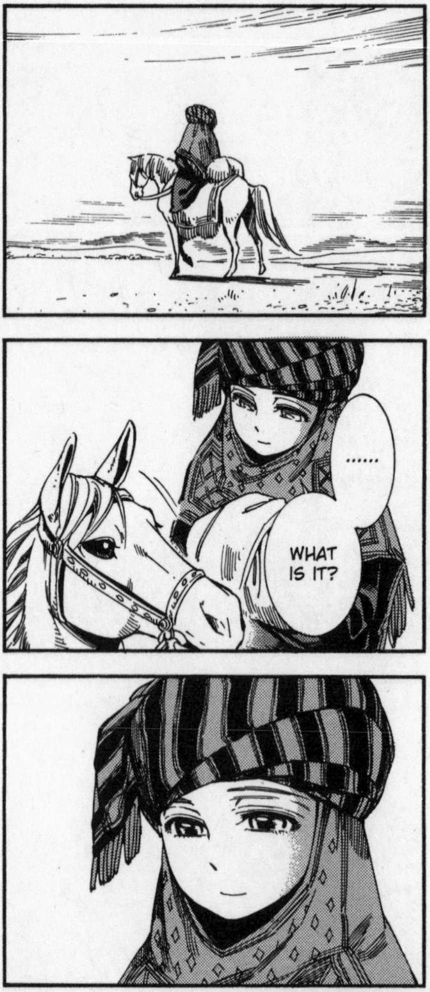
......
WHAT IS IT?
YOU'RE RIGHT.
WE CAN GO WHEREVER WE WANT.

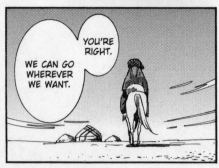

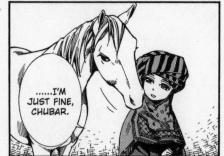

✦ SIDE STORY: END ✦

Chapter 52

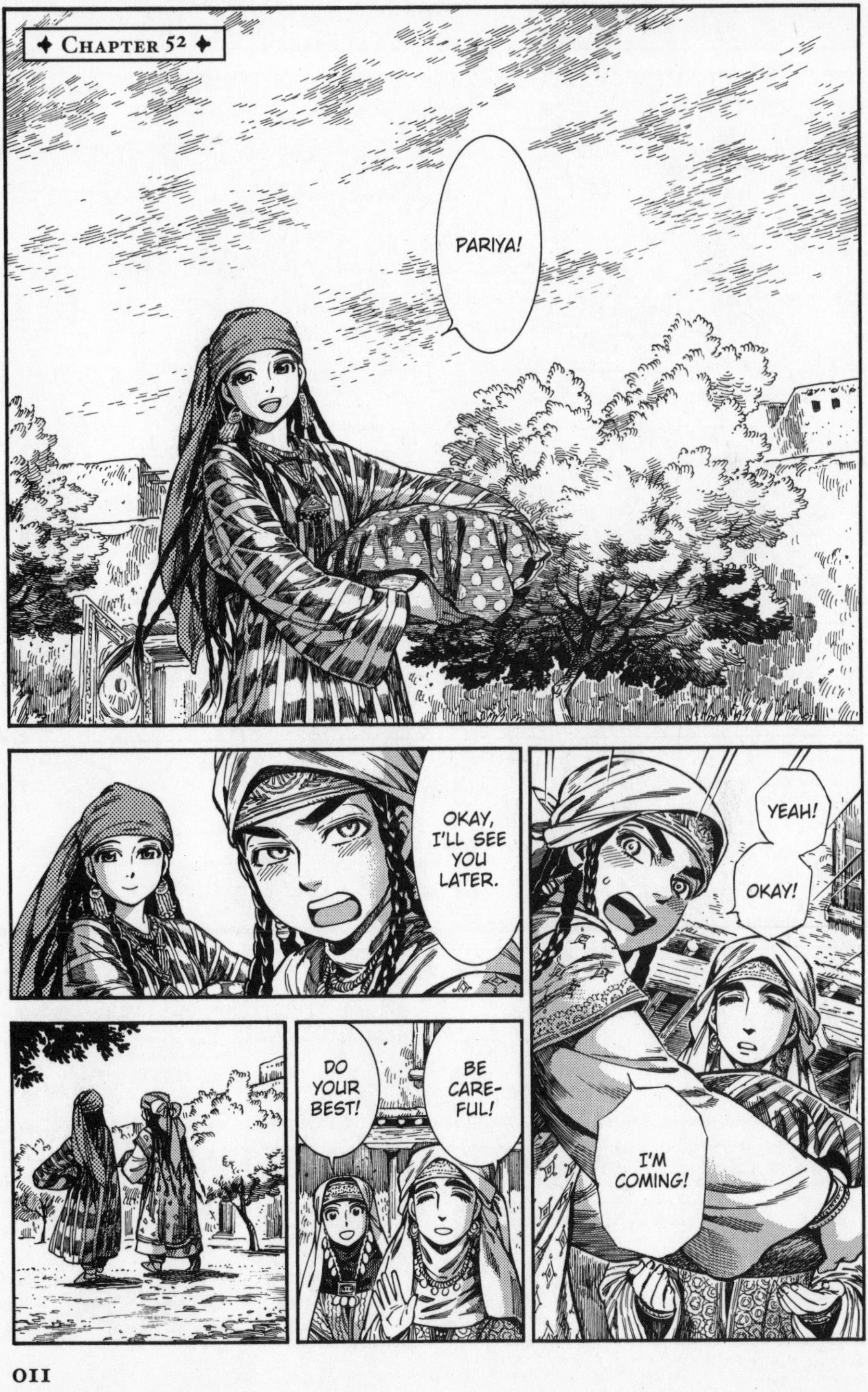
PARIYA!
YEAH!
OKAY!
I'M COMING!
OKAY, I'LL SEE YOU LATER.
BE CAREFUL!
DO YOUR BEST!

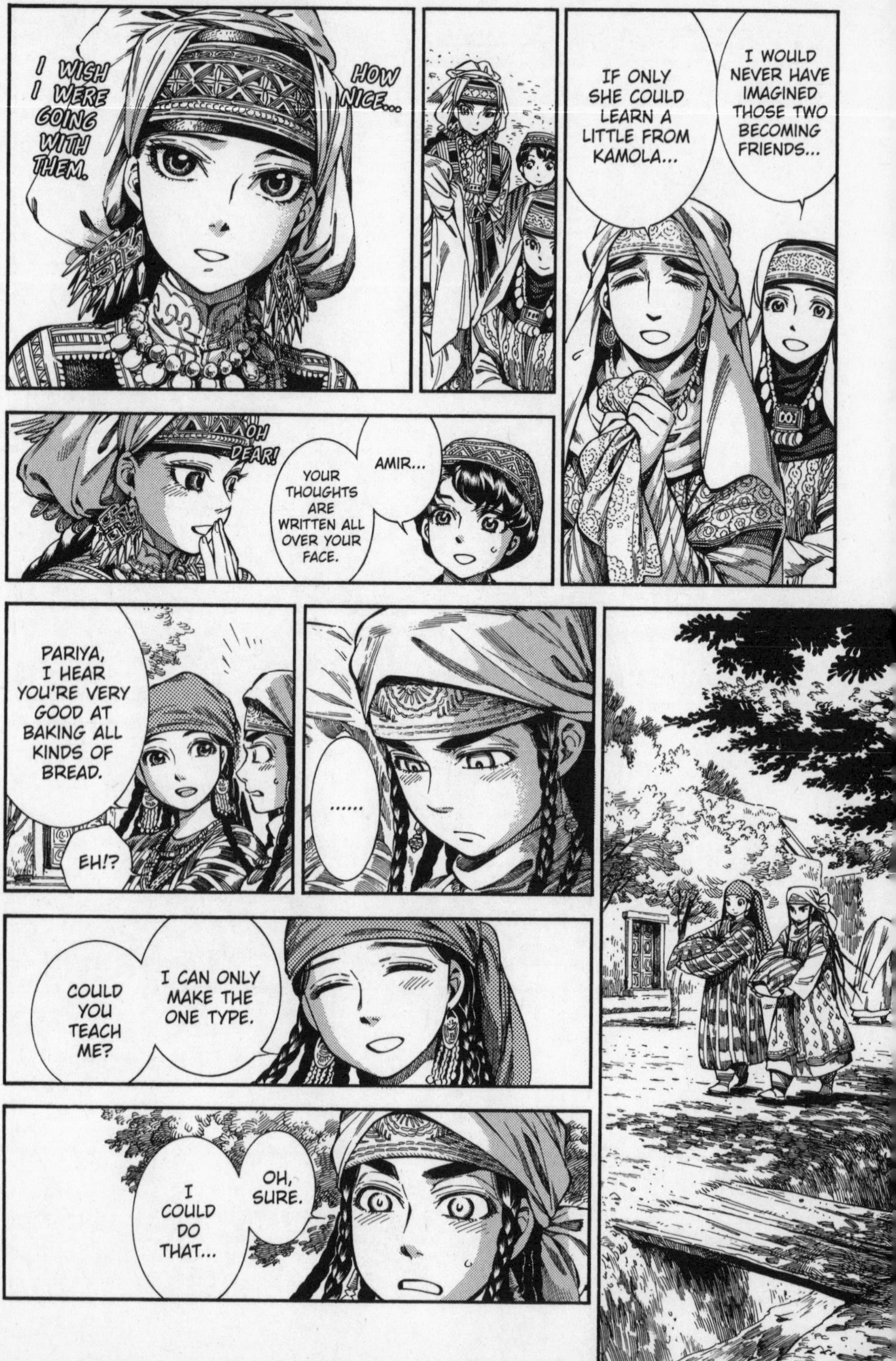
I WOULD NEVER HAVE IMAGINED THOSE TWO BECOMING FRIENDS...
IF ONLY SHE COULD LEARN A LITTLE FROM KAMOLA...
HOW NICE...
I WISH I WERE GOING WITH THEM.
AMIR...
YOUR THOUGHTS ARE WRITTEN ALL OVER YOUR FACE.
OH DEAR!
......
PARIYA, I HEAR YOU'RE VERY GOOD AT BAKING ALL KINDS OF BREAD.
EH!?
I CAN ONLY MAKE THE ONE TYPE.
COULD YOU TEACH ME?
OH, SURE.
I COULD DO THAT...

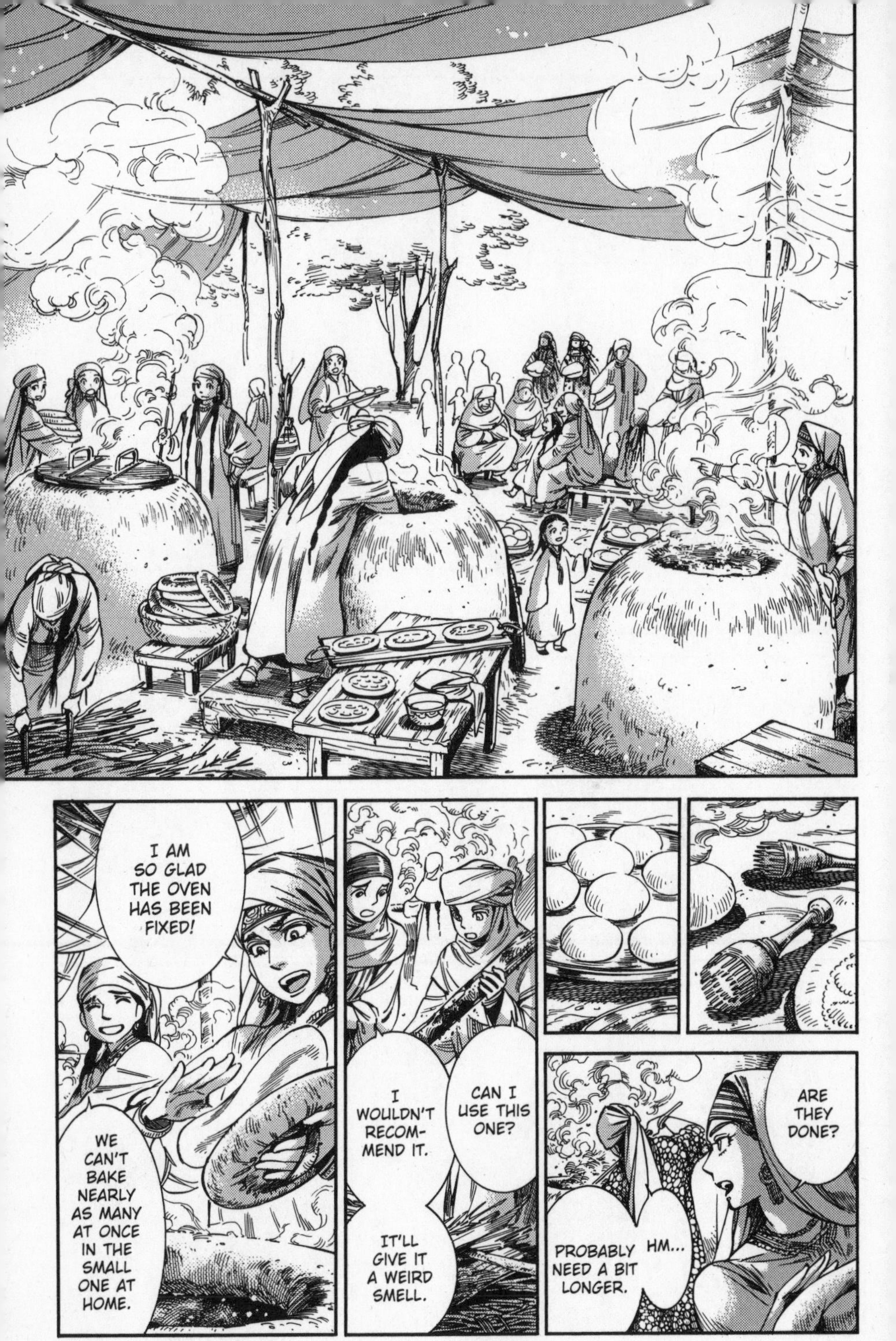
ARE THEY DONE?
HM...
PROBABLY NEED A BIT LONGER.
CAN I USE THIS ONE?
I WOULDN'T RECOMMEND IT.
IT'LL GIVE IT A WEIRD SMELL.
I AM SO GLAD THE OVEN HAS BEEN FIXED!
WE CAN'T BAKE NEARLY AS MANY AT ONCE IN THE SMALL ONE AT HOME.

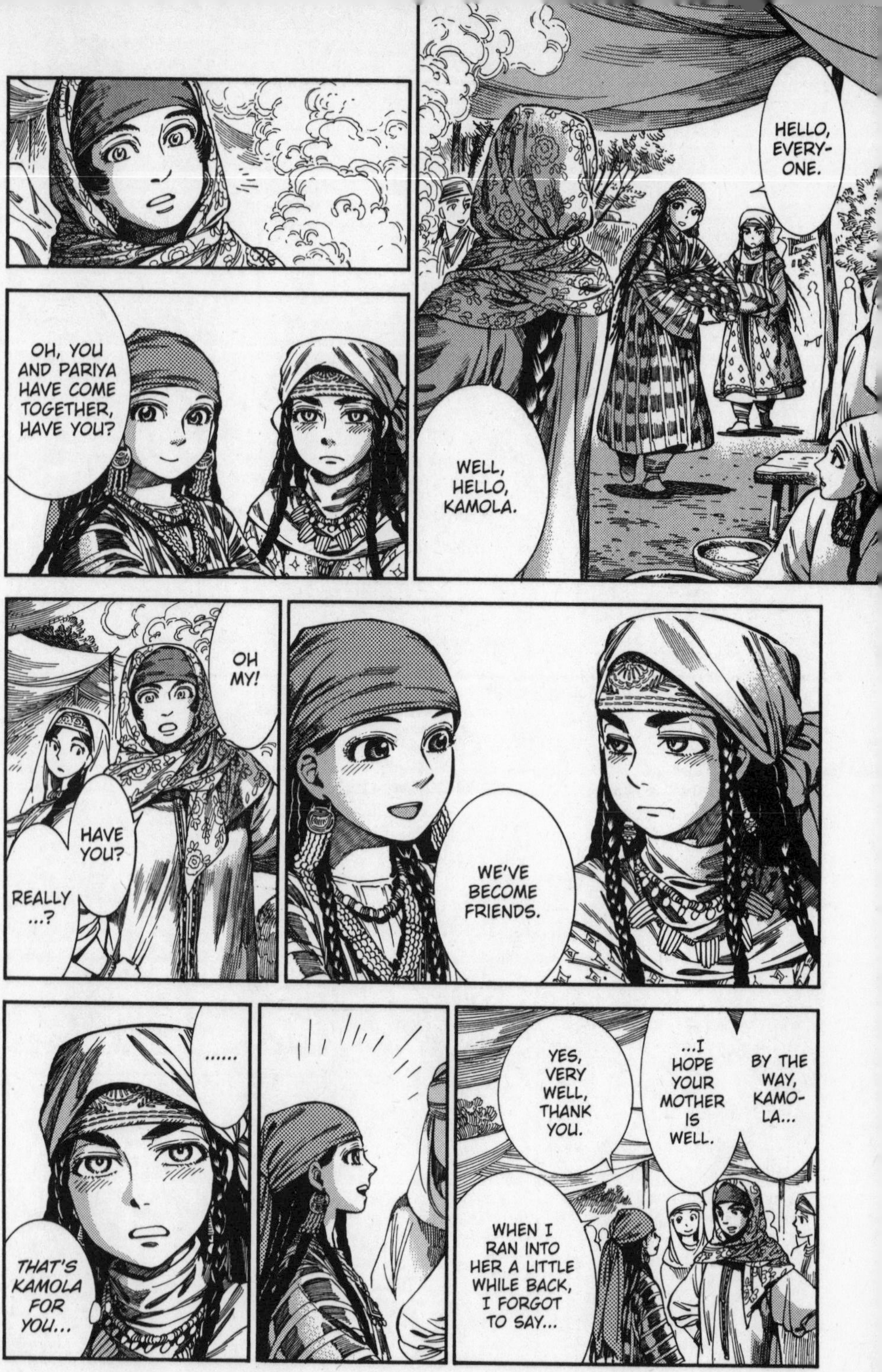
HELLO, EVERY-ONE.
WELL, HELLO, KAMOLA.
OH, YOU AND PARIYA HAVE COME TOGETHER, HAVE YOU?
WE'VE BECOME FRIENDS.
OH MY!
HAVE YOU?
REALLY ...?
BY THE WAY, KAMO-LA...
...I HOPE YOUR MOTHER IS WELL.
YES, VERY WELL, THANK YOU.
WHEN I RAN INTO HER A LITTLE WHILE BACK, I FORGOT TO SAY...
......
THAT'S KAMOLA FOR YOU...

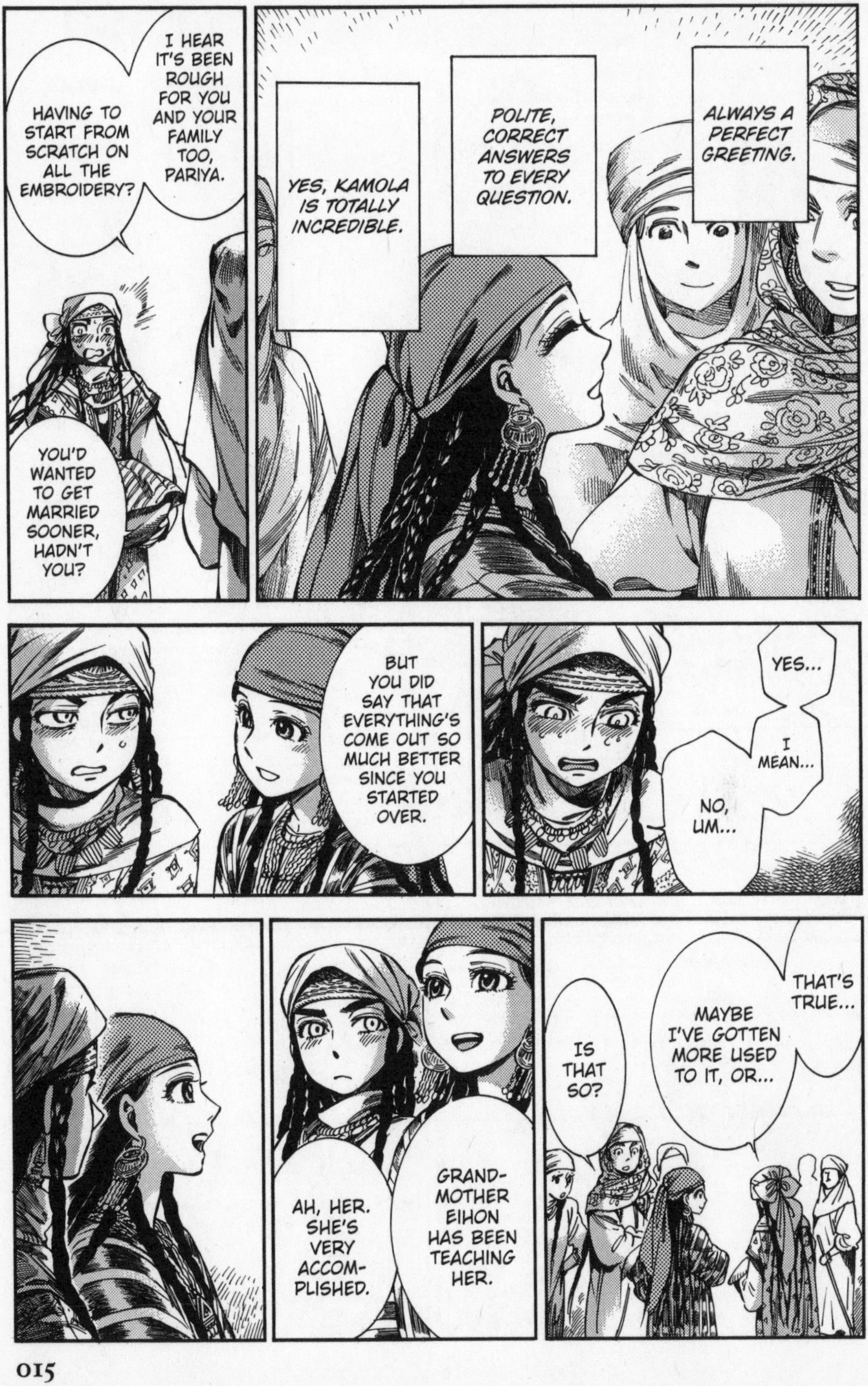
ALWAYS A PERFECT GREETING.
POLITE, CORRECT ANSWERS TO EVERY QUESTION.
YES, KAMOLA IS TOTALLY INCREDIBLE.
I HEAR IT'S BEEN ROUGH FOR YOU AND YOUR FAMILY TOO, PARIYA.
HAVING TO START FROM SCRATCH ON ALL THE EMBROIDERY?
YOU'D WANTED TO GET MARRIED SOONER, HADN'T YOU?
YES...
I MEAN...
NO, UM...
BUT YOU DID SAY THAT EVERYTHING'S COME OUT SO MUCH BETTER SINCE YOU STARTED OVER.
THAT'S TRUE...
MAYBE I'VE GOTTEN MORE USED TO IT, OR...
IS THAT SO?
GRAND-MOTHER EIHON HAS BEEN TEACHING HER.
AH, HER. SHE'S VERY ACCOM-PLISHED.

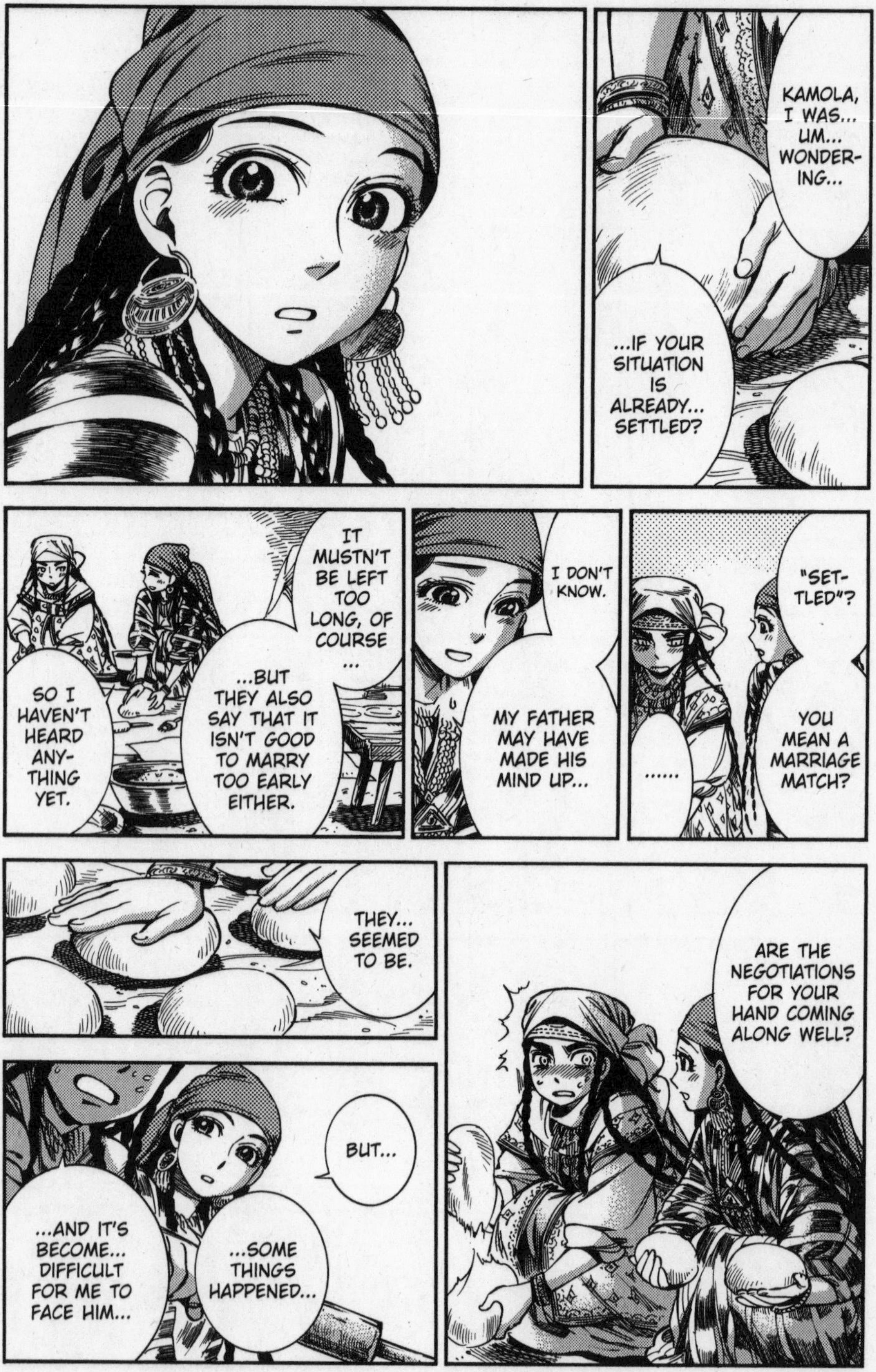
KAMOLA, I WAS... UM... WONDER-ING...
...IF YOUR SITUATION IS ALREADY... SETTLED?
"SET-TLED"?
YOU MEAN A MARRIAGE MATCH?
......
I DON'T KNOW.
MY FATHER MAY HAVE MADE HIS MIND UP...
IT MUSTN'T BE LEFT TOO LONG, OF COURSE...
...BUT THEY ALSO SAY THAT IT ISN'T GOOD TO MARRY TOO EARLY EITHER.
SO I HAVEN'T HEARD ANY-THING YET.
ARE THE NEGOTIATIONS FOR YOUR HAND COMING ALONG WELL?
THEY... SEEMED TO BE.
BUT...
...SOME THINGS HAPPENED...
...AND IT'S BECOME... DIFFICULT FOR ME TO FACE HIM...

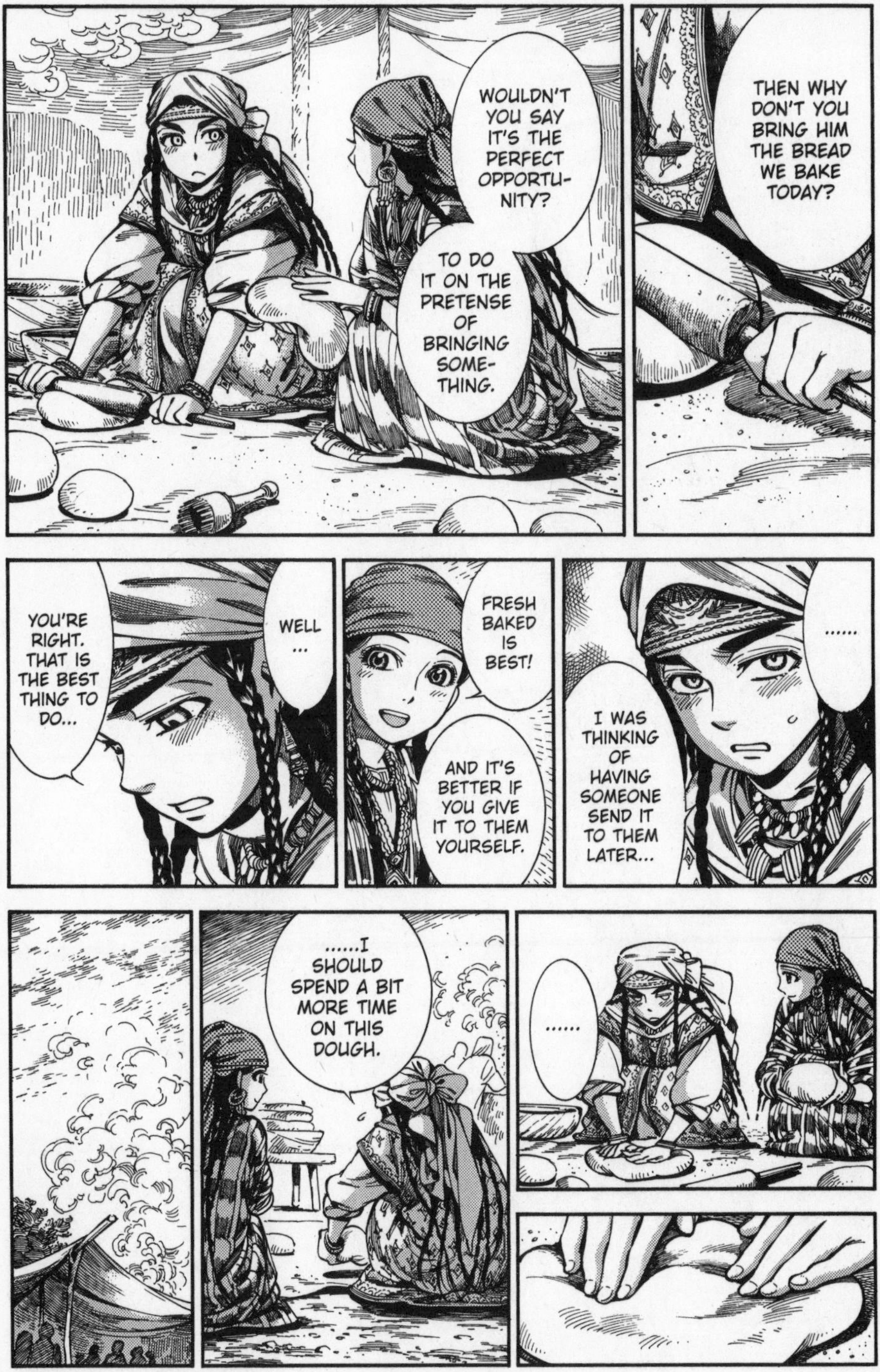
THEN WHY DON'T YOU BRING HIM THE BREAD WE BAKE TODAY?
WOULDN'T YOU SAY IT'S THE PERFECT OPPORTU-NITY?
TO DO IT ON THE PRETENSE OF BRINGING SOME-THING.
......
I WAS THINKING OF HAVING SOMEONE SEND IT TO THEM LATER...
FRESH BAKED IS BEST!
AND IT'S BETTER IF YOU GIVE IT TO THEM YOURSELF.
WELL ...
YOU'RE RIGHT. THAT IS THE BEST THING TO DO...
......
......I SHOULD SPEND A BIT MORE TIME ON THIS DOUGH.

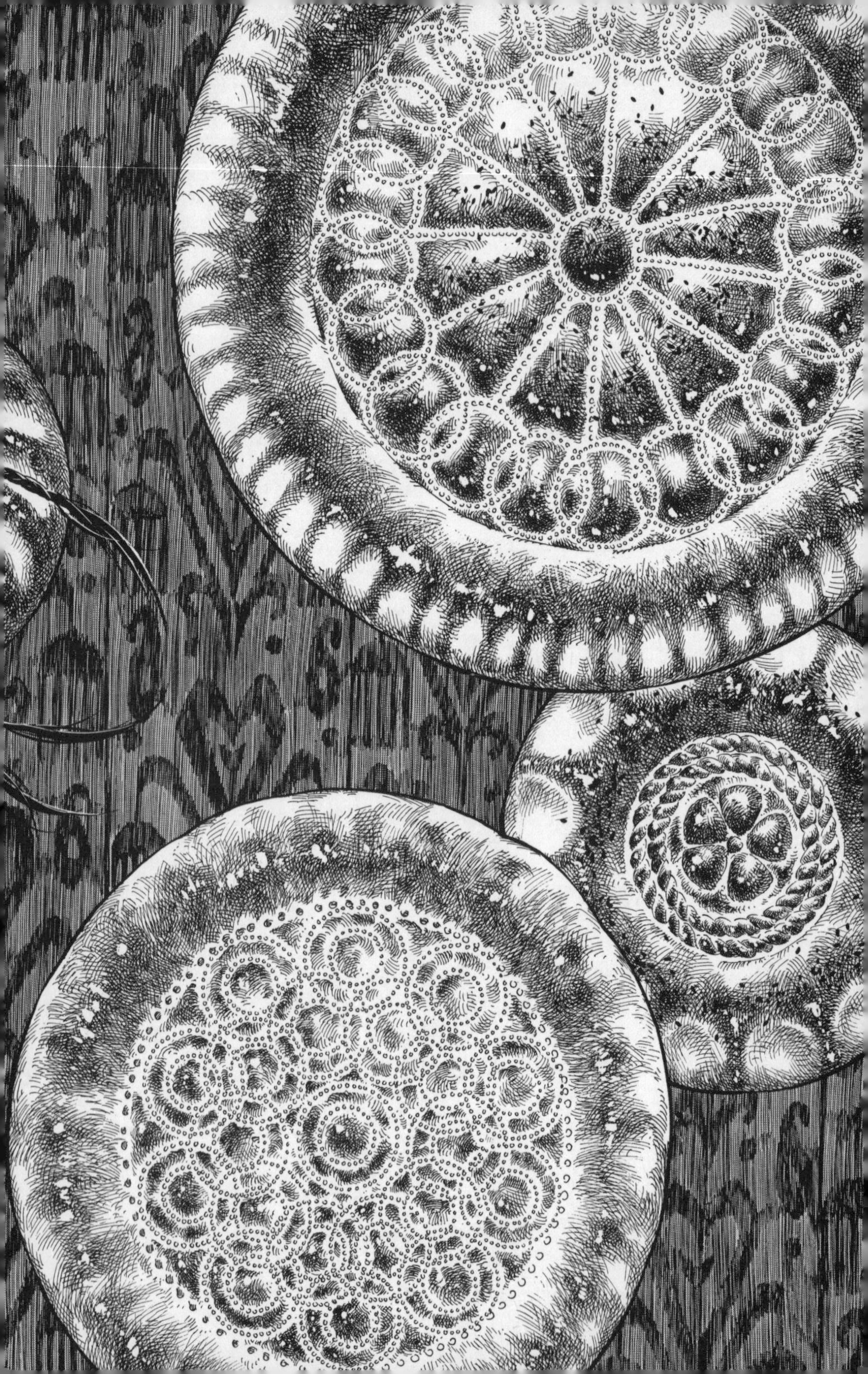

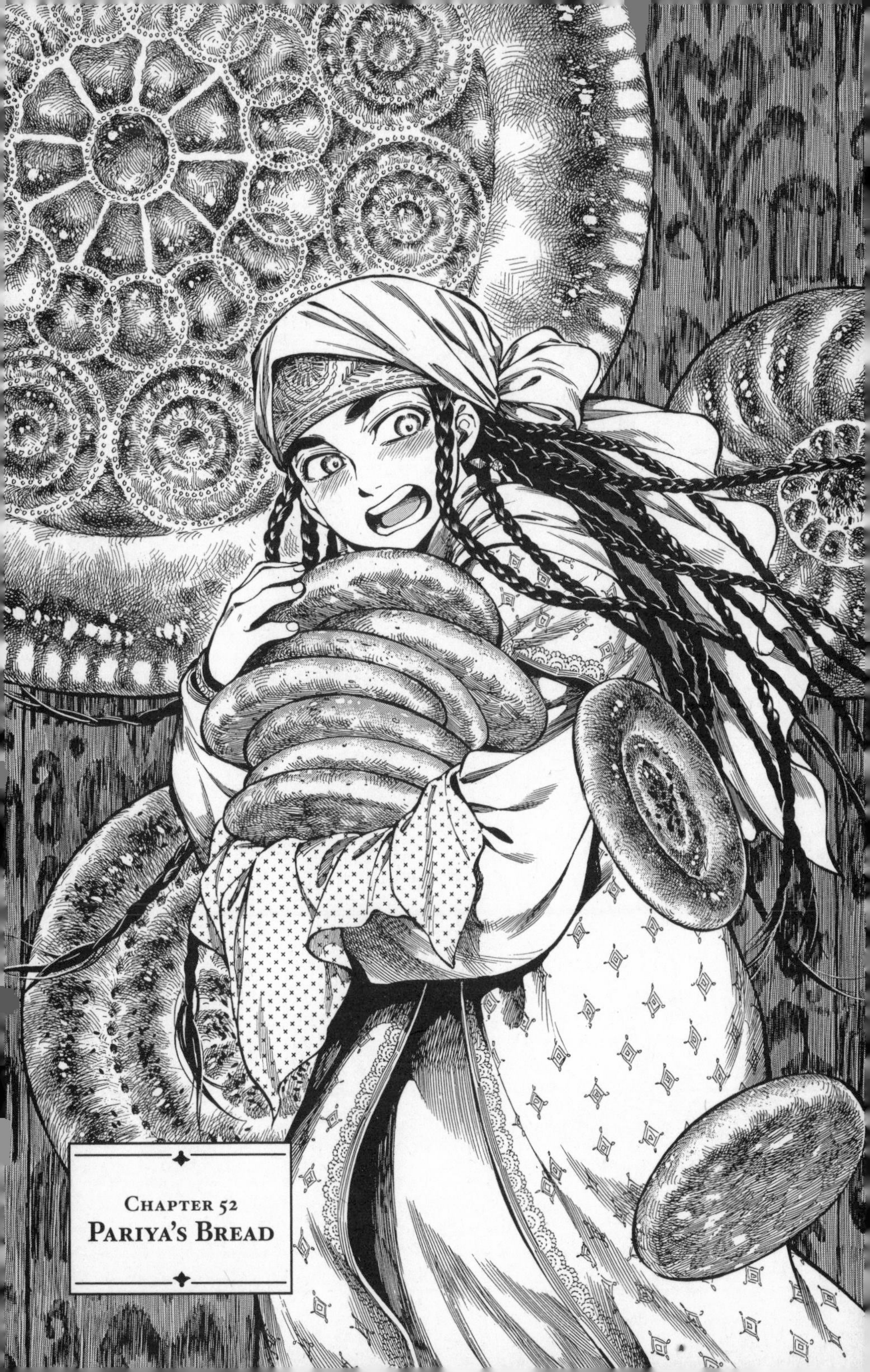
Chapter 52
Pariya's Bread

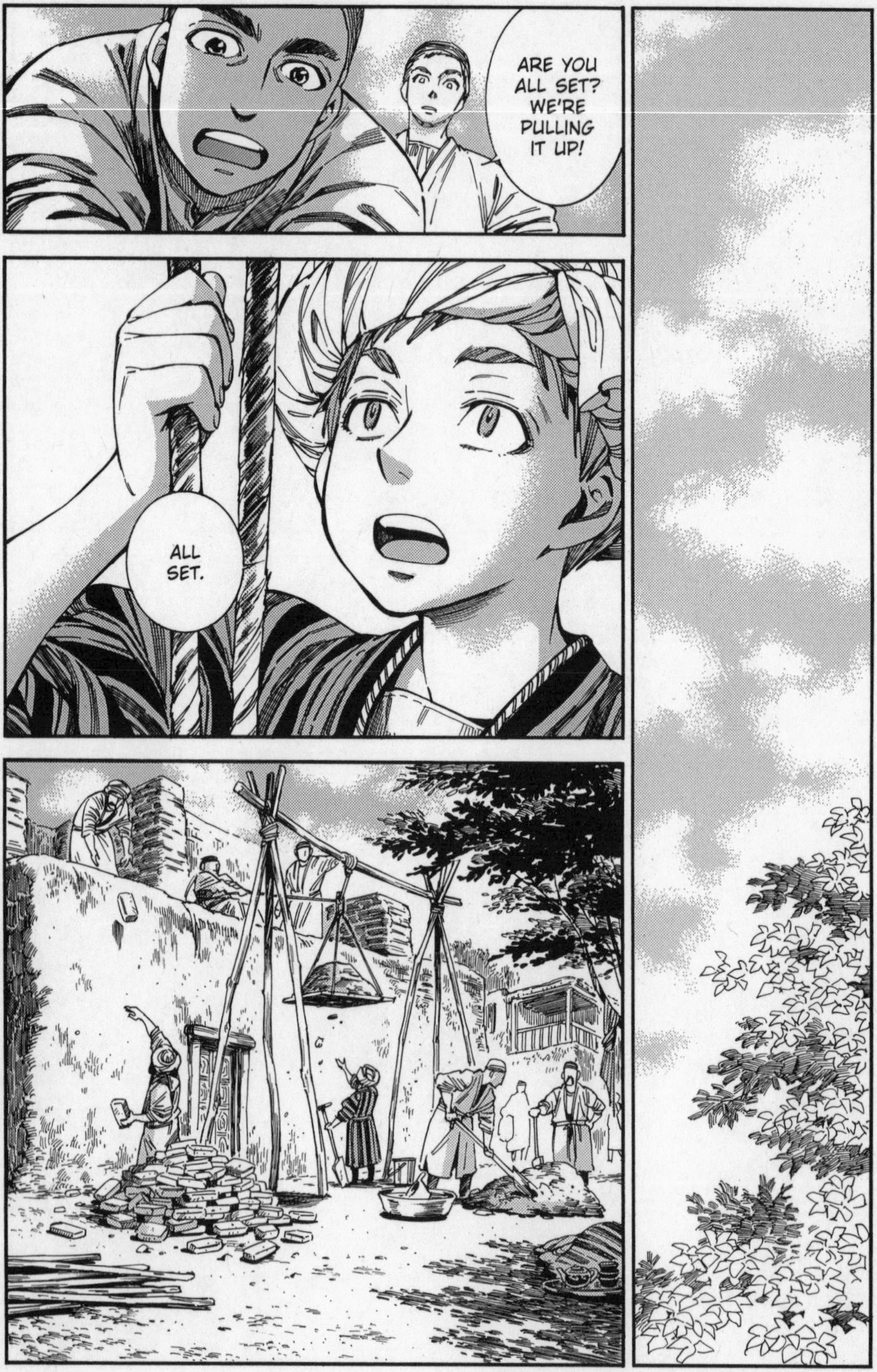
ARE YOU ALL SET? WE'RE PULLING IT UP!
ALL SET.

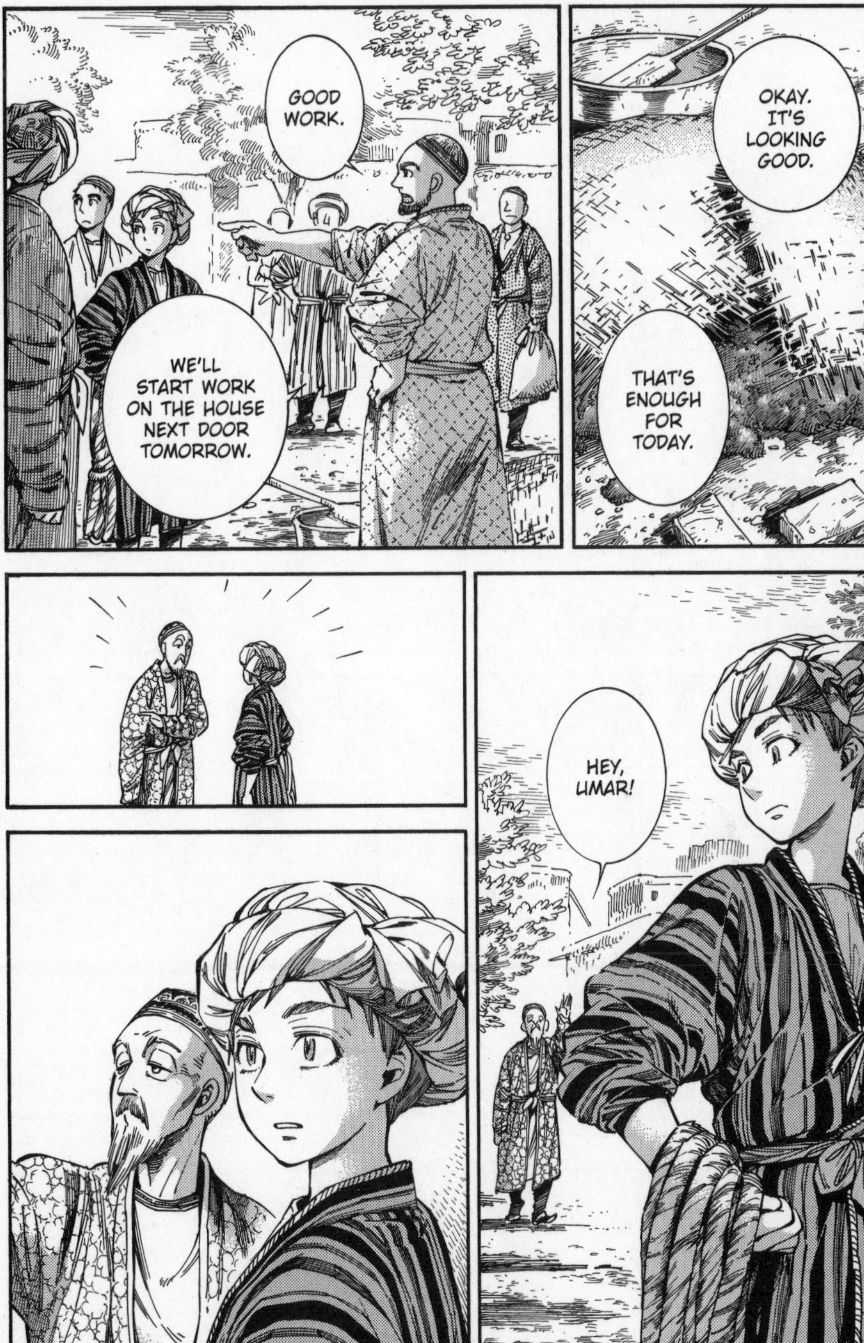
OKAY. IT'S LOOKING GOOD.
THAT'S ENOUGH FOR TODAY.
GOOD WORK.
WE'LL START WORK ON THE HOUSE NEXT DOOR TOMORROW.
HEY, UMAR!

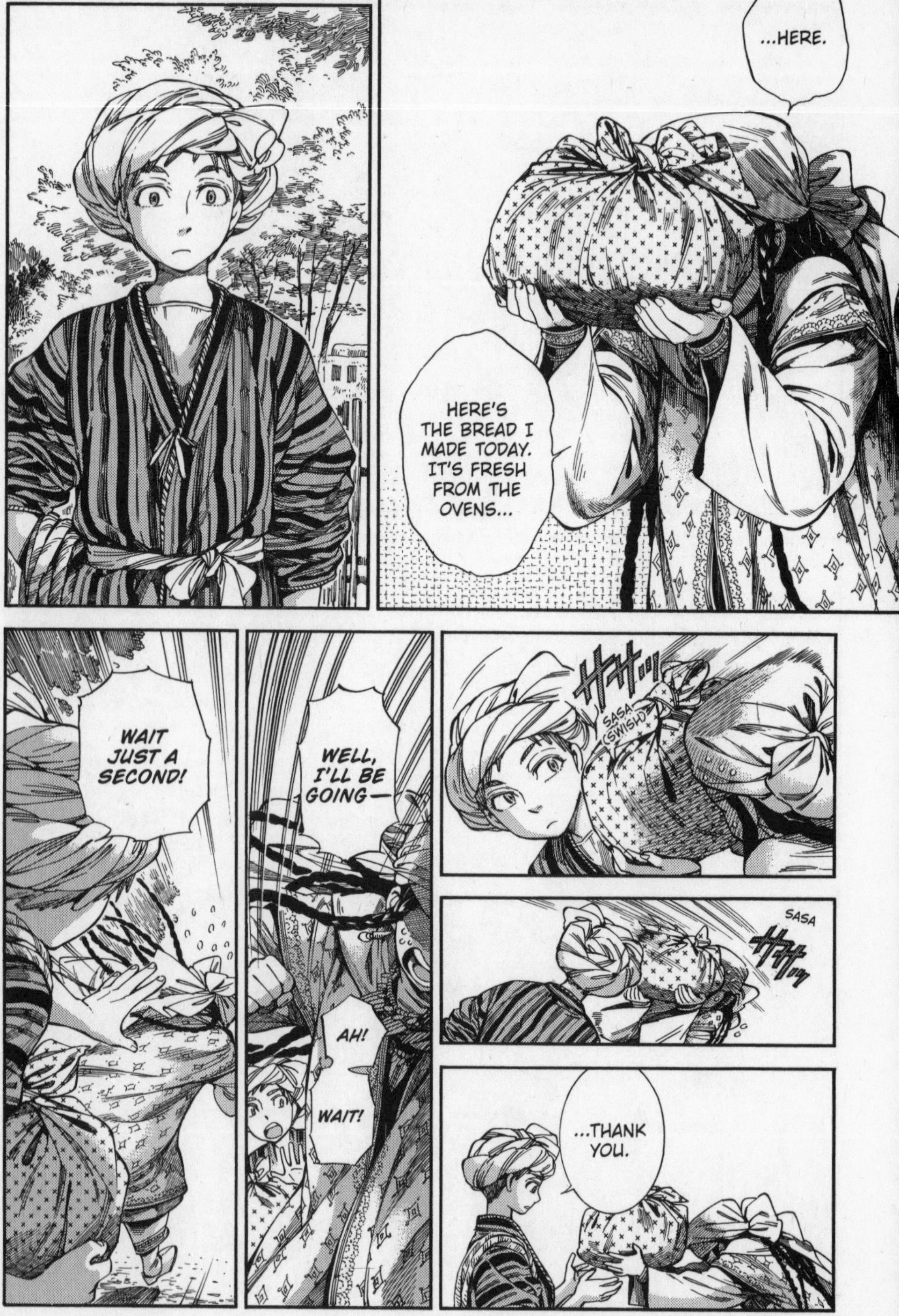
...HERE.
HERE'S THE BREAD I MADE TODAY. IT'S FRESH FROM THE OVENS...
SASA (SWISH)
SASA
...THANK YOU.
WELL, I'LL BE GOING—
AH!
WAIT!
WAIT JUST A SECOND!

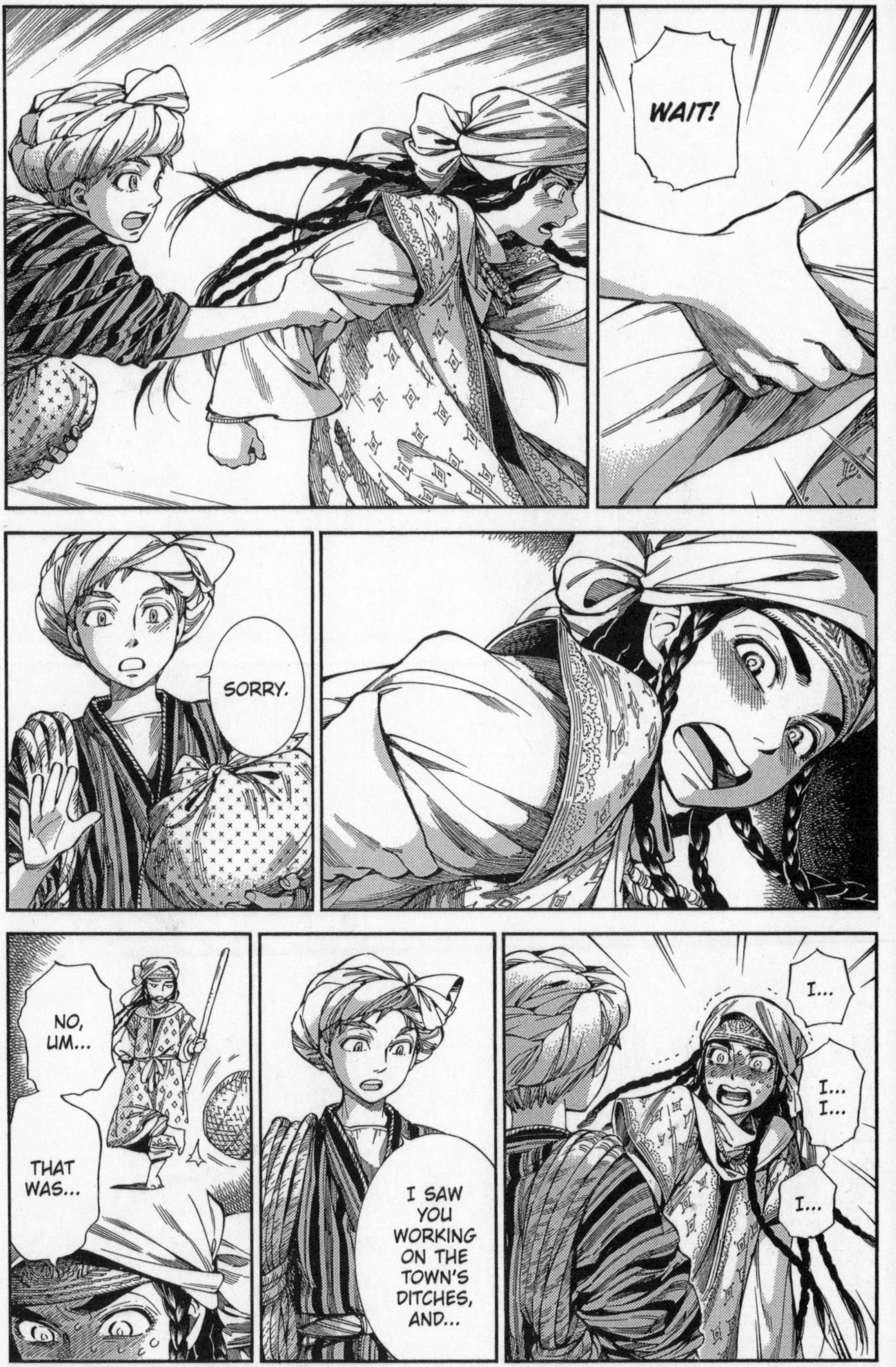
WAIT!
SORRY.
I...
I... I...
I...
I SAW YOU WORKING ON THE TOWN'S DITCHES, AND...
NO, UM...
THAT WAS...

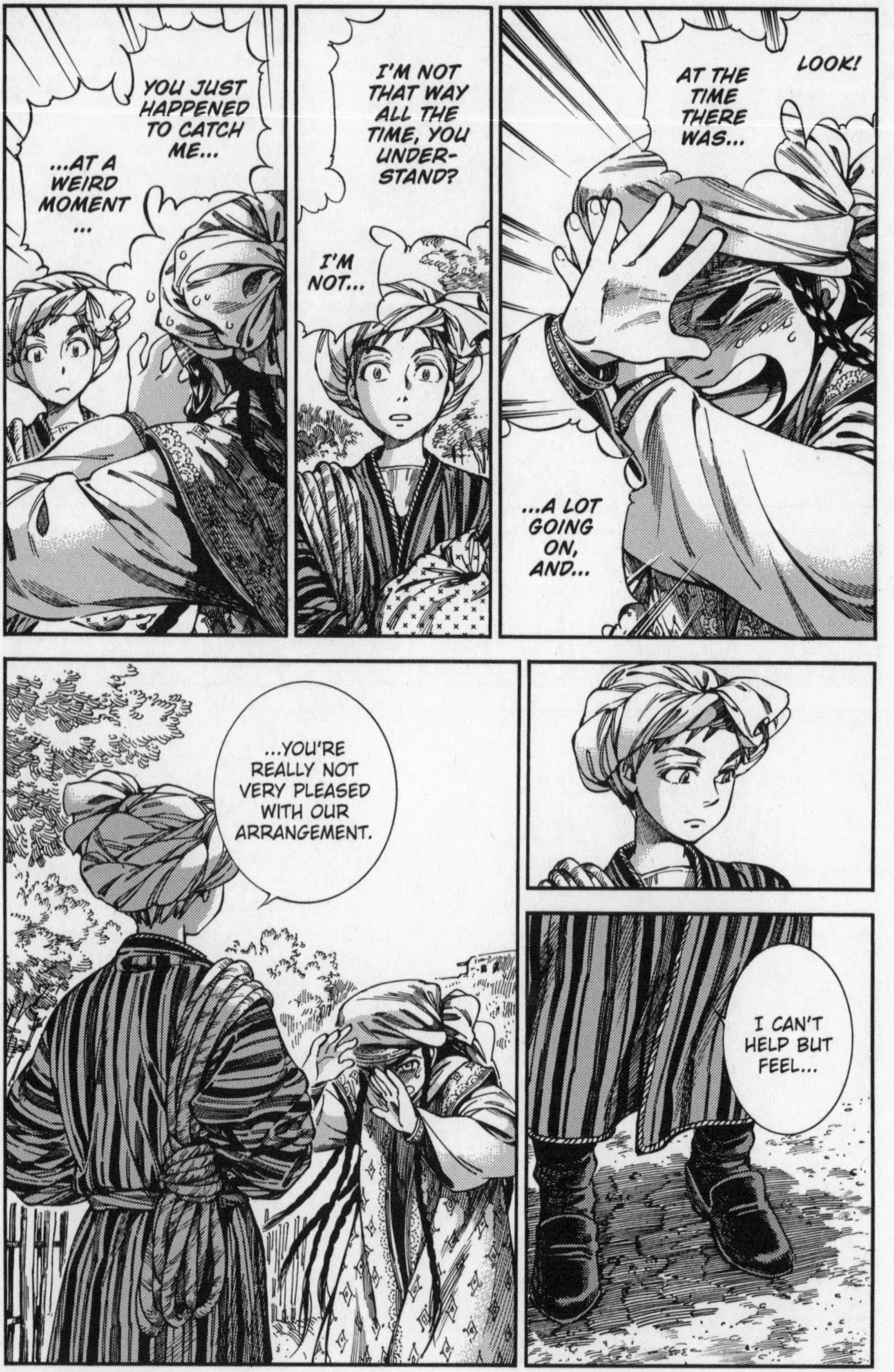
LOOK!
AT THE TIME THERE WAS...
...A LOT GOING ON, AND...
I'M NOT THAT WAY ALL THE TIME, YOU UNDERSTAND?
I'M NOT...
YOU JUST HAPPENED TO CATCH ME...
...AT A WEIRD MOMENT ...
I CAN'T HELP BUT FEEL...
...YOU'RE REALLY NOT VERY PLEASED WITH OUR ARRANGEMENT.

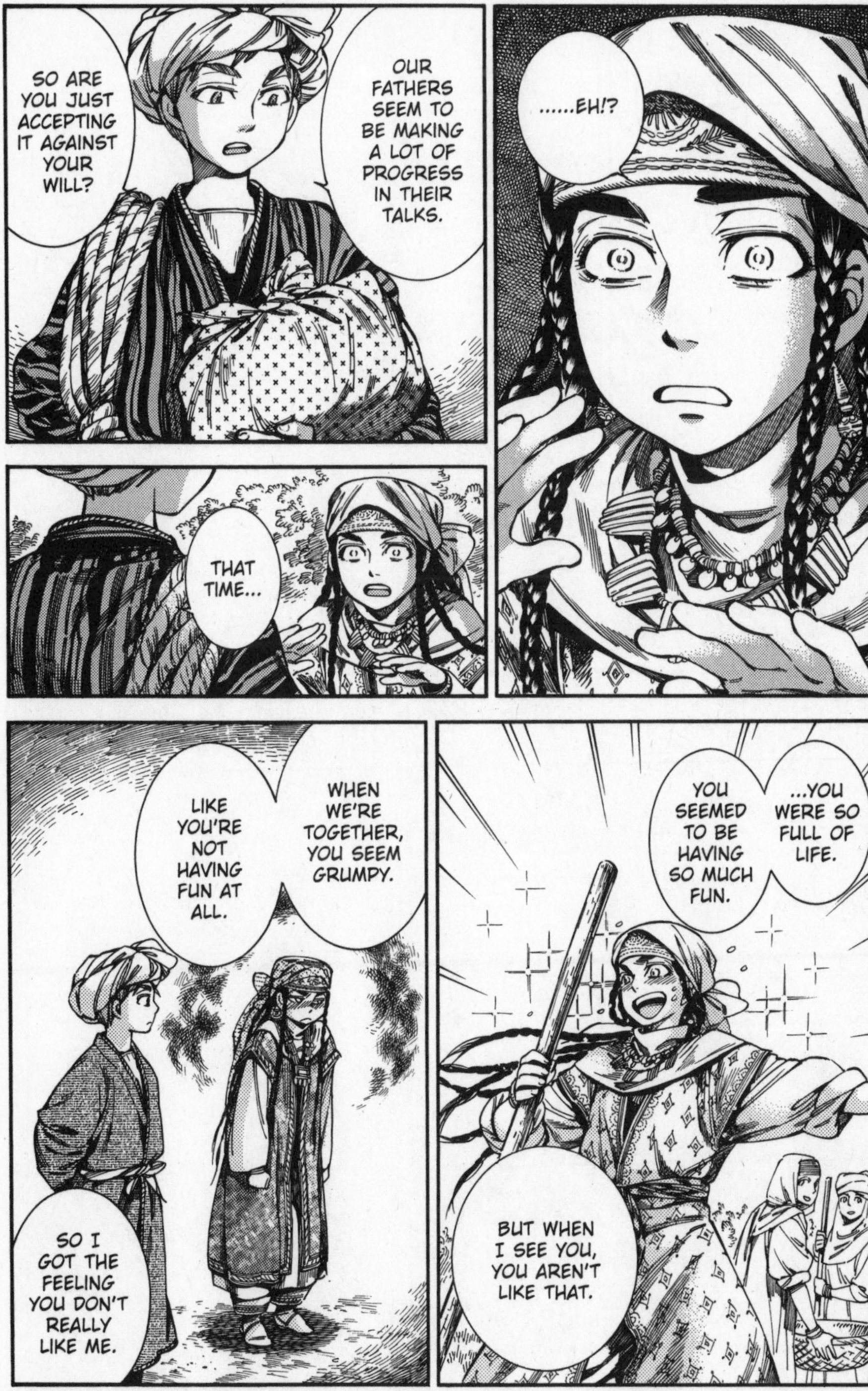
......EH!?
OUR FATHERS SEEM TO BE MAKING A LOT OF PROGRESS IN THEIR TALKS.
SO ARE YOU JUST ACCEPTING IT AGAINST YOUR WILL?
THAT TIME...
...YOU WERE SO FULL OF LIFE.
YOU SEEMED TO BE HAVING SO MUCH FUN.
BUT WHEN I SEE YOU, YOU AREN'T LIKE THAT.
WHEN WE'RE TOGETHER, YOU SEEM GRUMPY.
LIKE YOU'RE NOT HAVING FUN AT ALL.
SO I GOT THE FEELING YOU DON'T REALLY LIKE ME.

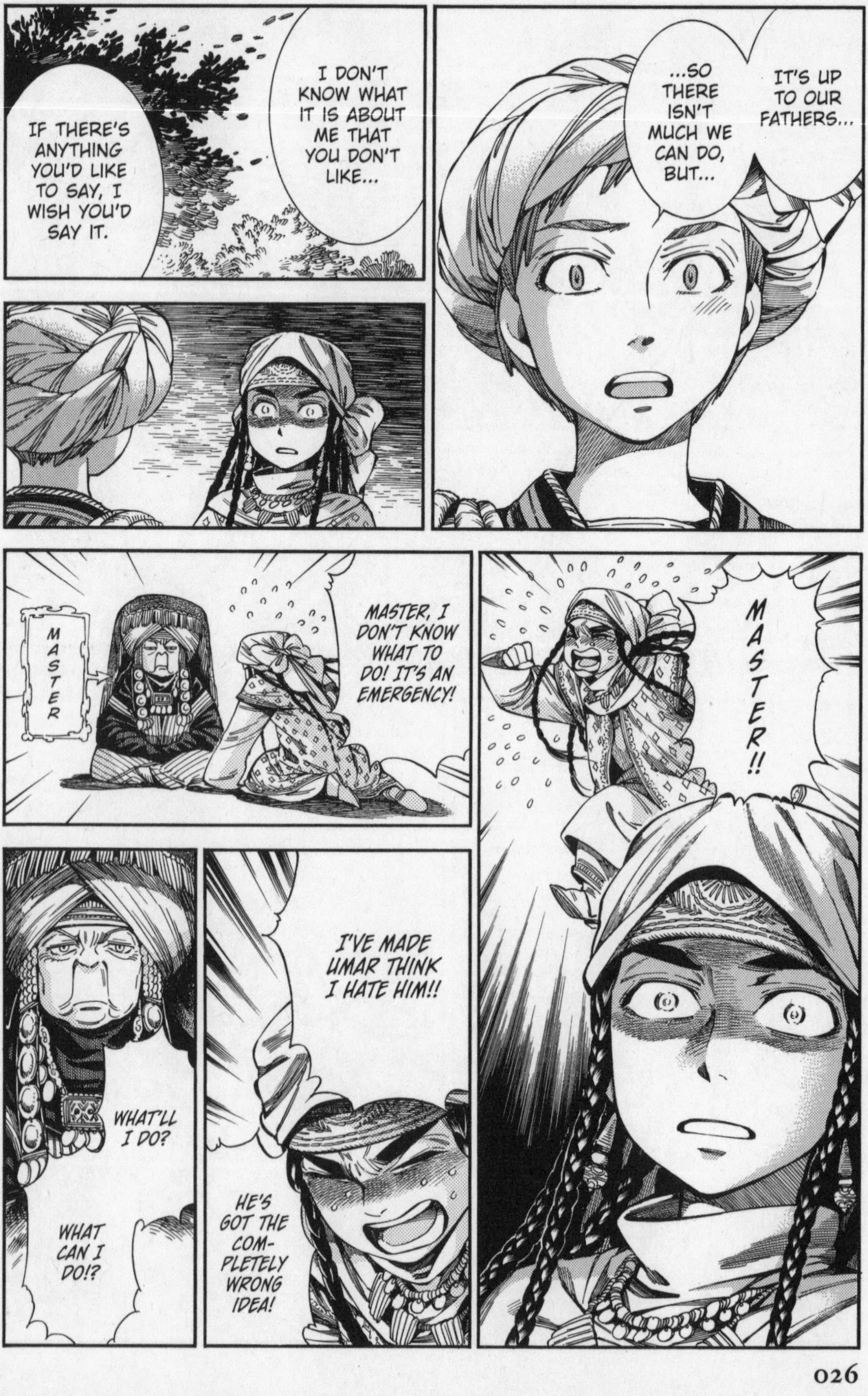
IT'S UP TO OUR FATHERS...
...SO THERE ISN'T MUCH WE CAN DO, BUT...
I DON'T KNOW WHAT IT IS ABOUT ME THAT YOU DON'T LIKE...
IF THERE'S ANYTHING YOU'D LIKE TO SAY, I WISH YOU'D SAY IT.
MASTER!!
MASTER, I DON'T KNOW WHAT TO DO! IT'S AN EMERGENCY!
MASTER
I'VE MADE UMAR THINK I HATE HIM!!
HE'S GOT THE COMPLETELY WRONG IDEA!
WHAT'LL I DO?
WHAT CAN I DO!?

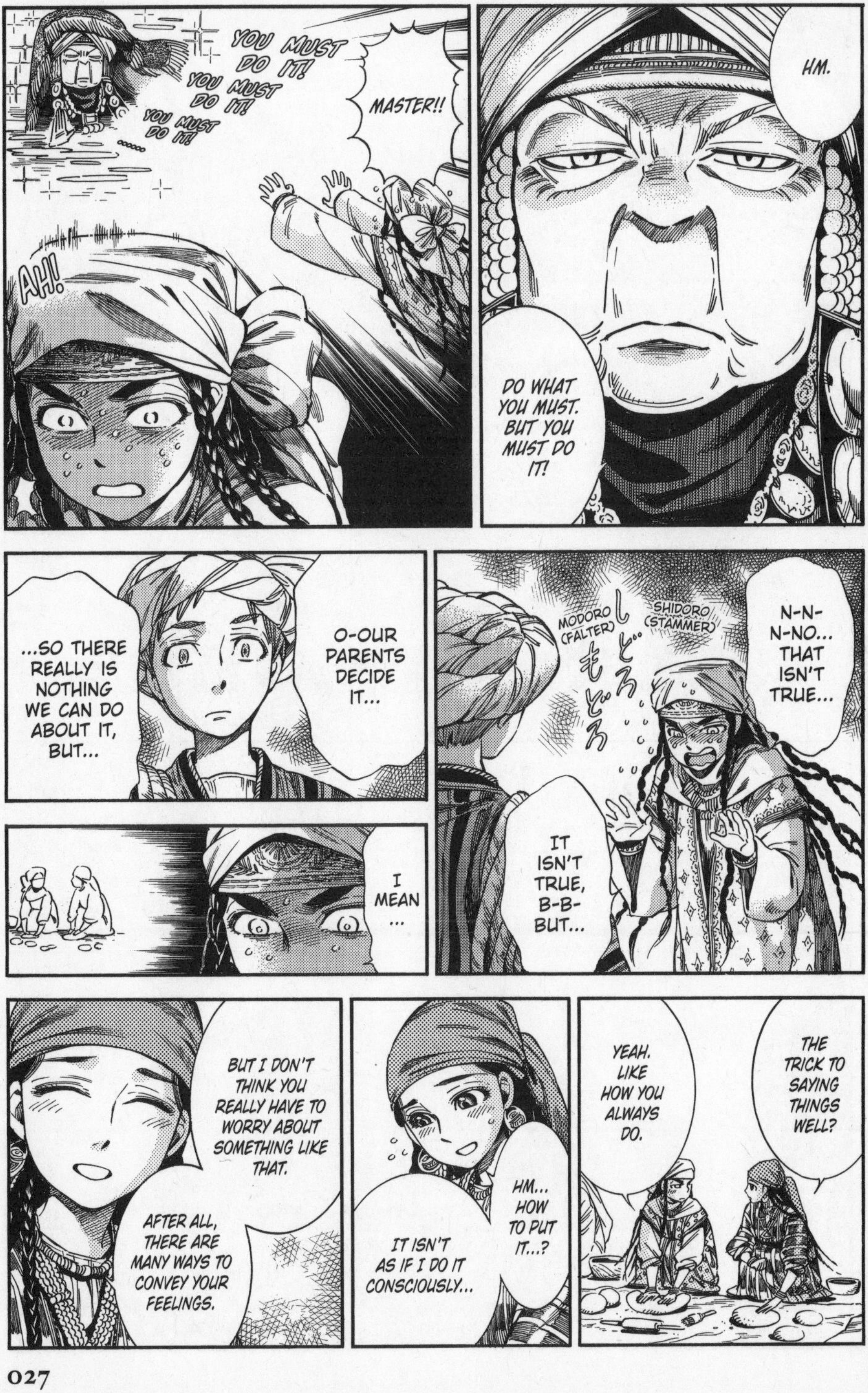
HM.
DO WHAT YOU MUST. BUT YOU MUST DO IT!
YOU MUST DO IT!
YOU MUST DO IT!
YOU MUST DO IT!
......
MASTER!!
AH!
N-N-N-NO... THAT ISN'T TRUE...
SHIDORO (STAMMER)
MODORO (FALTER)
しどろもどろ
IT ISN'T TRUE, B-B-BUT...
O-OUR PARENTS DECIDE IT...
...SO THERE REALLY IS NOTHING WE CAN DO ABOUT IT, BUT...
I MEAN ...
THE TRICK TO SAYING THINGS WELL?
YEAH. LIKE HOW YOU ALWAYS DO.
HM... HOW TO PUT IT...?
IT ISN'T AS IF I DO IT CONSCIOUSLY...
BUT I DON'T THINK YOU REALLY HAVE TO WORRY ABOUT SOMETHING LIKE THAT.
AFTER ALL, THERE ARE MANY WAYS TO CONVEY YOUR FEELINGS.

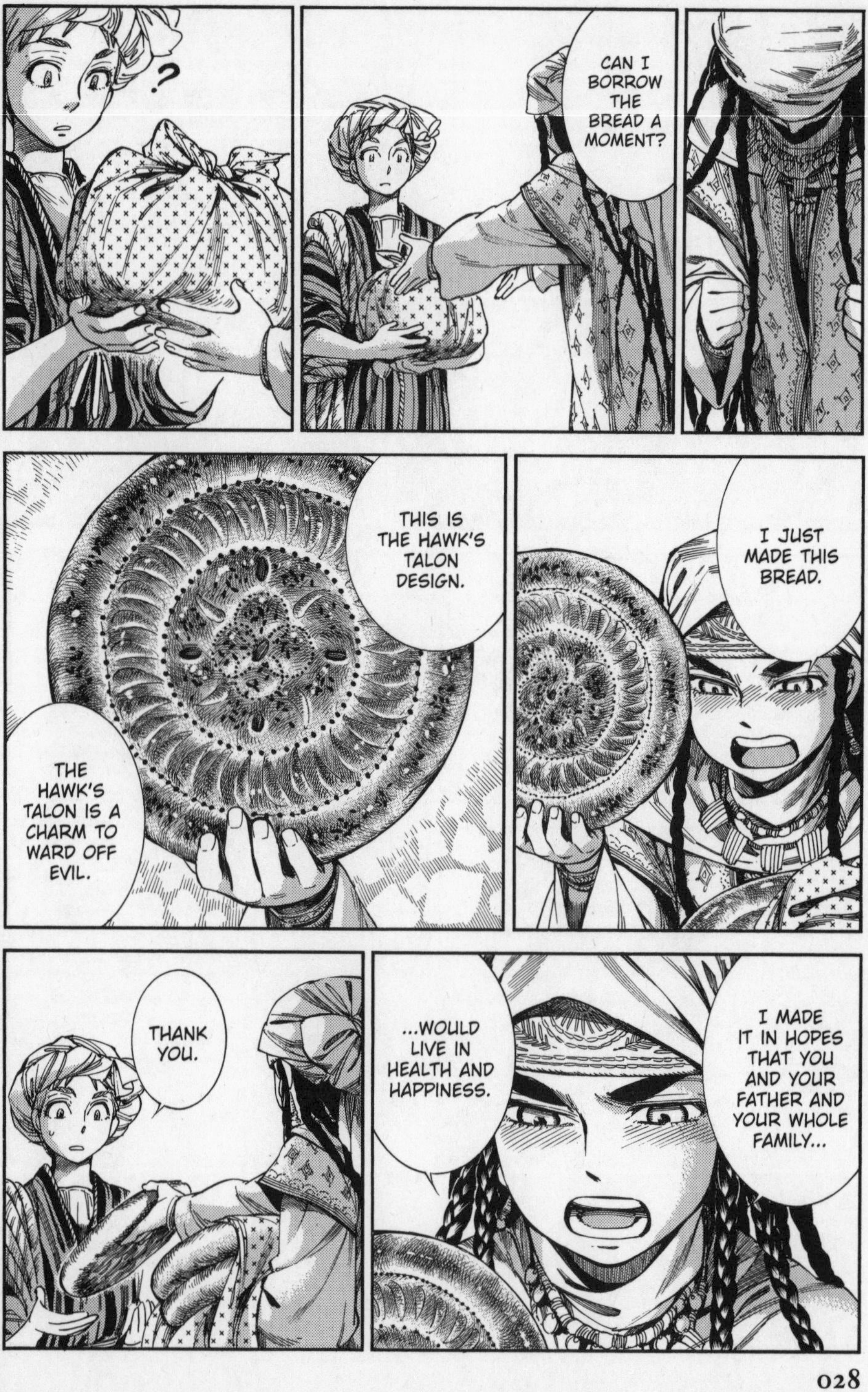
CAN I BORROW THE BREAD A MOMENT?
?
I JUST MADE THIS BREAD.
THIS IS THE HAWK'S TALON DESIGN.
THE HAWK'S TALON IS A CHARM TO WARD OFF EVIL.
I MADE IT IN HOPES THAT YOU AND YOUR FATHER AND YOUR WHOLE FAMILY...
...WOULD LIVE IN HEALTH AND HAPPINESS.
THANK YOU.

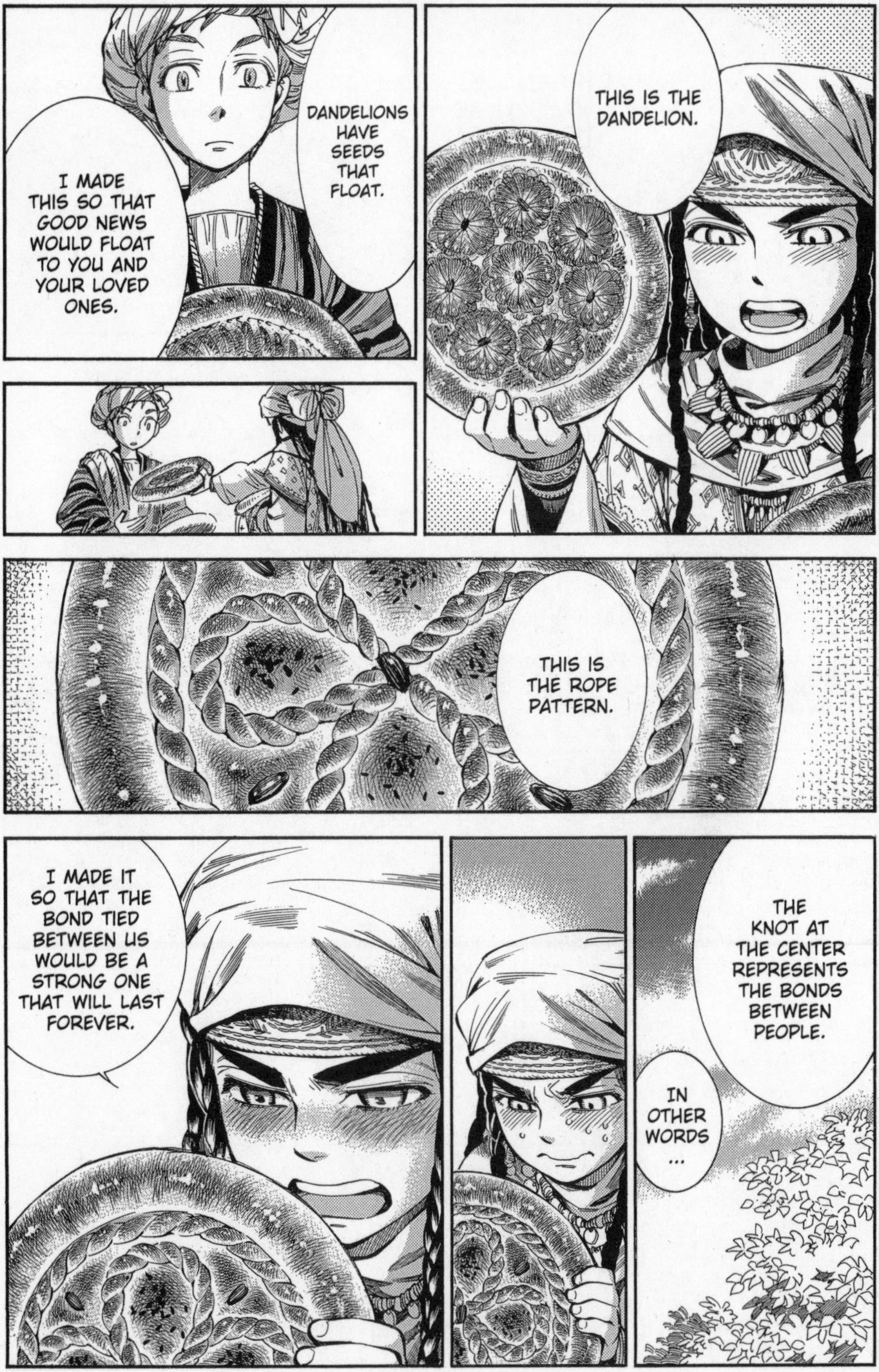
THIS IS THE DANDELION.
DANDELIONS HAVE SEEDS THAT FLOAT.
I MADE THIS SO THAT GOOD NEWS WOULD FLOAT TO YOU AND YOUR LOVED ONES.
THIS IS THE ROPE PATTERN.
THE KNOT AT THE CENTER REPRESENTS THE BONDS BETWEEN PEOPLE.
IN OTHER WORDS ...
I MADE IT SO THAT THE BOND TIED BETWEEN US WOULD BE A STRONG ONE THAT WILL LAST FOREVER.

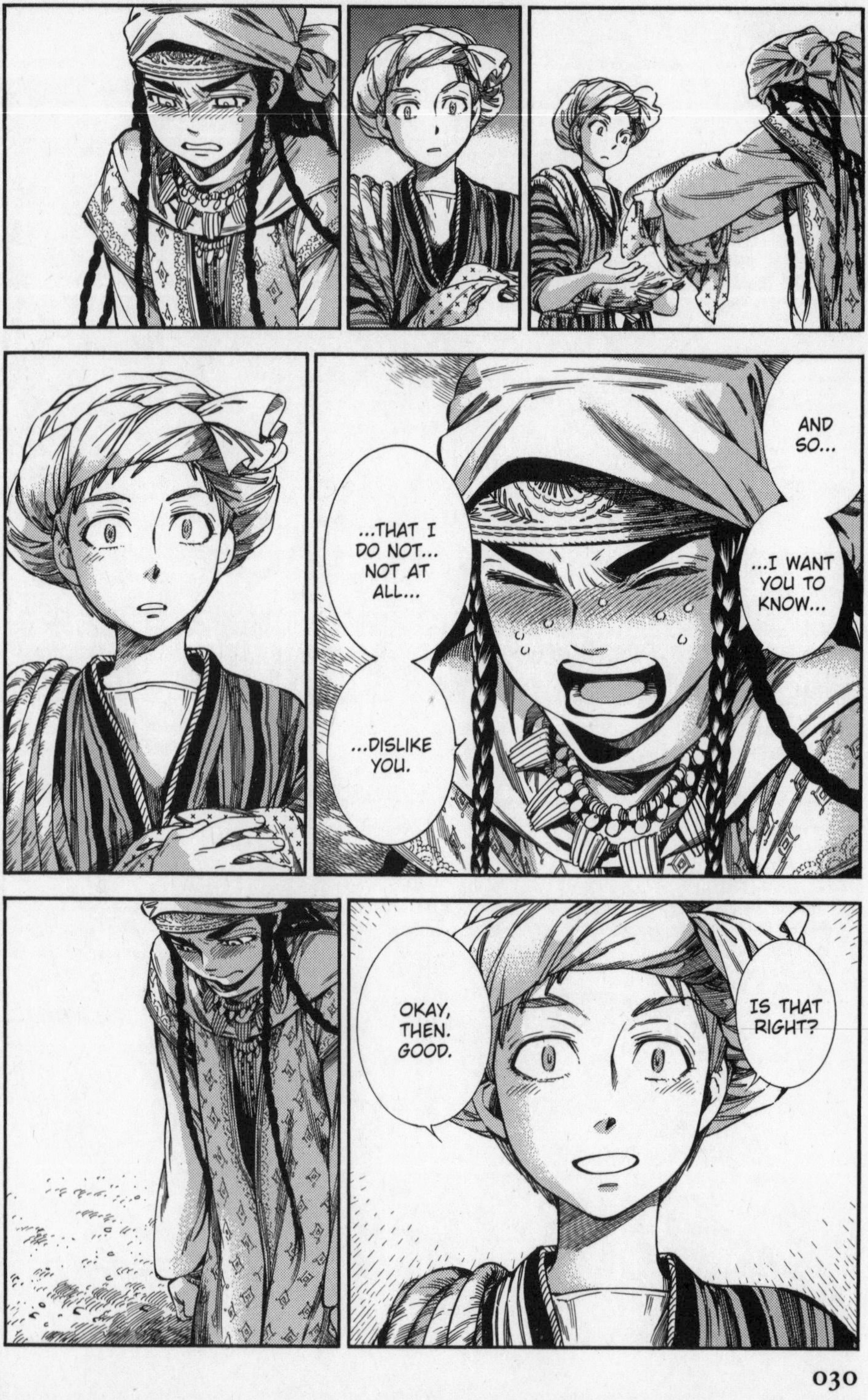
AND SO...
...I WANT YOU TO KNOW...
...THAT I DO NOT... NOT AT ALL...
...DISLIKE YOU.
IS THAT RIGHT?
OKAY, THEN. GOOD.

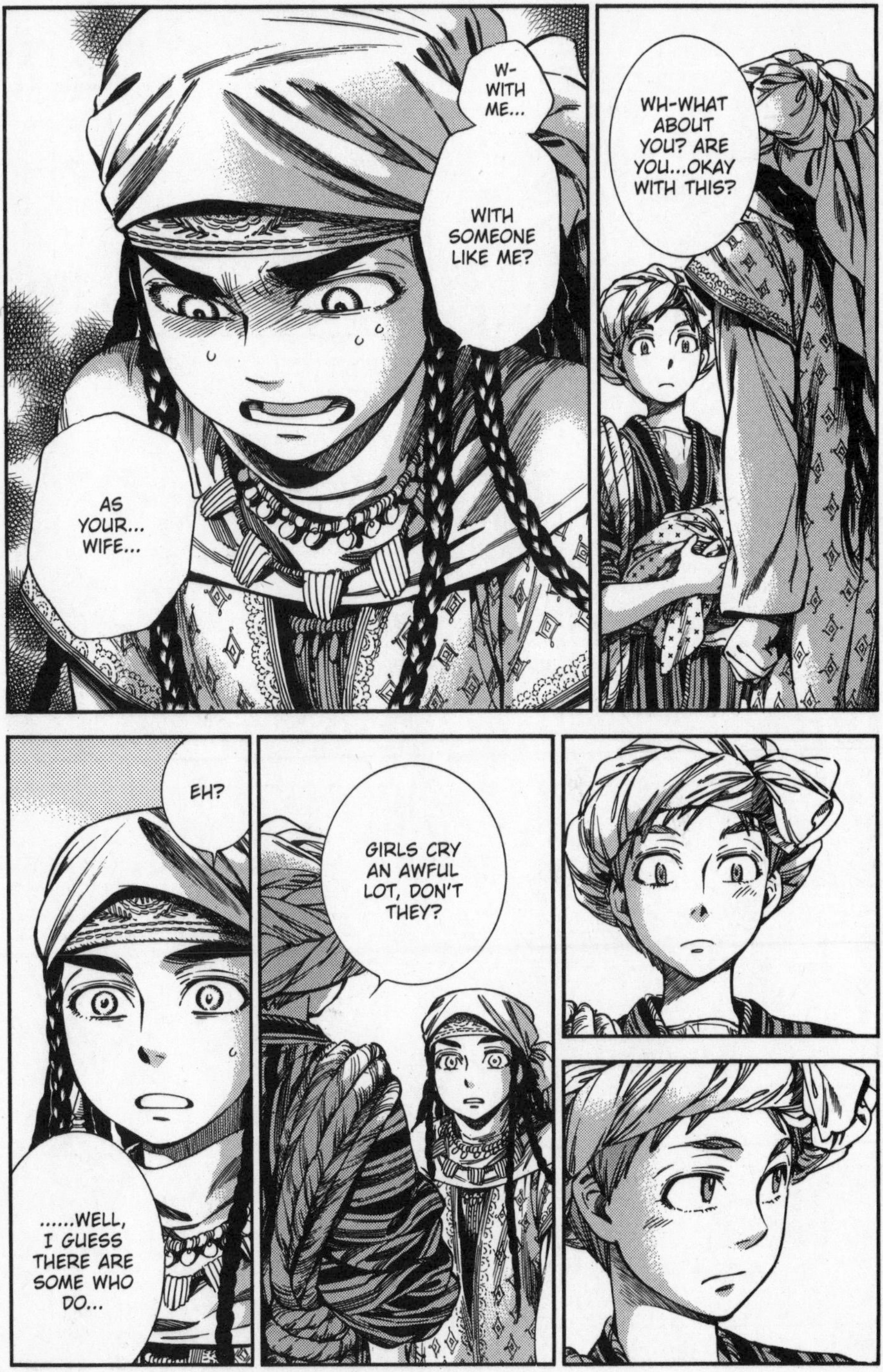
WH-WHAT ABOUT YOU? ARE YOU...OKAY WITH THIS?
W- WITH ME...
WITH SOMEONE LIKE ME?
AS YOUR... WIFE...
GIRLS CRY AN AWFUL LOT, DON'T THEY?
EH?
......WELL, I GUESS THERE ARE SOME WHO DO...

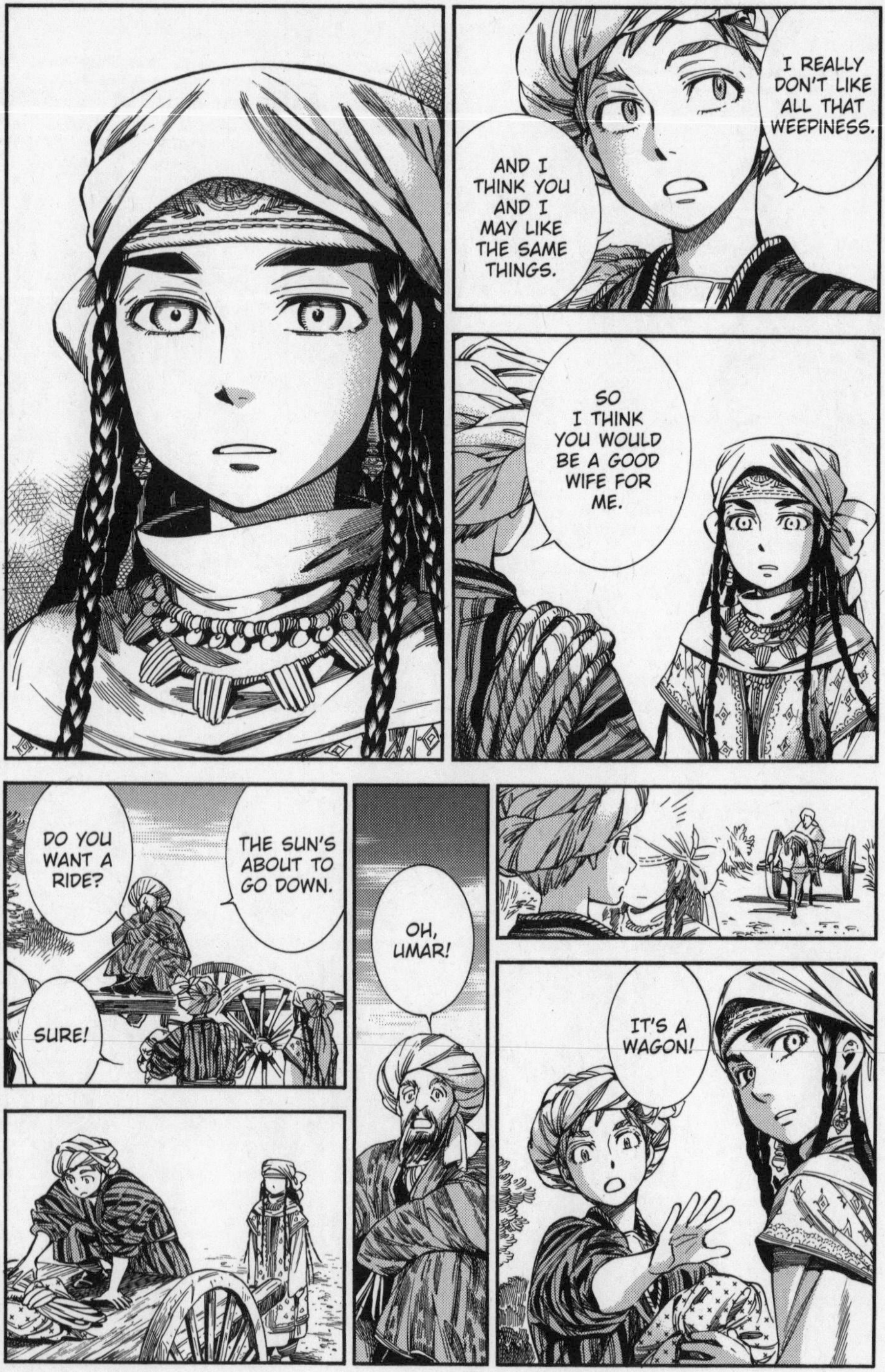
I REALLY DON'T LIKE ALL THAT WEEPINESS.
AND I THINK YOU AND I MAY LIKE THE SAME THINGS.
SO I THINK YOU WOULD BE A GOOD WIFE FOR ME.
IT'S A WAGON!
OH, UMAR!
THE SUN'S ABOUT TO GO DOWN.
DO YOU WANT A RIDE?
SURE!

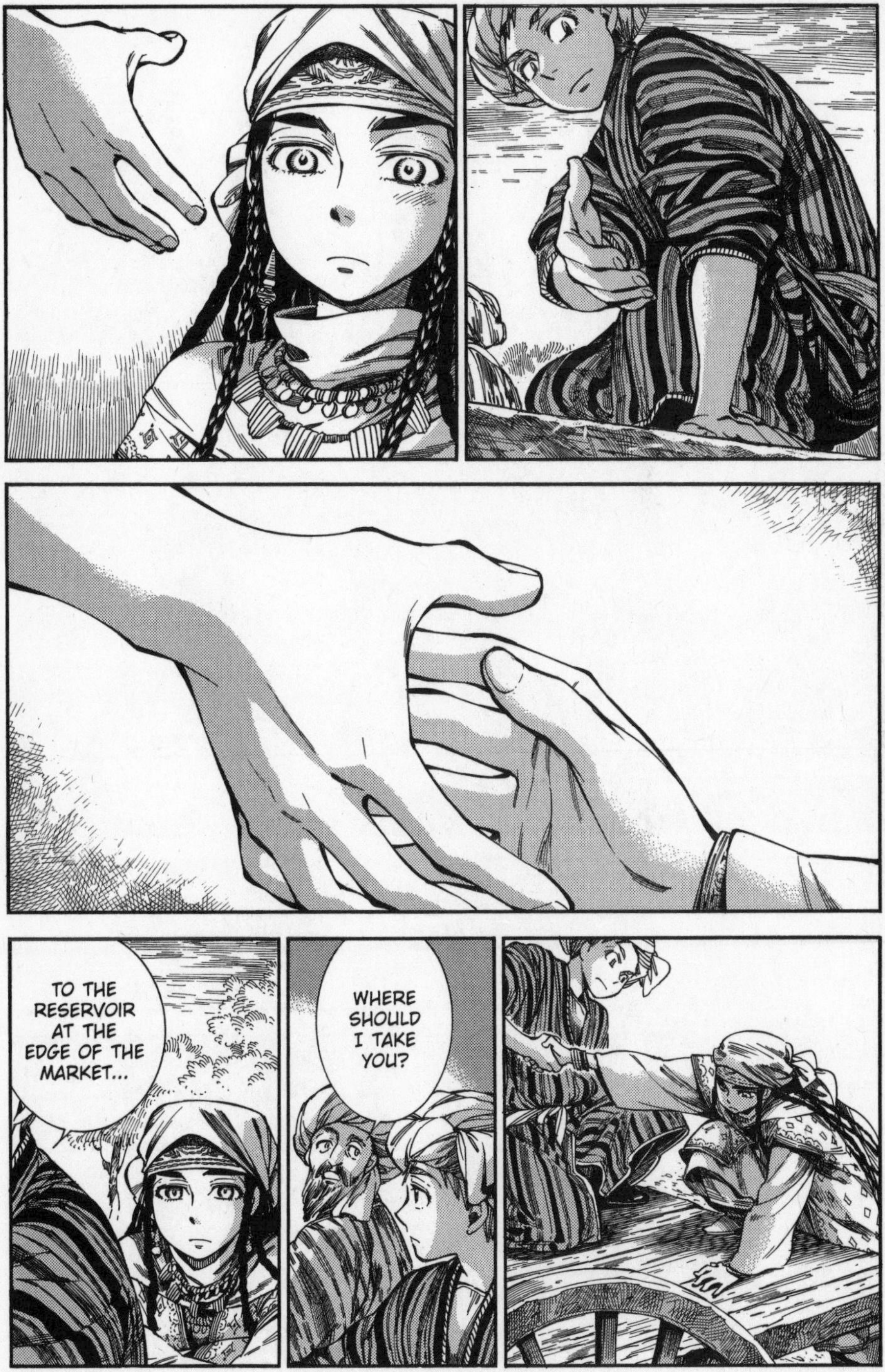
WHERE SHOULD I TAKE YOU?
TO THE RESERVOIR AT THE EDGE OF THE MARKET...

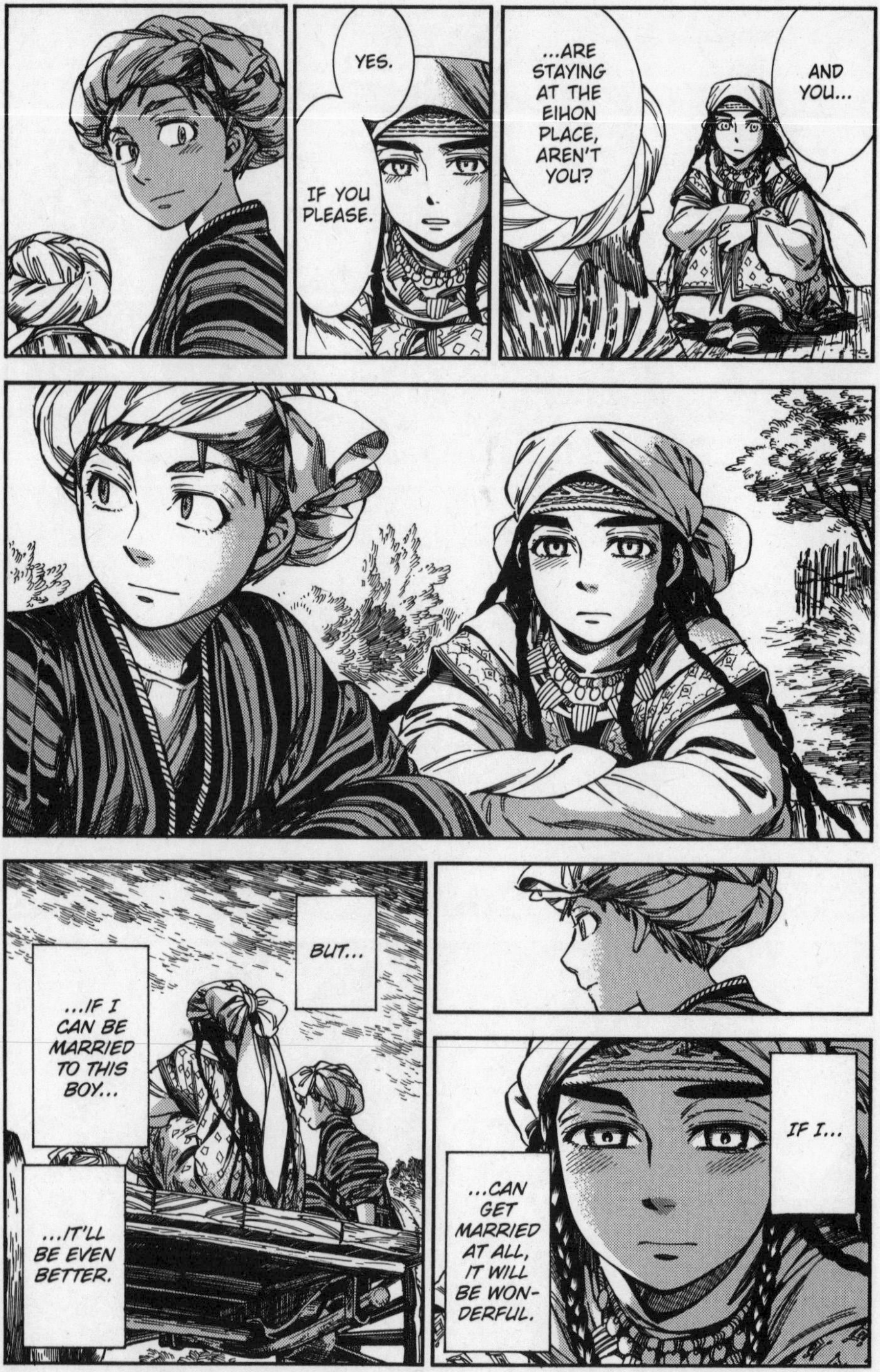
AND YOU...
...ARE STAYING AT THE EIHON PLACE, AREN'T YOU?
YES.
IF YOU PLEASE.
IF I...
...CAN GET MARRIED AT ALL, IT WILL BE WONDERFUL.
BUT...
...IF I CAN BE MARRIED TO THIS BOY...
...IT'LL BE EVEN BETTER.

✦ Chapter 52: End ✦

✦ Chapter 53 ✦

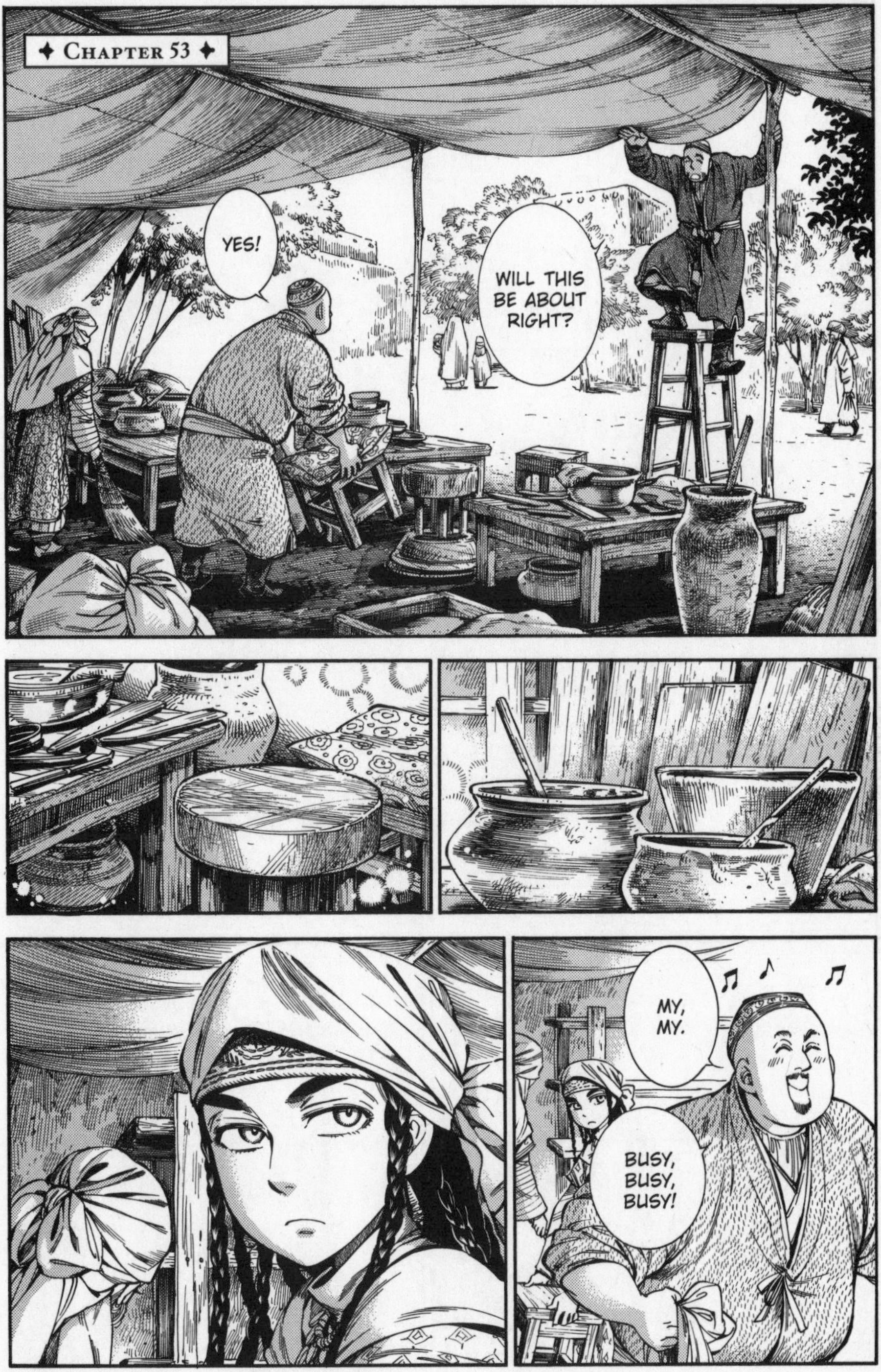
WILL THIS BE ABOUT RIGHT?
YES!
MY, MY.
BUSY, BUSY, BUSY!

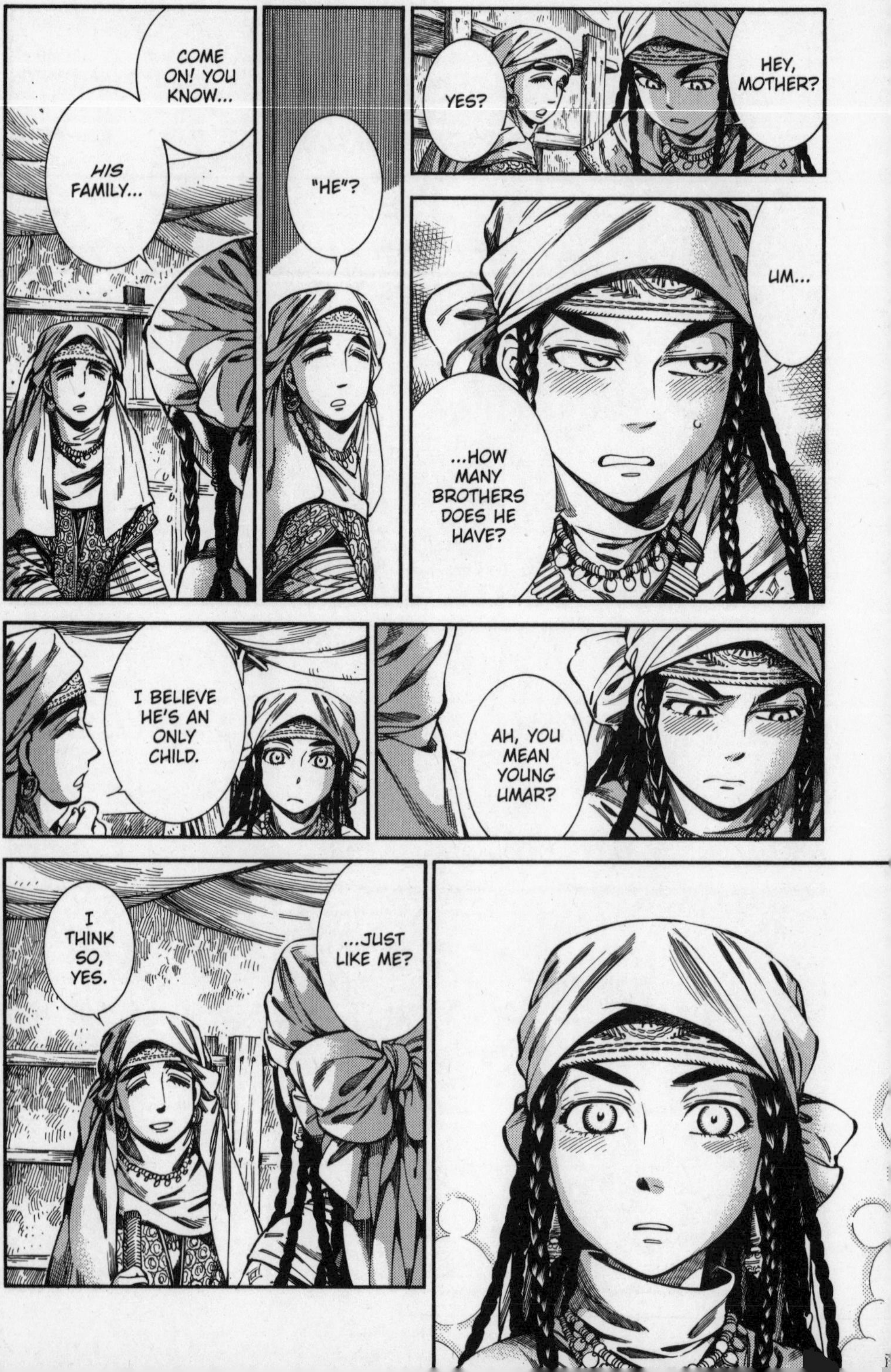
HEY, MOTHER?
YES?
UM...
...HOW MANY BROTHERS DOES HE HAVE?
"HE"?
COME ON! YOU KNOW...
HIS FAMILY...
AH, YOU MEAN YOUNG UMAR?
I BELIEVE HE'S AN ONLY CHILD.
...JUST LIKE ME?
I THINK SO, YES.

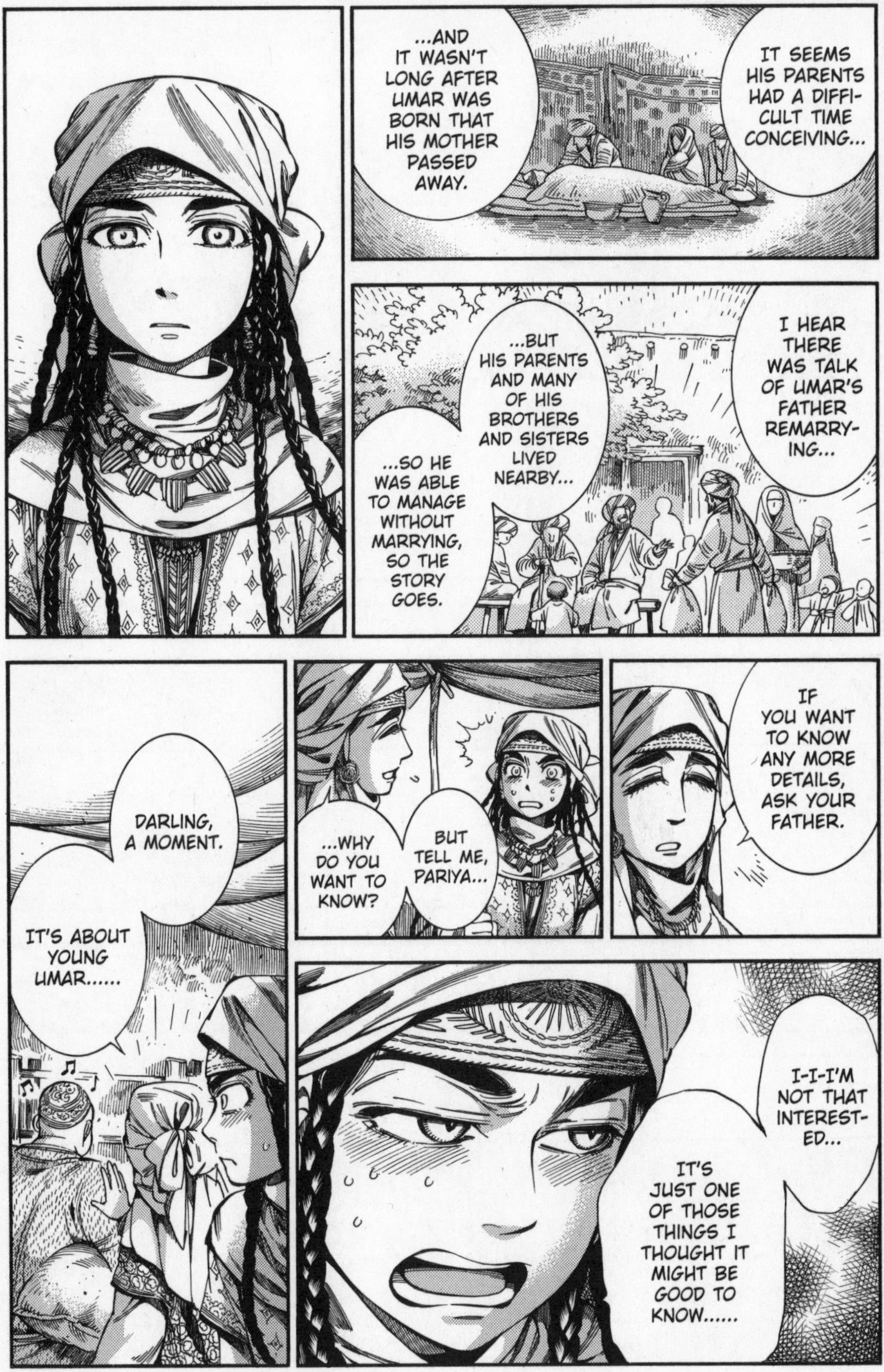
IT SEEMS HIS PARENTS HAD A DIFFI- CULT TIME CONCEIVING...
...AND IT WASN'T LONG AFTER UMAR WAS BORN THAT HIS MOTHER PASSED AWAY.
I HEAR THERE WAS TALK OF UMAR'S FATHER REMARRY- ING...
...BUT HIS PARENTS AND MANY OF HIS BROTHERS AND SISTERS LIVED NEARBY...
...SO HE WAS ABLE TO MANAGE WITHOUT MARRYING, SO THE STORY GOES.
IF YOU WANT TO KNOW ANY MORE DETAILS, ASK YOUR FATHER.
BUT TELL ME, PARIYA...
...WHY DO YOU WANT TO KNOW?
I-I-I'M NOT THAT INTEREST- ED...
IT'S JUST ONE OF THOSE THINGS I THOUGHT IT MIGHT BE GOOD TO KNOW......
DARLING, A MOMENT.
IT'S ABOUT YOUNG UMAR......

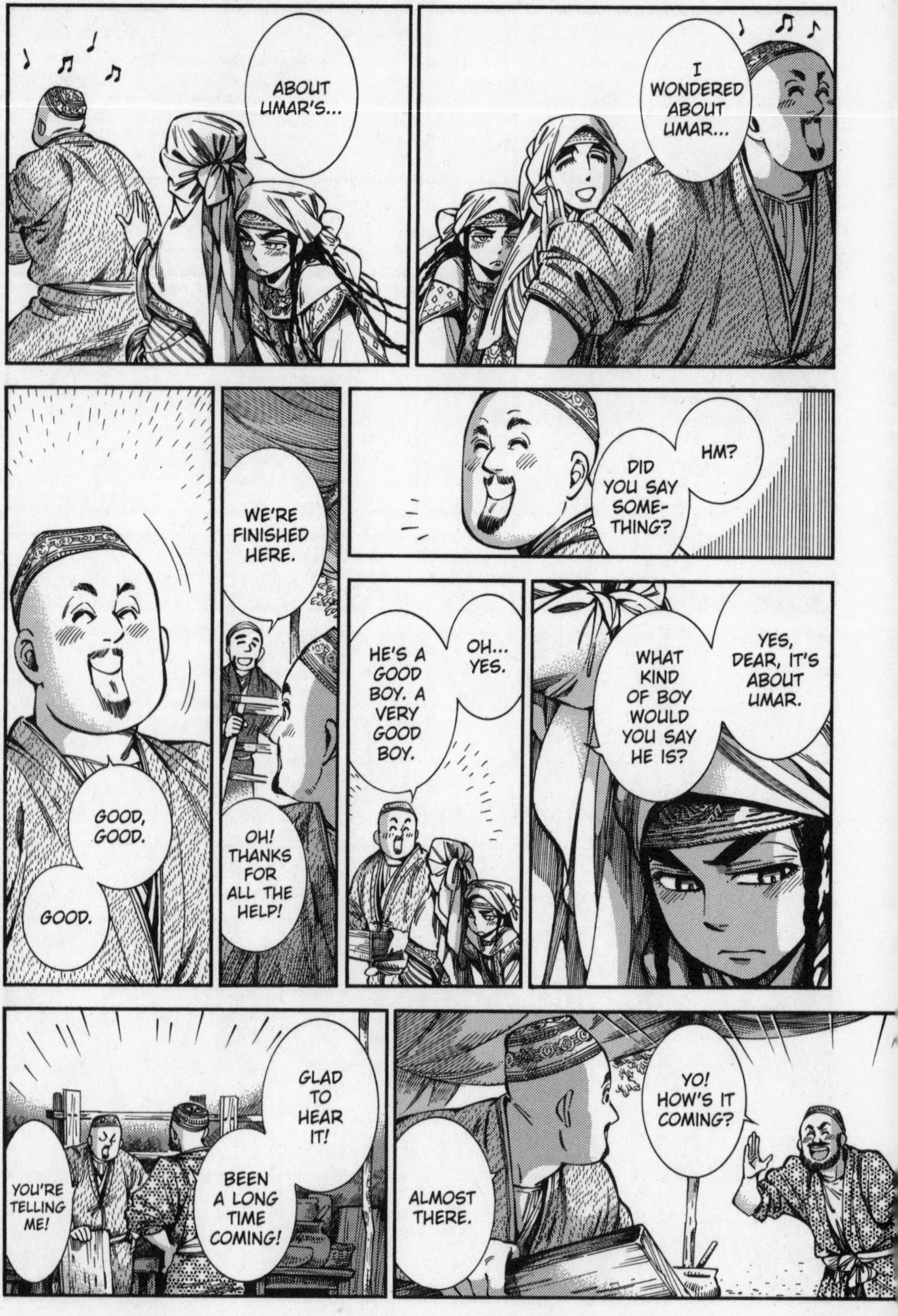
I WONDERED ABOUT UMAR...
ABOUT UMAR'S...
HM?
DID YOU SAY SOME-THING?
YES, DEAR, IT'S ABOUT UMAR.
WHAT KIND OF BOY WOULD YOU SAY HE IS?
OH... YES.
HE'S A GOOD BOY. A VERY GOOD BOY.
WE'RE FINISHED HERE.
OH! THANKS FOR ALL THE HELP!
GOOD, GOOD.
GOOD.
YO! HOW'S IT COMING?
ALMOST THERE.
GLAD TO HEAR IT!
BEEN A LONG TIME COMING!
YOU'RE TELLING ME!

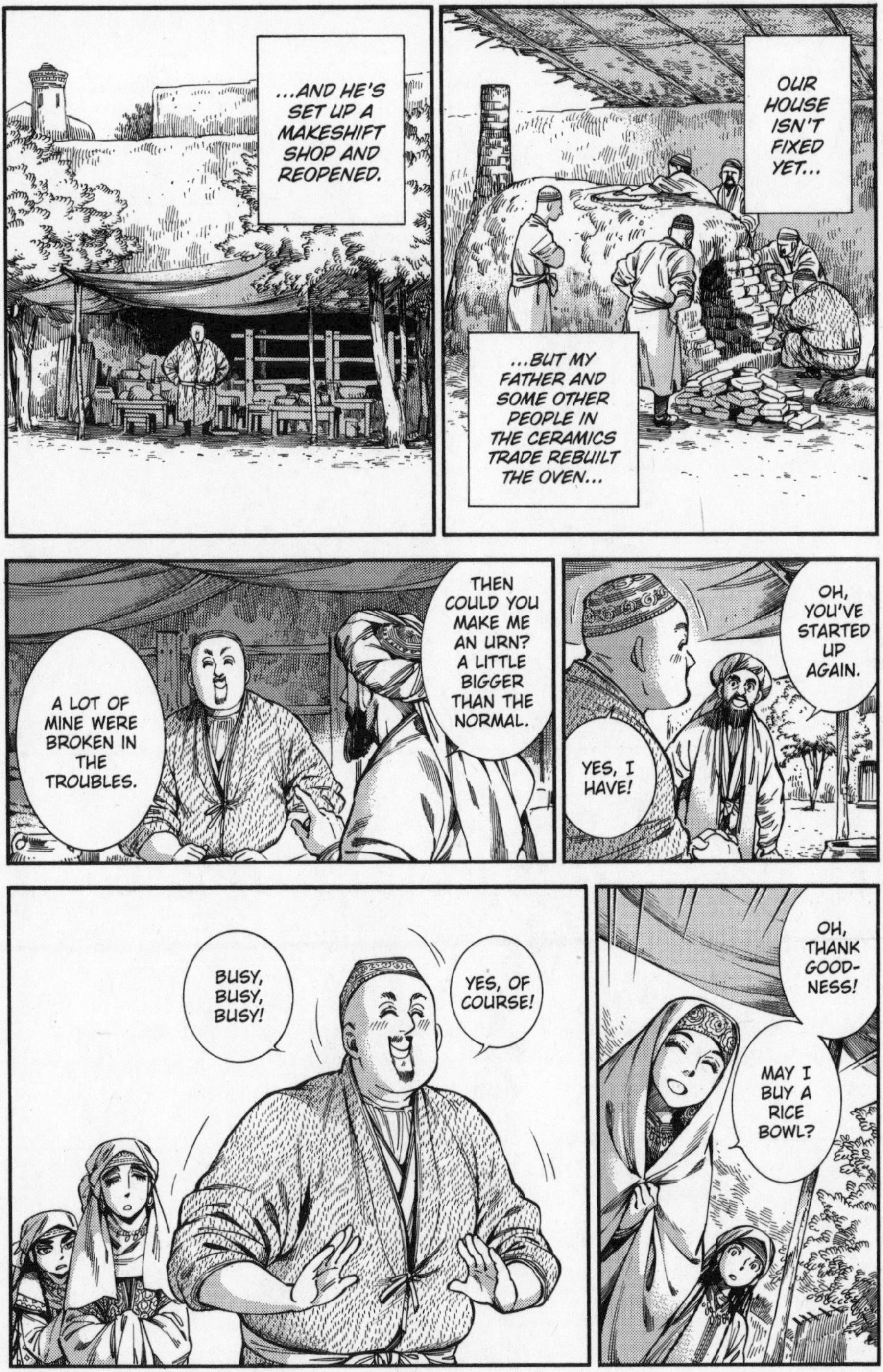
OUR HOUSE ISN'T FIXED YET...
...BUT MY FATHER AND SOME OTHER PEOPLE IN THE CERAMICS TRADE REBUILT THE OVEN...
...AND HE'S SET UP A MAKESHIFT SHOP AND REOPENED.
OH, YOU'VE STARTED UP AGAIN.
YES, I HAVE!
A LOT OF MINE WERE BROKEN IN THE TROUBLES.
THEN COULD YOU MAKE ME AN URN? A LITTLE BIGGER THAN THE NORMAL.
OH, THANK GOOD-NESS!
MAY I BUY A RICE BOWL?
YES, OF COURSE!
BUSY, BUSY, BUSY!

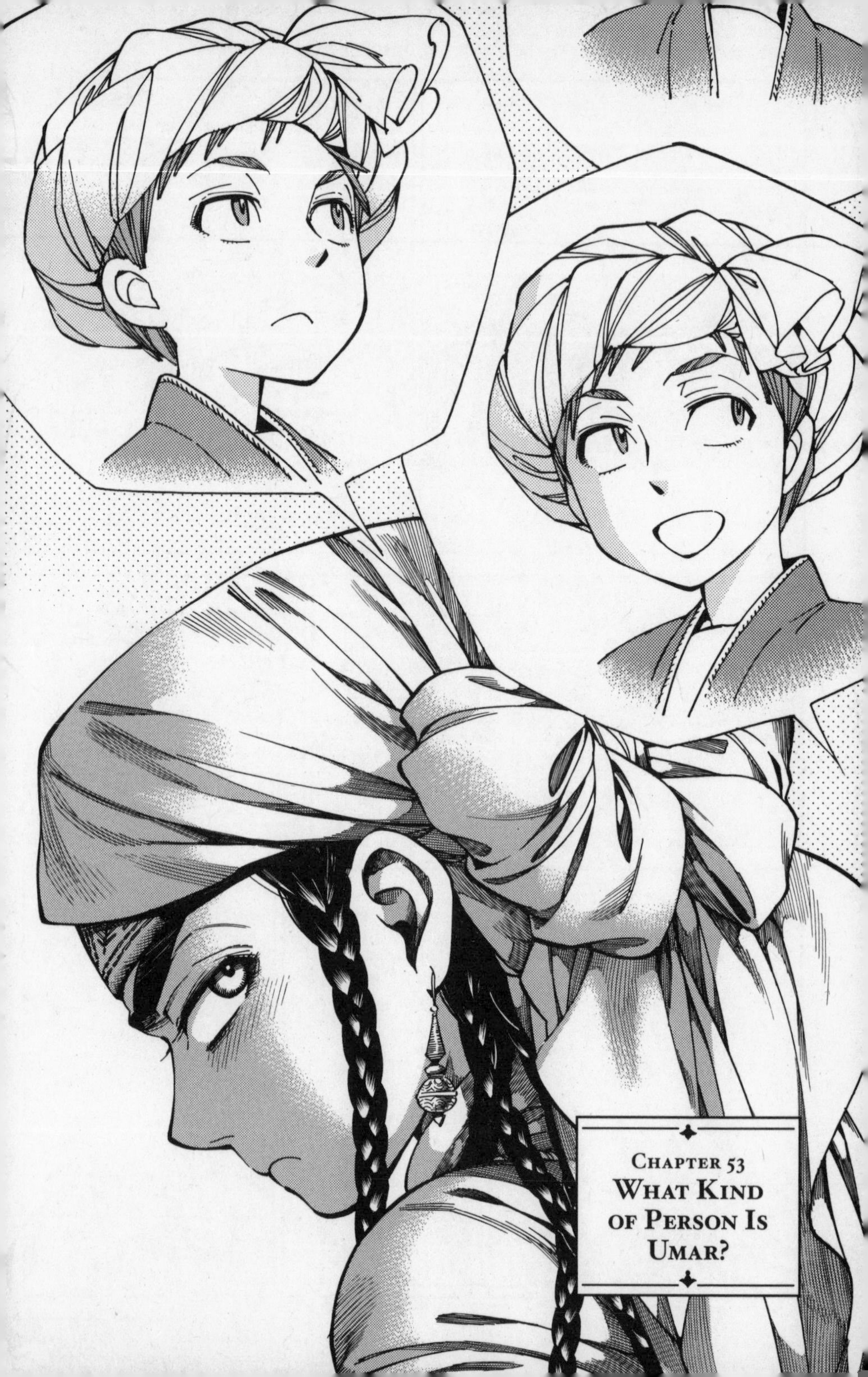
CHAPTER 53
WHAT KIND OF PERSON IS UMAR?

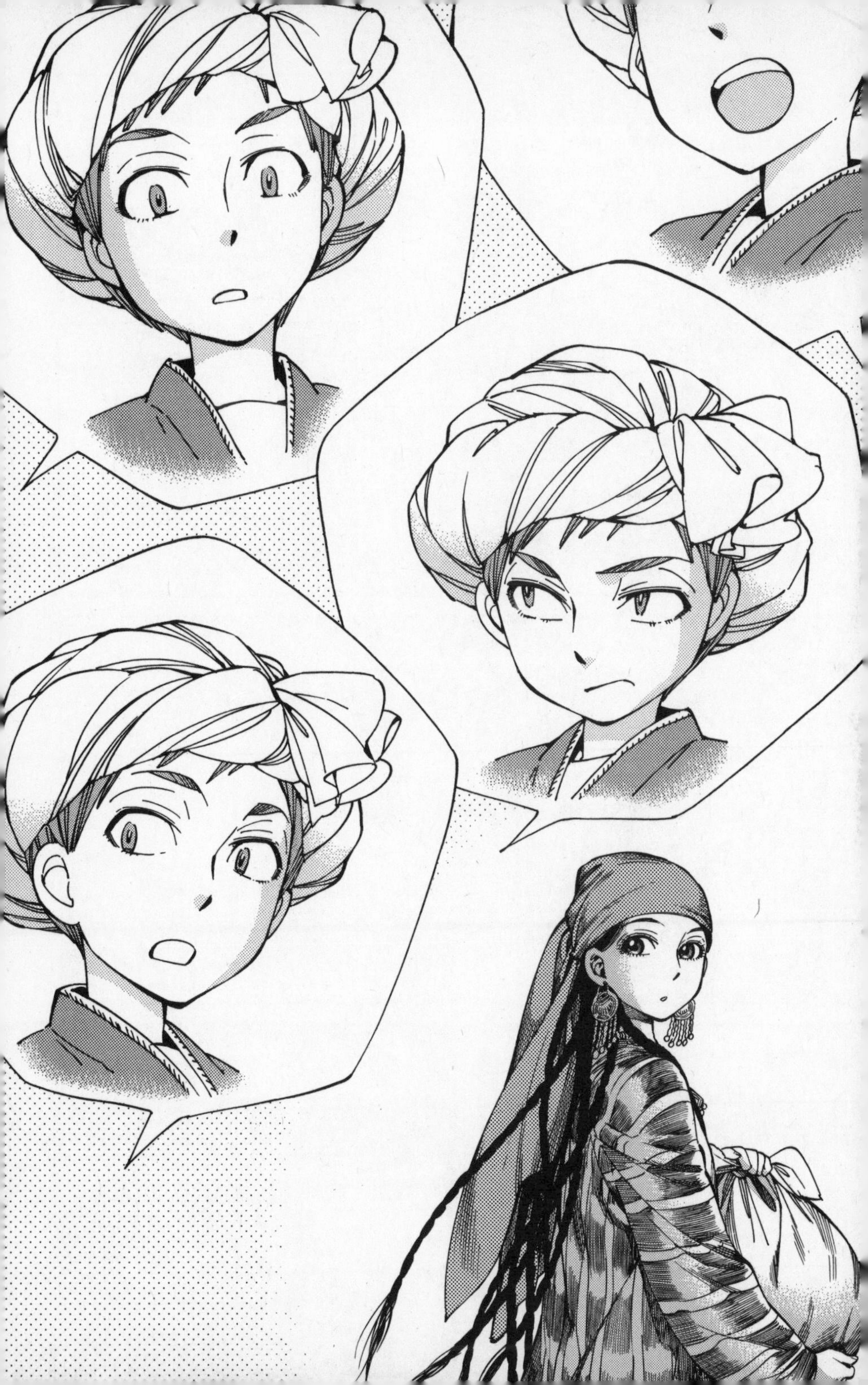

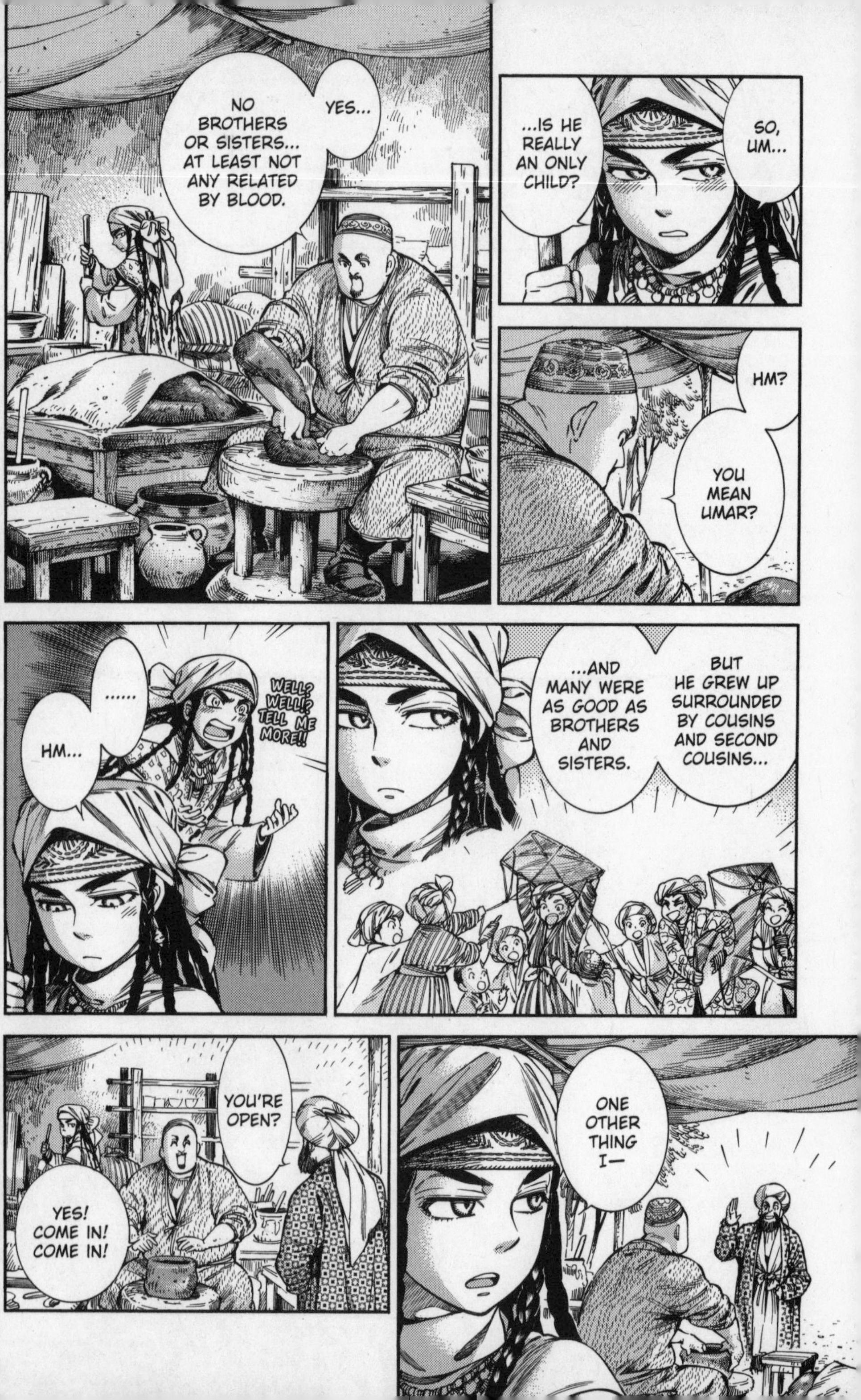
SO, UM...
...IS HE REALLY AN ONLY CHILD?
HM?
YOU MEAN UMAR?
YES...
NO BROTHERS OR SISTERS... AT LEAST NOT ANY RELATED BY BLOOD.
BUT HE GREW UP SURROUNDED BY COUSINS AND SECOND COUSINS...
...AND MANY WERE AS GOOD AS BROTHERS AND SISTERS.
WELL? WELL!? TELL ME MORE!!
......
HM...
ONE OTHER THING I—
YOU'RE OPEN?
YES! COME IN! COME IN!

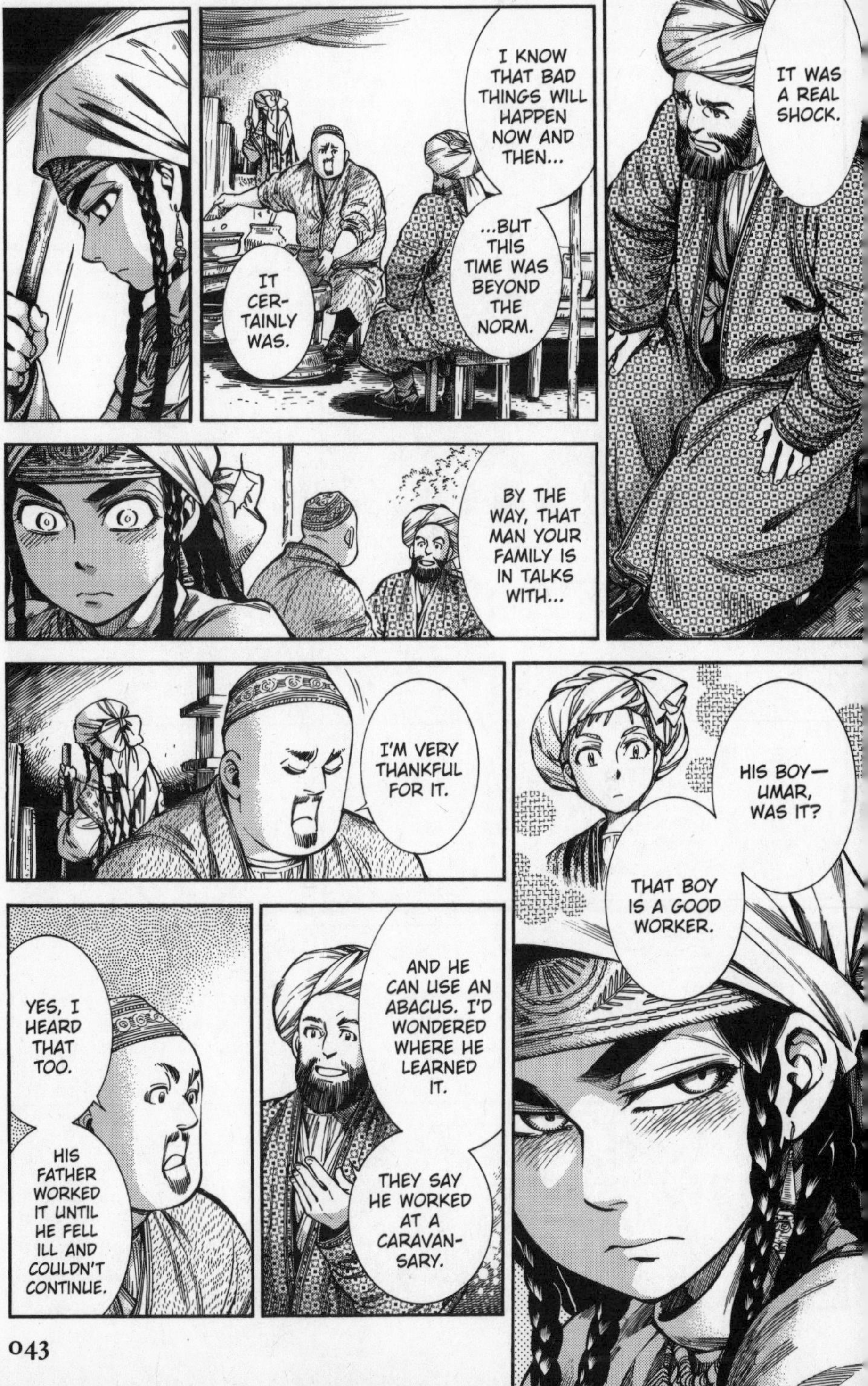

IT WAS A REAL SHOCK.
I KNOW THAT BAD THINGS WILL HAPPEN NOW AND THEN...
...BUT THIS TIME WAS BEYOND THE NORM.
IT CERTAINLY WAS.
BY THE WAY, THAT MAN YOUR FAMILY IS IN TALKS WITH...
HIS BOY— UMAR, WAS IT?
THAT BOY IS A GOOD WORKER.
I'M VERY THANKFUL FOR IT.
AND HE CAN USE AN ABACUS. I'D WONDERED WHERE HE LEARNED IT.
THEY SAY HE WORKED AT A CARAVAN-SARY.
YES, I HEARD THAT TOO.
HIS FATHER WORKED IT UNTIL HE FELL ILL AND COULDN'T CONTINUE.

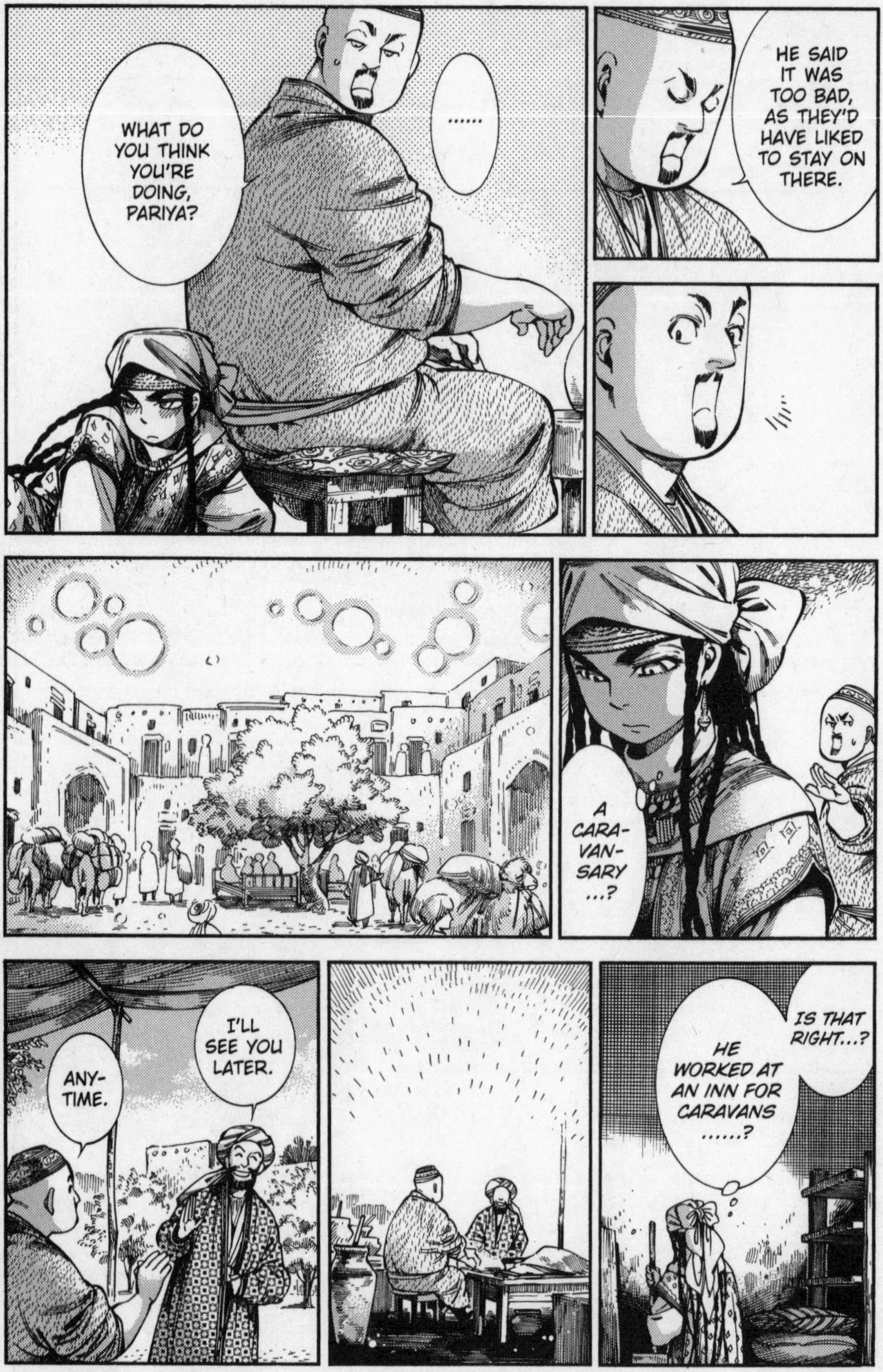
HE SAID IT WAS TOO BAD, AS THEY'D HAVE LIKED TO STAY ON THERE.
......
WHAT DO YOU THINK YOU'RE DOING, PARIYA?
A CARA-VAN-SARY ...?
IS THAT RIGHT...?
HE WORKED AT AN INN FOR CARAVANS ......?
I'LL SEE YOU LATER.
ANY-TIME.

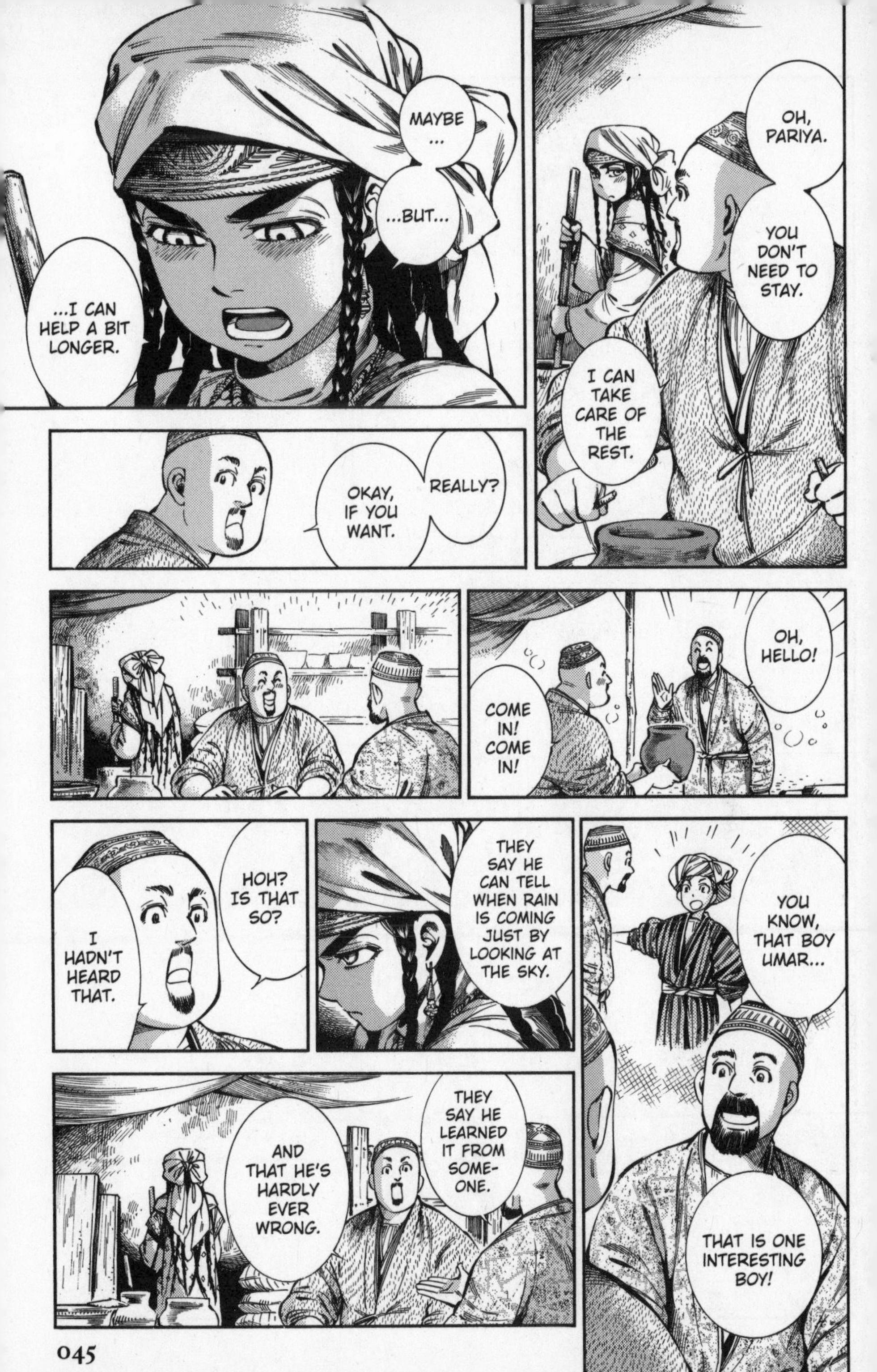
OH, PARIYA.
YOU DON'T NEED TO STAY.
I CAN TAKE CARE OF THE REST.
MAYBE ...
...BUT...
...I CAN HELP A BIT LONGER.
REALLY?
OKAY, IF YOU WANT.
OH, HELLO!
COME IN! COME IN!
YOU KNOW, THAT BOY UMAR...
THAT IS ONE INTERESTING BOY!
THEY SAY HE CAN TELL WHEN RAIN IS COMING JUST BY LOOKING AT THE SKY.
HOH? IS THAT SO?
I HADN'T HEARD THAT.
THEY SAY HE LEARNED IT FROM SOME-ONE.
AND THAT HE'S HARDLY EVER WRONG.

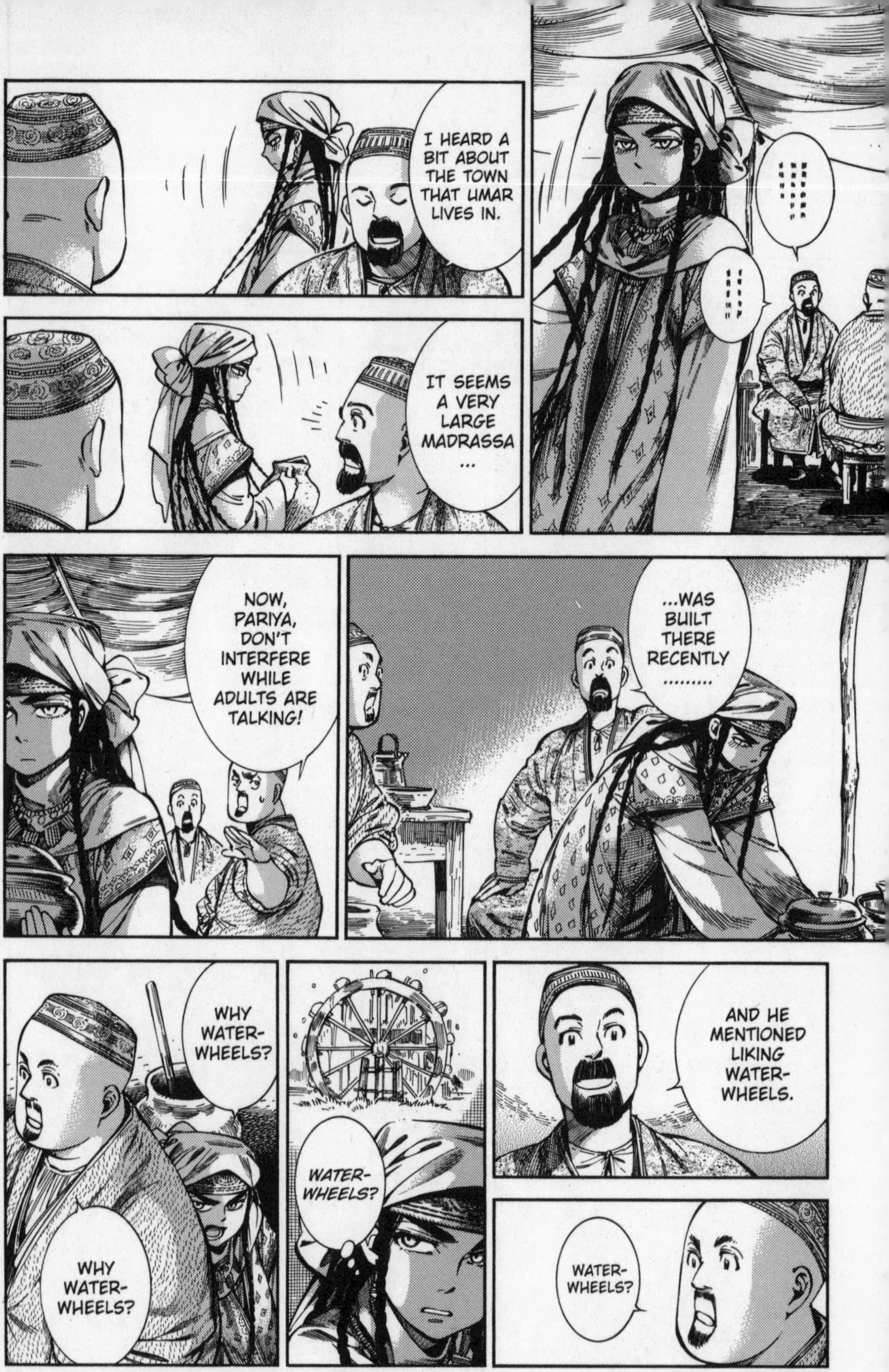
......
......
I HEARD A BIT ABOUT THE TOWN THAT UMAR LIVES IN.
IT SEEMS A VERY LARGE MADRASSA ...
...WAS BUILT THERE RECENTLY ....
NOW, PARIYA, DON'T INTERFERE WHILE ADULTS ARE TALKING!
AND HE MENTIONED LIKING WATER-WHEELS.
WATER-WHEELS?
WATER-WHEELS?
WHY WATER-WHEELS?
WHY WATER-WHEELS?

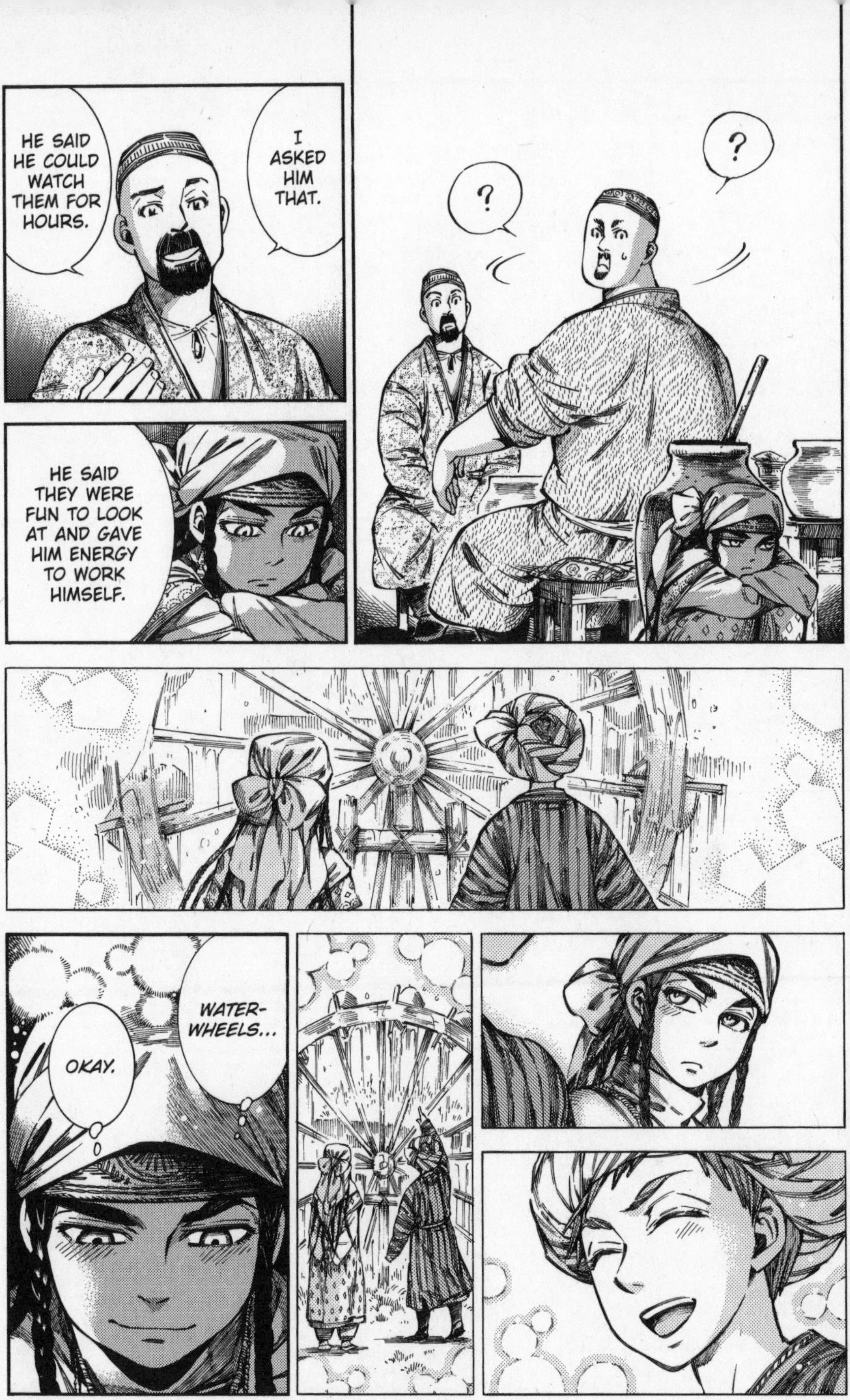
?
?
I ASKED HIM THAT.
HE SAID HE COULD WATCH THEM FOR HOURS.
HE SAID THEY WERE FUN TO LOOK AT AND GAVE HIM ENERGY TO WORK HIMSELF.
WATER-WHEELS...
OKAY.

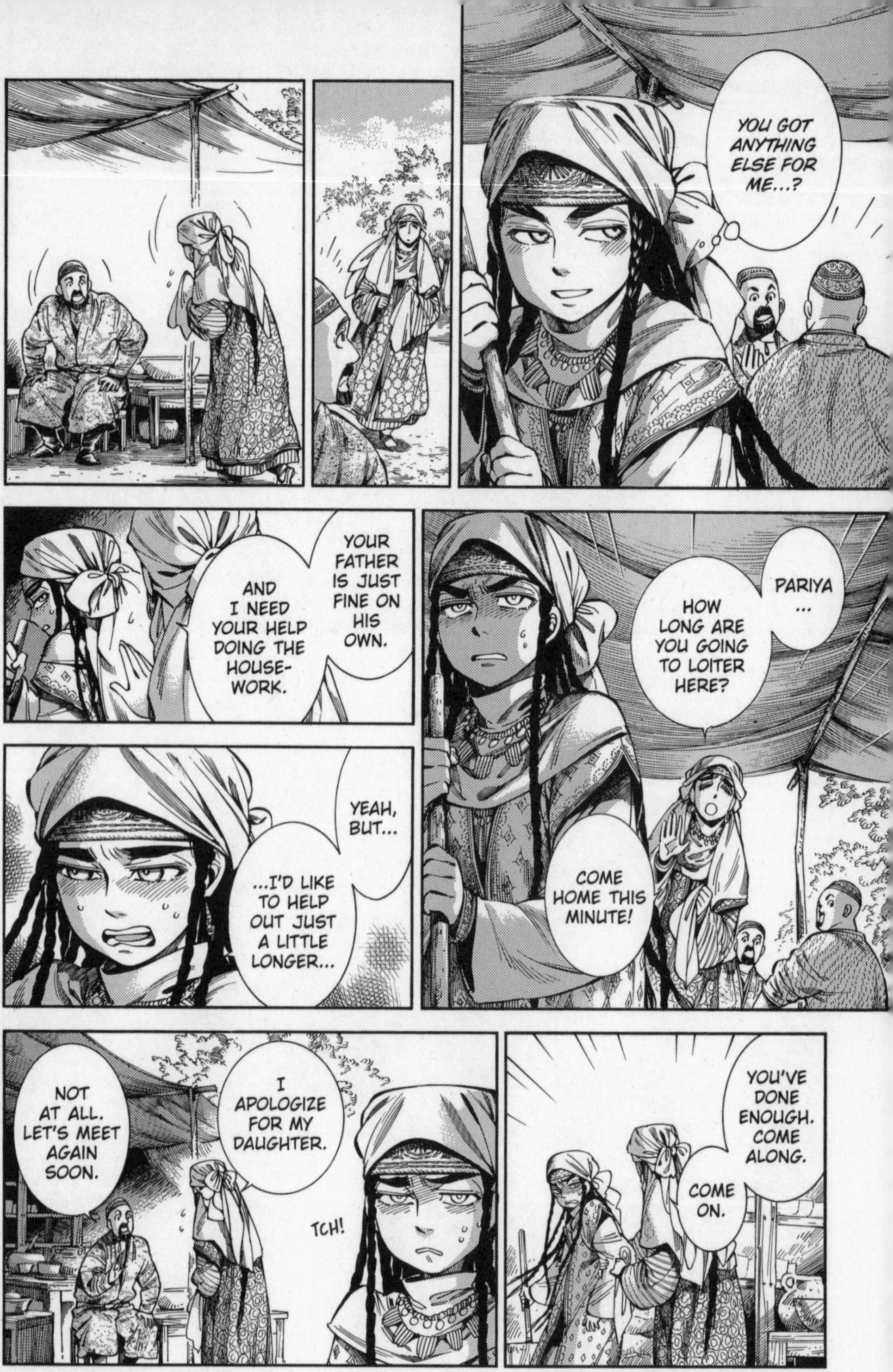
YOU GOT ANYTHING ELSE FOR ME...?
PARIYA ...
HOW LONG ARE YOU GOING TO LOITER HERE?
COME HOME THIS MINUTE!
YOUR FATHER IS JUST FINE ON HIS OWN.
AND I NEED YOUR HELP DOING THE HOUSE-WORK.
YEAH, BUT...
...I'D LIKE TO HELP OUT JUST A LITTLE LONGER...
YOU'VE DONE ENOUGH. COME ALONG.
COME ON.
I APOLOGIZE FOR MY DAUGHTER.
NOT AT ALL. LET'S MEET AGAIN SOON.
TCH!

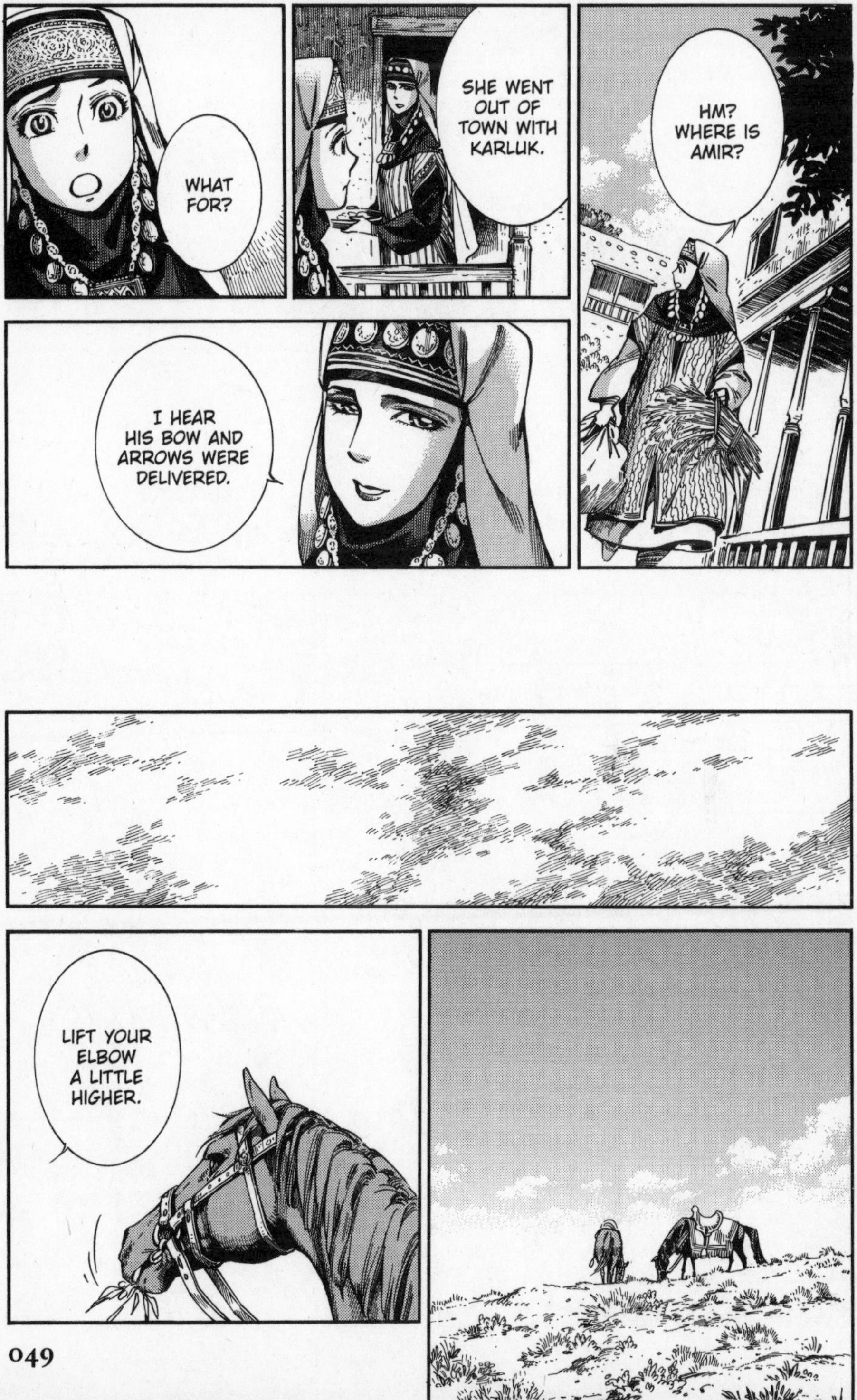
HM? WHERE IS AMIR?
SHE WENT OUT OF TOWN WITH KARLUK.
WHAT FOR?
I HEAR HIS BOW AND ARROWS WERE DELIVERED.
LIFT YOUR ELBOW A LITTLE HIGHER.

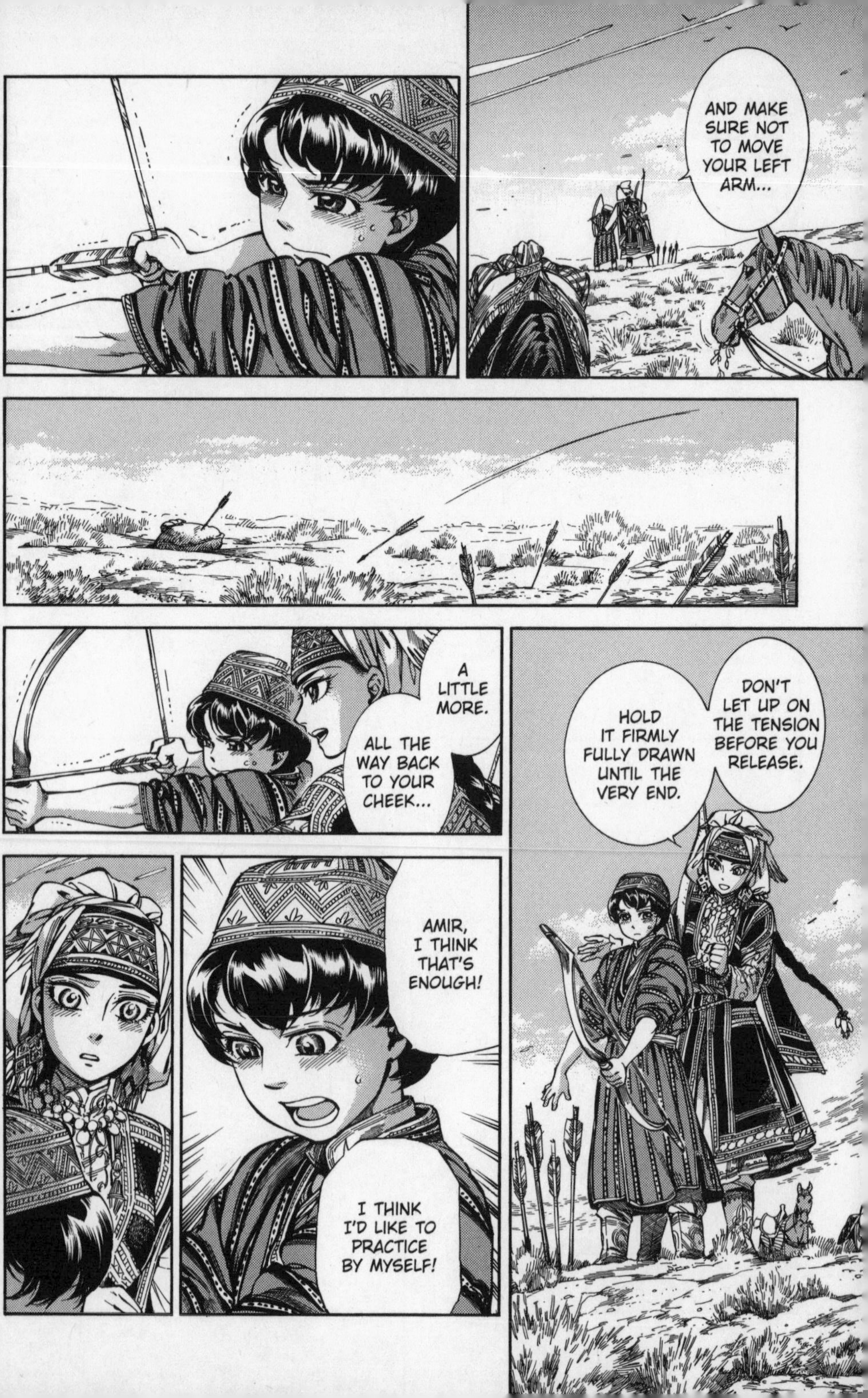
AND MAKE SURE NOT TO MOVE YOUR LEFT ARM...
DON'T LET UP ON THE TENSION BEFORE YOU RELEASE.
HOLD IT FIRMLY FULLY DRAWN UNTIL THE VERY END.
A LITTLE MORE.
ALL THE WAY BACK TO YOUR CHEEK...
AMIR, I THINK THAT'S ENOUGH!
I THINK I'D LIKE TO PRACTICE BY MYSELF!

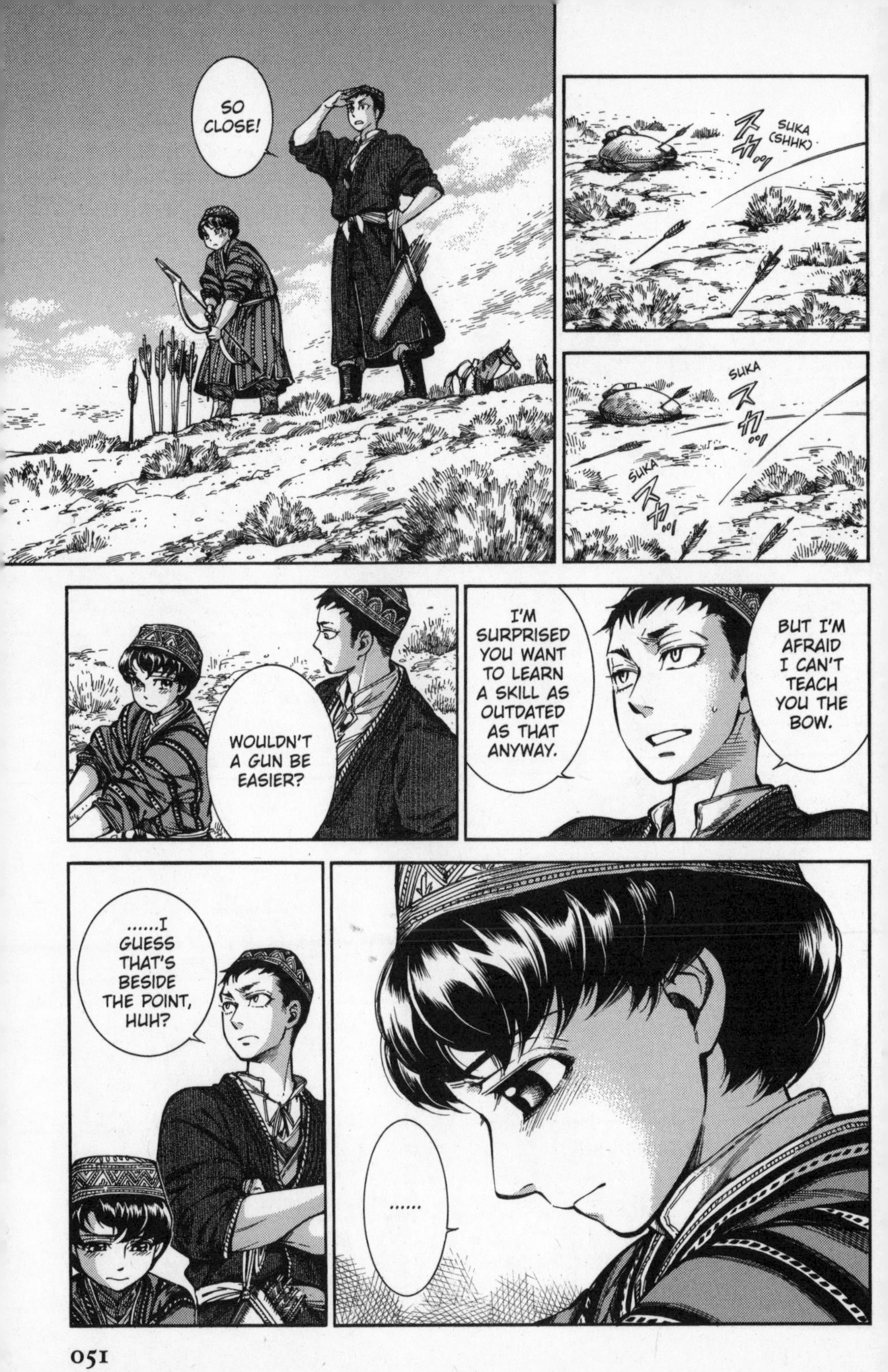
スカッ
SUKA (SHHK)
スカッ
SUKA
スカッ
SUKA
SO CLOSE!
BUT I'M AFRAID I CAN'T TEACH YOU THE BOW.
I'M SURPRISED YOU WANT TO LEARN A SKILL AS OUTDATED AS THAT ANYWAY.
WOULDN'T A GUN BE EASIER?
......
......I GUESS THAT'S BESIDE THE POINT, HUH?

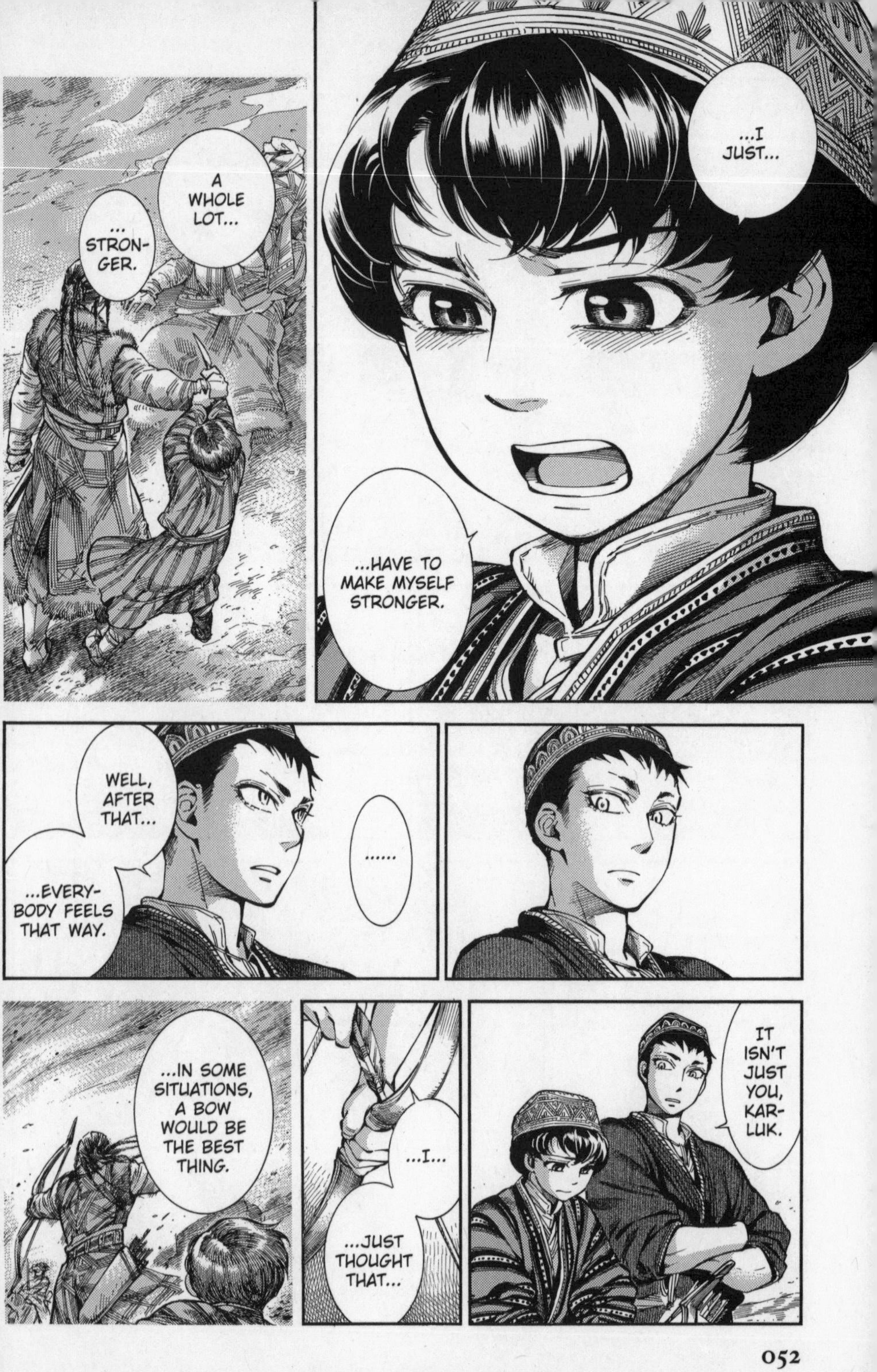
...I JUST...
...HAVE TO MAKE MYSELF STRONGER.
A WHOLE LOT...
...STRON-GER.
WELL, AFTER THAT...
...EVERY-BODY FEELS THAT WAY.
......
IT ISN'T JUST YOU, KAR-LUK.
...I...
...JUST THOUGHT THAT...
...IN SOME SITUATIONS, A BOW WOULD BE THE BEST THING.

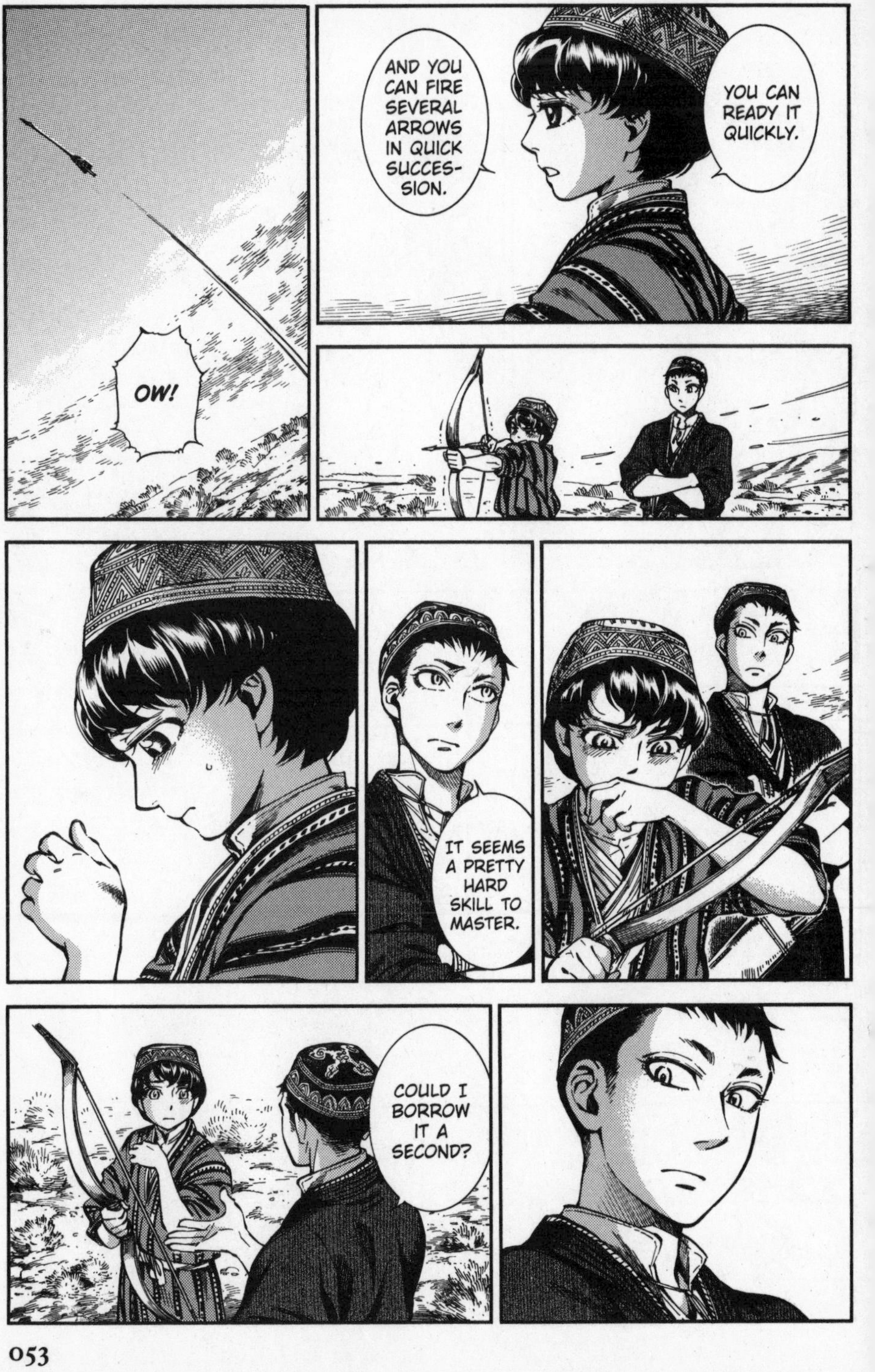
YOU CAN READY IT QUICKLY.
AND YOU CAN FIRE SEVERAL ARROWS IN QUICK SUCCESSION.
OW!
IT SEEMS A PRETTY HARD SKILL TO MASTER.
COULD I BORROW IT A SECOND?

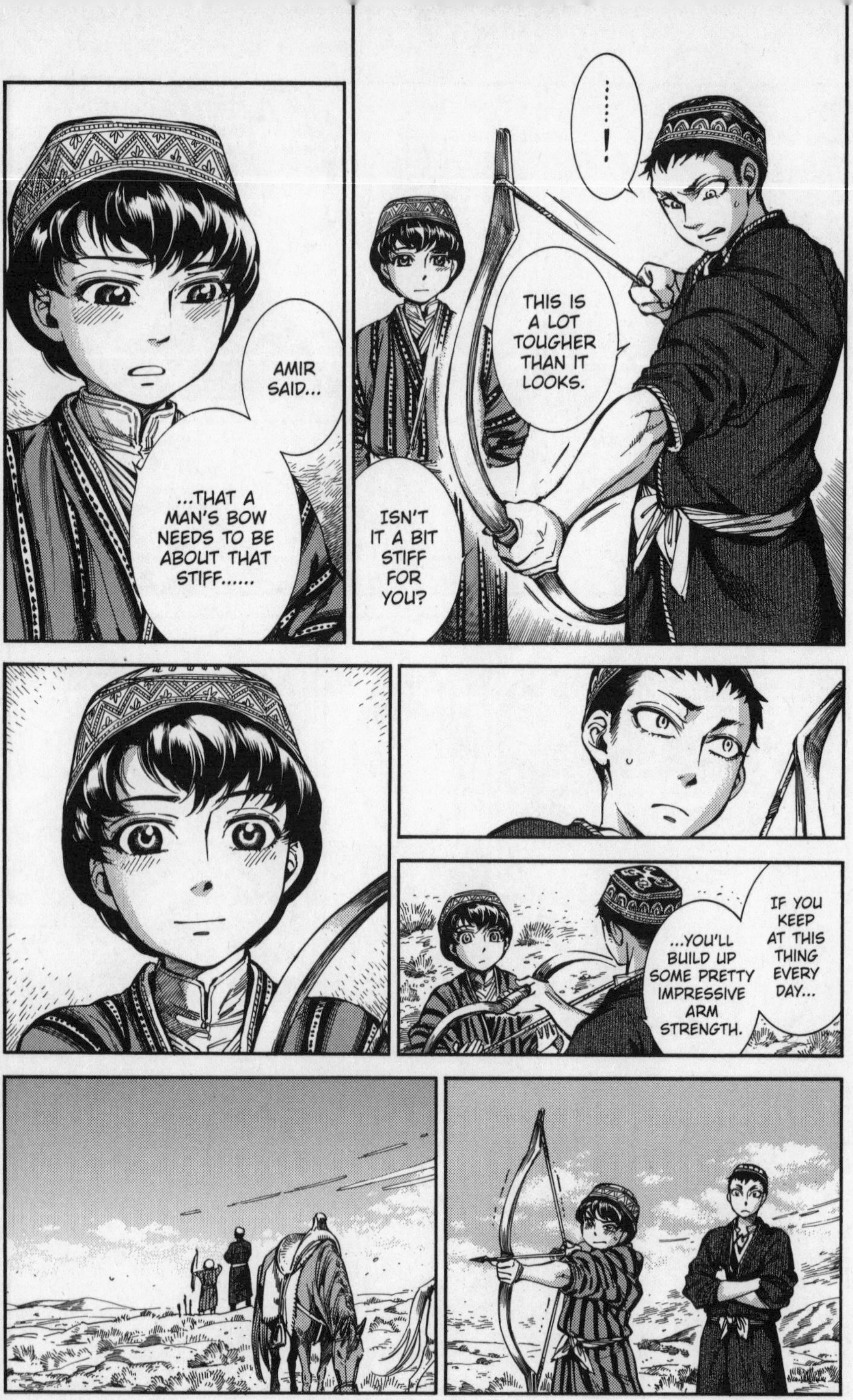

......!
THIS IS A LOT TOUGHER THAN IT LOOKS.
ISN'T IT A BIT STIFF FOR YOU?
AMIR SAID...
...THAT A MAN'S BOW NEEDS TO BE ABOUT THAT STIFF......
IF YOU KEEP AT THIS THING EVERY DAY...
...YOU'LL BUILD UP SOME PRETTY IMPRESSIVE ARM STRENGTH.

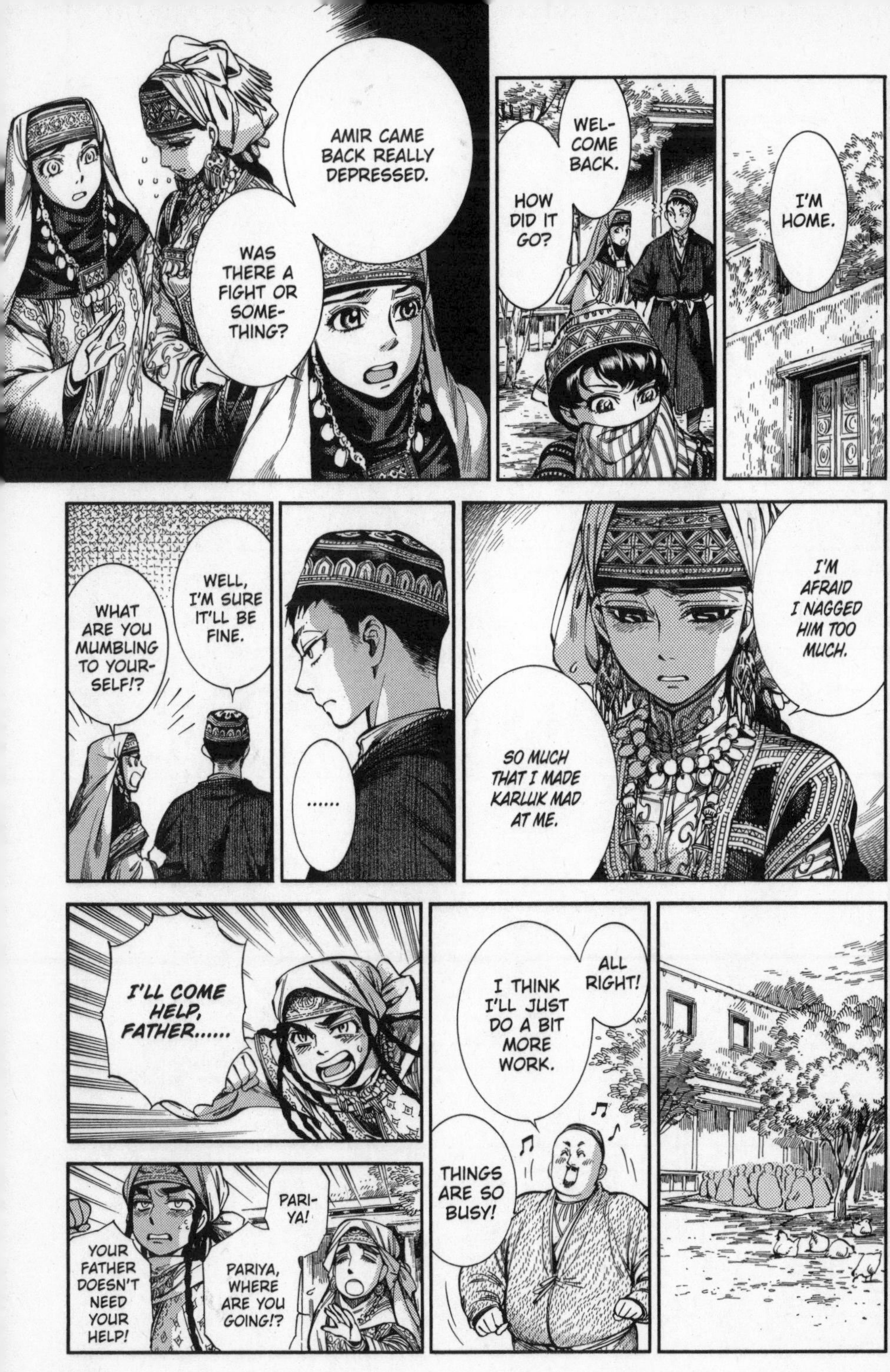
I'M HOME.
WEL-COME BACK.
HOW DID IT GO?
AMIR CAME BACK REALLY DEPRESSED.
WAS THERE A FIGHT OR SOME-THING?
I'M AFRAID I NAGGED HIM TOO MUCH.
SO MUCH THAT I MADE KARLUK MAD AT ME.
......
WELL, I'M SURE IT'LL BE FINE.
WHAT ARE YOU MUMBLING TO YOUR-SELF!?
ALL RIGHT!
I THINK I'LL JUST DO A BIT MORE WORK.
THINGS ARE SO BUSY!
I'LL COME HELP, FATHER......
PARI-YA!
PARIYA, WHERE ARE YOU GOING!?
YOUR FATHER DOESN'T NEED YOUR HELP!

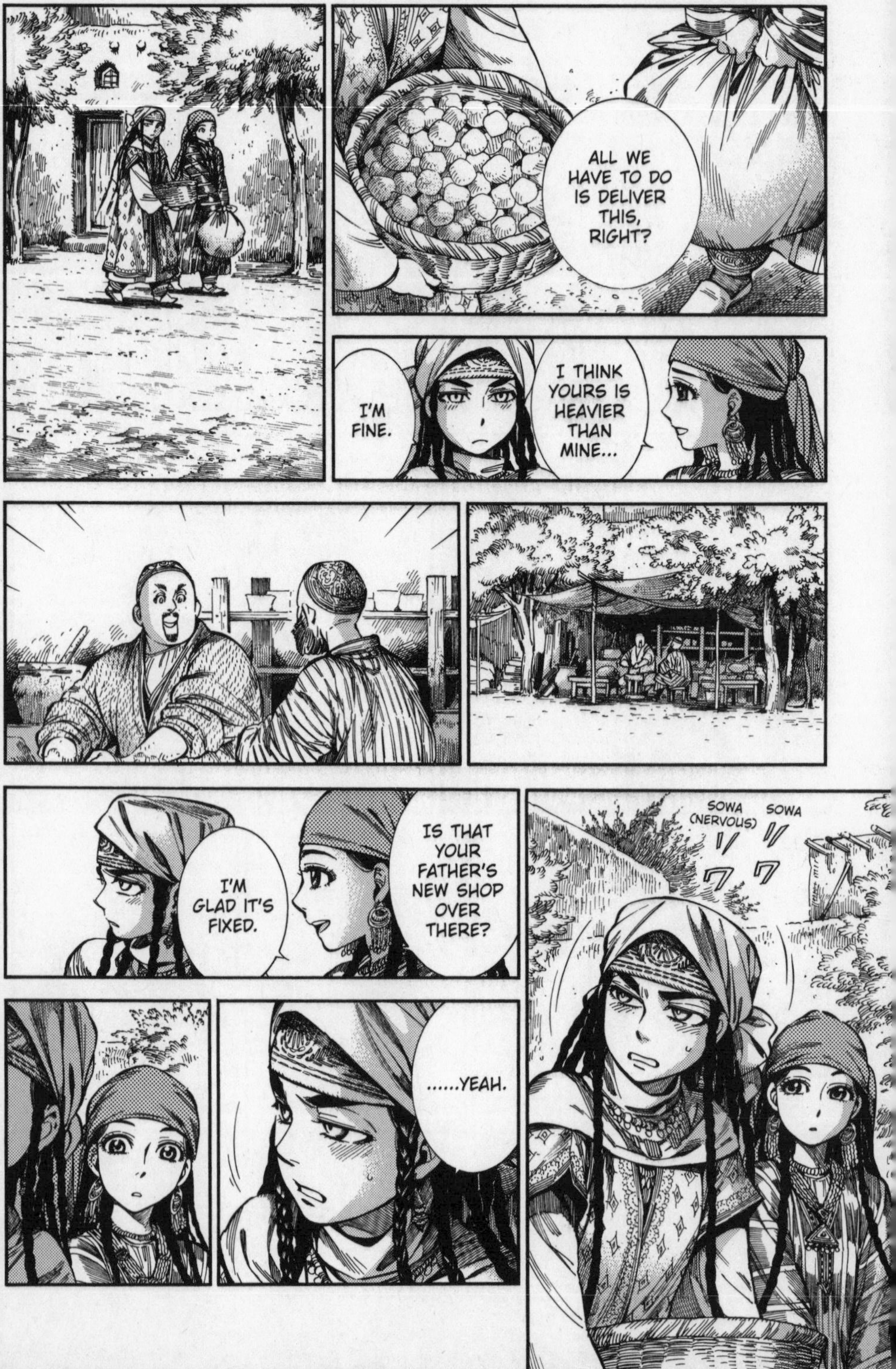
ALL WE HAVE TO DO IS DELIVER THIS, RIGHT?
I THINK YOURS IS HEAVIER THAN MINE...
I'M FINE.
SOWA
SOWA (NERVOUS)
IS THAT YOUR FATHER'S NEW SHOP OVER THERE?
I'M GLAD IT'S FIXED.
......YEAH.

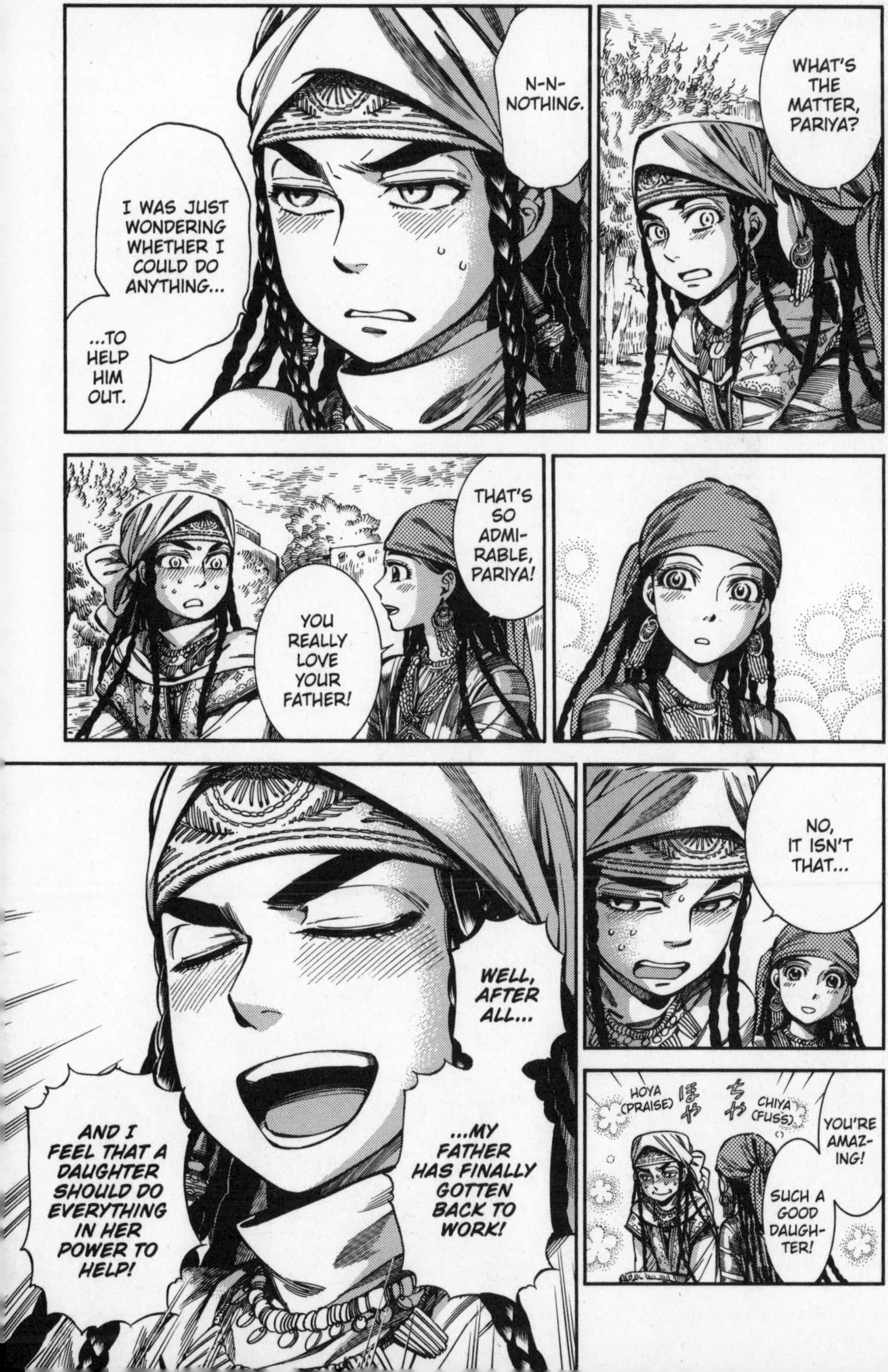
WHAT'S THE MATTER, PARIYA?
N-N-NOTHING.
I WAS JUST WONDERING WHETHER I COULD DO ANYTHING...
...TO HELP HIM OUT.
THAT'S SO ADMIRABLE, PARIYA!
YOU REALLY LOVE YOUR FATHER!
NO, IT ISN'T THAT...
HOYA (PRAISE) ほや
ちや CHIYA (FUSS)
YOU'RE AMAZING!
SUCH A GOOD DAUGHTER!
WELL, AFTER ALL...
...MY FATHER HAS FINALLY GOTTEN BACK TO WORK!
AND I FEEL THAT A DAUGHTER SHOULD DO EVERYTHING IN HER POWER TO HELP!

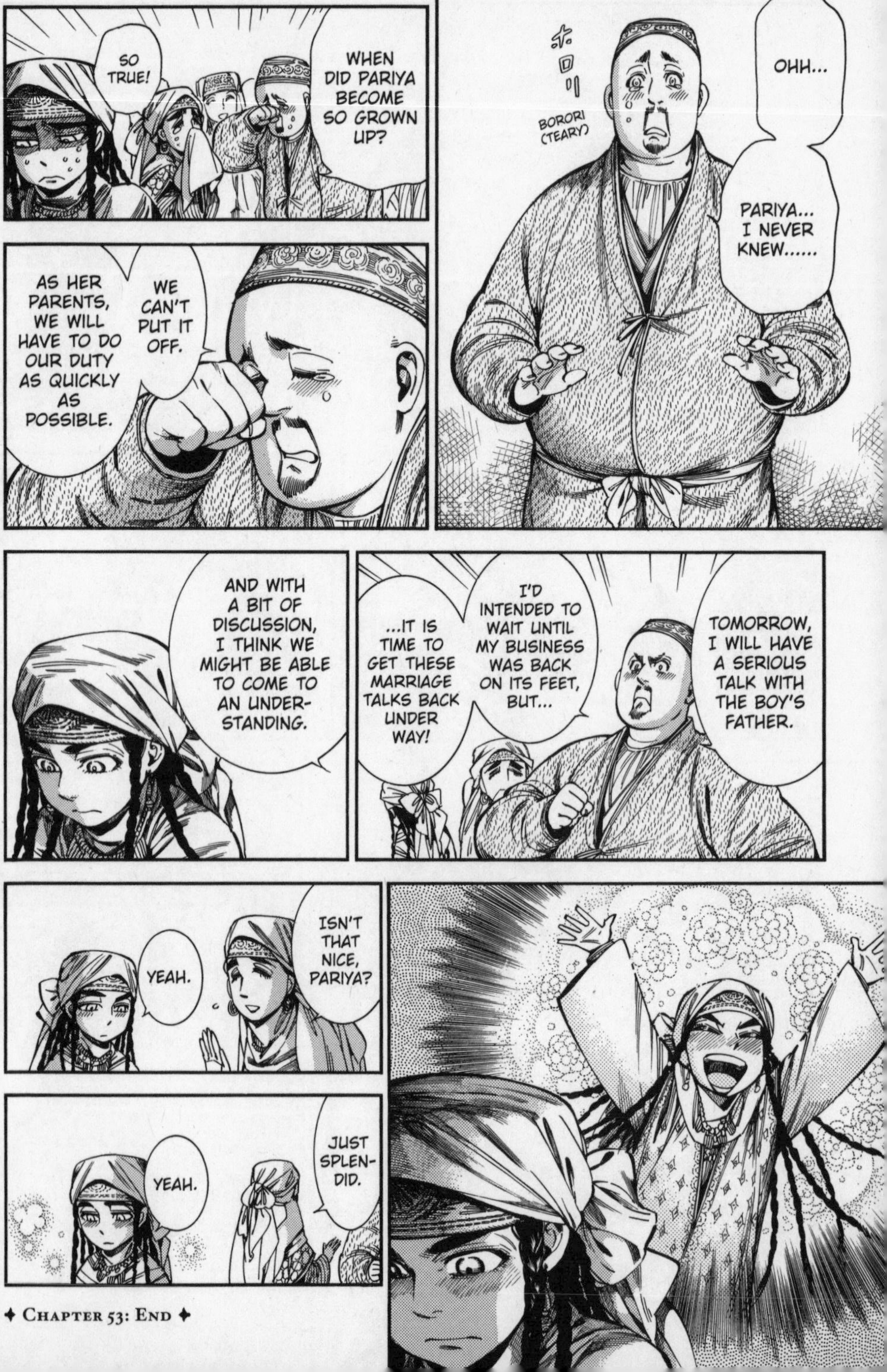
ボロリ
BORORI (TEARY)
OHH...
PARIYA... I NEVER KNEW......
WHEN DID PARIYA BECOME SO GROWN UP?
SO TRUE!
WE CAN'T PUT IT OFF.
AS HER PARENTS, WE WILL HAVE TO DO OUR DUTY AS QUICKLY AS POSSIBLE.
TOMORROW, I WILL HAVE A SERIOUS TALK WITH THE BOY'S FATHER.
I'D INTENDED TO WAIT UNTIL MY BUSINESS WAS BACK ON ITS FEET, BUT...
...IT IS TIME TO GET THESE MARRIAGE TALKS BACK UNDER WAY!
AND WITH A BIT OF DISCUSSION, I THINK WE MIGHT BE ABLE TO COME TO AN UNDER-STANDING.
ISN'T THAT NICE, PARIYA?
YEAH.
JUST SPLEND-ID.
YEAH.

✦ Chapter 53: End ✦

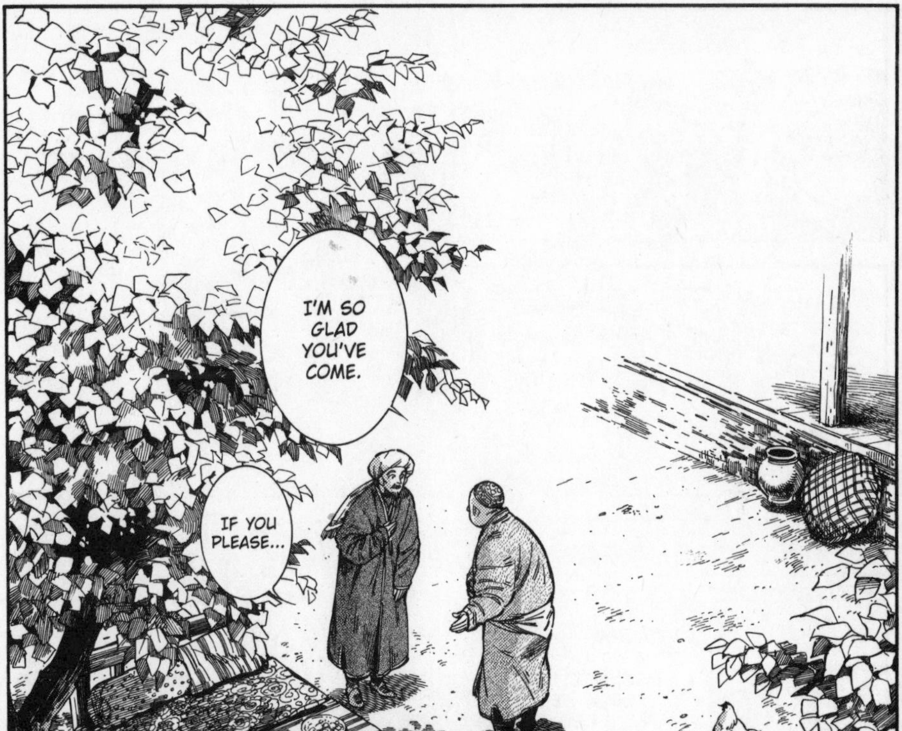
I'M SO GLAD YOU'VE COME.
IF YOU PLEASE...
CHAPTER 54
CONVERSATION
(PART 1)

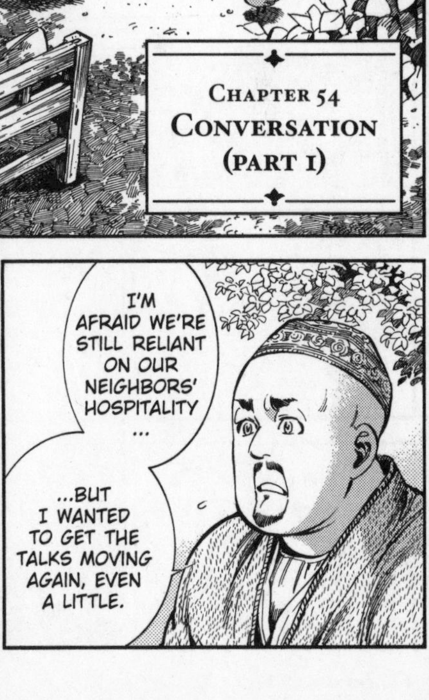
I'M AFRAID WE'RE STILL RELIANT ON OUR NEIGHBORS' HOSPITALITY ...
...BUT I WANTED TO GET THE TALKS MOVING AGAIN, EVEN A LITTLE.

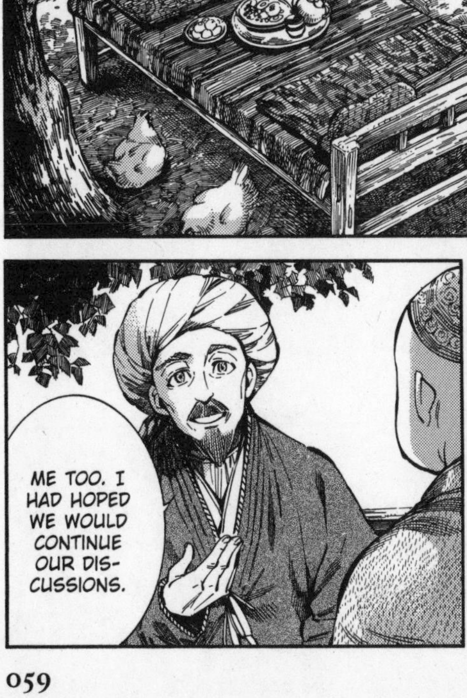
ME TOO. I HAD HOPED WE WOULD CONTINUE OUR DIS-CUSSIONS.

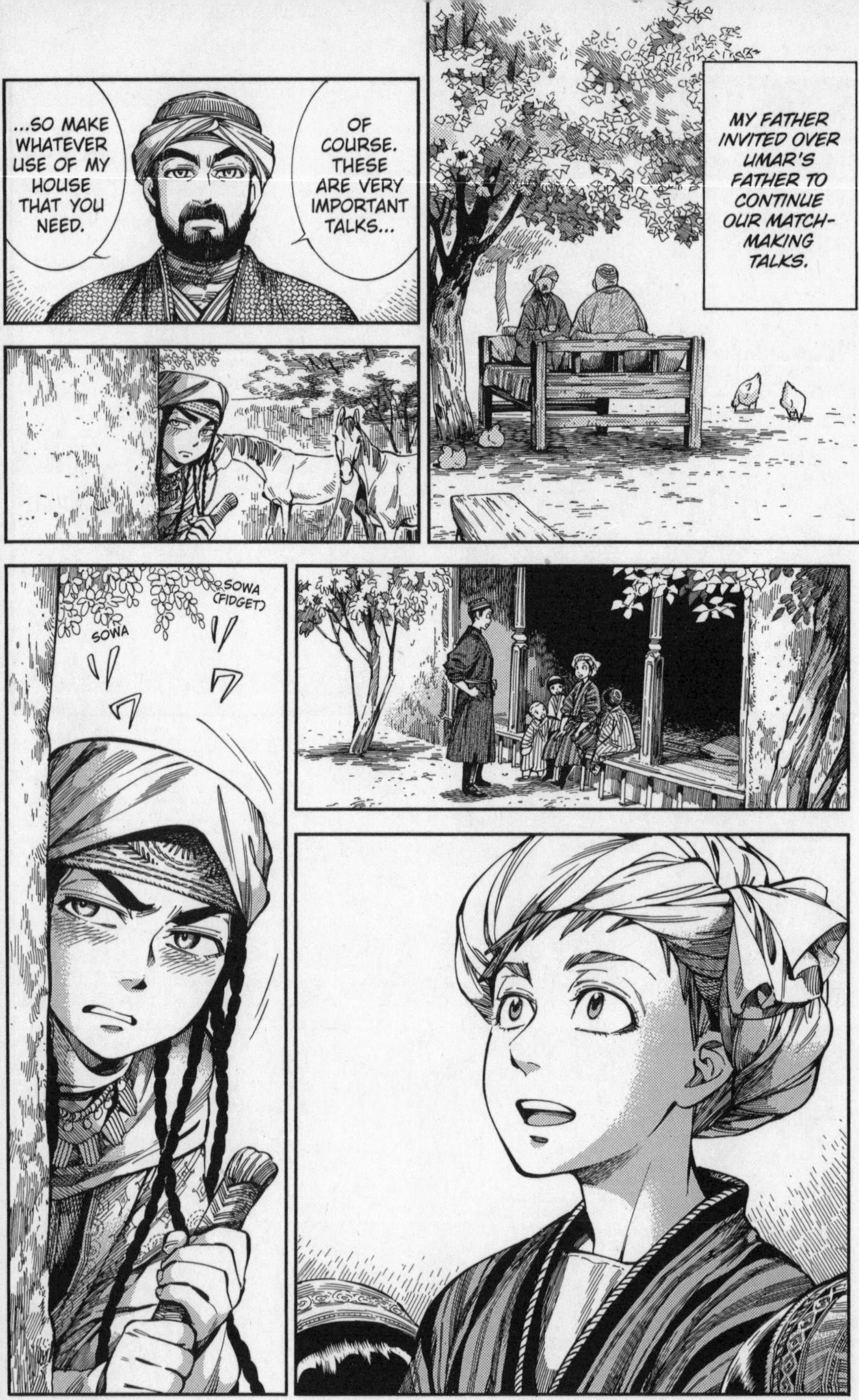
MY FATHER INVITED OVER UMAR'S FATHER TO CONTINUE OUR MATCH-MAKING TALKS.
OF COURSE. THESE ARE VERY IMPORTANT TALKS...
...SO MAKE WHATEVER USE OF MY HOUSE THAT YOU NEED.
SOWA (FIDGET)
SOWA

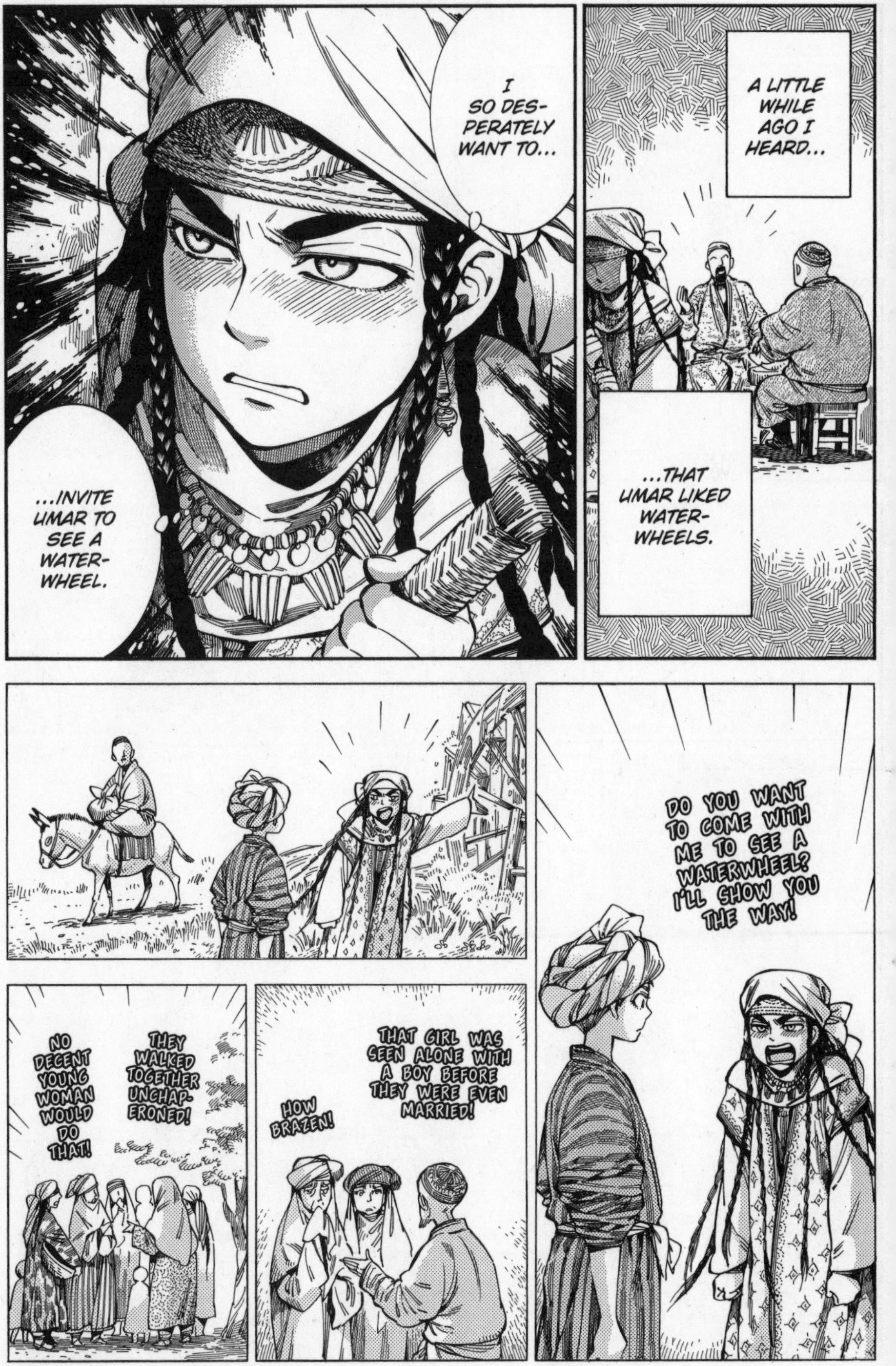
A LITTLE WHILE AGO I HEARD...
...THAT UMAR LIKED WATER-WHEELS.
I SO DES-PERATELY WANT TO...
...INVITE UMAR TO SEE A WATER-WHEEL.
DO YOU WANT TO COME WITH ME TO SEE A WATERWHEEL? I'LL SHOW YOU THE WAY!
THAT GIRL WAS SEEN ALONE WITH A BOY BEFORE THEY WERE EVEN MARRIED!
HOW BRAZEN!
THEY WALKED TOGETHER UNCHAP-ERONED!
NO DECENT YOUNG WOMAN WOULD DO THAT!

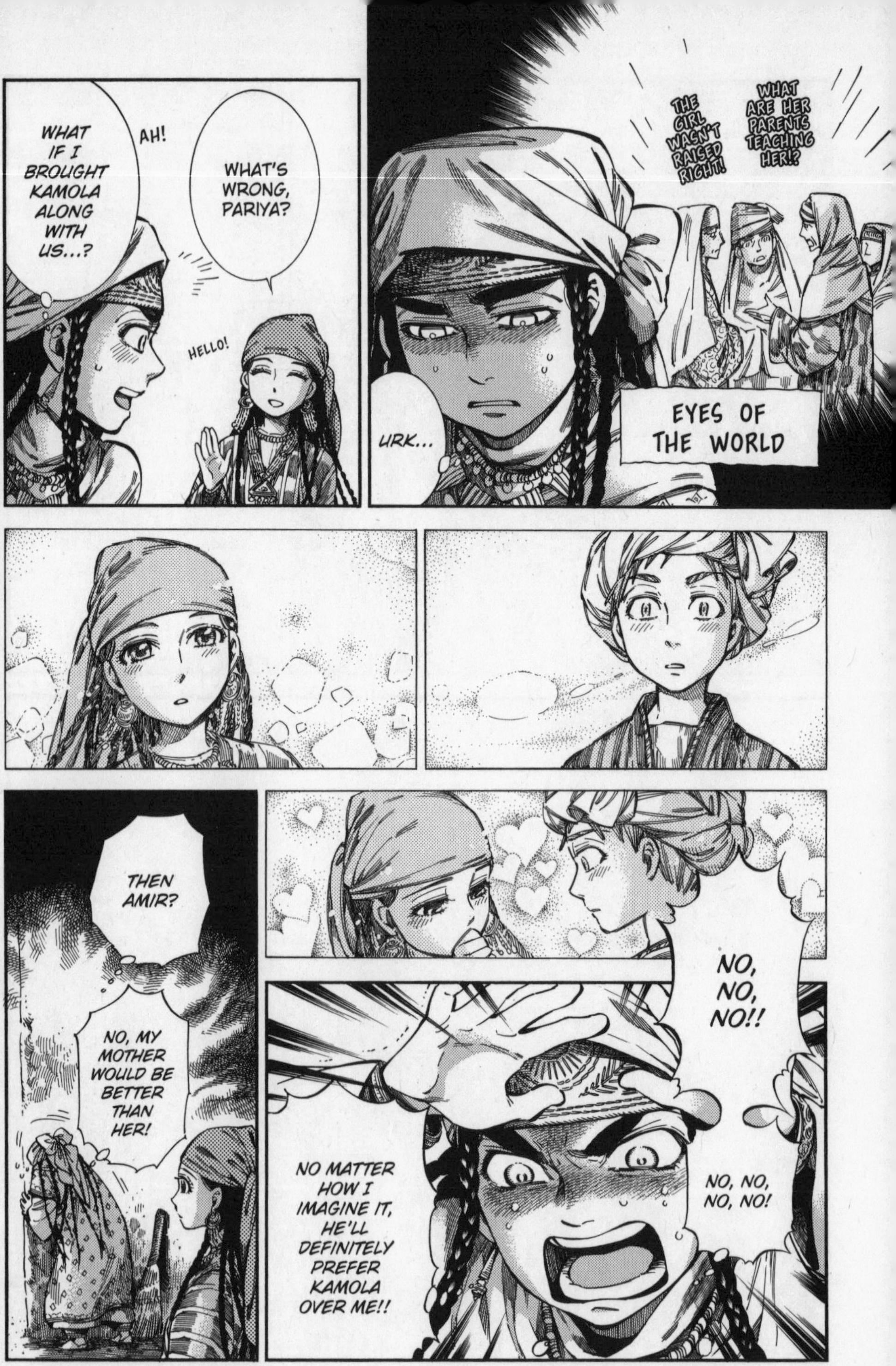
WHAT ARE HER PARENTS TEACHING HER!?
THE GIRL WASN'T RAISED RIGHT!
URK...
EYES OF THE WORLD
WHAT'S WRONG, PARIYA?
AH!
WHAT IF I BROUGHT KAMOLA ALONG WITH US...?
HELLO!
NO, NO, NO!!
NO, NO, NO, NO!
NO MATTER HOW I IMAGINE IT, HE'LL DEFINITELY PREFER KAMOLA OVER ME!!
THEN AMIR?
NO, MY MOTHER WOULD BE BETTER THAN HER!

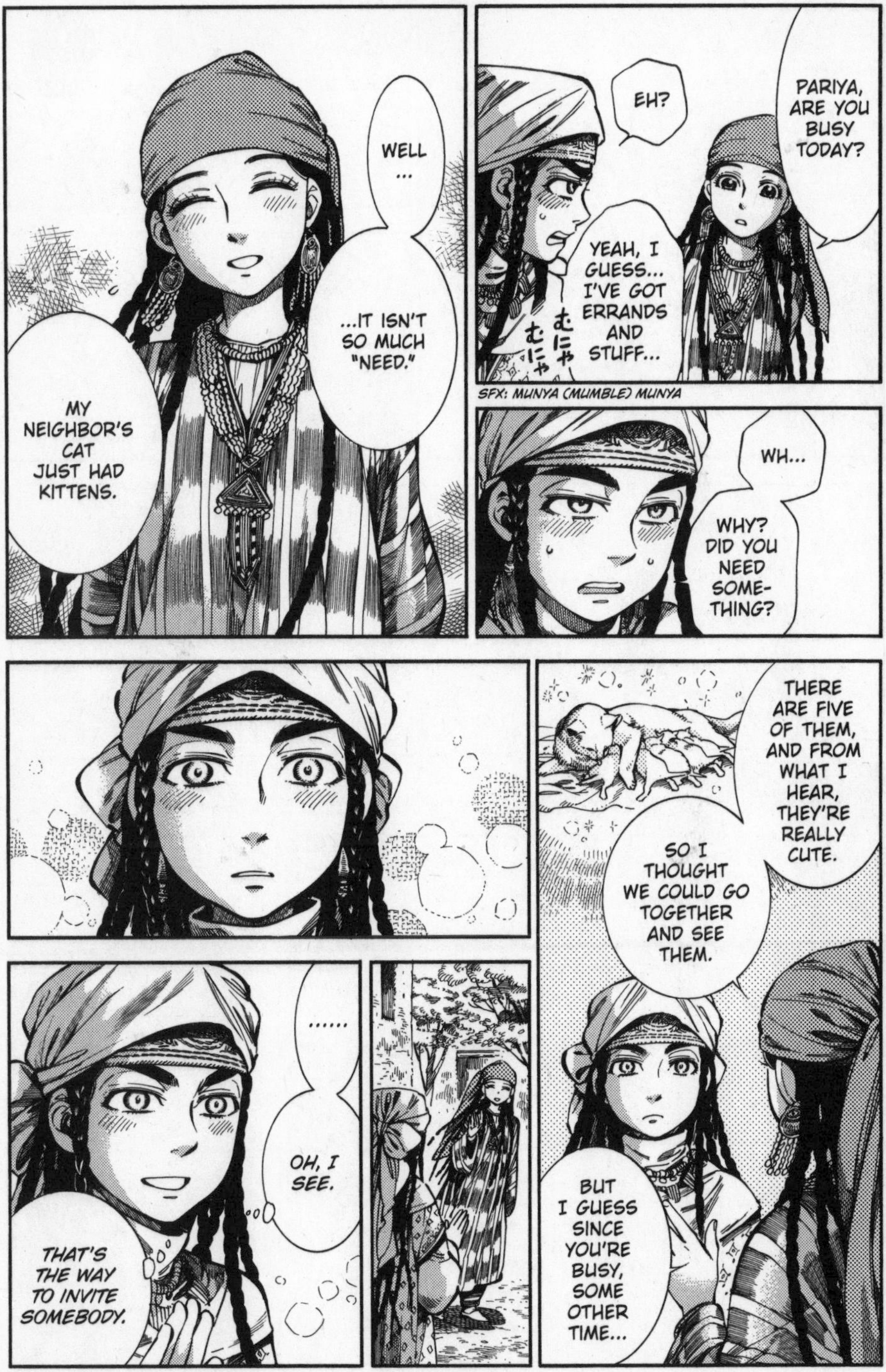
PARIYA, ARE YOU BUSY TODAY?
EH?
YEAH, I GUESS... I'VE GOT ERRANDS AND STUFF...
むにゃ むにゃ
SFX: MUNYA (MUMBLE) MUNYA
WH...
WHY? DID YOU NEED SOME-THING?
WELL ...
...IT ISN'T SO MUCH "NEED."
MY NEIGHBOR'S CAT JUST HAD KITTENS.
THERE ARE FIVE OF THEM, AND FROM WHAT I HEAR, THEY'RE REALLY CUTE.
SO I THOUGHT WE COULD GO TOGETHER AND SEE THEM.
BUT I GUESS SINCE YOU'RE BUSY, SOME OTHER TIME...
......
OH, I SEE.
THAT'S THE WAY TO INVITE SOMEBODY.

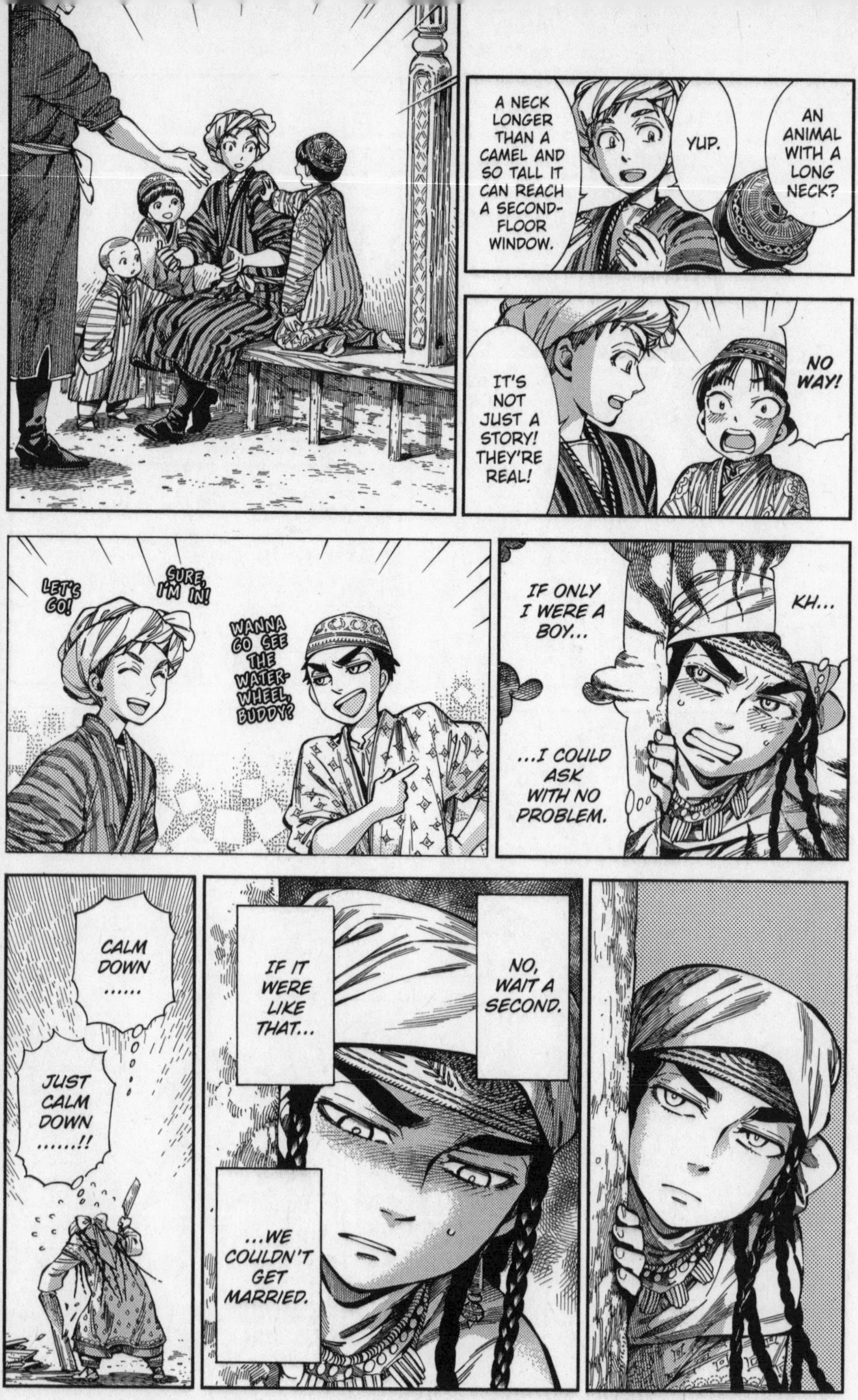

AN ANIMAL WITH A LONG NECK?
YUP.
A NECK LONGER THAN A CAMEL AND SO TALL IT CAN REACH A SECOND-FLOOR WINDOW.
NO WAY!
IT'S NOT JUST A STORY! THEY'RE REAL!
KH...
IF ONLY I WERE A BOY...
...I COULD ASK WITH NO PROBLEM.
WANNA GO SEE THE WATER-WHEEL, BUDDY?
SURE, I'M IN!
LET'S GO!
NO, WAIT A SECOND.
IF IT WERE LIKE THAT...
...WE COULDN'T GET MARRIED.
CALM DOWN......
JUST CALM DOWN......!!

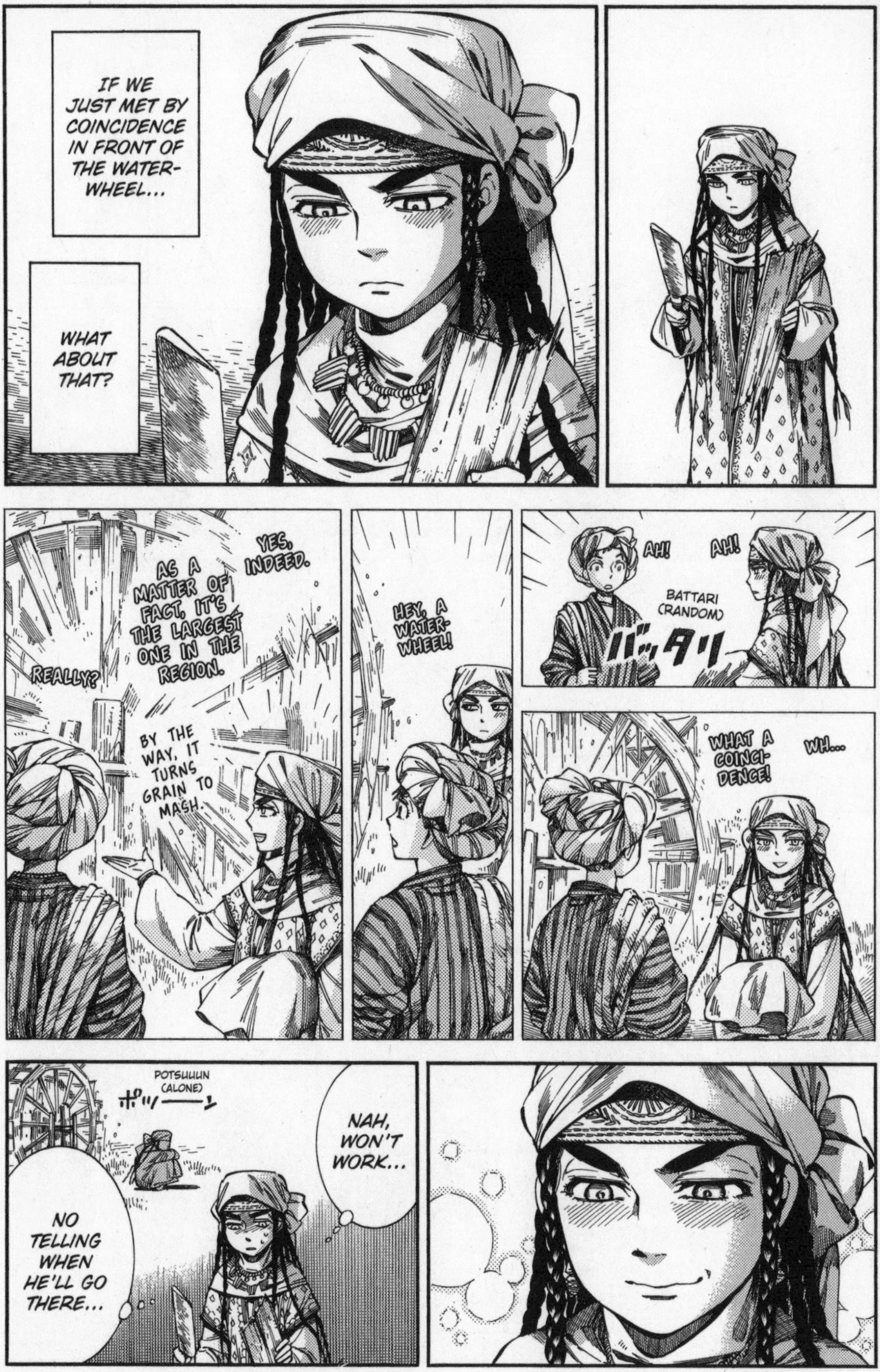
IF WE JUST MET BY COINCIDENCE IN FRONT OF THE WATER-WHEEL...
WHAT ABOUT THAT?
AH!
AH!
BATTARI (RANDOM)
バッタリ
WH...
WHAT A COINCIDENCE!
HEY, A WATER-WHEEL!
YES, INDEED.
AS A MATTER OF FACT, IT'S THE LARGEST ONE IN THE REGION.
REALLY?
BY THE WAY, IT TURNS GRAIN TO MASH.
NAH, WON'T WORK...
POTSUUUN (ALONE)
ポツーーン
NO TELLING WHEN HE'LL GO THERE...

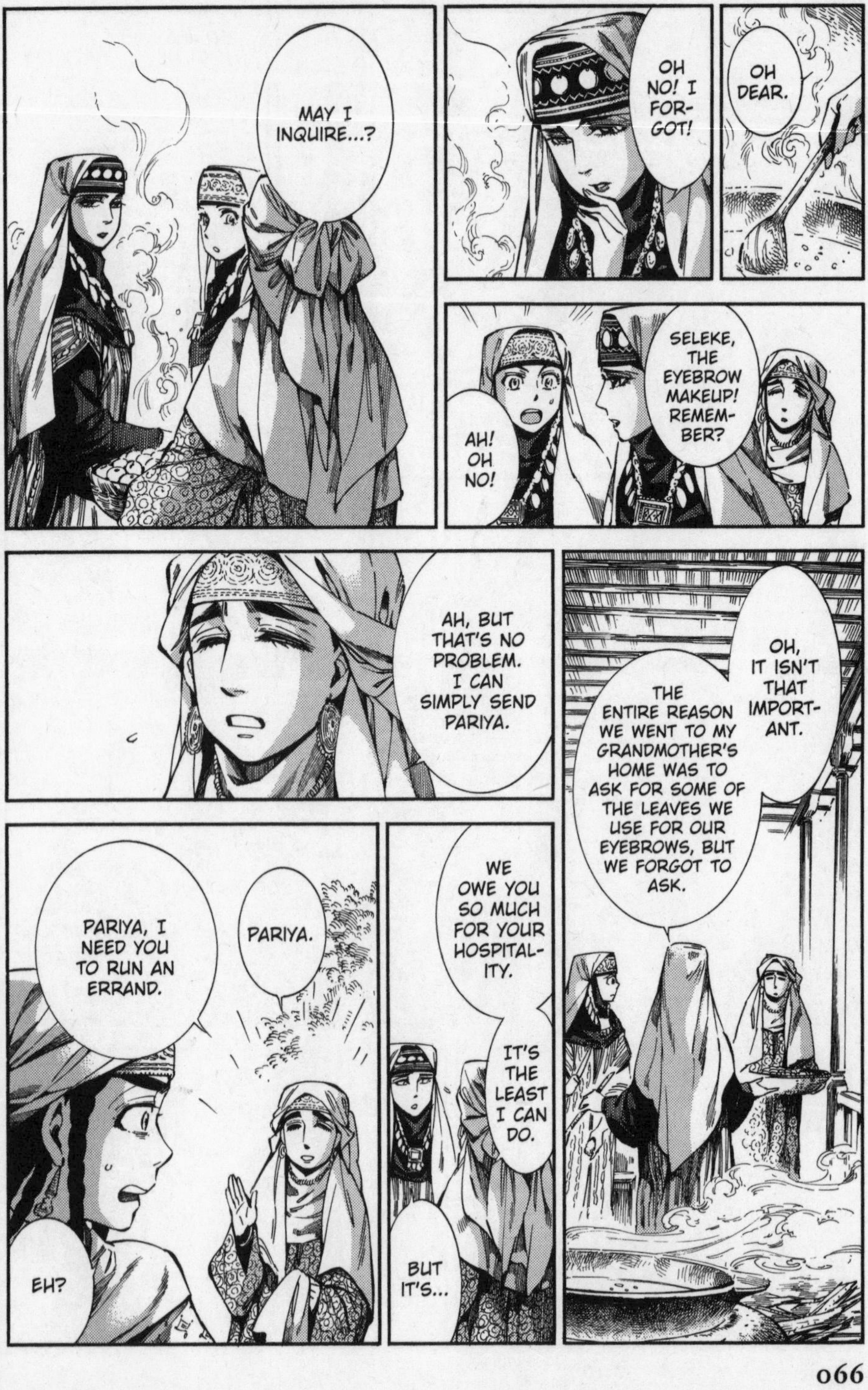
OH DEAR.
OH NO! I FORGOT!
SELEKE, THE EYEBROW MAKEUP! REMEMBER?
AH! OH NO!
MAY I INQUIRE...?
OH, IT ISN'T THAT IMPORTANT.
THE ENTIRE REASON WE WENT TO MY GRANDMOTHER'S HOME WAS TO ASK FOR SOME OF THE LEAVES WE USE FOR OUR EYEBROWS, BUT WE FORGOT TO ASK.
AH, BUT THAT'S NO PROBLEM. I CAN SIMPLY SEND PARIYA.
WE OWE YOU SO MUCH FOR YOUR HOSPITAL-ITY.
IT'S THE LEAST I CAN DO.
BUT IT'S...
PARIYA.
PARIYA, I NEED YOU TO RUN AN ERRAND.
EH?

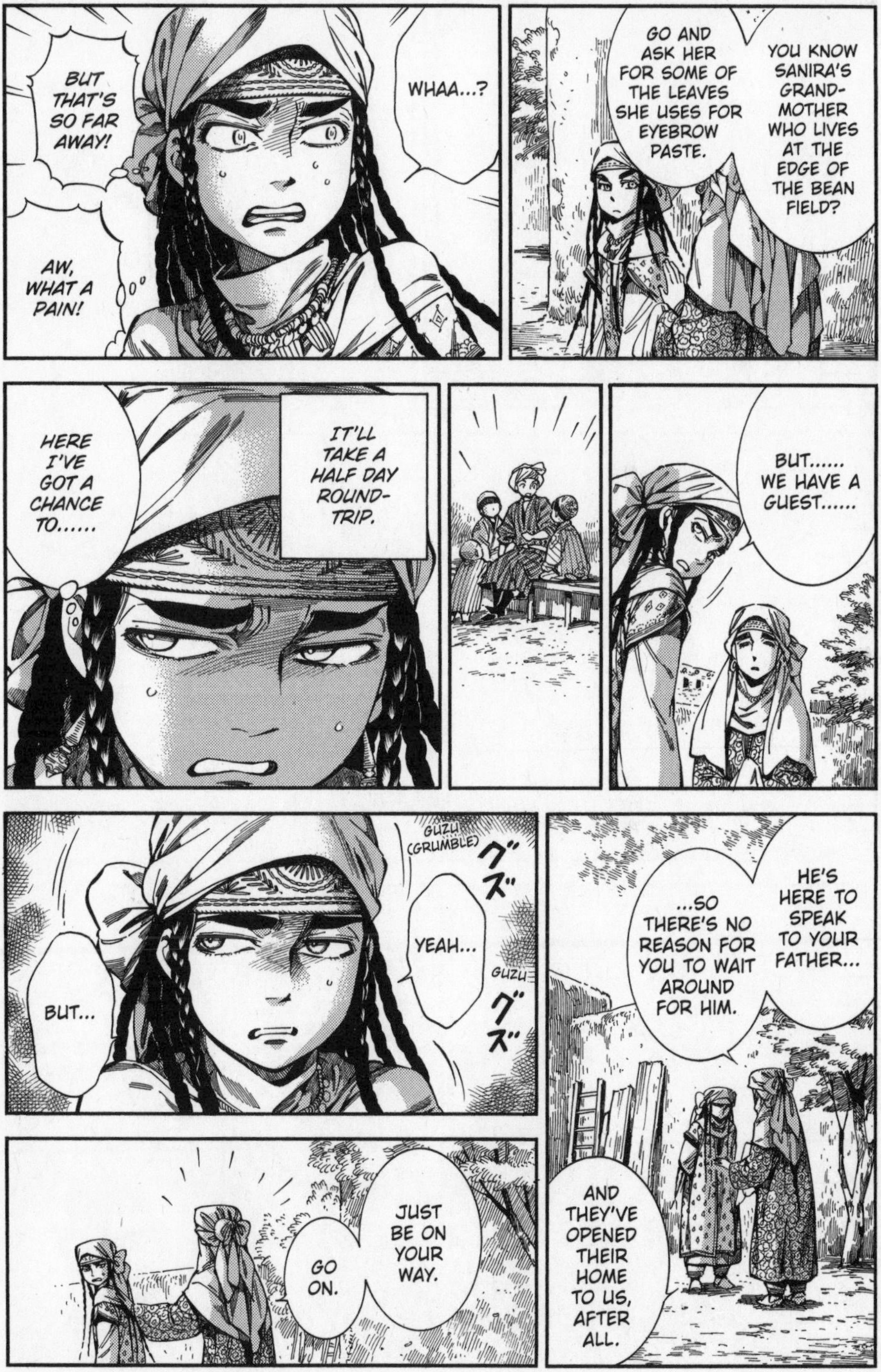
YOU KNOW SANIRA'S GRAND-MOTHER WHO LIVES AT THE EDGE OF THE BEAN FIELD?
GO AND ASK HER FOR SOME OF THE LEAVES SHE USES FOR EYEBROW PASTE.
WHAA...?
BUT THAT'S SO FAR AWAY!
AW, WHAT A PAIN!
BUT...... WE HAVE A GUEST......
IT'LL TAKE A HALF DAY ROUND-TRIP.
HERE I'VE GOT A CHANCE TO......
HE'S HERE TO SPEAK TO YOUR FATHER...
...SO THERE'S NO REASON FOR YOU TO WAIT AROUND FOR HIM.
AND THEY'VE OPENED THEIR HOME TO US, AFTER ALL.
GUZU (GRUMBLE)
グズ
YEAH...
GUZU
グズ
BUT...
JUST BE ON YOUR WAY.
GO ON.

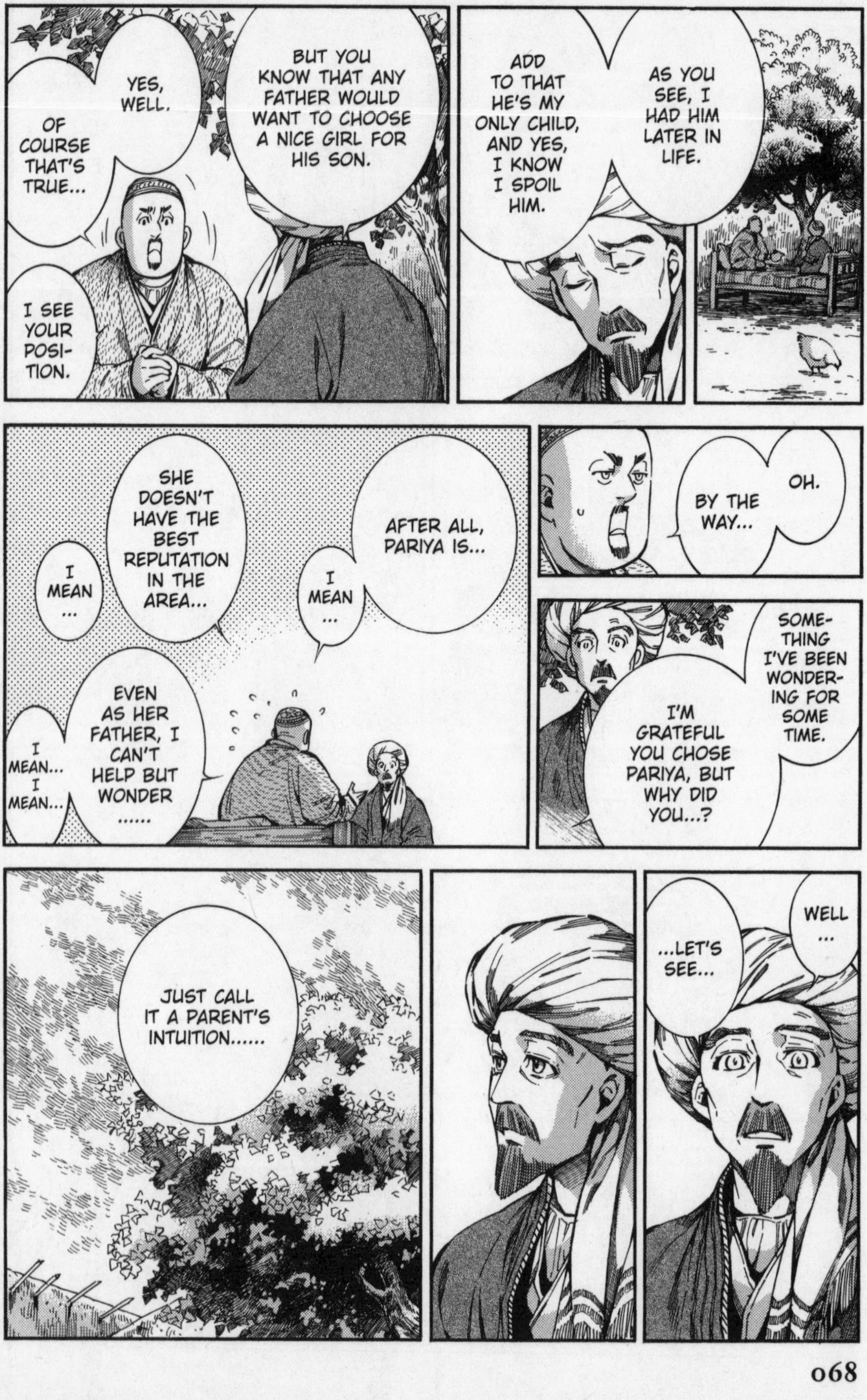
AS YOU SEE, I HAD HIM LATER IN LIFE.
ADD TO THAT HE'S MY ONLY CHILD, AND YES, I KNOW I SPOIL HIM.
BUT YOU KNOW THAT ANY FATHER WOULD WANT TO CHOOSE A NICE GIRL FOR HIS SON.
YES, WELL.
OF COURSE THAT'S TRUE...
I SEE YOUR POSITION.
OH.
BY THE WAY...
SOMETHING I'VE BEEN WONDERING FOR SOME TIME.
I'M GRATEFUL YOU CHOSE PARIYA, BUT WHY DID YOU...?
AFTER ALL, PARIYA IS...
I MEAN ...
SHE DOESN'T HAVE THE BEST REPUTATION IN THE AREA...
I MEAN ...
EVEN AS HER FATHER, I CAN'T HELP BUT WONDER ......
I MEAN... I MEAN...
WELL ...
...LET'S SEE...
JUST CALL IT A PARENT'S INTUITION......

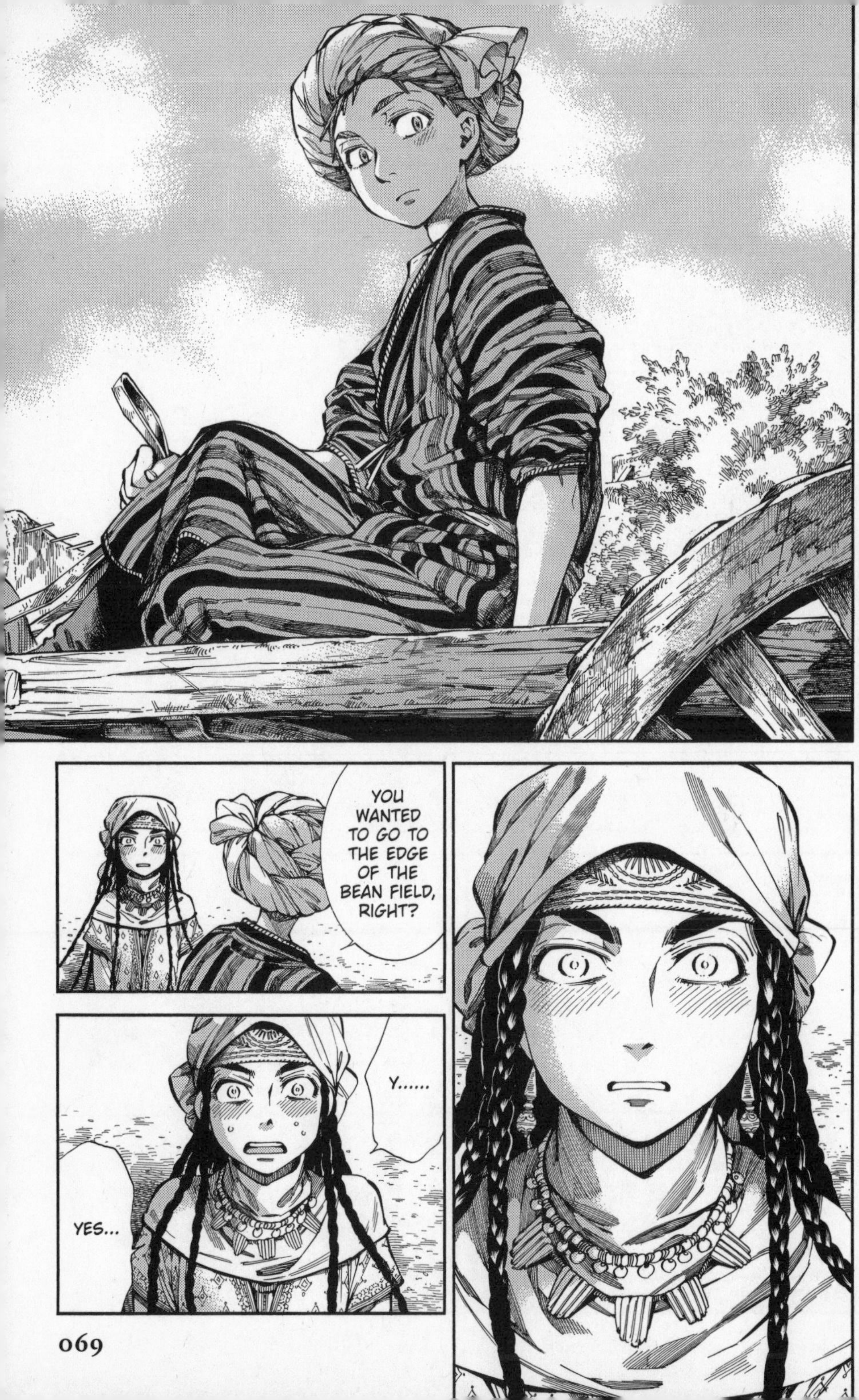
YOU WANTED TO GO TO THE EDGE OF THE BEAN FIELD, RIGHT?
Y......
YES...

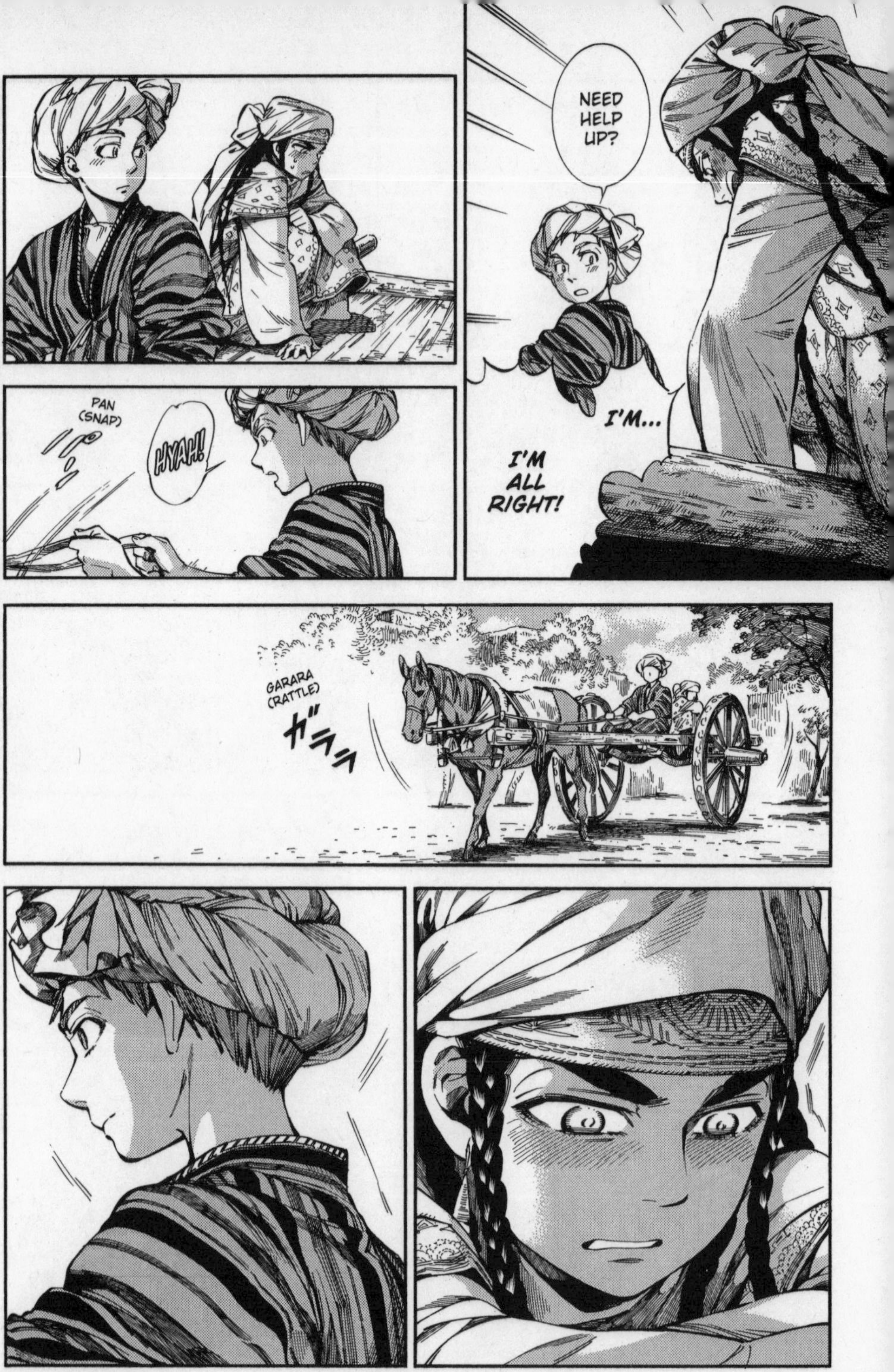
NEED HELP UP?
I'M...
I'M ALL RIGHT!
PAN (SNAP)
HYAH!
GARARA (RATTLE)
ガララ

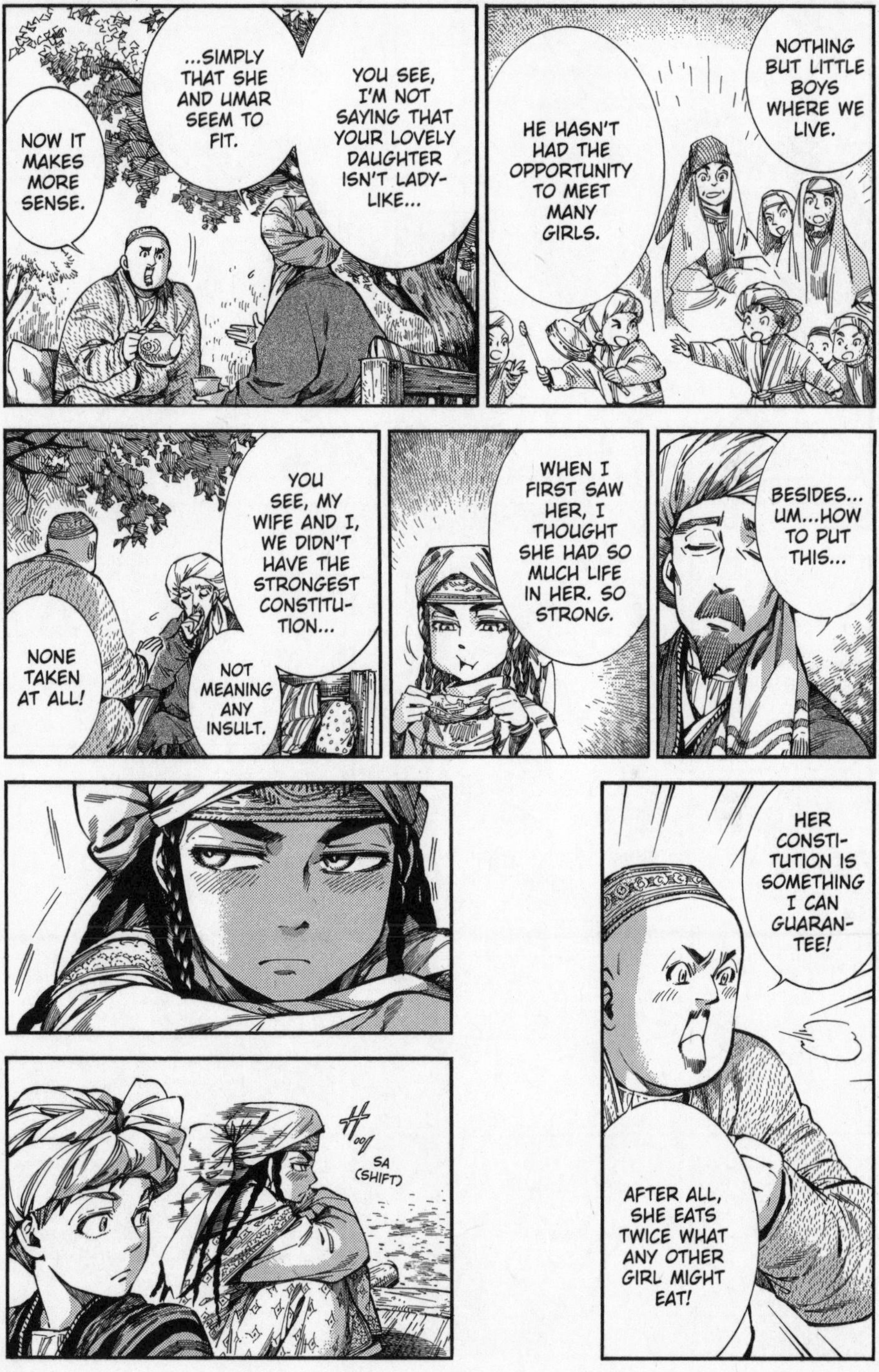
NOTHING BUT LITTLE BOYS WHERE WE LIVE.
HE HASN'T HAD THE OPPORTUNITY TO MEET MANY GIRLS.
YOU SEE, I'M NOT SAYING THAT YOUR LOVELY DAUGHTER ISN'T LADY-LIKE...
...SIMPLY THAT SHE AND UMAR SEEM TO FIT.
NOW IT MAKES MORE SENSE.
BESIDES... UM...HOW TO PUT THIS...
WHEN I FIRST SAW HER, I THOUGHT SHE HAD SO MUCH LIFE IN HER. SO STRONG.
YOU SEE, MY WIFE AND I, WE DIDN'T HAVE THE STRONGEST CONSTITUTION...
NOT MEANING ANY INSULT.
NONE TAKEN AT ALL!
HER CONSTITUTION IS SOMETHING I CAN GUARANTEE!
AFTER ALL, SHE EATS TWICE WHAT ANY OTHER GIRL MIGHT EAT!
SA (SHIFT)

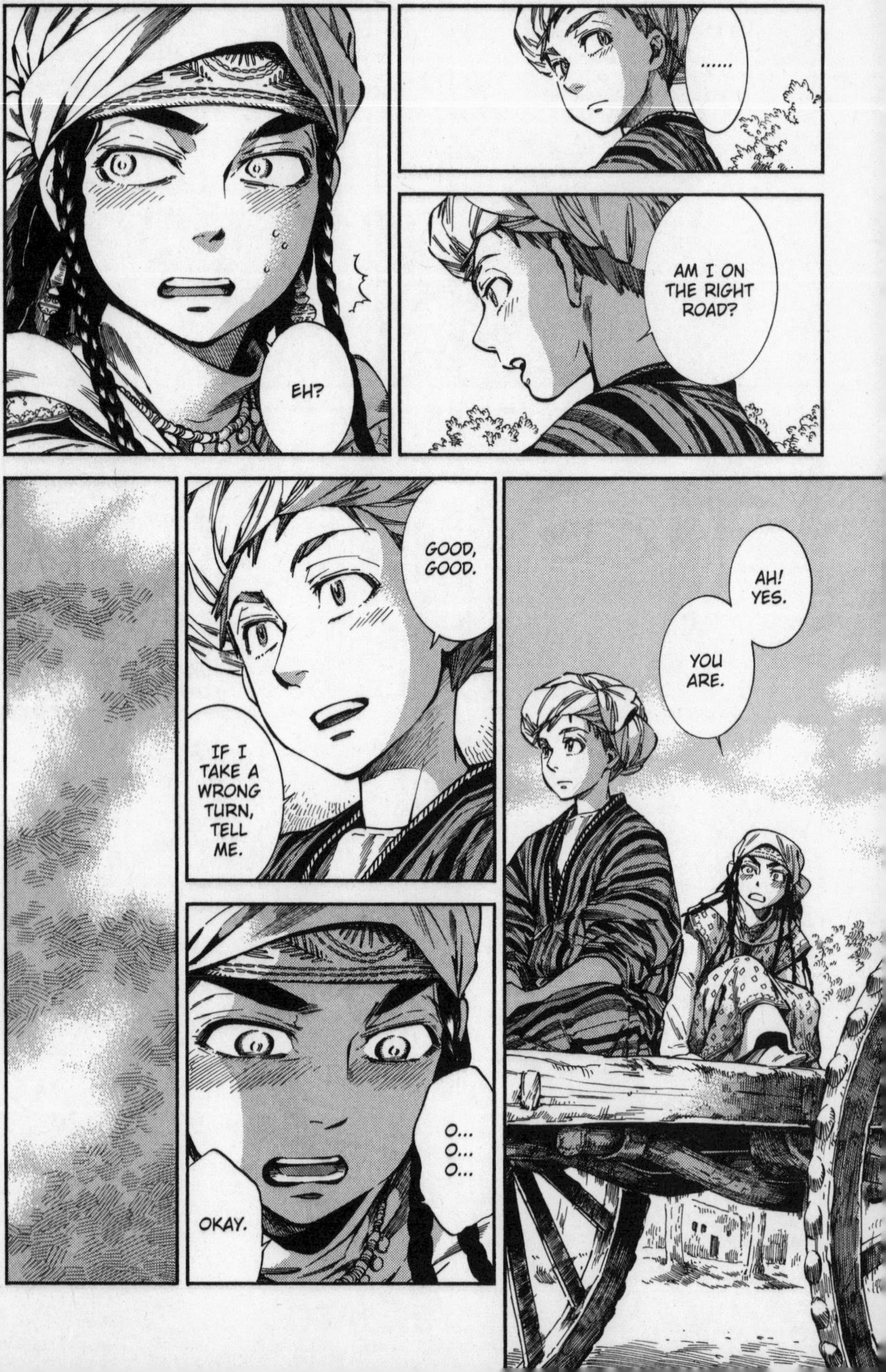
......
AM I ON THE RIGHT ROAD?
EH?
AH! YES.
YOU ARE.
GOOD, GOOD.
IF I TAKE A WRONG TURN, TELL ME.
O... O... O...
OKAY.

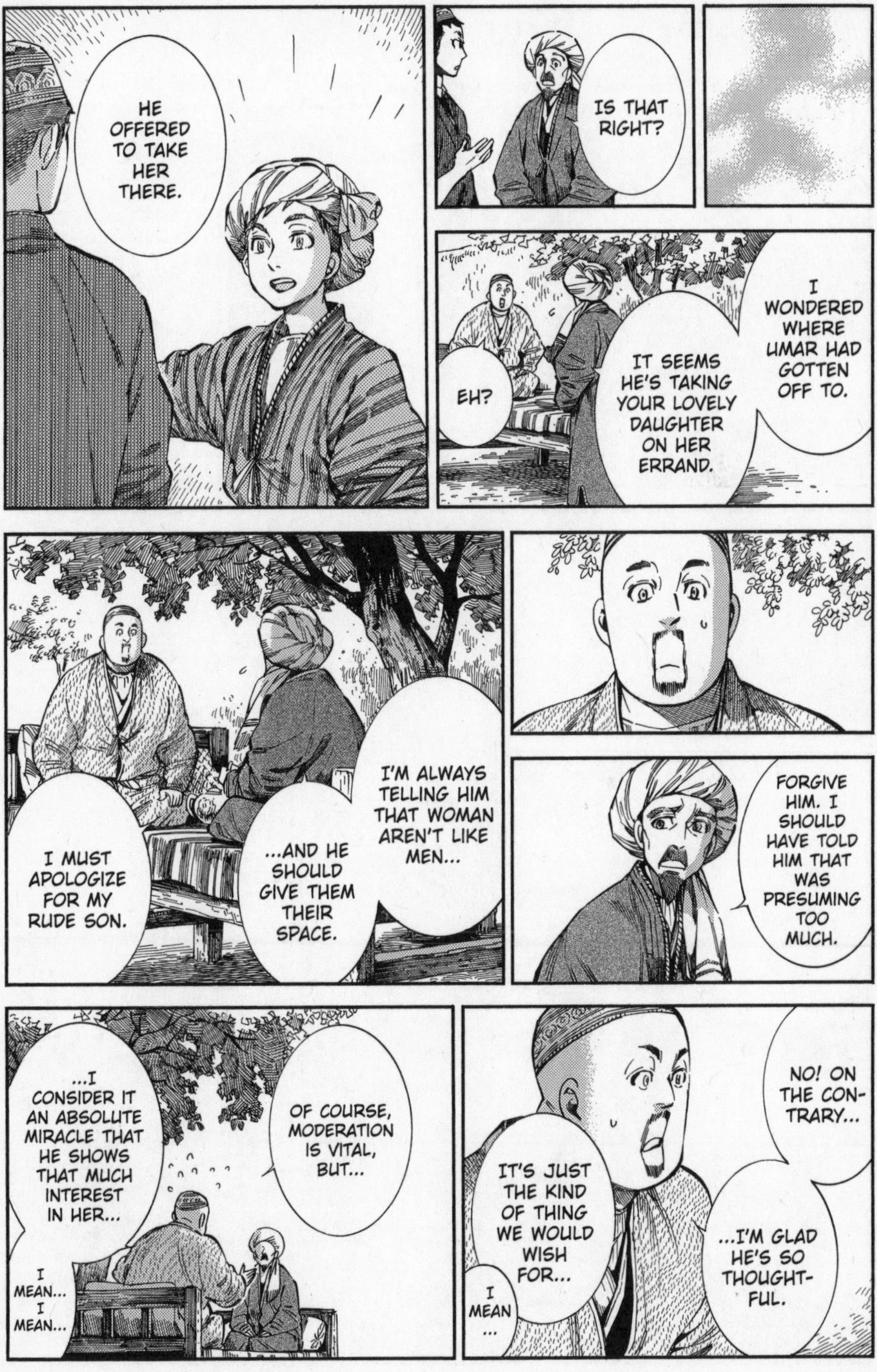
IS THAT RIGHT?
I WONDERED WHERE UMAR HAD GOTTEN OFF TO.
IT SEEMS HE'S TAKING YOUR LOVELY DAUGHTER ON HER ERRAND.
EH?
HE OFFERED TO TAKE HER THERE.
FORGIVE HIM. I SHOULD HAVE TOLD HIM THAT WAS PRESUMING TOO MUCH.
I'M ALWAYS TELLING HIM THAT WOMAN AREN'T LIKE MEN...
...AND HE SHOULD GIVE THEM THEIR SPACE.
I MUST APOLOGIZE FOR MY RUDE SON.
NO! ON THE CON-TRARY...
...I'M GLAD HE'S SO THOUGHT-FUL.
IT'S JUST THE KIND OF THING WE WOULD WISH FOR...
I MEAN ...
OF COURSE, MODERATION IS VITAL, BUT...
...I CONSIDER IT AN ABSOLUTE MIRACLE THAT HE SHOWS THAT MUCH INTEREST IN HER...
I MEAN... I MEAN...

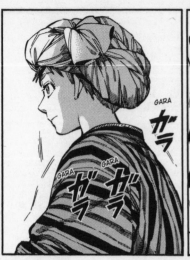

GARA
GARA (CLATTER)
ガラ
ガラ
GARA
ガラ
GARA
GARA
ガラ
ガラ
GARA
ガラ
GARA
GARA
ガラ
ガラ
THE ROAD TO THEIR GRAND-MOTHER'S PLACE IS...
...REALLY LONG.
A ROUND-TRIP...
...TAKES HALF A DAY.
A FULL...
...HALF DAY OF TIME!!

✦ Chapter 54: End ✦

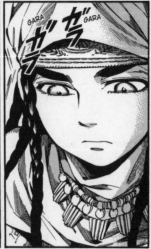

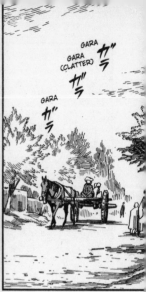

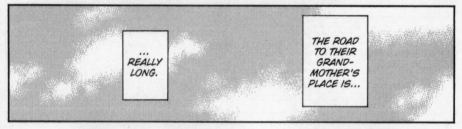

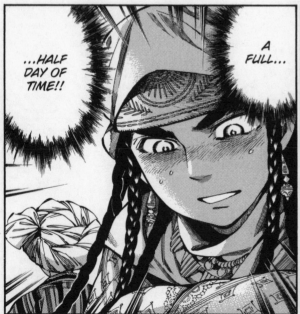

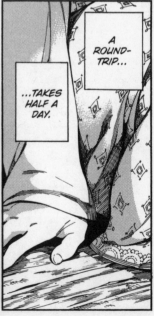

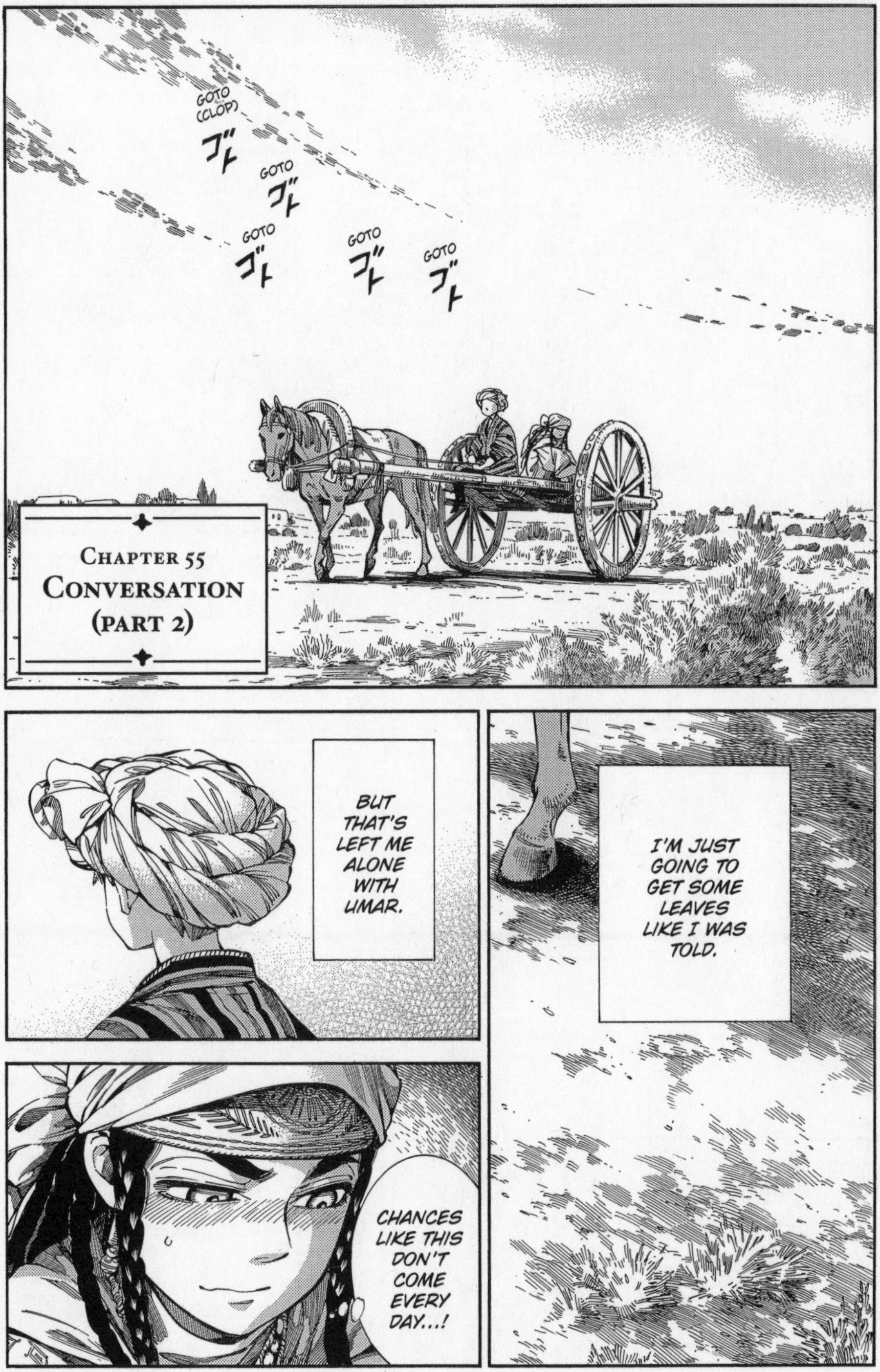
GOTO (CLOP)
ゴト
GOTO
ゴト
GOTO
ゴト
GOTO
ゴト
GOTO
ゴト
CHAPTER 55
CONVERSATION (PART 2)
I'M JUST GOING TO GET SOME LEAVES LIKE I WAS TOLD.
BUT THAT'S LEFT ME ALONE WITH UMAR.
CHANCES LIKE THIS DON'T COME EVERY DAY...!

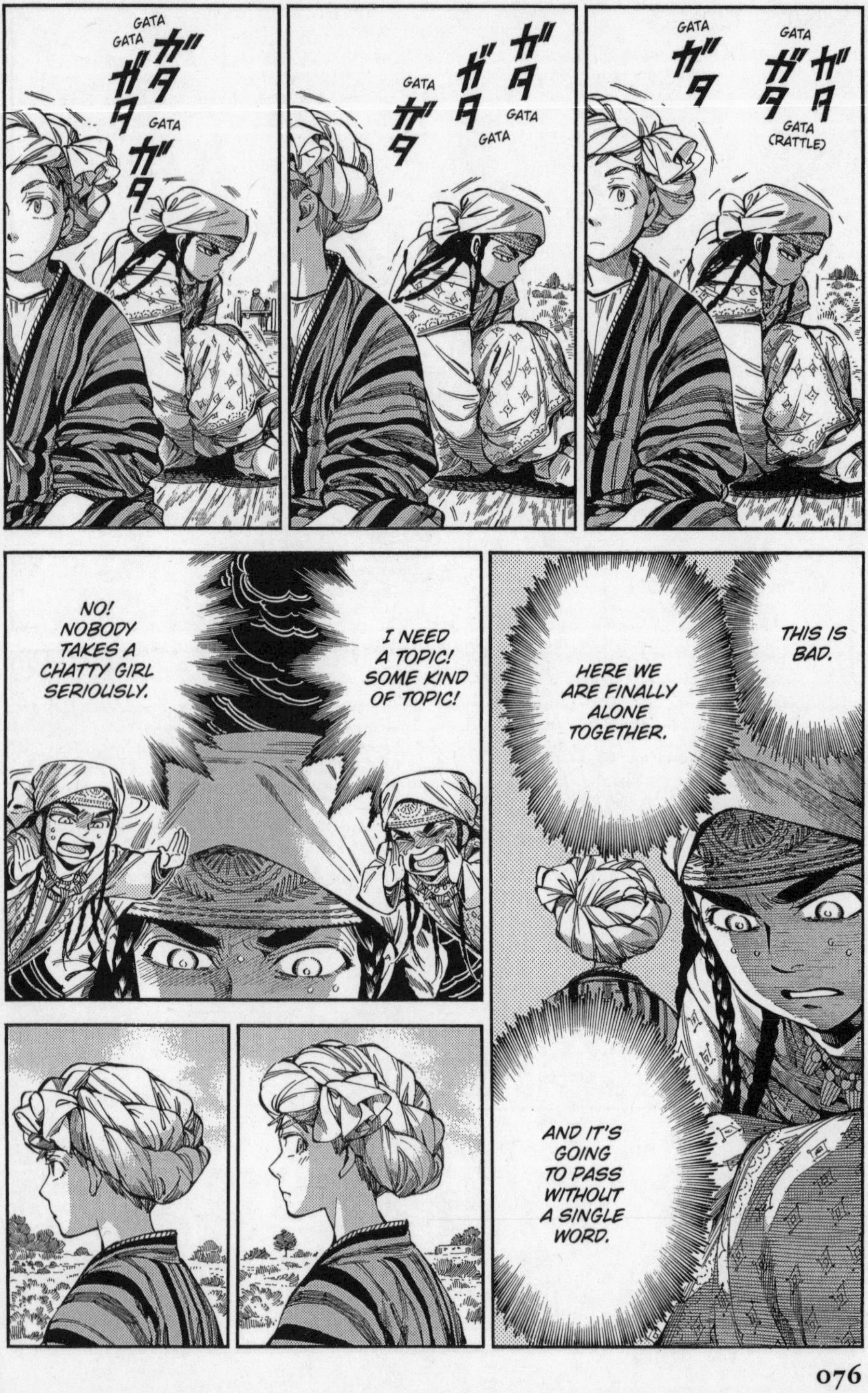
GATA
ガタ
GATA
ガタ
GATA (RATTLE)
ガタ
ガタ
GATA
ガタ
GATA
GATA
ガタ
GATA
GATA
ガタ
GATA
ガタ
GATA
ガタ
THIS IS BAD.
HERE WE ARE FINALLY ALONE TOGETHER.
AND IT'S GOING TO PASS WITHOUT A SINGLE WORD.
I NEED A TOPIC! SOME KIND OF TOPIC!
NO! NOBODY TAKES A CHATTY GIRL SERIOUSLY.

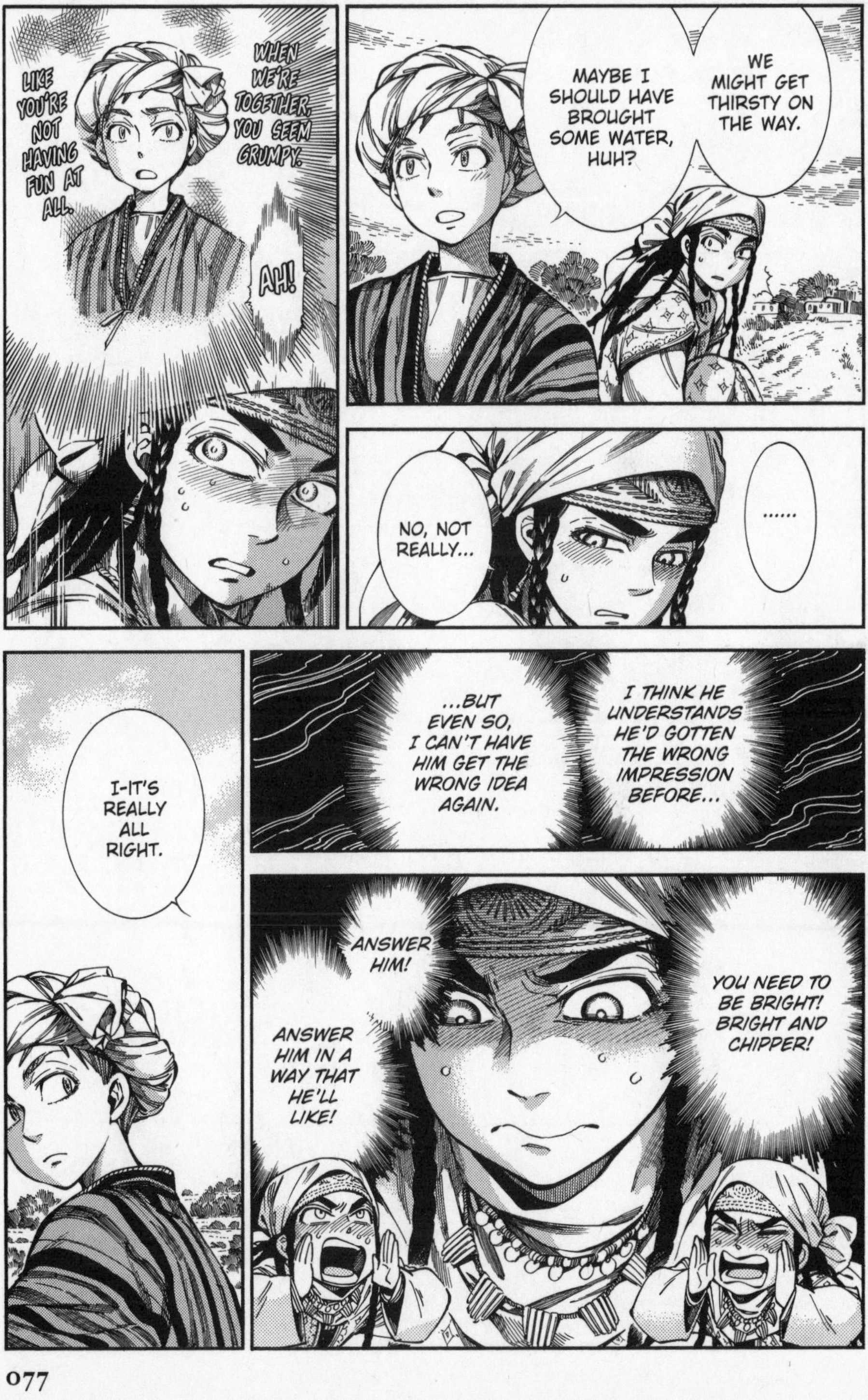
WE MIGHT GET THIRSTY ON THE WAY.
MAYBE I SHOULD HAVE BROUGHT SOME WATER, HUH?
......
NO, NOT REALLY...
WHEN WE'RE TOGETHER, YOU SEEM GRUMPY.
LIKE YOU'RE NOT HAVING FUN AT ALL.
AH!
I THINK HE UNDERSTANDS HE'D GOTTEN THE WRONG IMPRESSION BEFORE...
...BUT EVEN SO, I CAN'T HAVE HIM GET THE WRONG IDEA AGAIN.
YOU NEED TO BE BRIGHT! BRIGHT AND CHIPPER!
ANSWER HIM!
ANSWER HIM IN A WAY THAT HE'LL LIKE!
I-IT'S REALLY ALL RIGHT.

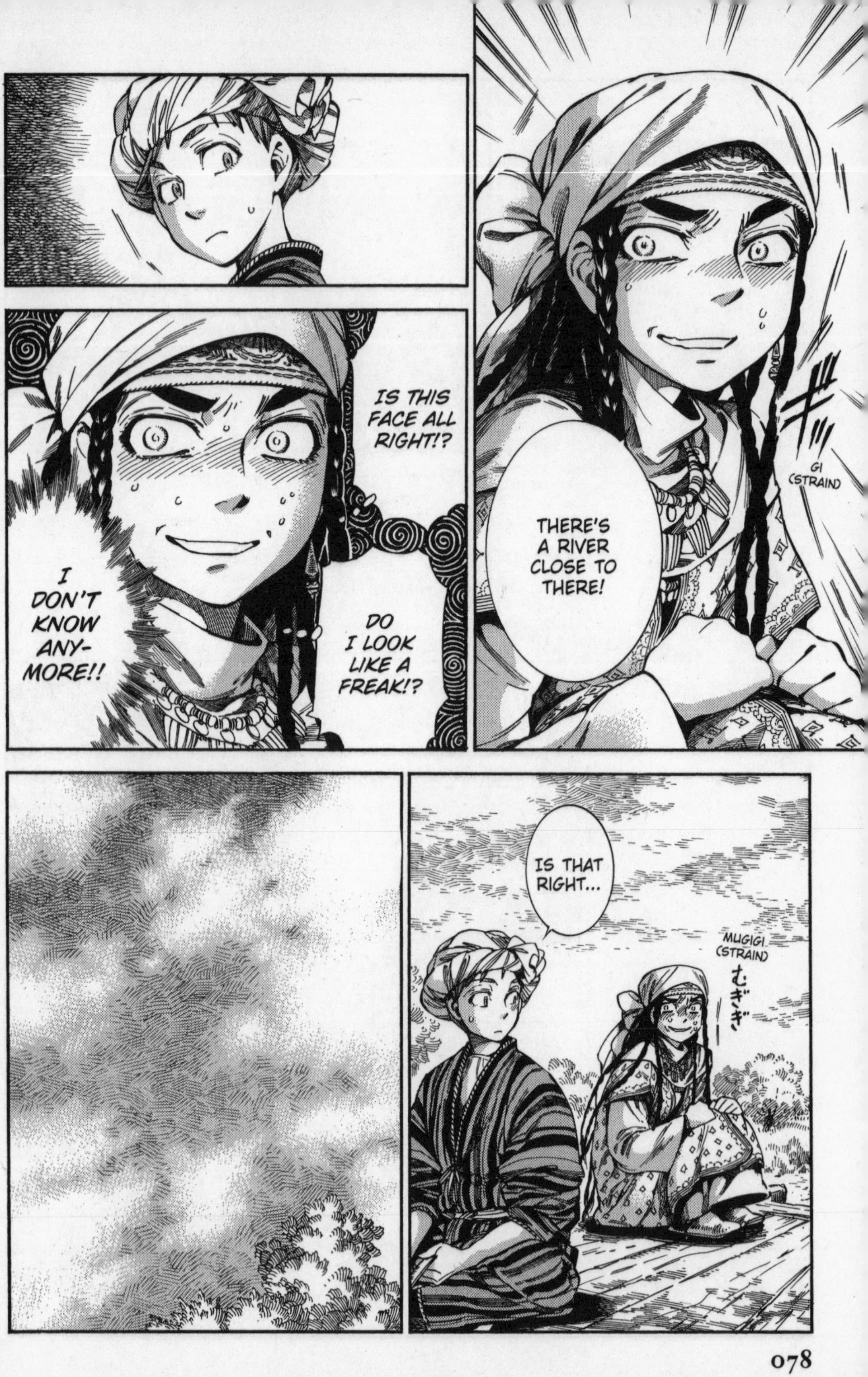
THERE'S A RIVER CLOSE TO THERE!
GI (STRAIN)
IS THIS FACE ALL RIGHT!?
DO I LOOK LIKE A FREAK!?
I DON'T KNOW ANY-MORE!!
IS THAT RIGHT...
MUGIGI (STRAIN)
むぎぎ

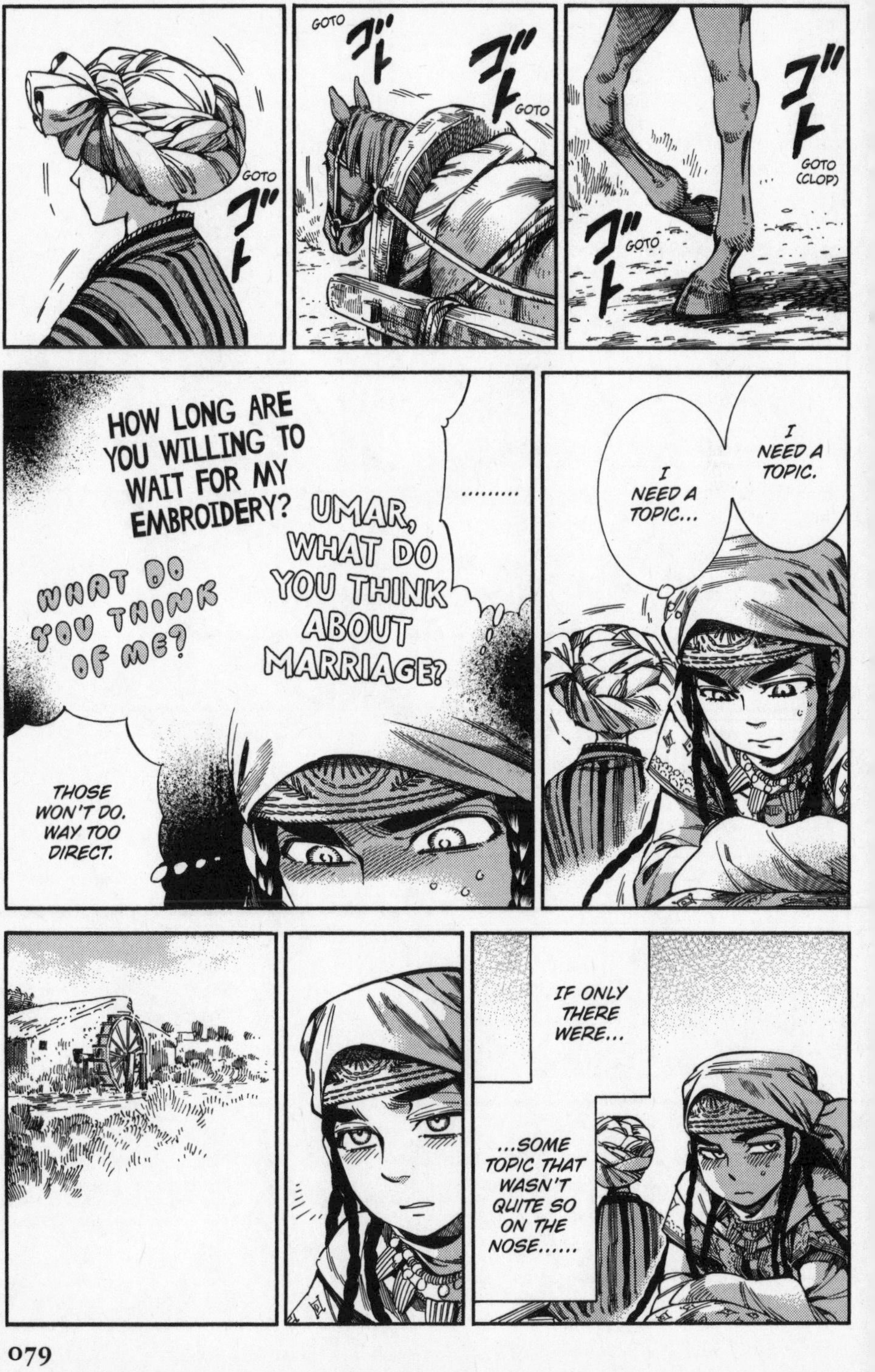
ゴト
GOTO (CLOP)
ゴト
GOTO
GOTO
ゴト
ゴト
GOTO
GOTO
ゴト
I NEED A TOPIC.
I NEED A TOPIC...
....
UMAR, WHAT DO YOU THINK ABOUT MARRIAGE?
HOW LONG ARE YOU WILLING TO WAIT FOR MY EMBROIDERY?
WHAT DO YOU THINK OF ME?
THOSE WON'T DO. WAY TOO DIRECT.
IF ONLY THERE WERE...
...SOME TOPIC THAT WASN'T QUITE SO ON THE NOSE......

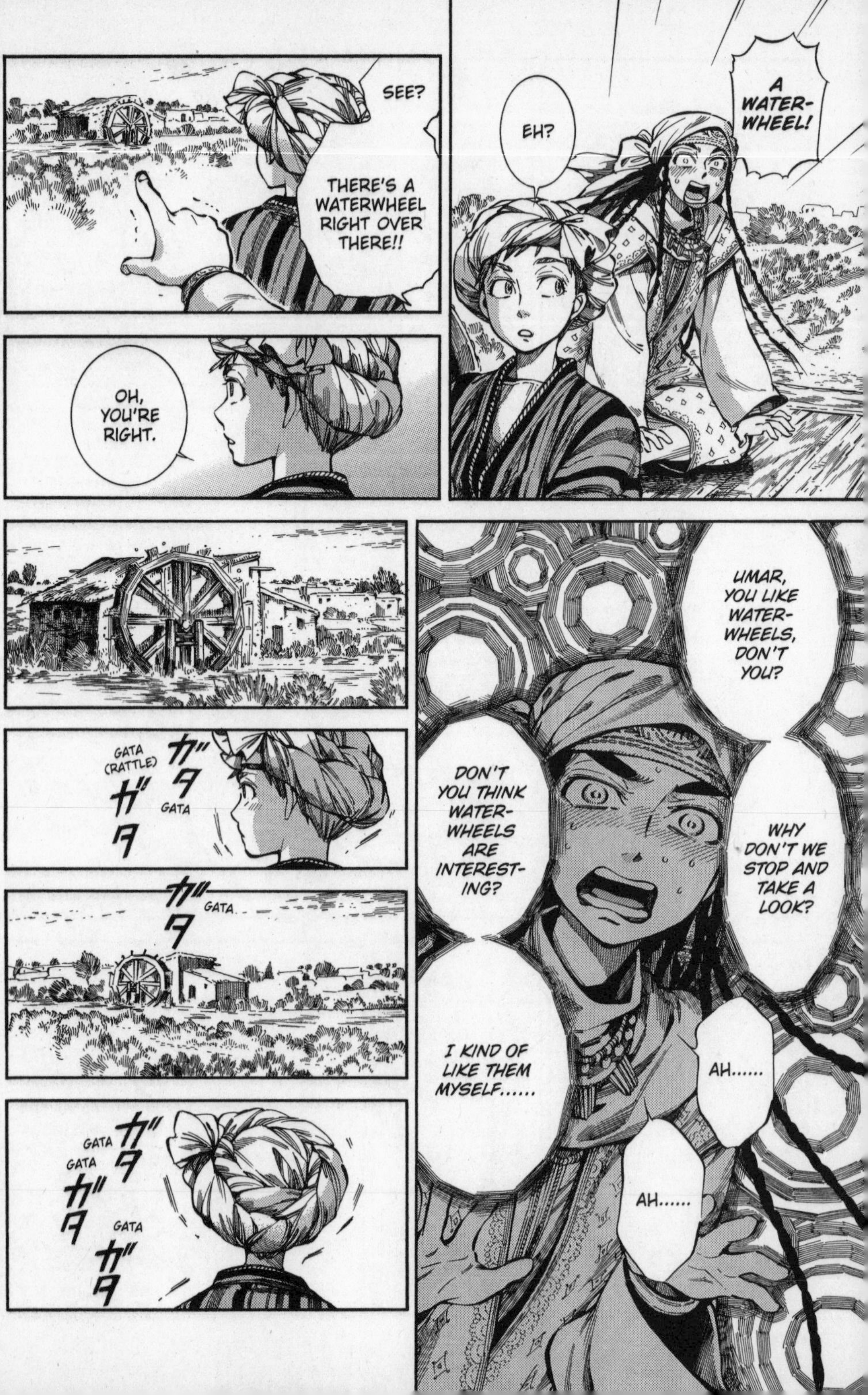
A WATER-WHEEL!
EH?
SEE?
THERE'S A WATERWHEEL RIGHT OVER THERE!!
OH, YOU'RE RIGHT.
UMAR, YOU LIKE WATER-WHEELS, DON'T YOU?
WHY DON'T WE STOP AND TAKE A LOOK?
DON'T YOU THINK WATER-WHEELS ARE INTEREST-ING?
AH......
I KIND OF LIKE THEM MYSELF......
AH......
ガタ GATA (RATTLE)
ガタ GATA
ガタ GATA
ガタ GATA
ガタ GATA
ガタ GATA

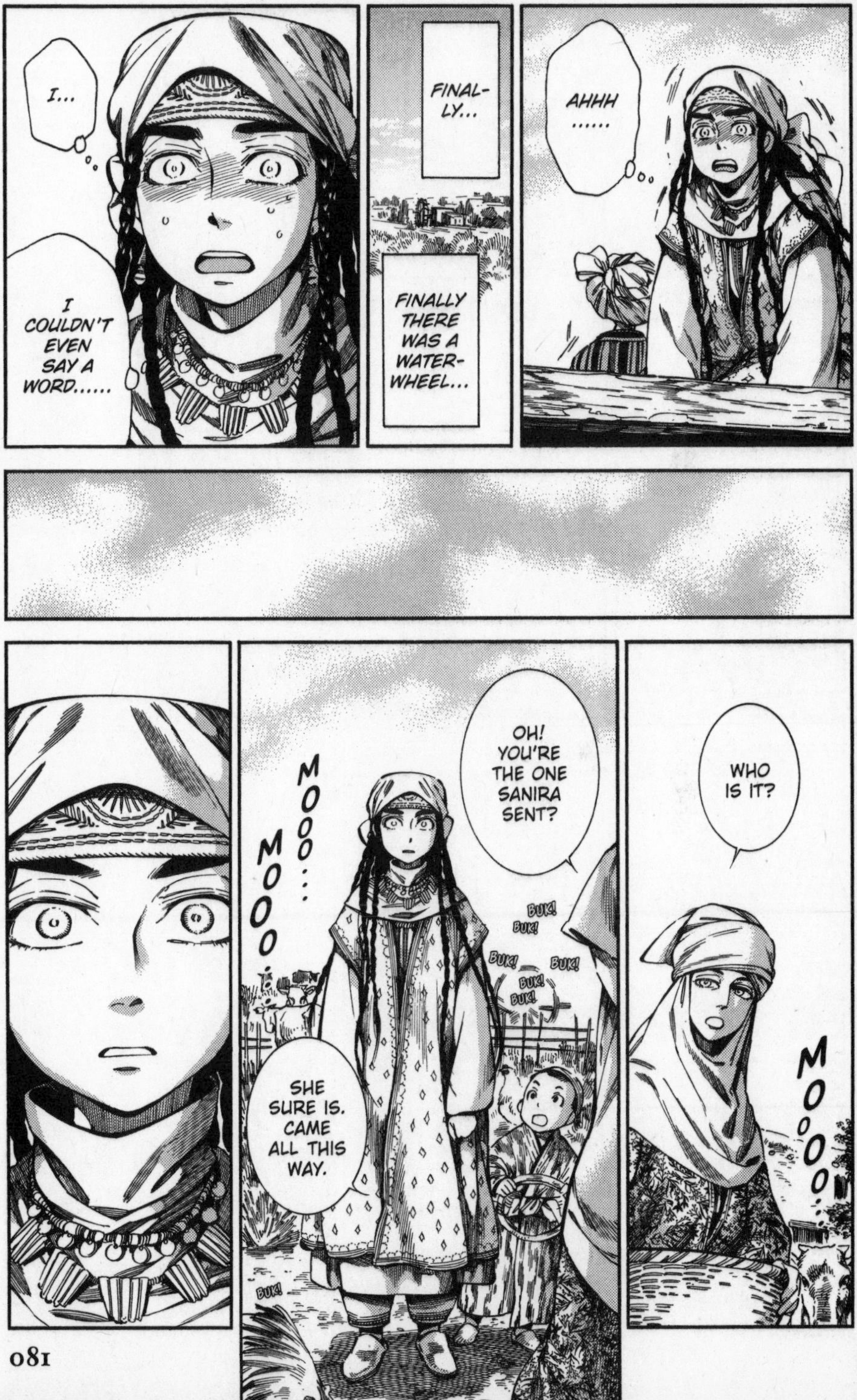
AHHH ......
FINAL-LY...
FINALLY THERE WAS A WATER-WHEEL...
I...
I COULDN'T EVEN SAY A WORD......
WHO IS IT?
MOOOO...
OH! YOU'RE THE ONE SANIRA SENT?
BUK! BUK! BUK! BUK! BUK! BUK!
MOOOO...
MOOOO...
SHE SURE IS. CAME ALL THIS WAY.
BUK!

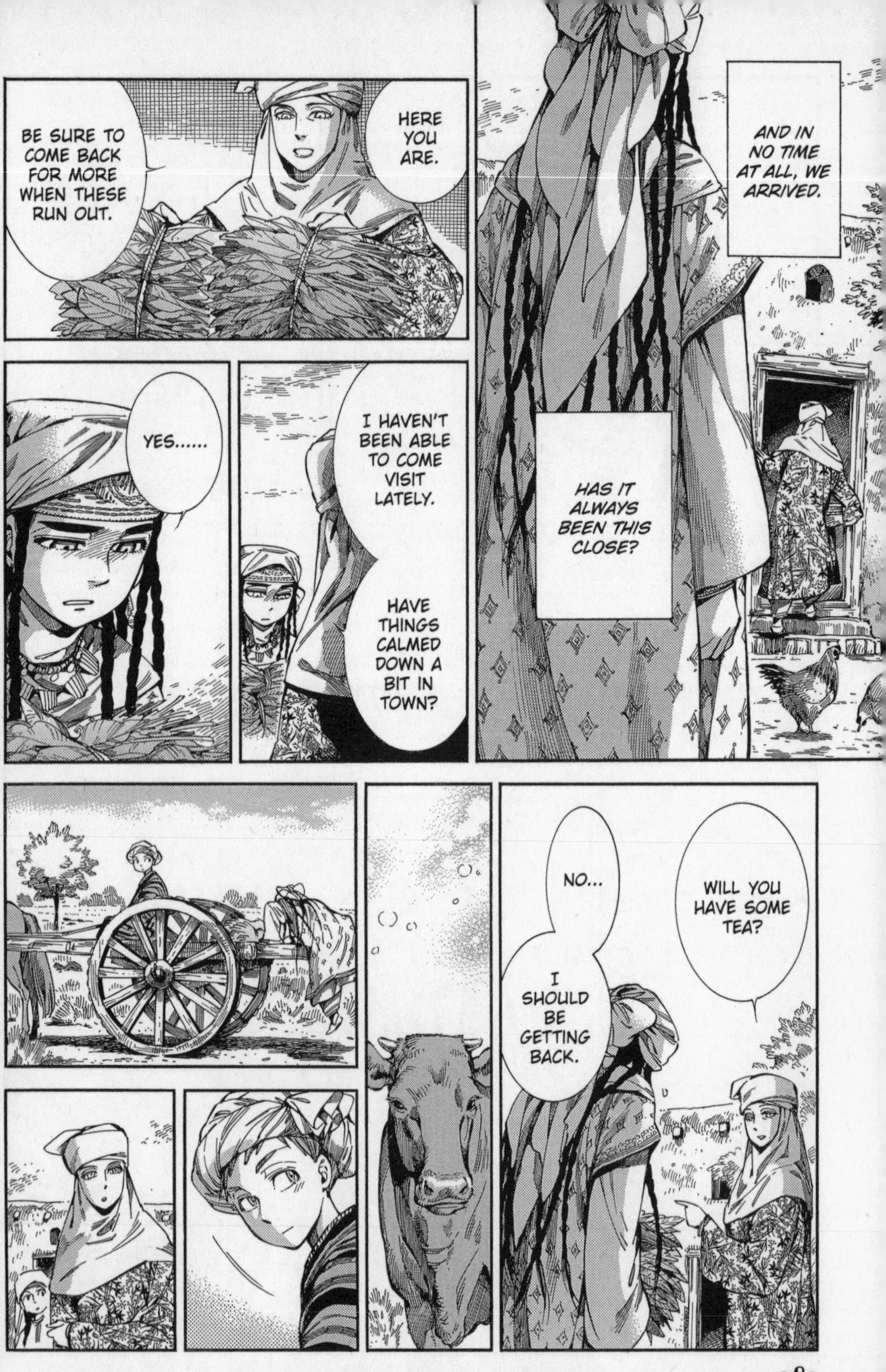
AND IN NO TIME AT ALL, WE ARRIVED.
HAS IT ALWAYS BEEN THIS CLOSE?
HERE YOU ARE.
BE SURE TO COME BACK FOR MORE WHEN THESE RUN OUT.
I HAVEN'T BEEN ABLE TO COME VISIT LATELY.
HAVE THINGS CALMED DOWN A BIT IN TOWN?
YES......
WILL YOU HAVE SOME TEA?
NO...
I SHOULD BE GETTING BACK.

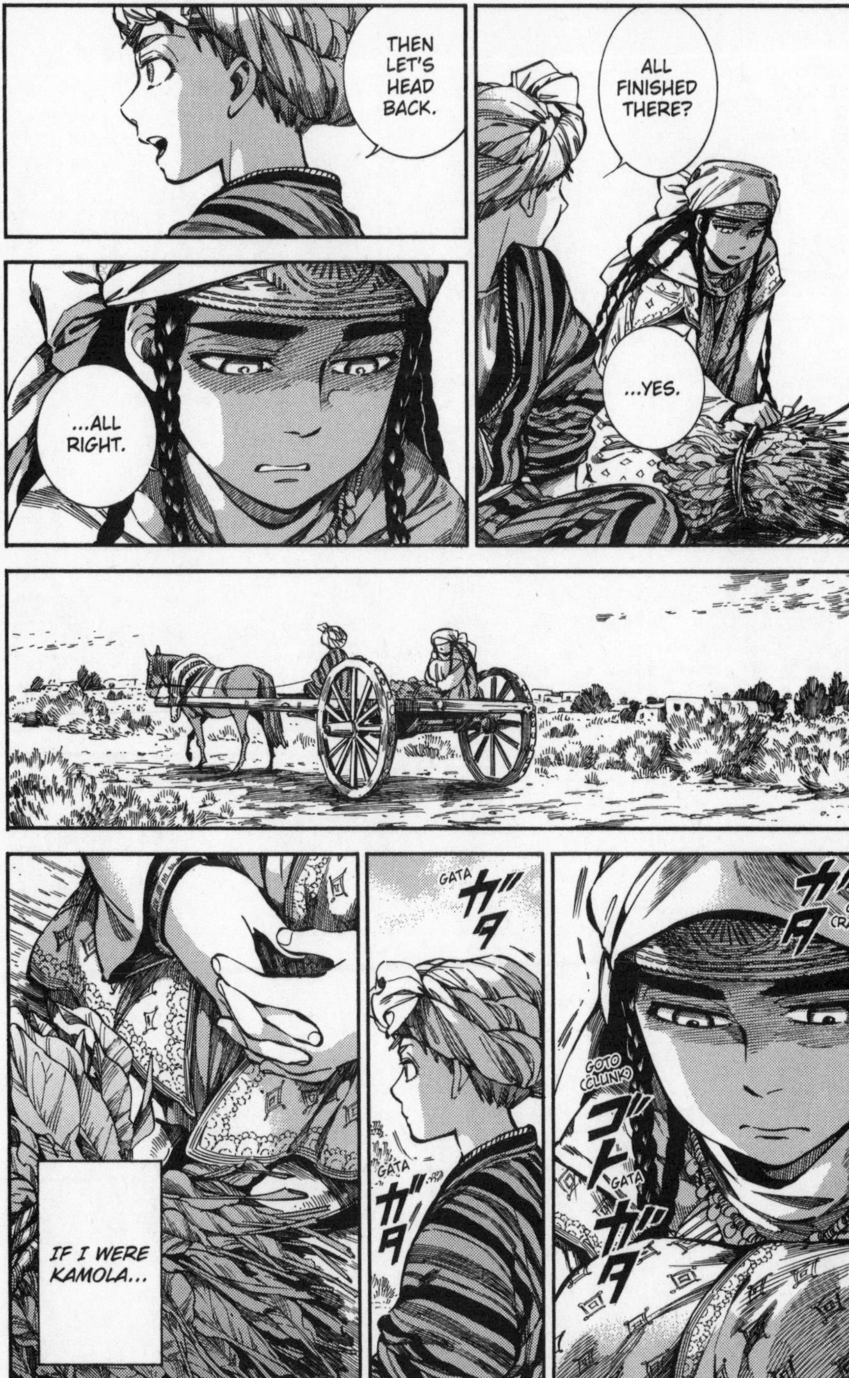
ALL FINISHED THERE?
...YES.
THEN LET'S HEAD BACK.
...ALL RIGHT.
ガタ
GATA (RATTLE)
ゴト
GOTO (CLUNK)
ガタ
GATA
ガタ
GATA
ガタ
GATA
IF I WERE KAMOLA...

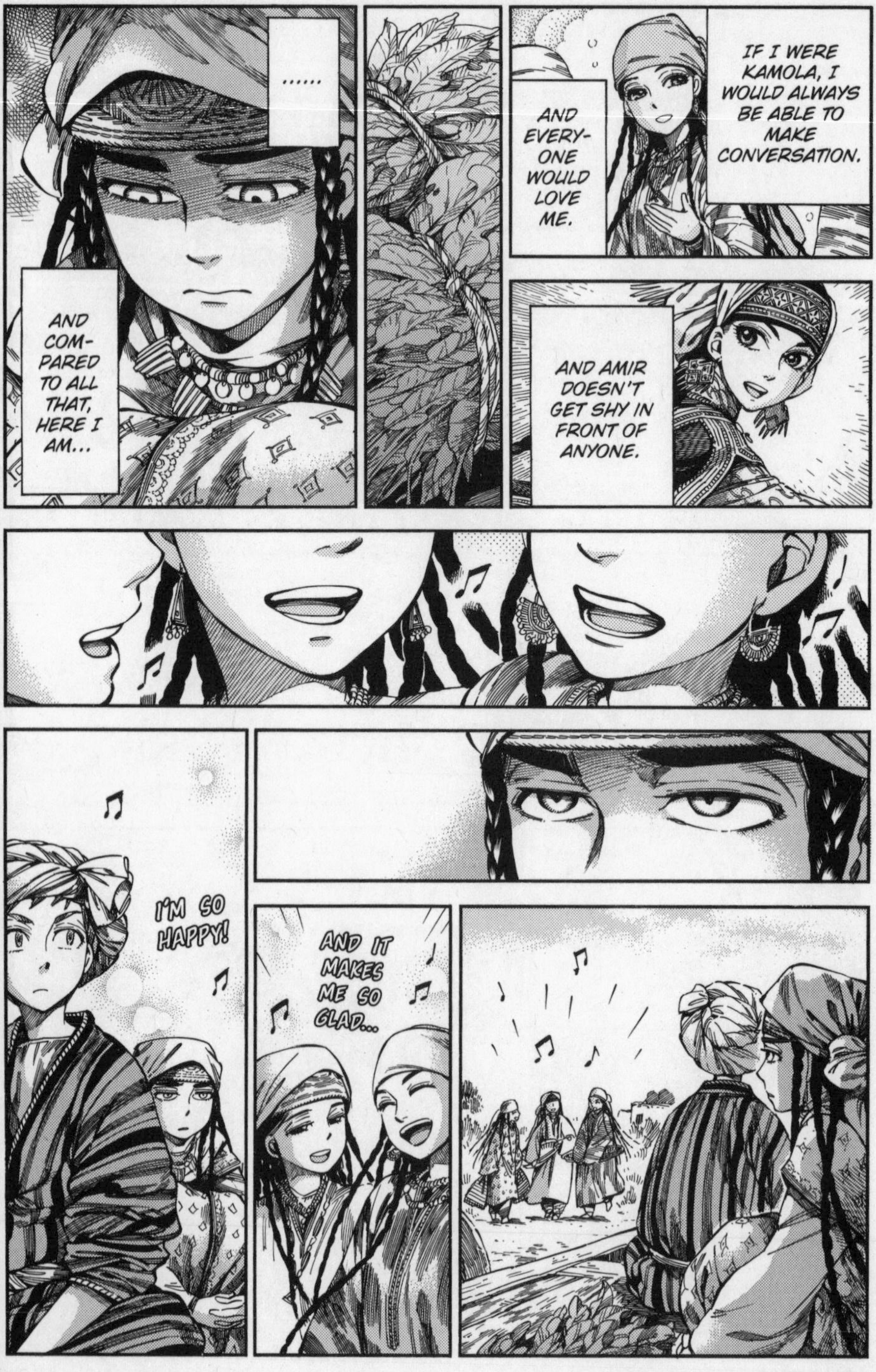
IF I WERE KAMOLA, I WOULD ALWAYS BE ABLE TO MAKE CONVERSATION.
AND EVERY-ONE WOULD LOVE ME.
AND AMIR DOESN'T GET SHY IN FRONT OF ANYONE.
......
AND COM-PARED TO ALL THAT, HERE I AM...
AND IT MAKES ME SO GLAD...
I'M SO HAPPY!

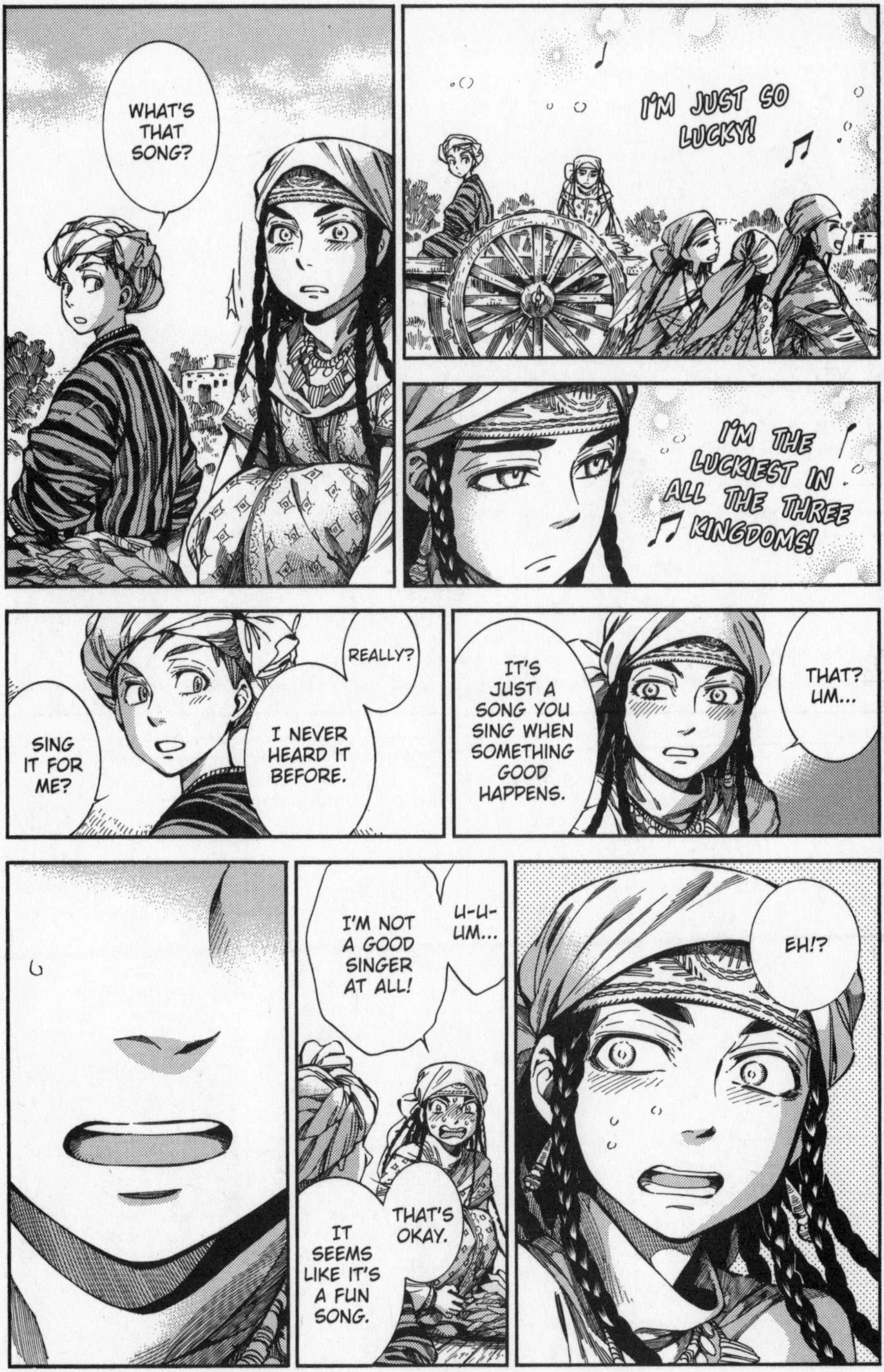
I'M JUST SO LUCKY!
I'M THE LUCKIEST IN ALL THE THREE KINGDOMS!
WHAT'S THAT SONG?
THAT? UM...
IT'S JUST A SONG YOU SING WHEN SOMETHING GOOD HAPPENS.
REALLY?
I NEVER HEARD IT BEFORE.
SING IT FOR ME?
EH!?
U-U-UM...
I'M NOT A GOOD SINGER AT ALL!
THAT'S OKAY.
IT SEEMS LIKE IT'S A FUN SONG.

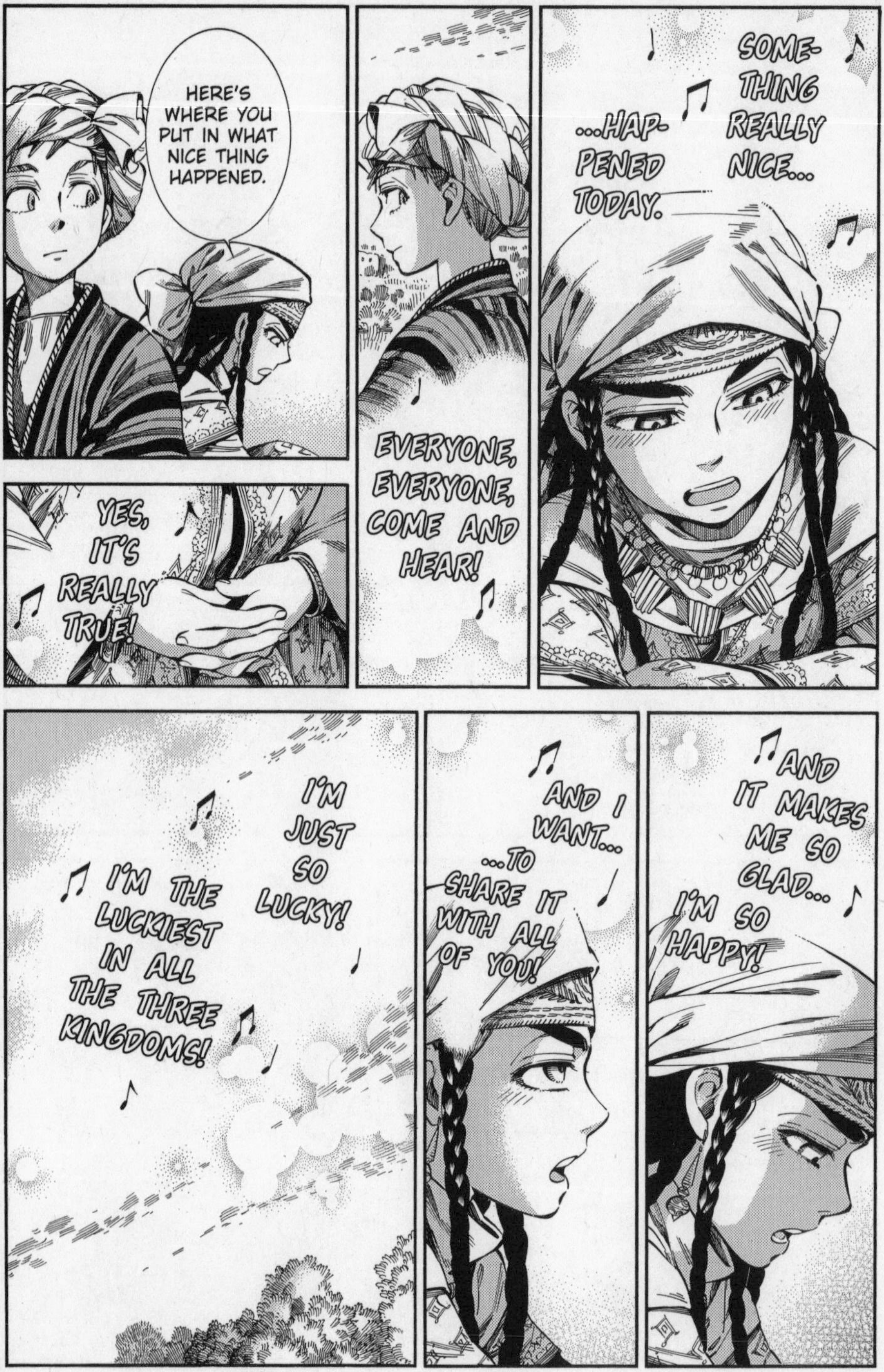
SOME-THING REALLY NICE...
...HAP-PENED TODAY.
EVERYONE, EVERYONE, COME AND HEAR!
HERE'S WHERE YOU PUT IN WHAT NICE THING HAPPENED.
YES, IT'S REALLY TRUE!
AND IT MAKES ME SO GLAD...
I'M SO HAPPY!
AND I WANT...
...TO SHARE IT WITH ALL OF YOU!
I'M JUST SO LUCKY!
I'M THE LUCKIEST IN ALL THE THREE KINGDOMS!

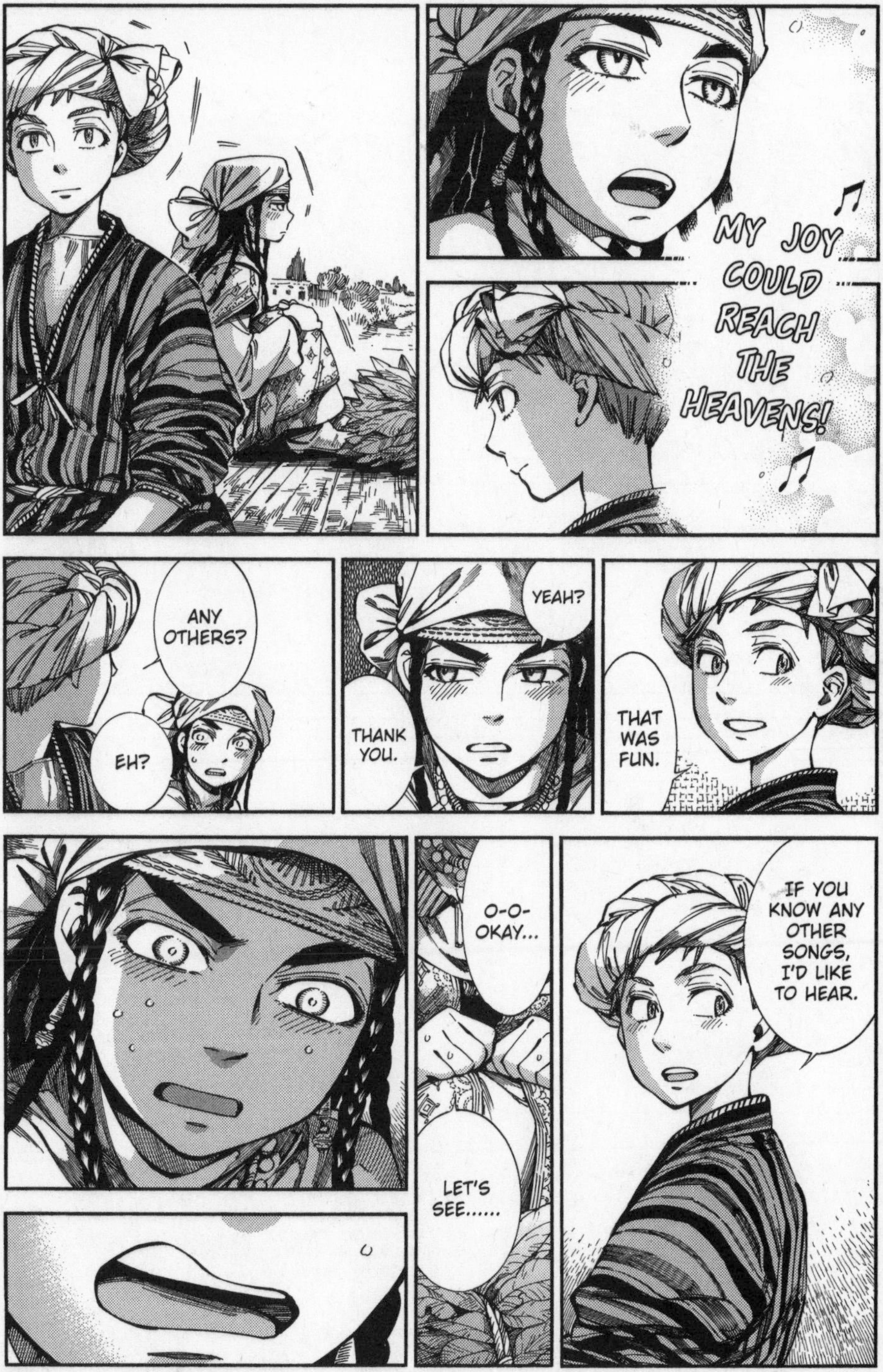

MY JOY COULD REACH THE HEAVENS!
THAT WAS FUN.
YEAH?
THANK YOU.
ANY OTHERS?
EH?
IF YOU KNOW ANY OTHER SONGS, I'D LIKE TO HEAR.
O-O-OKAY...
LET'S SEE......

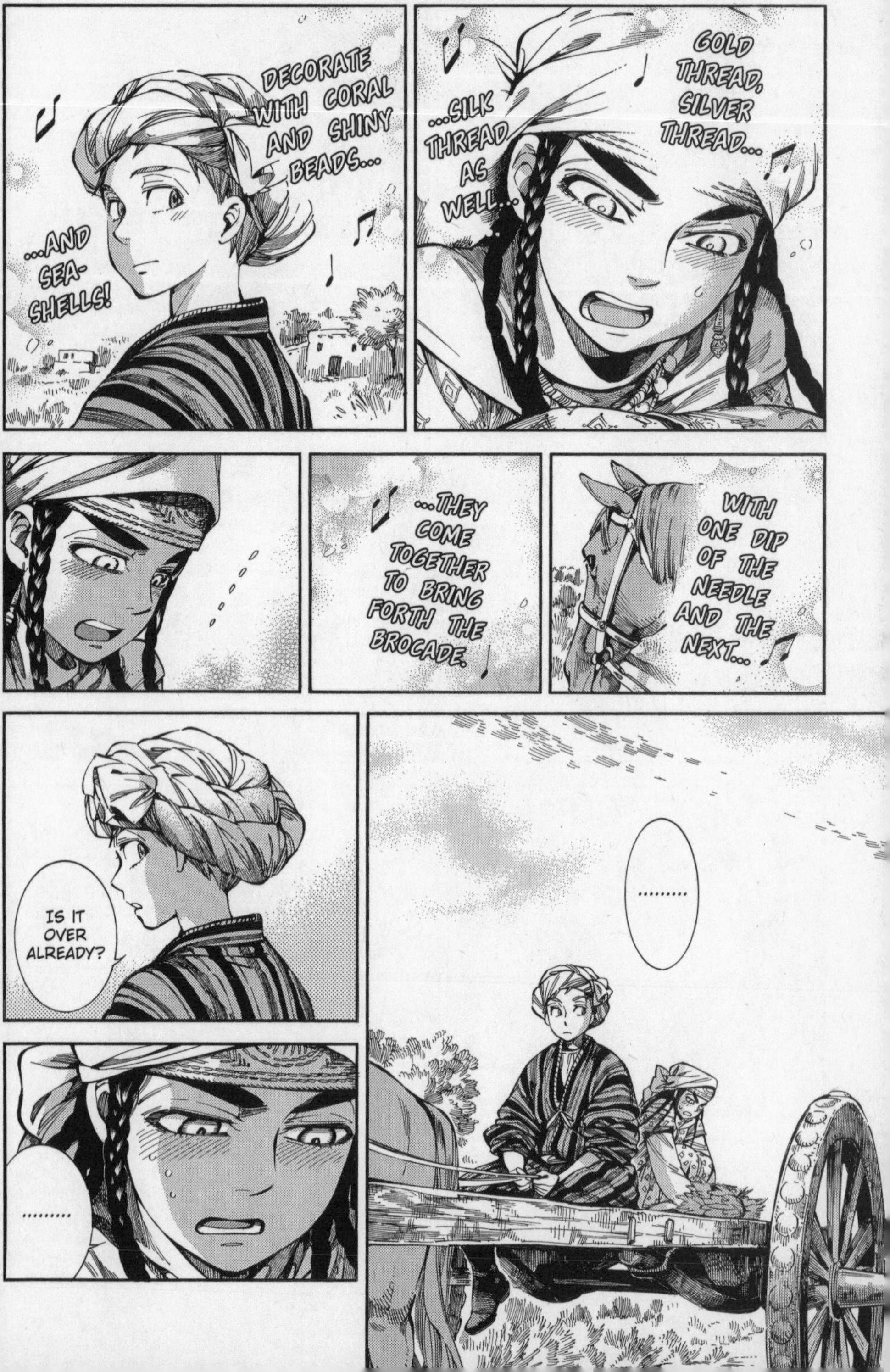
DECORATE WITH CORAL AND SHINY BEADS...
...AND SEA-SHELLS!
...SILK THREAD AS WELL...
GOLD THREAD, SILVER THREAD...
...THEY COME TOGETHER TO BRING FORTH THE BROCADE.
WITH ONE DIP OF THE NEEDLE AND THE NEXT...
IS IT OVER ALREADY?
....
....

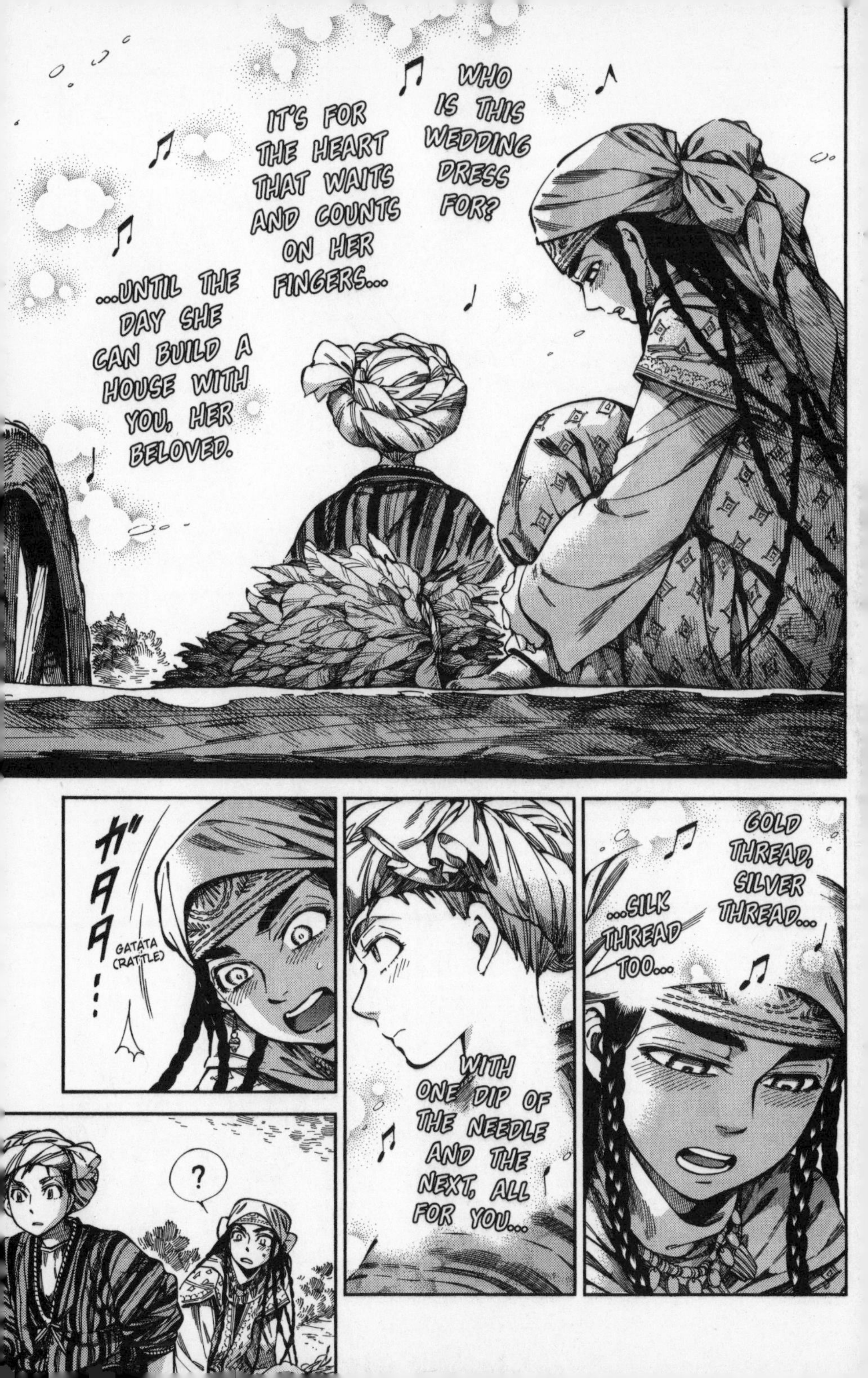
WHO IS THIS WEDDING DRESS FOR?
IT'S FOR THE HEART THAT WAITS AND COUNTS ON HER FINGERS...
...UNTIL THE DAY SHE CAN BUILD A HOUSE WITH YOU, HER BELOVED.
GOLD THREAD, SILVER THREAD...
...SILK THREAD TOO...
WITH ONE DIP OF THE NEEDLE AND THE NEXT, ALL FOR YOU...
ガタタ!!
GATATA (RATTLE)
?

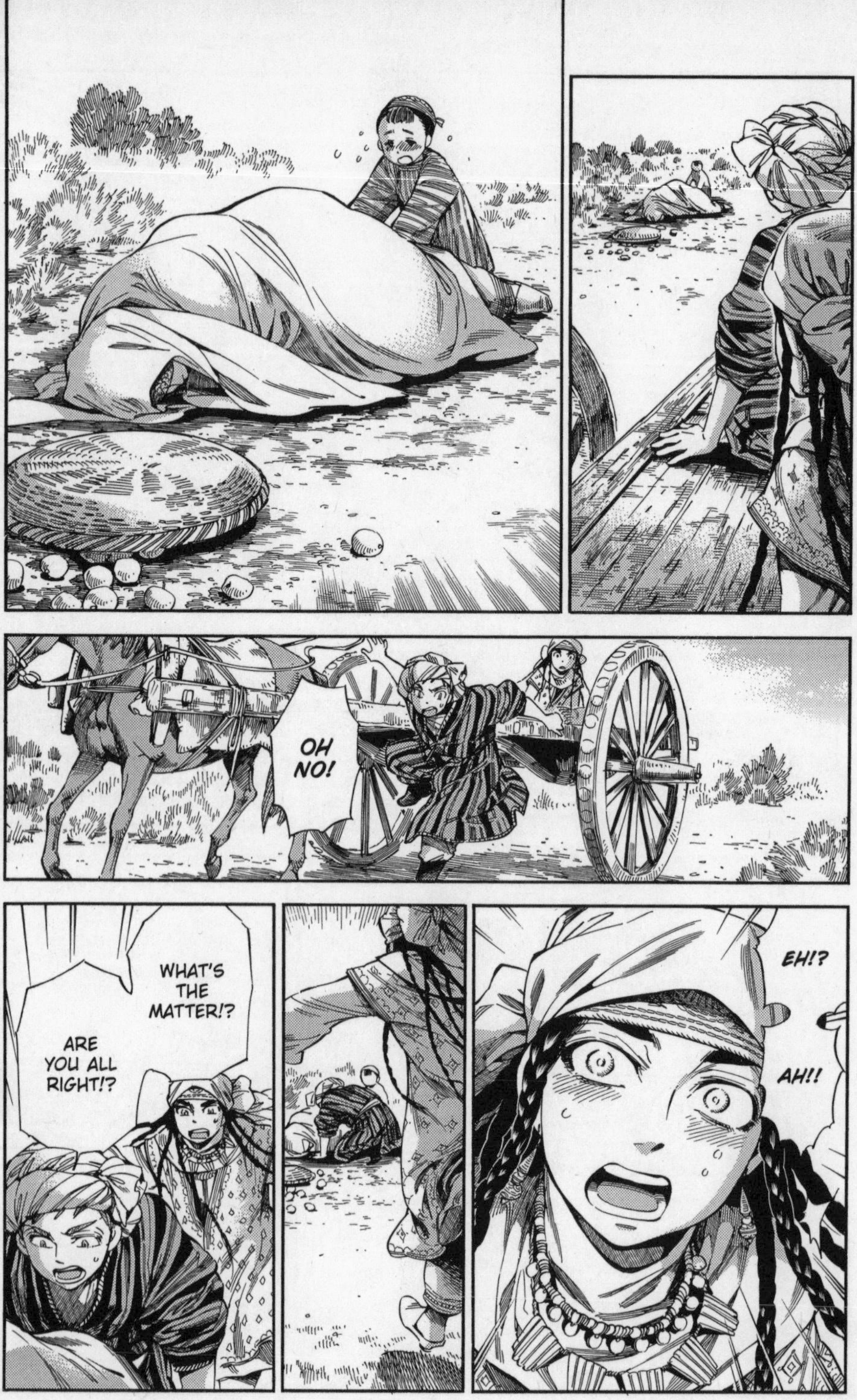
OH NO!
EH!?
AH!!
WHAT'S THE MATTER!?
ARE YOU ALL RIGHT!?

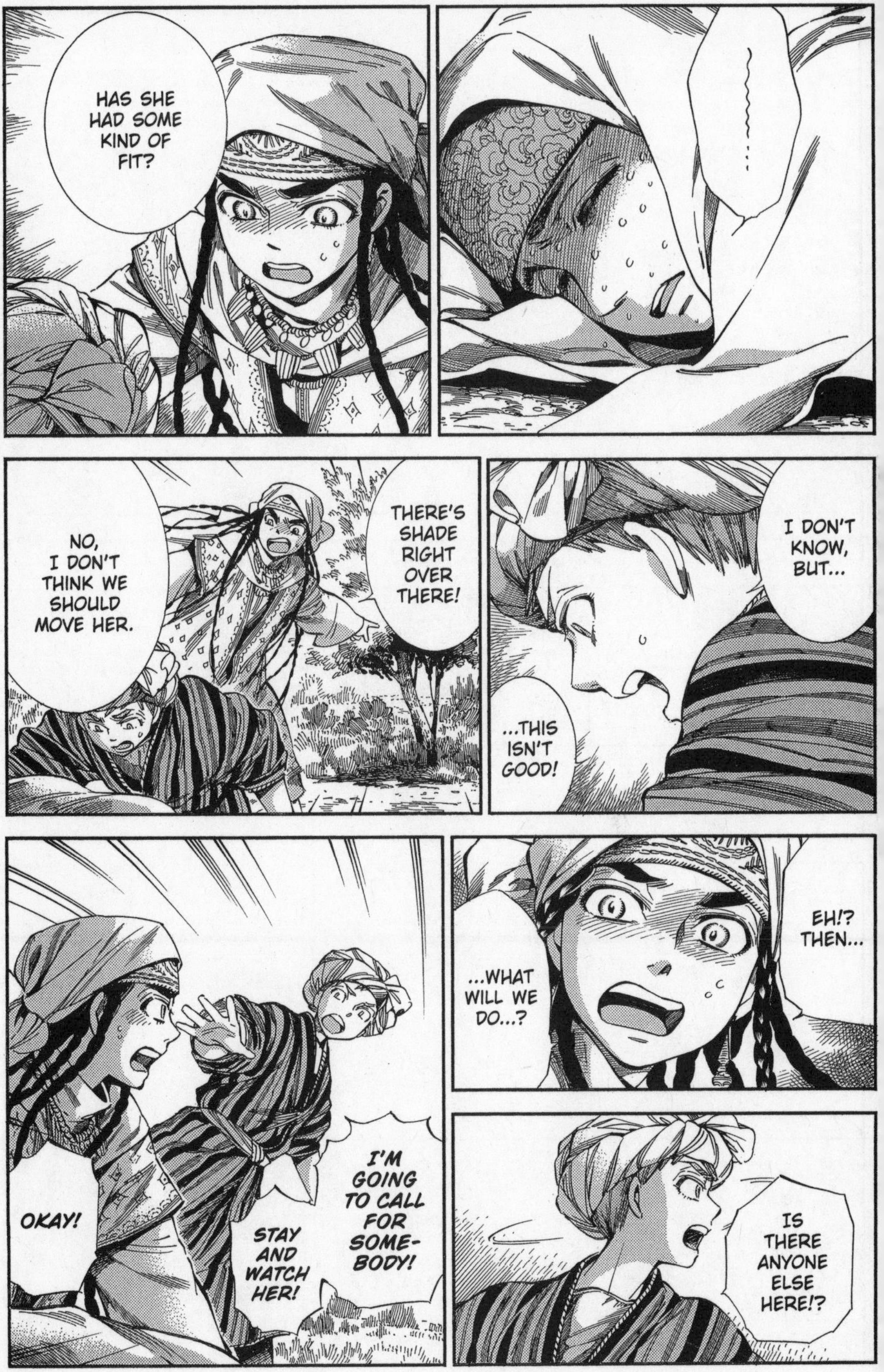
......
HAS SHE HAD SOME KIND OF FIT?
I DON'T KNOW, BUT...
...THIS ISN'T GOOD!
THERE'S SHADE RIGHT OVER THERE!
NO, I DON'T THINK WE SHOULD MOVE HER.
EH!? THEN...
...WHAT WILL WE DO...?
IS THERE ANYONE ELSE HERE!?
I'M GOING TO CALL FOR SOME-BODY!
STAY AND WATCH HER!
OKAY!

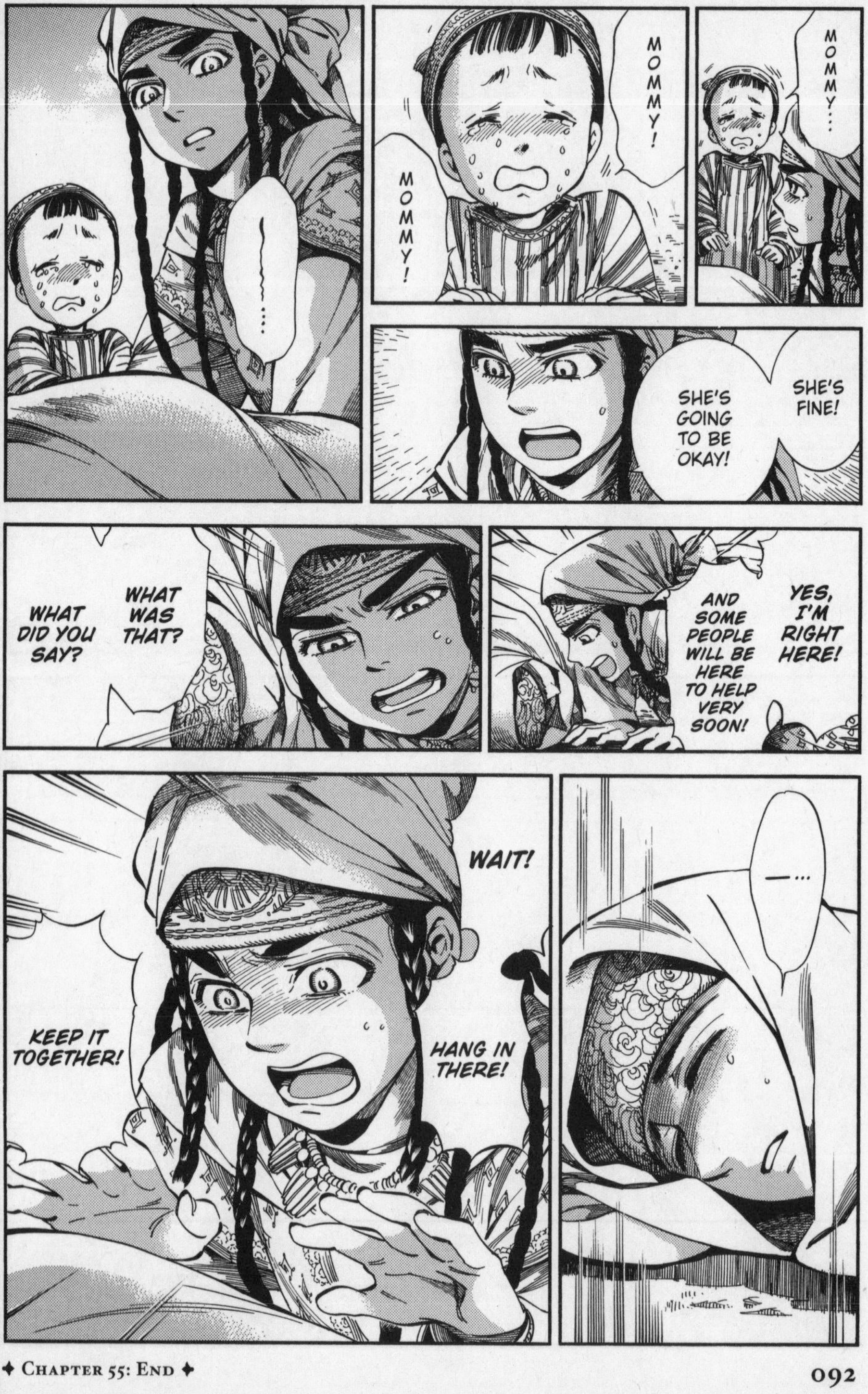
MOMMY...
MOMMY!
MOMMY!
SHE'S FINE!
SHE'S GOING TO BE OKAY!
—...
YES, I'M RIGHT HERE!
AND SOME PEOPLE WILL BE HERE TO HELP VERY SOON!
WHAT WAS THAT?
WHAT DID YOU SAY?
—...
WAIT!
HANG IN THERE!
KEEP IT TOGETHER!

✦ Chapter 55: End ✦

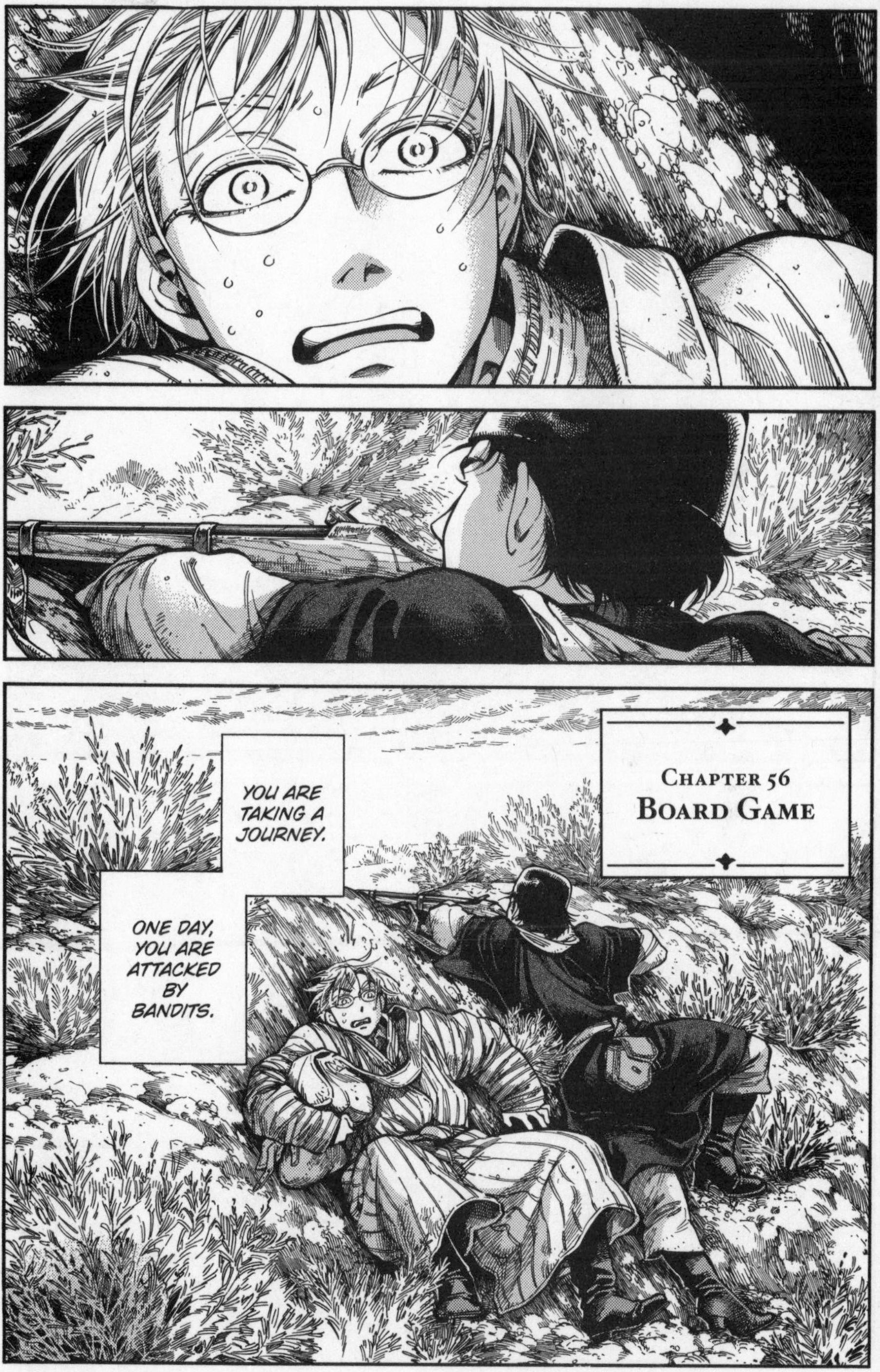
CHAPTER 56
BOARD GAME
YOU ARE TAKING A JOURNEY.
ONE DAY, YOU ARE ATTACKED BY BANDITS.

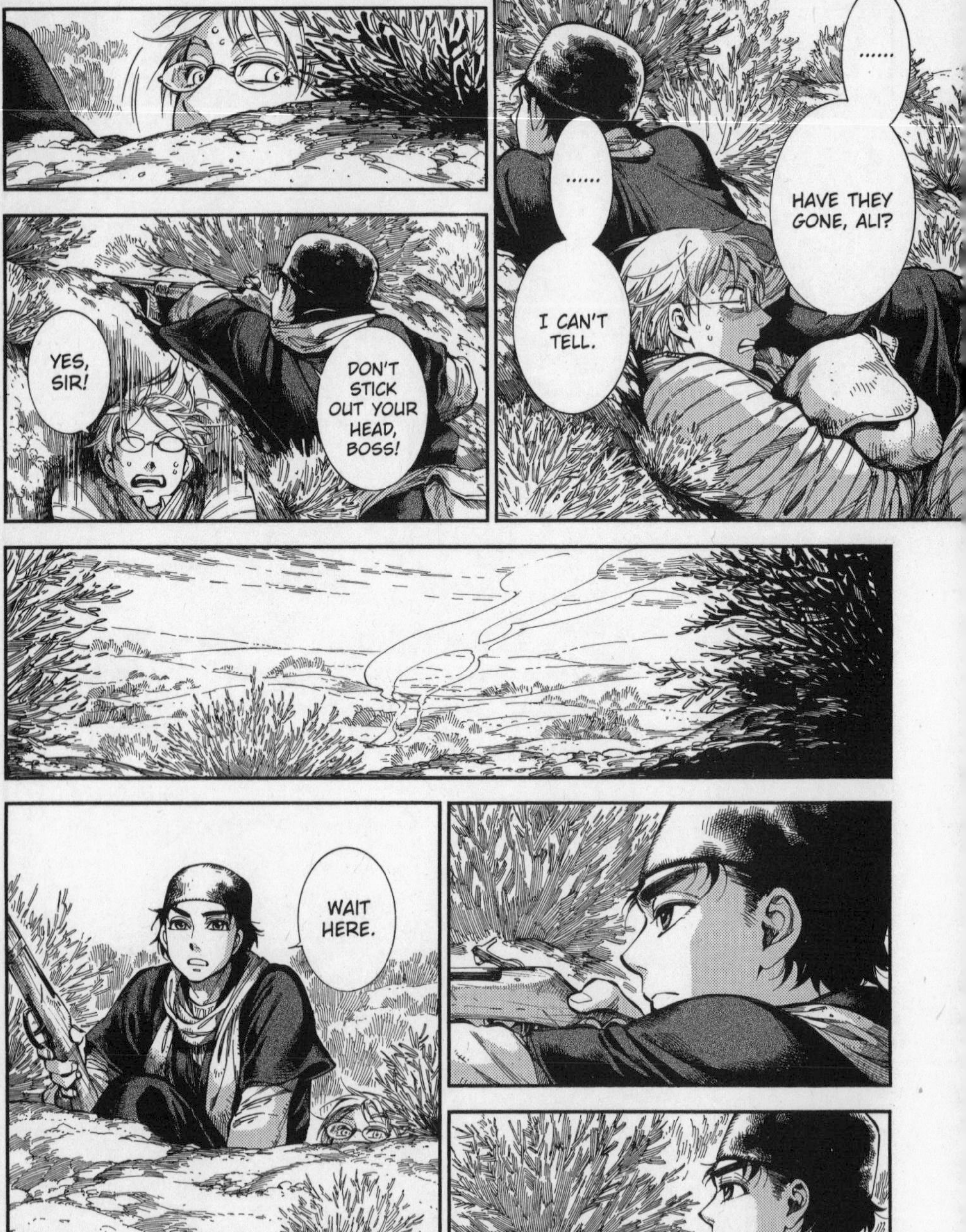
......
HAVE THEY GONE, ALI?
......
I CAN'T TELL.
DON'T STICK OUT YOUR HEAD, BOSS!
YES, SIR!
WAIT HERE.

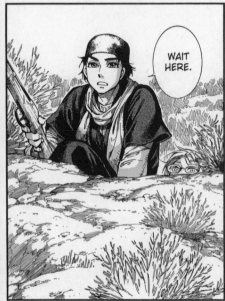

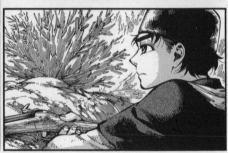

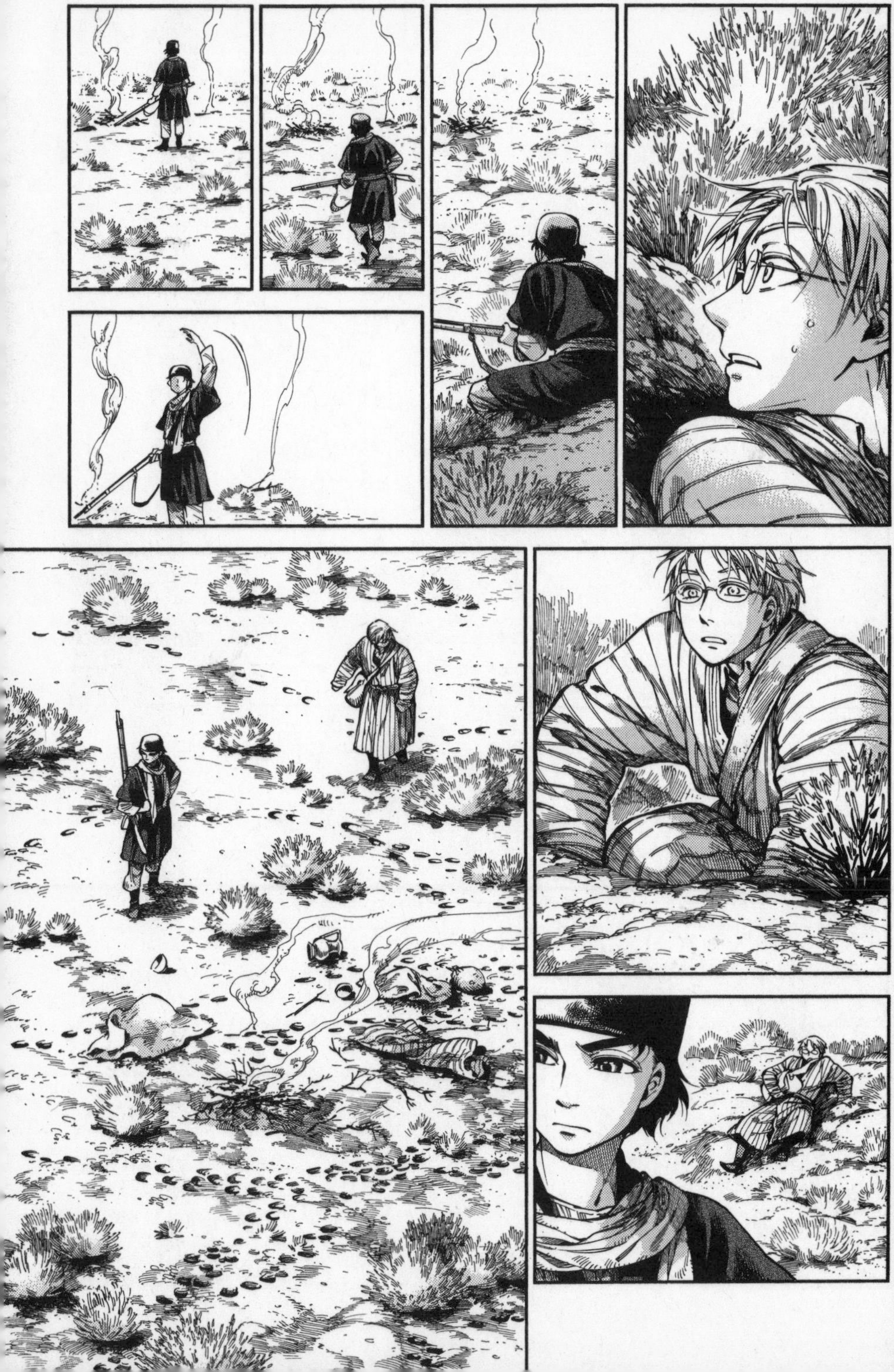

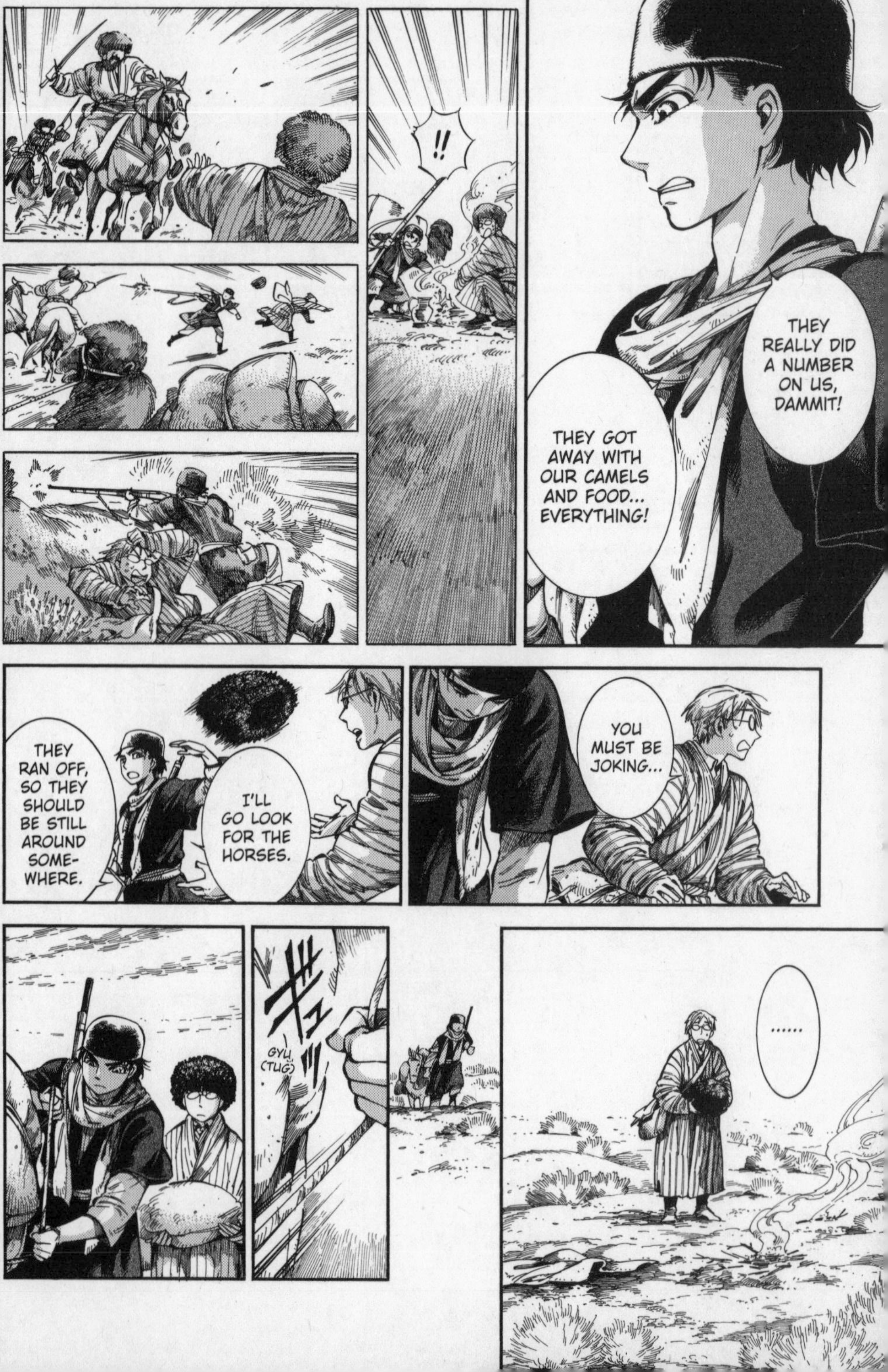
THEY REALLY DID A NUMBER ON US, DAMMIT!
THEY GOT AWAY WITH OUR CAMELS AND FOOD... EVERYTHING!
!!
YOU MUST BE JOKING...
I'LL GO LOOK FOR THE HORSES.
THEY RAN OFF, SO THEY SHOULD BE STILL AROUND SOME-WHERE.
......
ギュ
GYU (TUG)

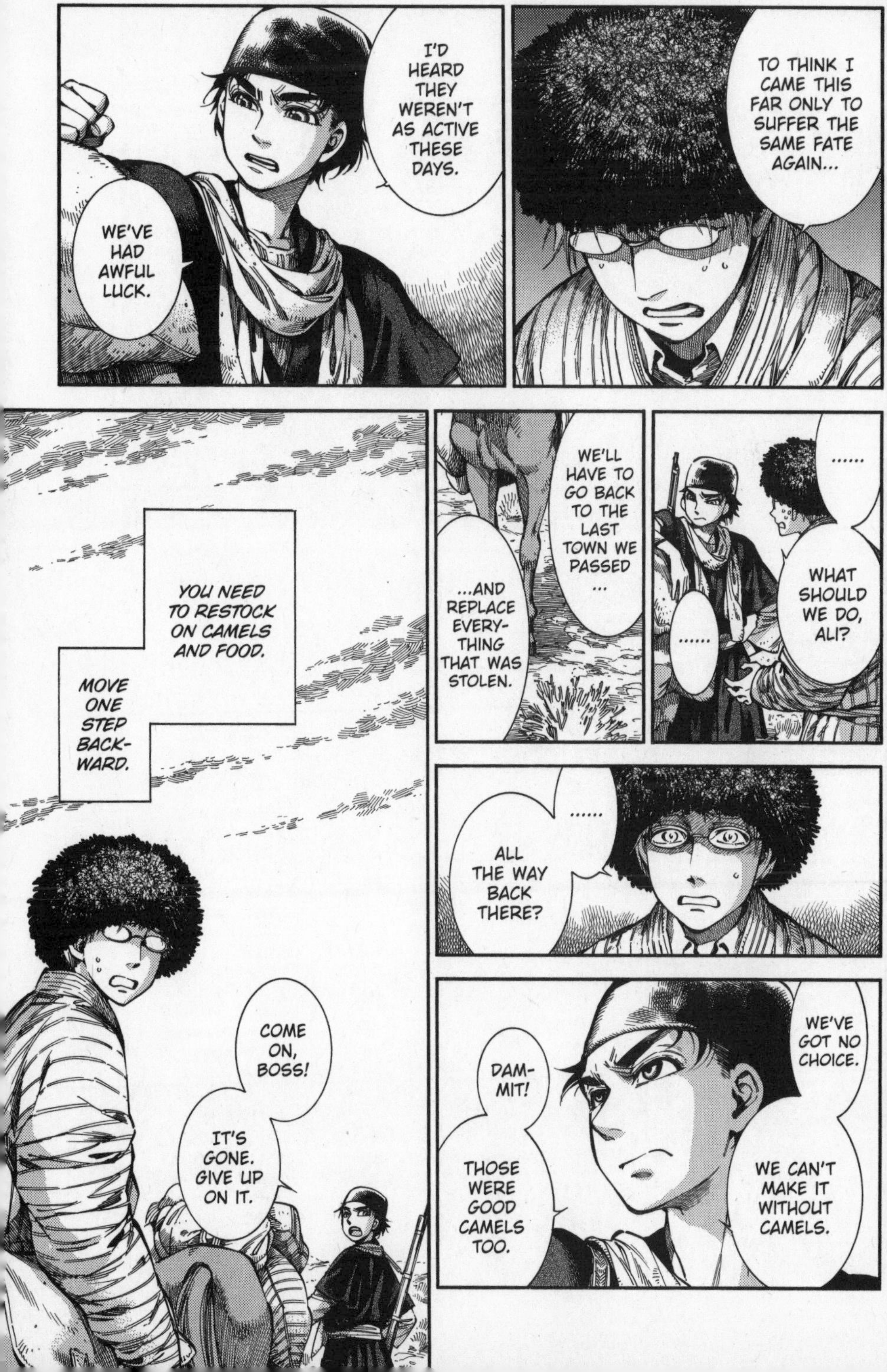
TO THINK I CAME THIS FAR ONLY TO SUFFER THE SAME FATE AGAIN...
I'D HEARD THEY WEREN'T AS ACTIVE THESE DAYS.
WE'VE HAD AWFUL LUCK.
......
WHAT SHOULD WE DO, ALI?
......
WE'LL HAVE TO GO BACK TO THE LAST TOWN WE PASSED...
...AND REPLACE EVERY-THING THAT WAS STOLEN.
......
ALL THE WAY BACK THERE?
WE'VE GOT NO CHOICE.
WE CAN'T MAKE IT WITHOUT CAMELS.
DAM-MIT!
THOSE WERE GOOD CAMELS TOO.
YOU NEED TO RESTOCK ON CAMELS AND FOOD.
MOVE ONE STEP BACK-WARD.
COME ON, BOSS!
IT'S GONE. GIVE UP ON IT.

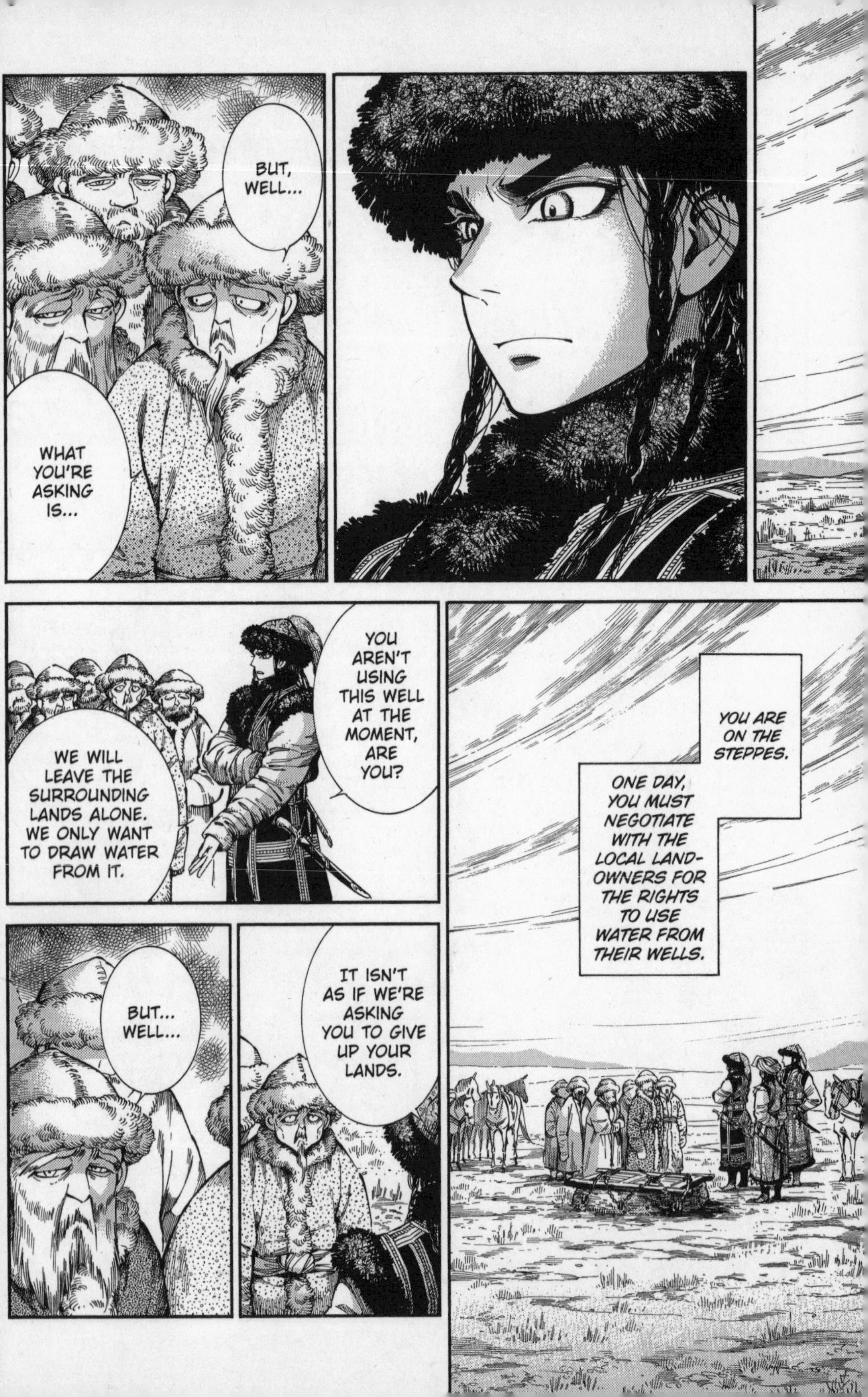
BUT, WELL...
WHAT YOU'RE ASKING IS...
YOU ARE ON THE STEPPES.
ONE DAY, YOU MUST NEGOTIATE WITH THE LOCAL LAND-OWNERS FOR THE RIGHTS TO USE WATER FROM THEIR WELLS.
YOU AREN'T USING THIS WELL AT THE MOMENT, ARE YOU?
WE WILL LEAVE THE SURROUNDING LANDS ALONE. WE ONLY WANT TO DRAW WATER FROM IT.
IT ISN'T AS IF WE'RE ASKING YOU TO GIVE UP YOUR LANDS.
BUT... WELL...

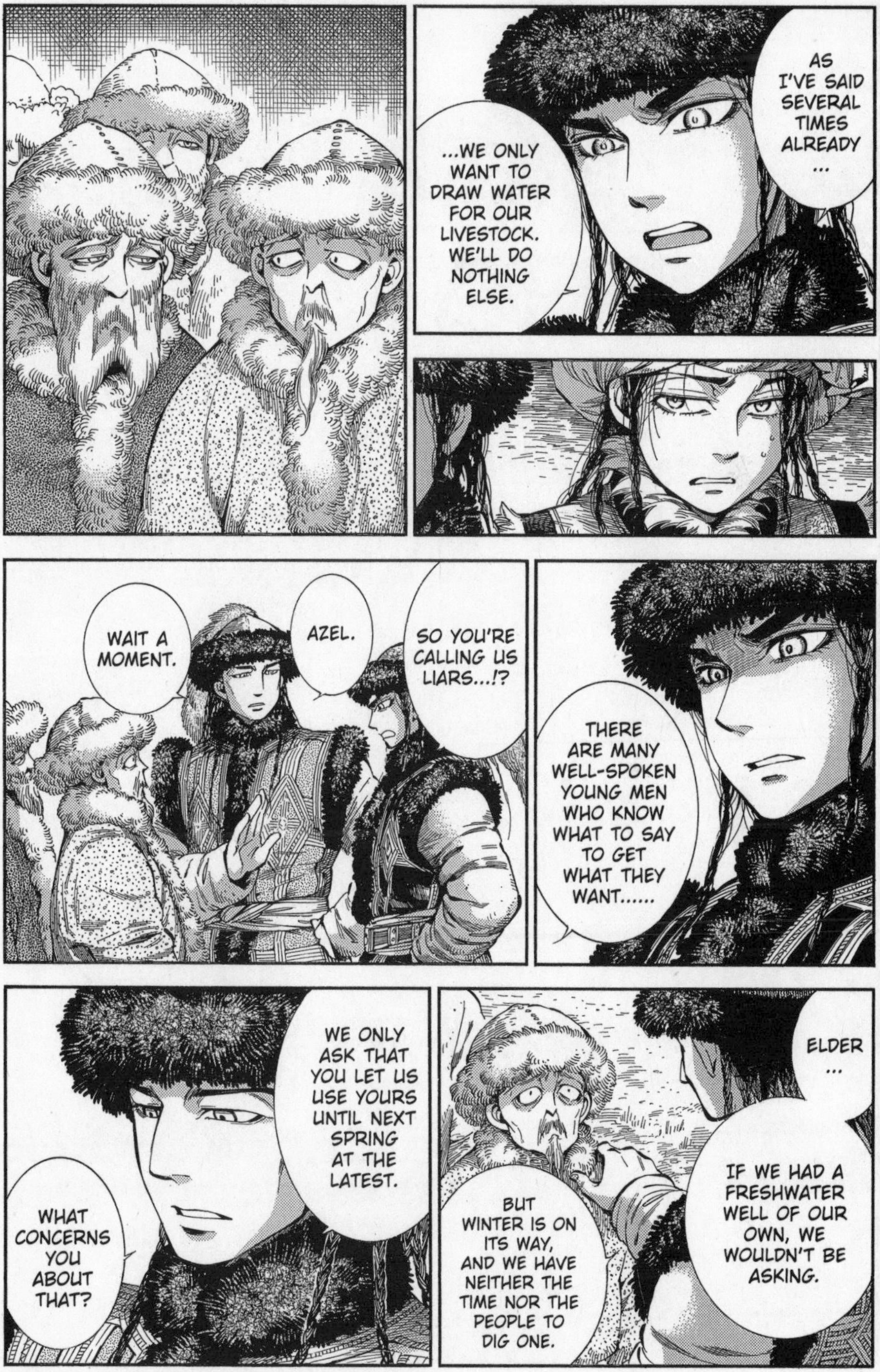
AS I'VE SAID SEVERAL TIMES ALREADY...
...WE ONLY WANT TO DRAW WATER FOR OUR LIVESTOCK. WE'LL DO NOTHING ELSE.
THERE ARE MANY WELL-SPOKEN YOUNG MEN WHO KNOW WHAT TO SAY TO GET WHAT THEY WANT......
SO YOU'RE CALLING US LIARS...!?
AZEL.
WAIT A MOMENT.
ELDER...
IF WE HAD A FRESHWATER WELL OF OUR OWN, WE WOULDN'T BE ASKING.
BUT WINTER IS ON ITS WAY, AND WE HAVE NEITHER THE TIME NOR THE PEOPLE TO DIG ONE.
WE ONLY ASK THAT YOU LET US USE YOURS UNTIL NEXT SPRING AT THE LATEST.
WHAT CONCERNS YOU ABOUT THAT?

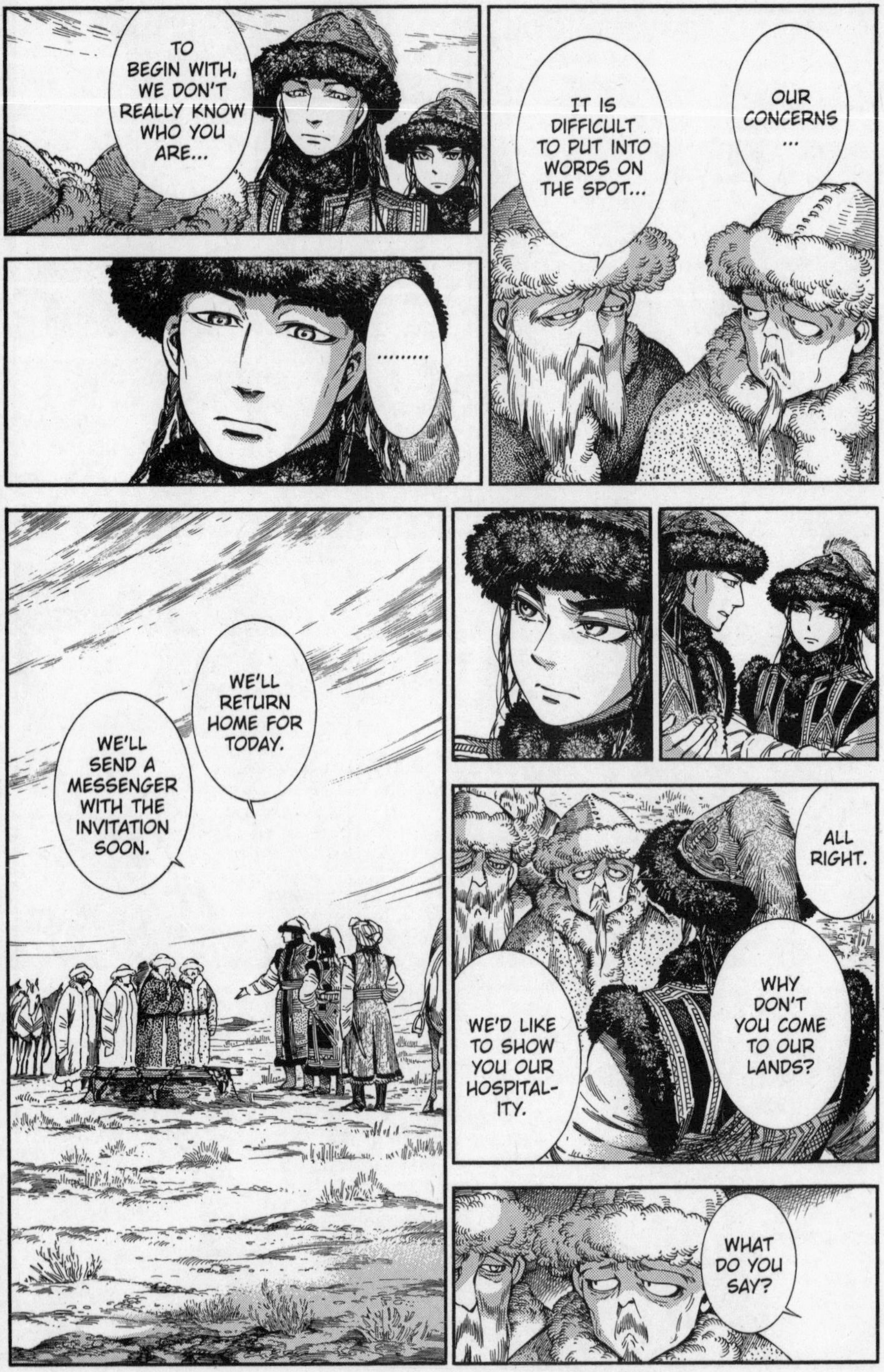
OUR CONCERNS ...
IT IS DIFFICULT TO PUT INTO WORDS ON THE SPOT...
TO BEGIN WITH, WE DON'T REALLY KNOW WHO YOU ARE...
....
ALL RIGHT.
WHY DON'T YOU COME TO OUR LANDS?
WE'D LIKE TO SHOW YOU OUR HOSPITAL-ITY.
WHAT DO YOU SAY?
WE'LL RETURN HOME FOR TODAY.
WE'LL SEND A MESSENGER WITH THE INVITATION SOON.

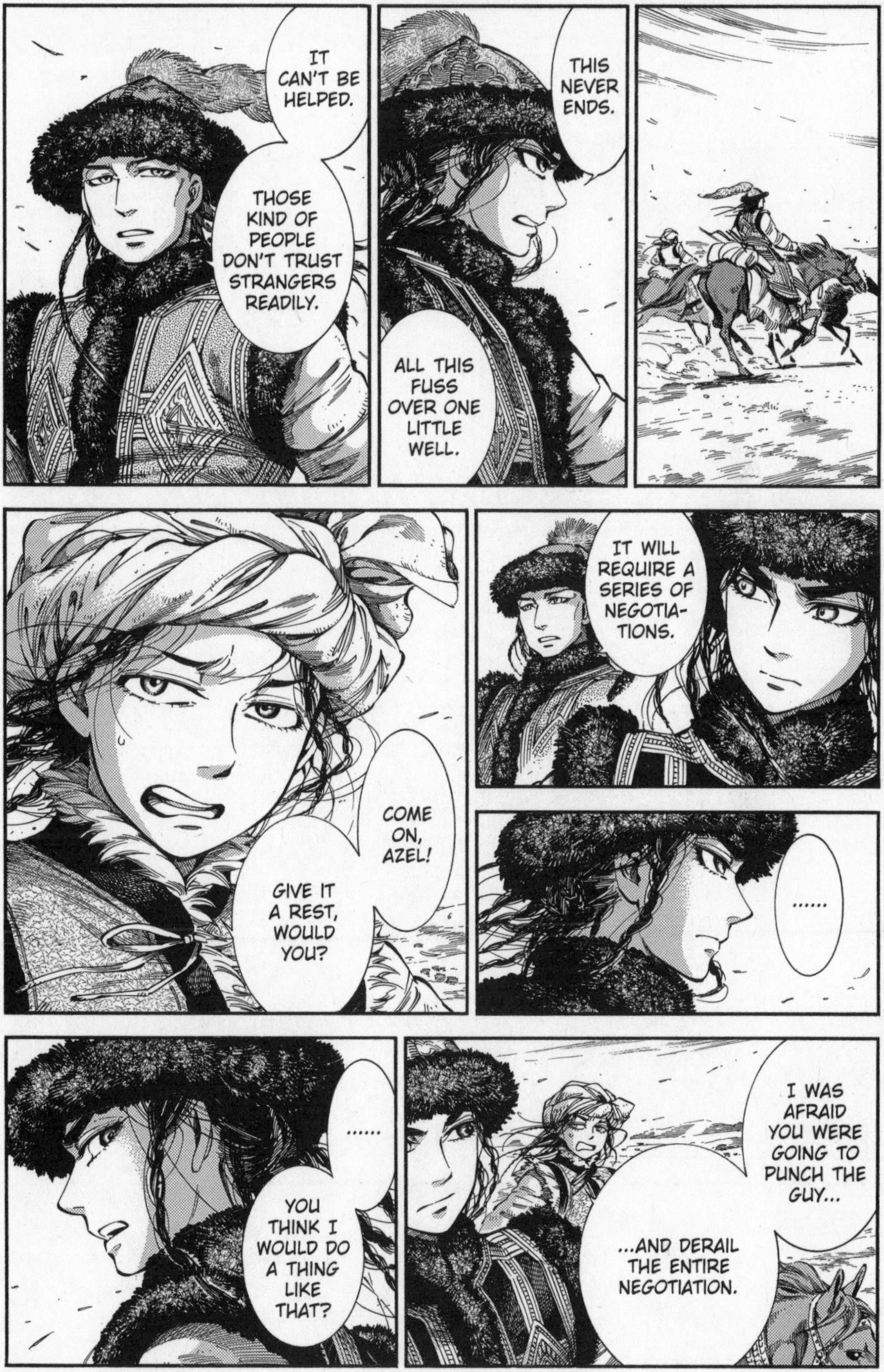
THIS NEVER ENDS.
ALL THIS FUSS OVER ONE LITTLE WELL.
IT CAN'T BE HELPED.
THOSE KIND OF PEOPLE DON'T TRUST STRANGERS READILY.
IT WILL REQUIRE A SERIES OF NEGOTIATIONS.
......
COME ON, AZEL!
GIVE IT A REST, WOULD YOU?
I WAS AFRAID YOU WERE GOING TO PUNCH THE GUY...
...AND DERAIL THE ENTIRE NEGOTIATION.
......
YOU THINK I WOULD DO A THING LIKE THAT?

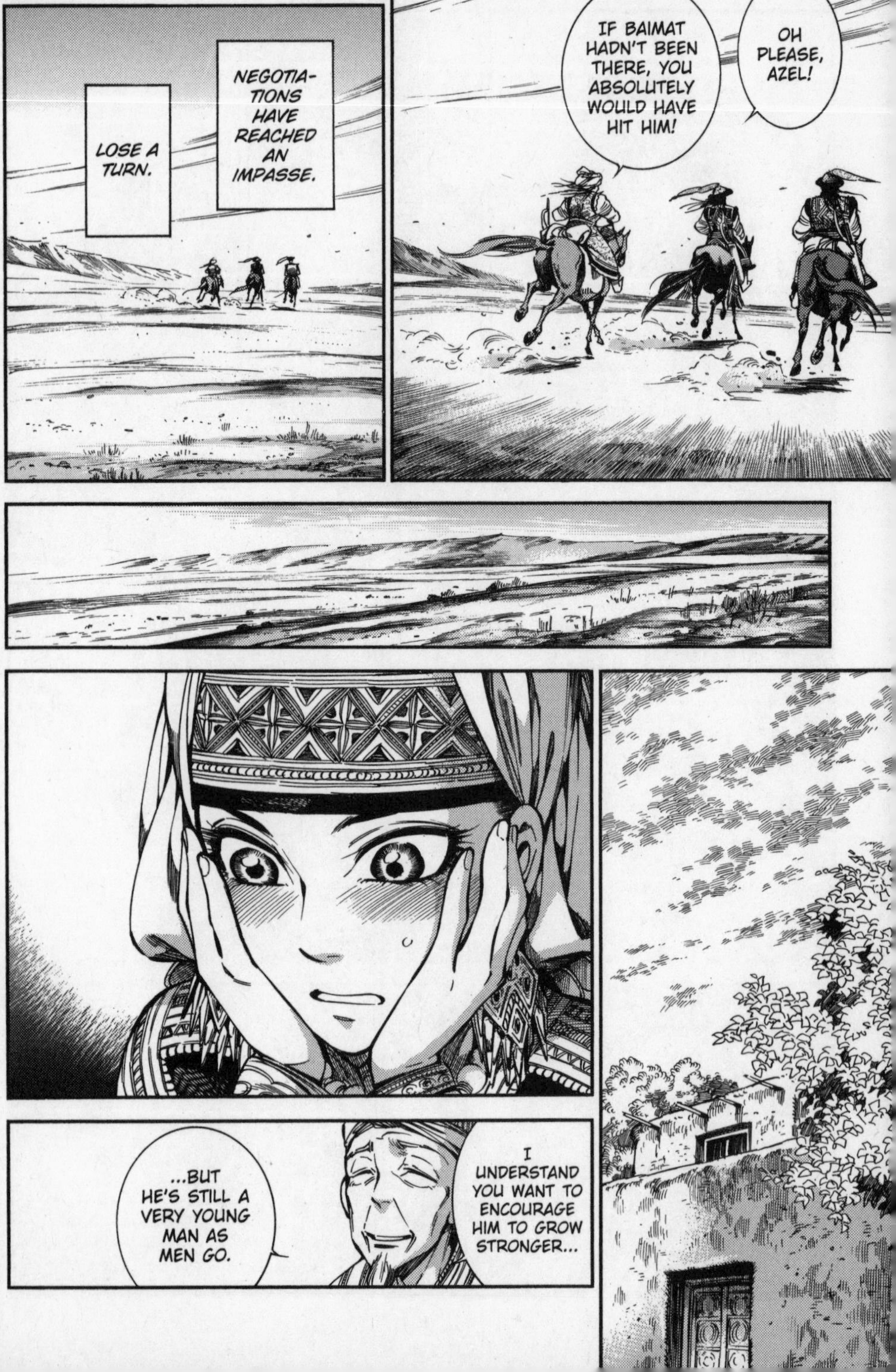
OH PLEASE, AZEL!
IF BAIMAT HADN'T BEEN THERE, YOU ABSOLUTELY WOULD HAVE HIT HIM!
NEGOTIA-TIONS HAVE REACHED AN IMPASSE.
LOSE A TURN.
I UNDERSTAND YOU WANT TO ENCOURAGE HIM TO GROW STRONGER...
...BUT HE'S STILL A VERY YOUNG MAN AS MEN GO.

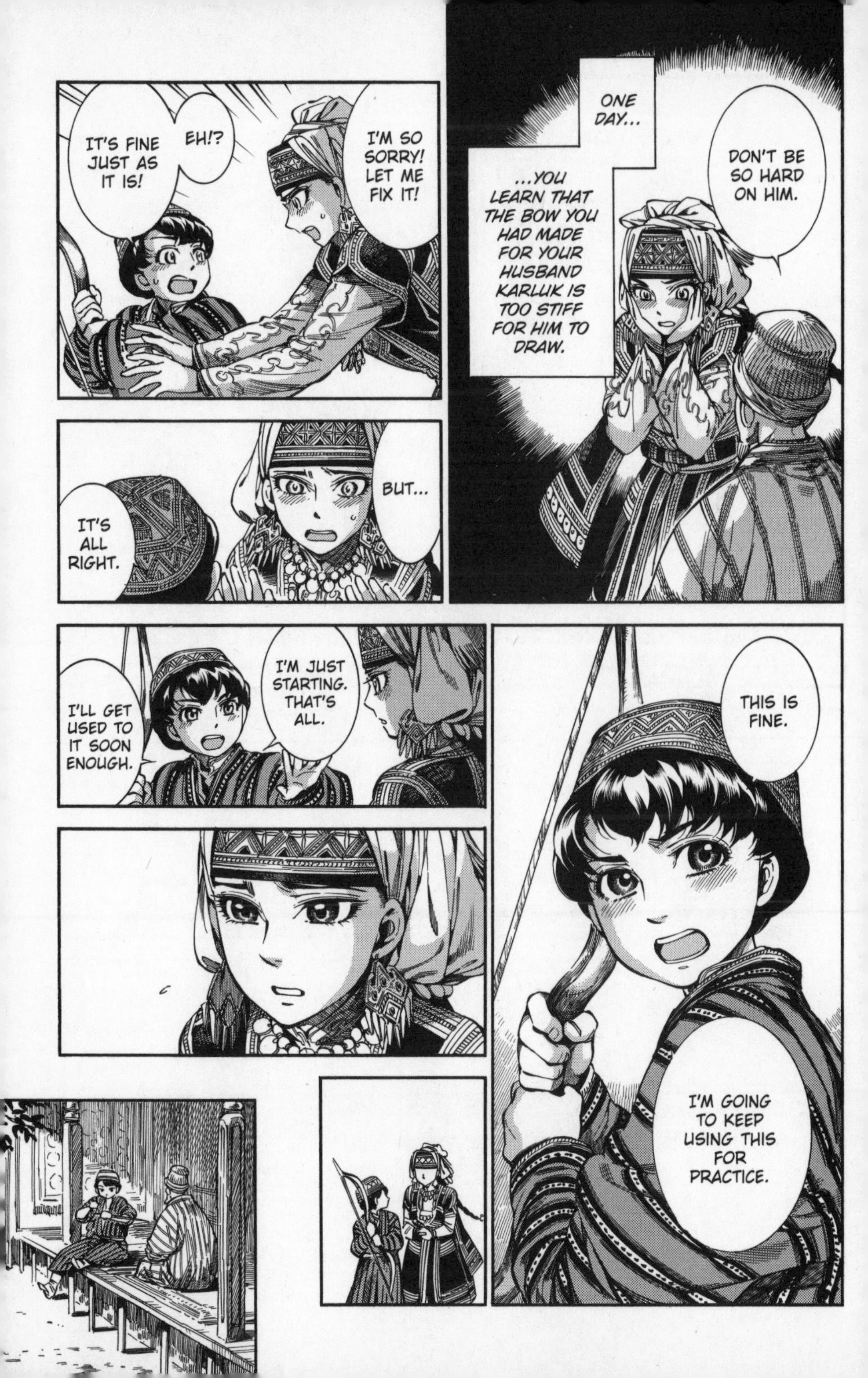
ONE DAY...
...YOU LEARN THAT THE BOW YOU HAD MADE FOR YOUR HUSBAND KARLUK IS TOO STIFF FOR HIM TO DRAW.
DON'T BE SO HARD ON HIM.
I'M SO SORRY! LET ME FIX IT!
EH!?
IT'S FINE JUST AS IT IS!
BUT...
IT'S ALL RIGHT.
THIS IS FINE.
I'M GOING TO KEEP USING THIS FOR PRACTICE.
I'M JUST STARTING. THAT'S ALL.
I'LL GET USED TO IT SOON ENOUGH.

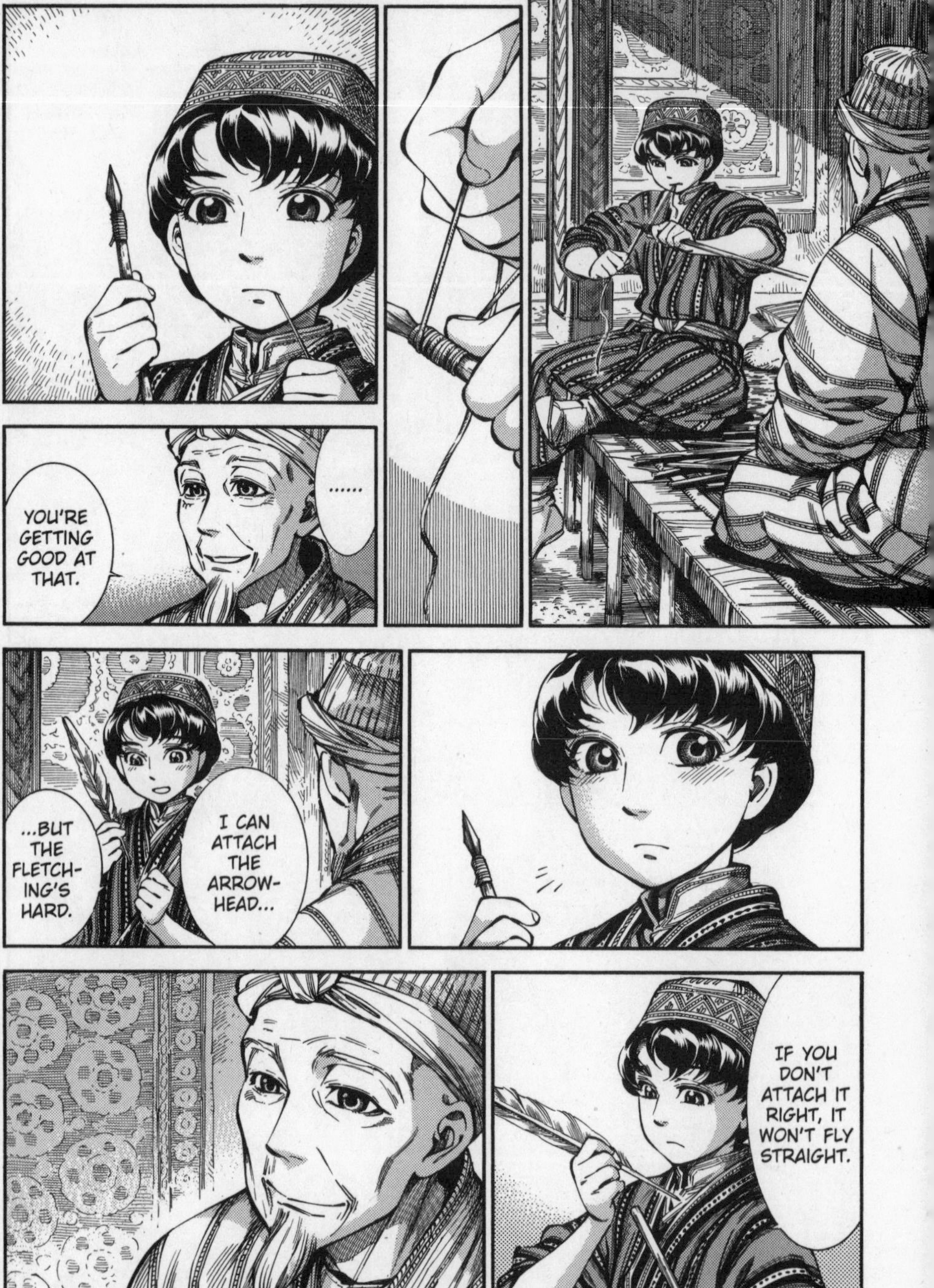
......
YOU'RE GETTING GOOD AT THAT.
I CAN ATTACH THE ARROWHEAD...
...BUT THE FLETCHING'S HARD.
IF YOU DON'T ATTACH IT RIGHT, IT WON'T FLY STRAIGHT.

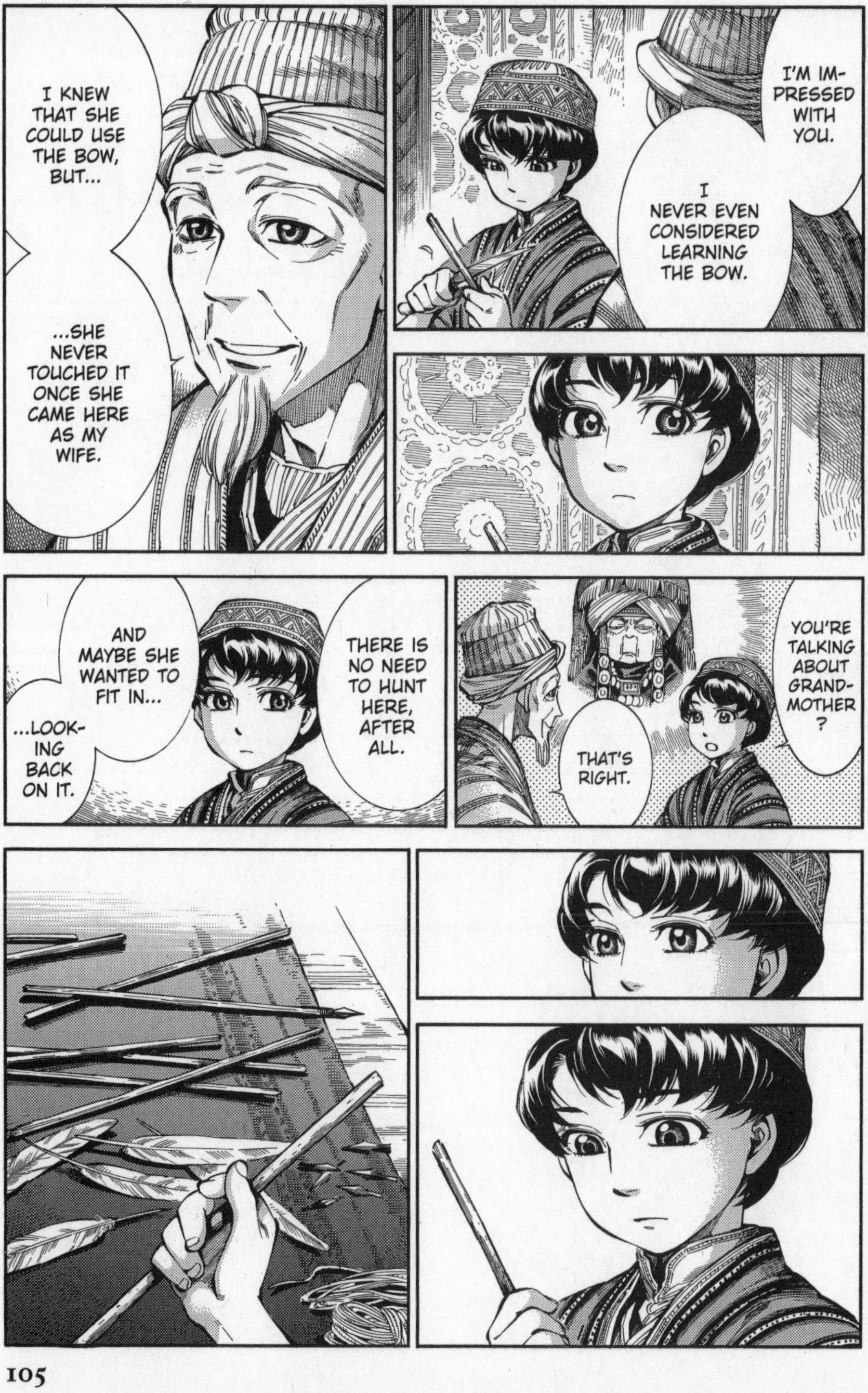
I'M IMPRESSED WITH YOU.
I NEVER EVEN CONSIDERED LEARNING THE BOW.
I KNEW THAT SHE COULD USE THE BOW, BUT...
...SHE NEVER TOUCHED IT ONCE SHE CAME HERE AS MY WIFE.
YOU'RE TALKING ABOUT GRANDMOTHER?
THAT'S RIGHT.
THERE IS NO NEED TO HUNT HERE, AFTER ALL.
AND MAYBE SHE WANTED TO FIT IN...
...LOOKING BACK ON IT.

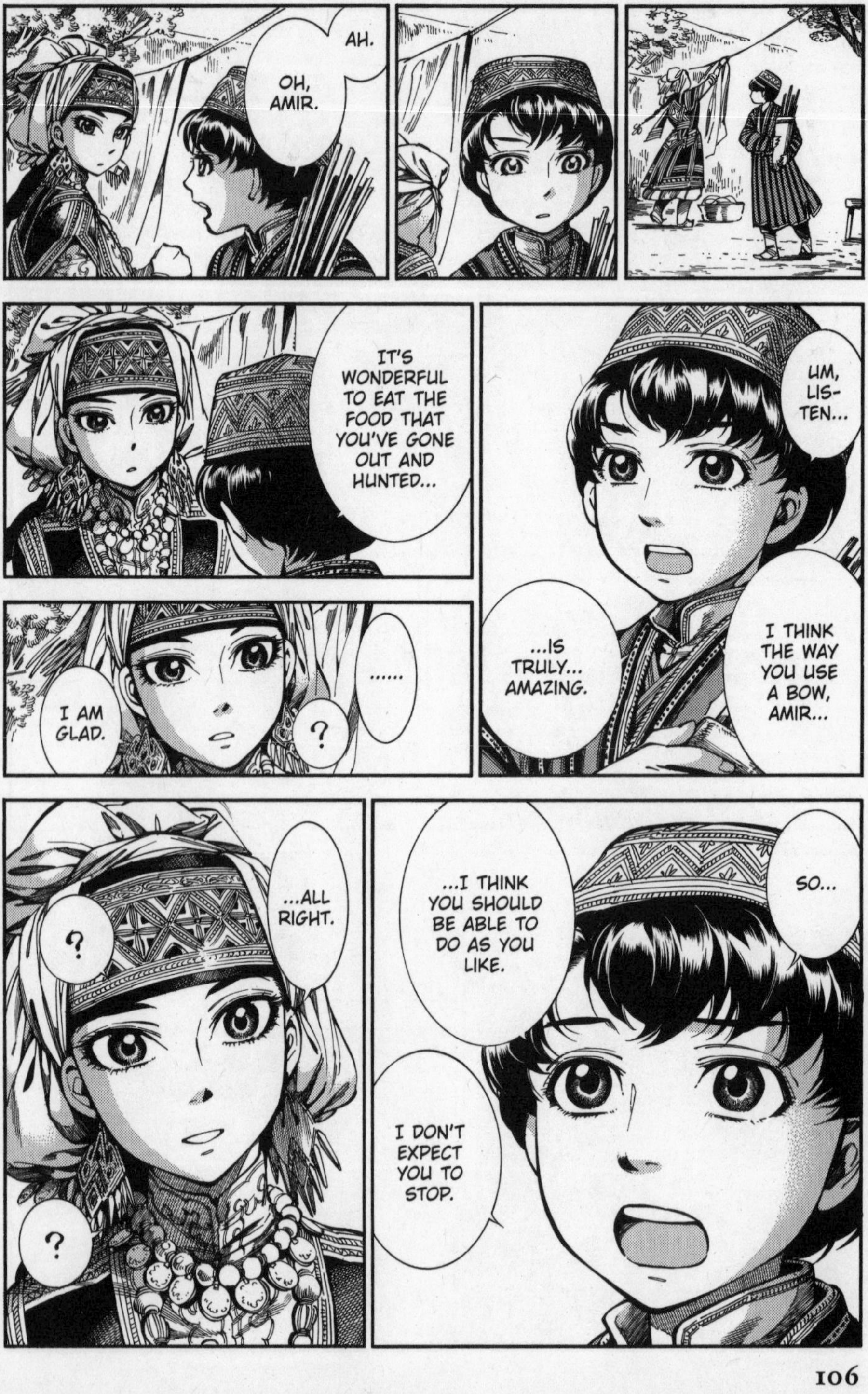
AH.
OH, AMIR.
UM, LIS- TEN...
I THINK THE WAY YOU USE A BOW, AMIR...
...IS TRULY... AMAZING.
IT'S WONDERFUL TO EAT THE FOOD THAT YOU'VE GONE OUT AND HUNTED...
......
?
I AM GLAD.
SO...
...I THINK YOU SHOULD BE ABLE TO DO AS YOU LIKE.
I DON'T EXPECT YOU TO STOP.
...ALL RIGHT.
?
?

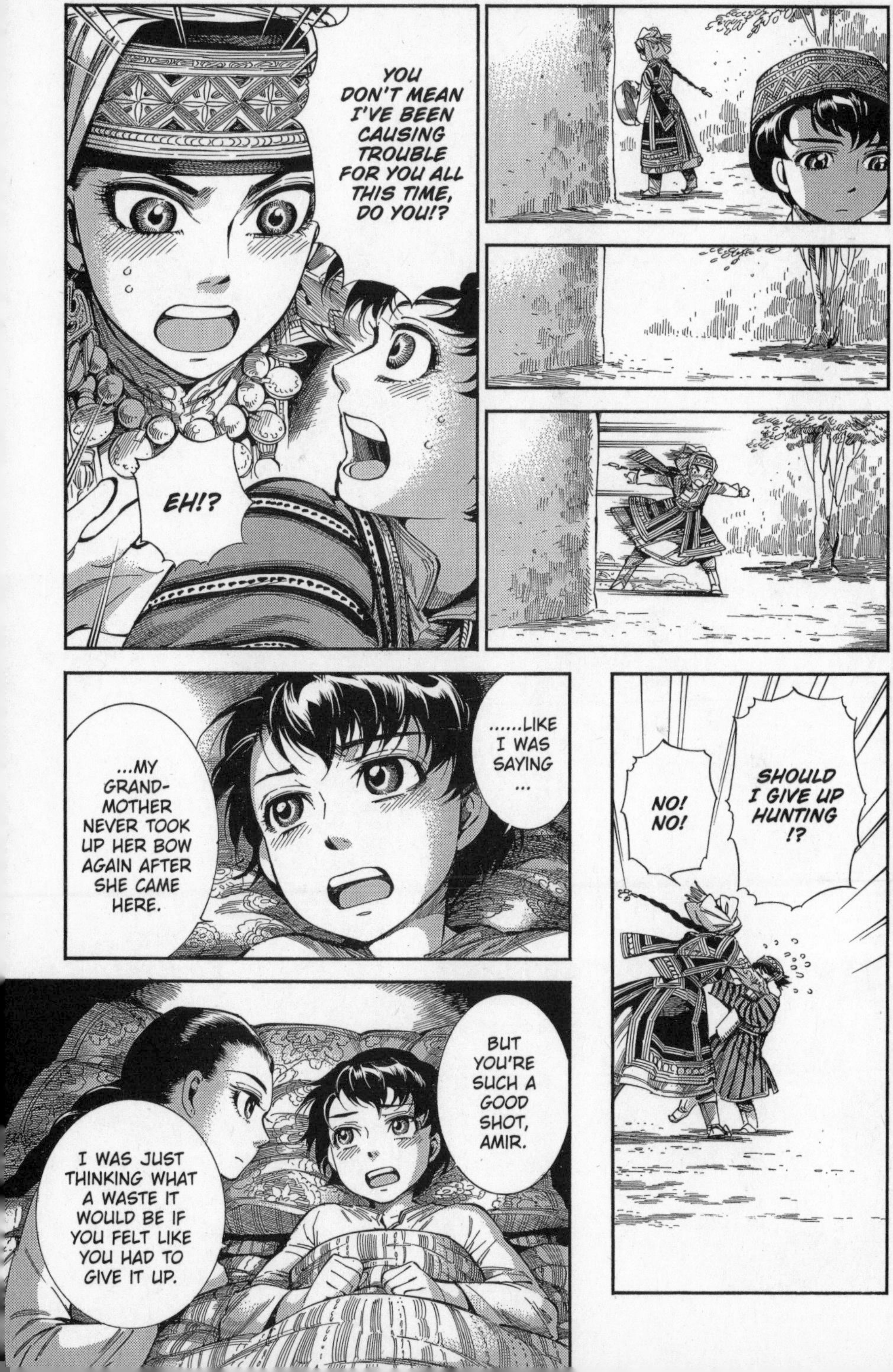
YOU DON'T MEAN I'VE BEEN CAUSING TROUBLE FOR YOU ALL THIS TIME, DO YOU!?
EH!?
SHOULD I GIVE UP HUNTING !?
NO! NO!
......LIKE I WAS SAYING ...
...MY GRAND-MOTHER NEVER TOOK UP HER BOW AGAIN AFTER SHE CAME HERE.
BUT YOU'RE SUCH A GOOD SHOT, AMIR.
I WAS JUST THINKING WHAT A WASTE IT WOULD BE IF YOU FELT LIKE YOU HAD TO GIVE IT UP.

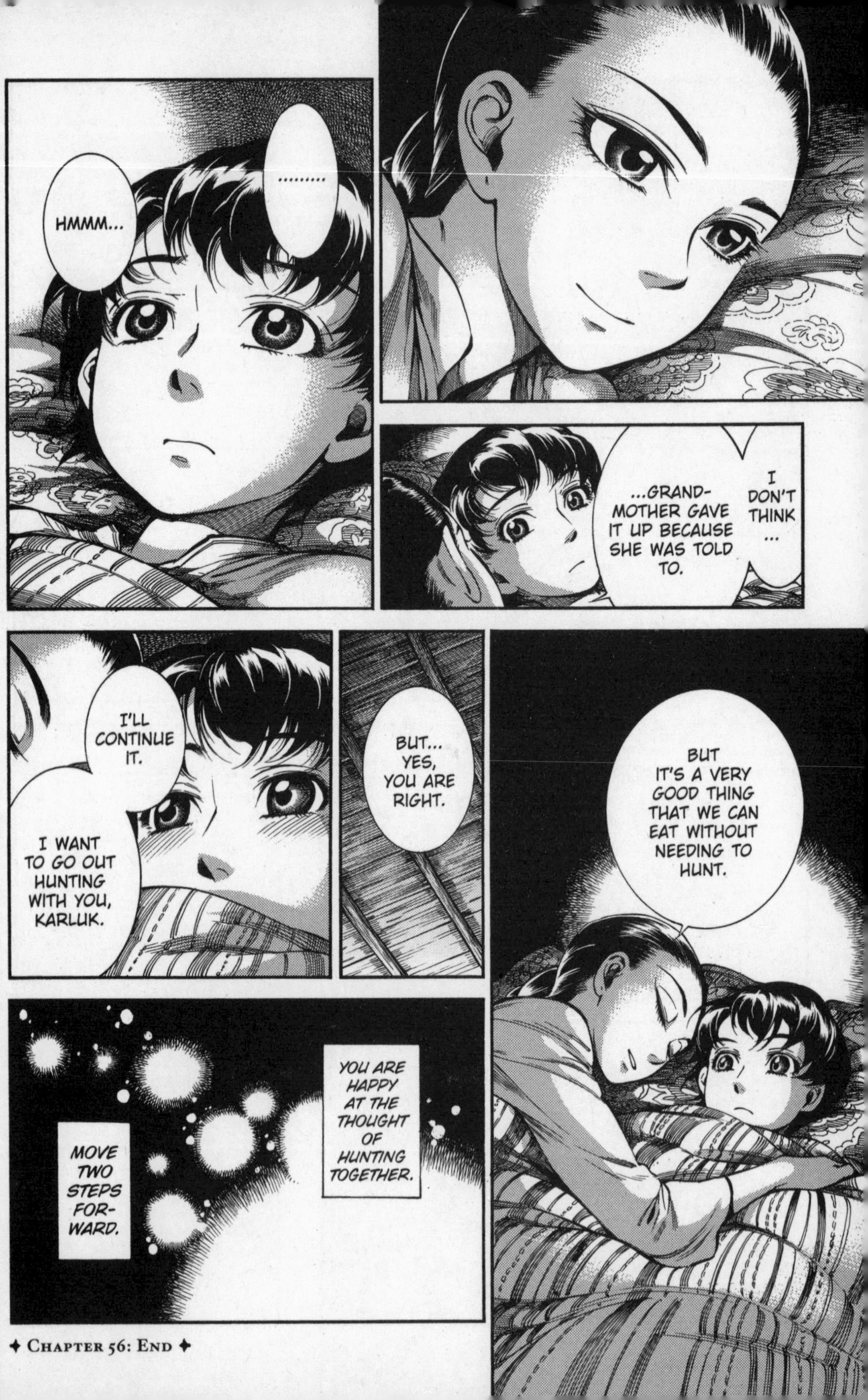
I DON'T THINK...
...GRAND-MOTHER GAVE IT UP BECAUSE SHE WAS TOLD TO.
....
HMMM...
BUT IT'S A VERY GOOD THING THAT WE CAN EAT WITHOUT NEEDING TO HUNT.
BUT... YES, YOU ARE RIGHT.
I'LL CONTINUE IT.
I WANT TO GO OUT HUNTING WITH YOU, KARLUK.
YOU ARE HAPPY AT THE THOUGHT OF HUNTING TOGETHER.
MOVE TWO STEPS FOR-WARD.

✦ CHAPTER 56: END ✦

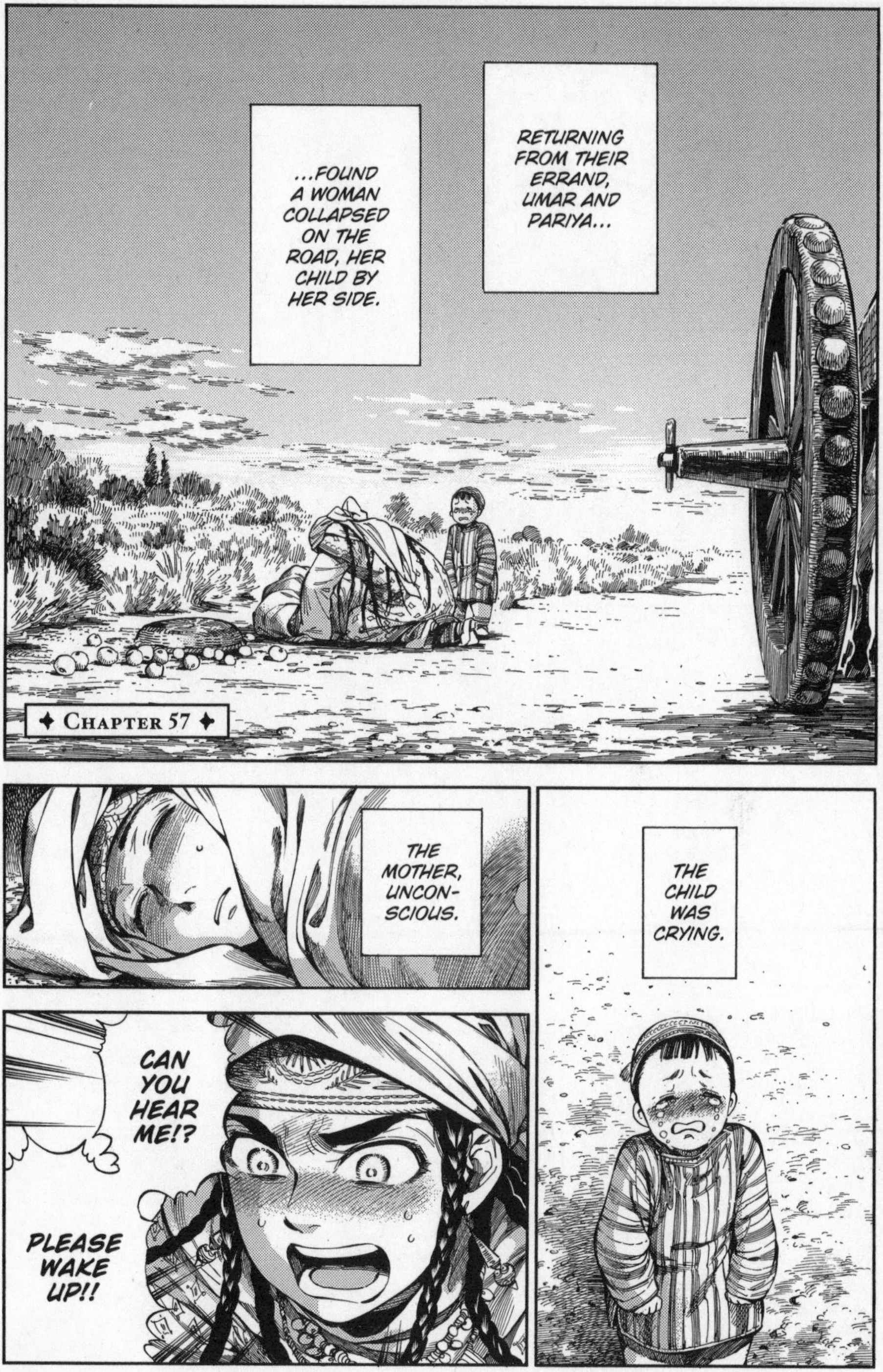
RETURNING FROM THEIR ERRAND, UMAR AND PARIYA...
...FOUND A WOMAN COLLAPSED ON THE ROAD, HER CHILD BY HER SIDE.
✦ CHAPTER 57 ✦
THE CHILD WAS CRYING.
THE MOTHER, UNCONSCIOUS.
CAN YOU HEAR ME!?
PLEASE WAKE UP!!

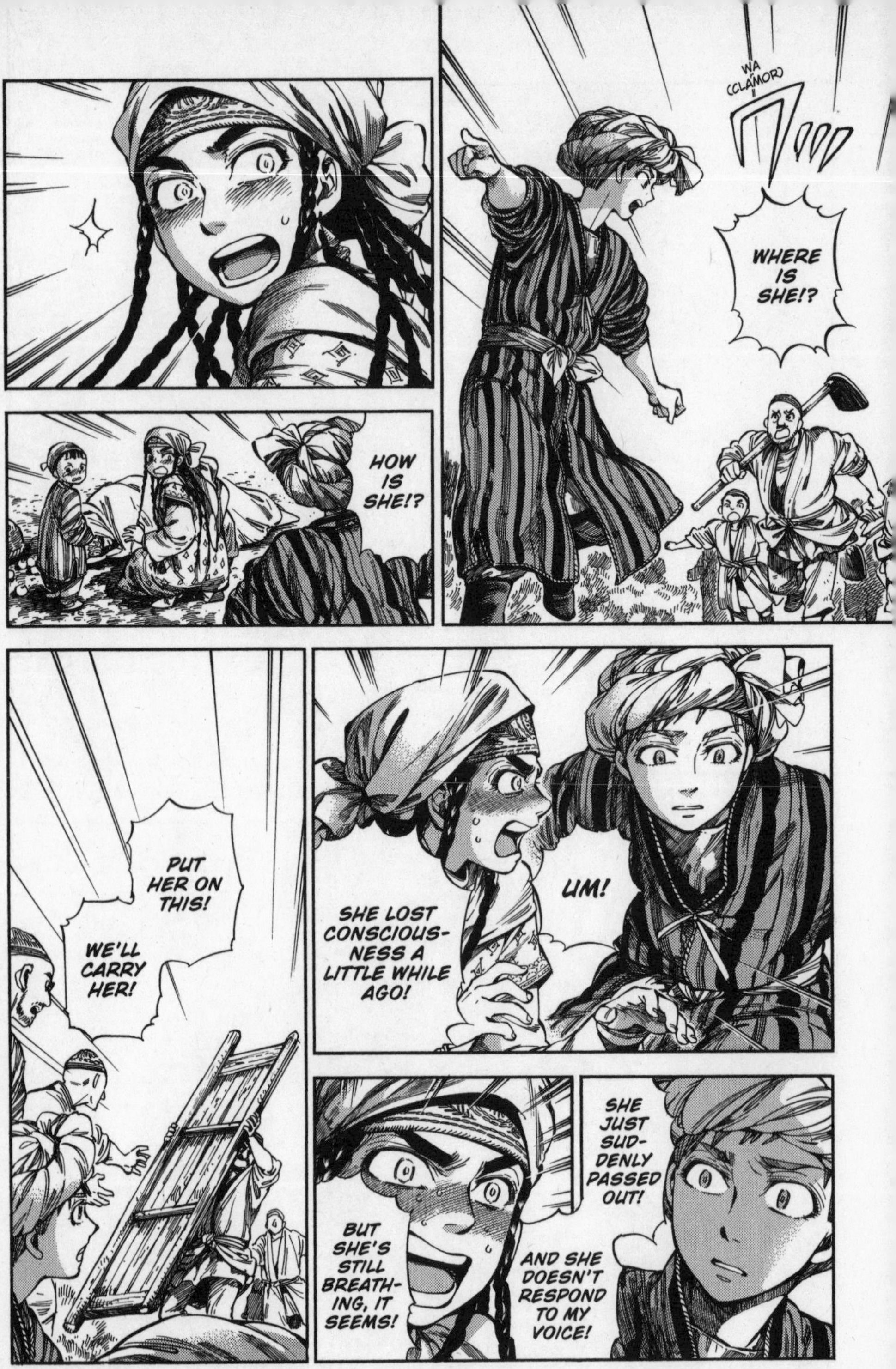
WA (CLAMOR)
WHERE IS SHE!?
HOW IS SHE!?
UM!
SHE LOST CONSCIOUS-NESS A LITTLE WHILE AGO!
SHE JUST SUD-DENLY PASSED OUT!
AND SHE DOESN'T RESPOND TO MY VOICE!
BUT SHE'S STILL BREATH-ING, IT SEEMS!
PUT HER ON THIS!
WE'LL CARRY HER!

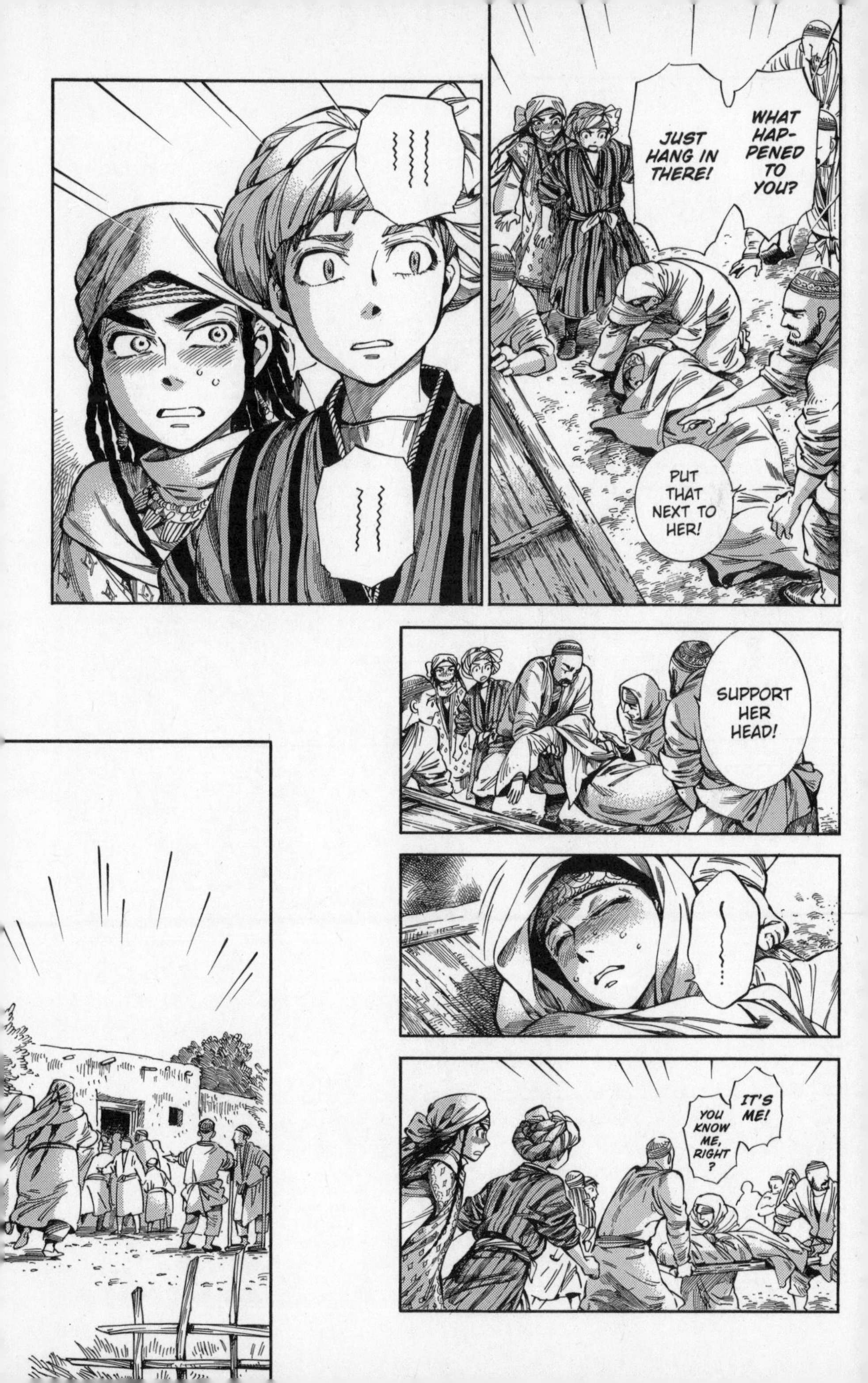
WHAT HAP-PENED TO YOU?
JUST HANG IN THERE!
PUT THAT NEXT TO HER!
SUPPORT HER HEAD!
IT'S ME!
YOU KNOW ME, RIGHT?

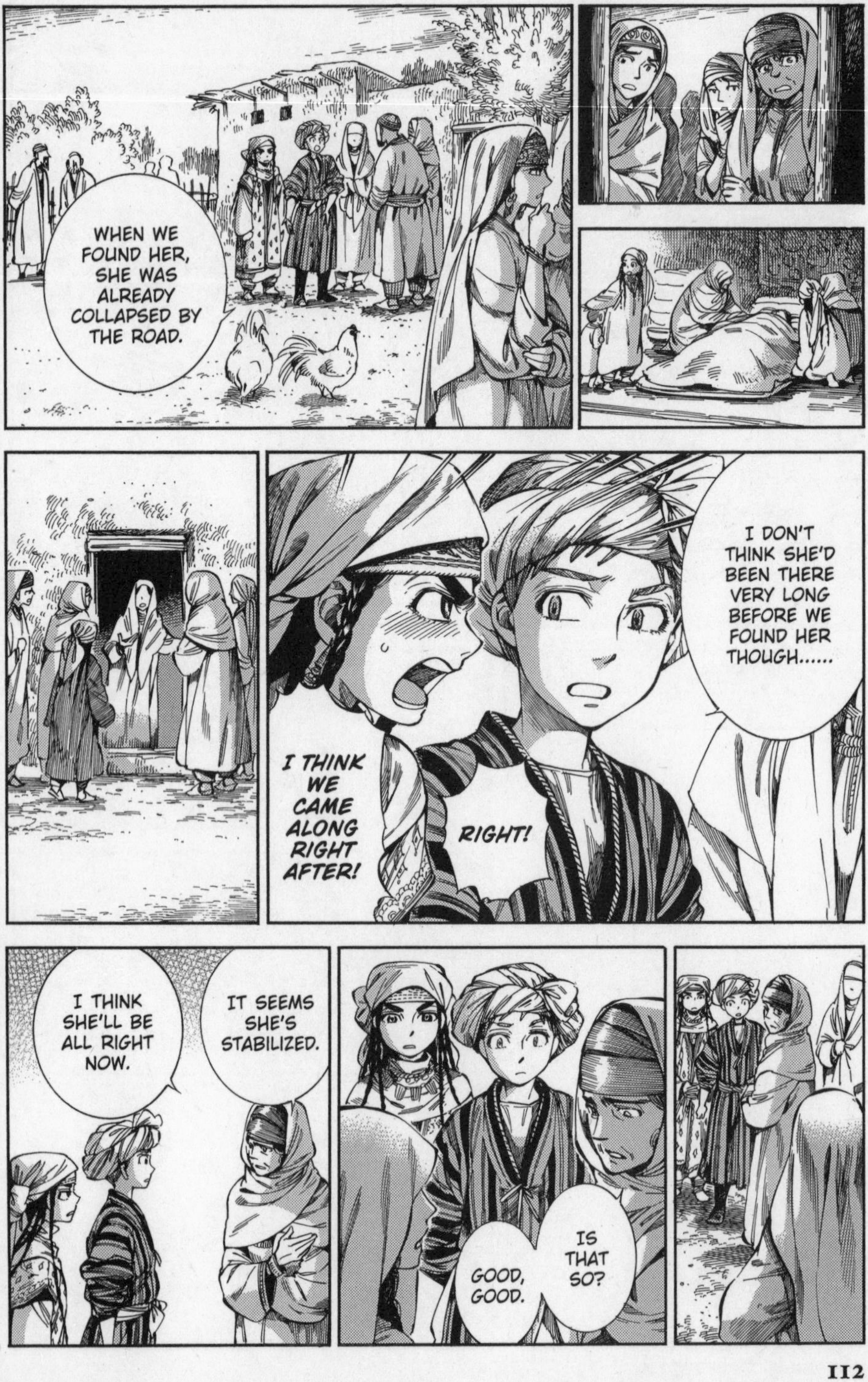
WHEN WE FOUND HER, SHE WAS ALREADY COLLAPSED BY THE ROAD.
I DON'T THINK SHE'D BEEN THERE VERY LONG BEFORE WE FOUND HER THOUGH......
RIGHT!
I THINK WE CAME ALONG RIGHT AFTER!
IS THAT SO?
GOOD, GOOD.
IT SEEMS SHE'S STABILIZED.
I THINK SHE'LL BE ALL RIGHT NOW.

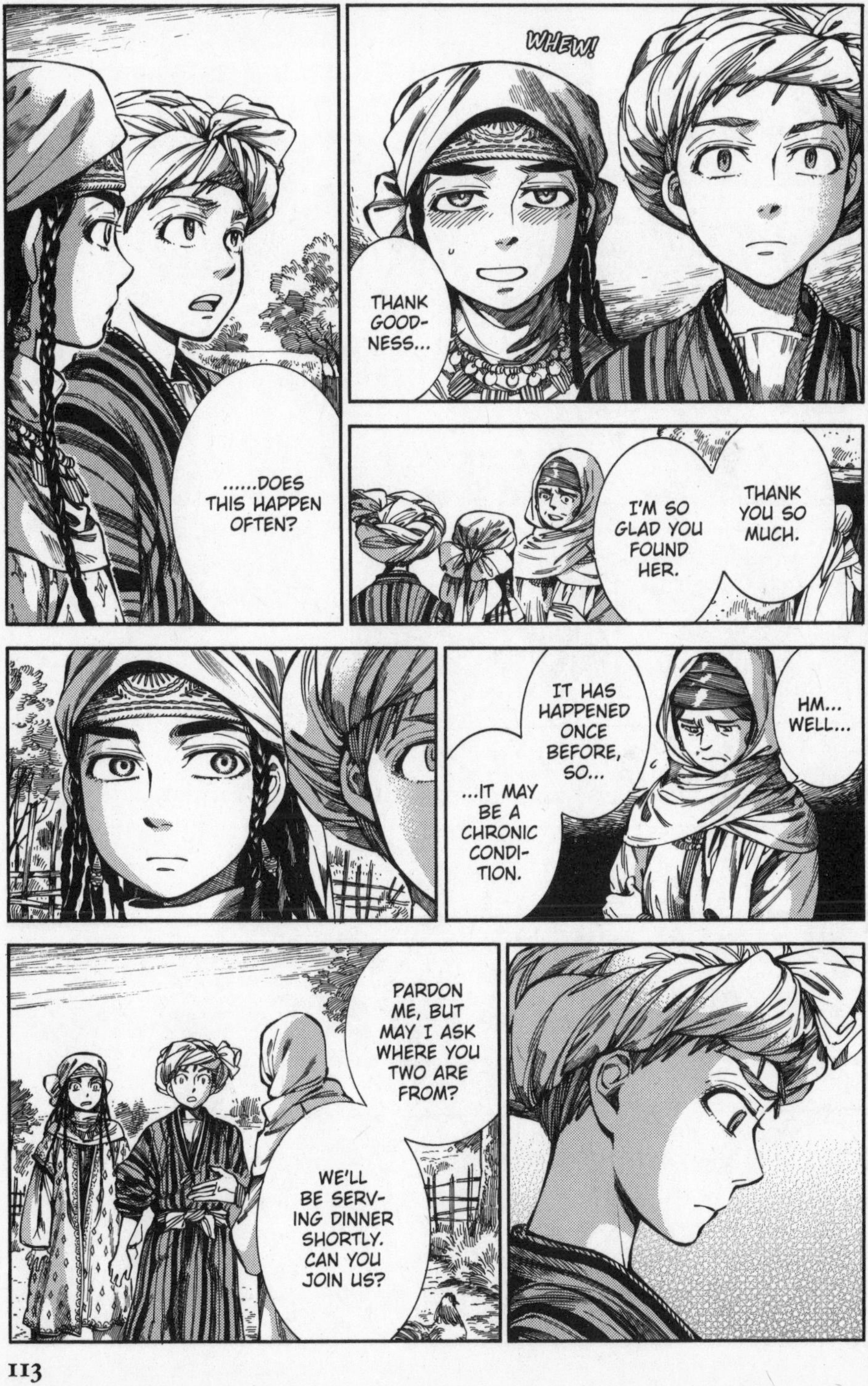
WHEW!
THANK GOODNESS...
THANK YOU SO MUCH.
I'M SO GLAD YOU FOUND HER.
......DOES THIS HAPPEN OFTEN?
HM... WELL...
IT HAS HAPPENED ONCE BEFORE, SO...
...IT MAY BE A CHRONIC CONDITION.
PARDON ME, BUT MAY I ASK WHERE YOU TWO ARE FROM?
WE'LL BE SERVING DINNER SHORTLY. CAN YOU JOIN US?

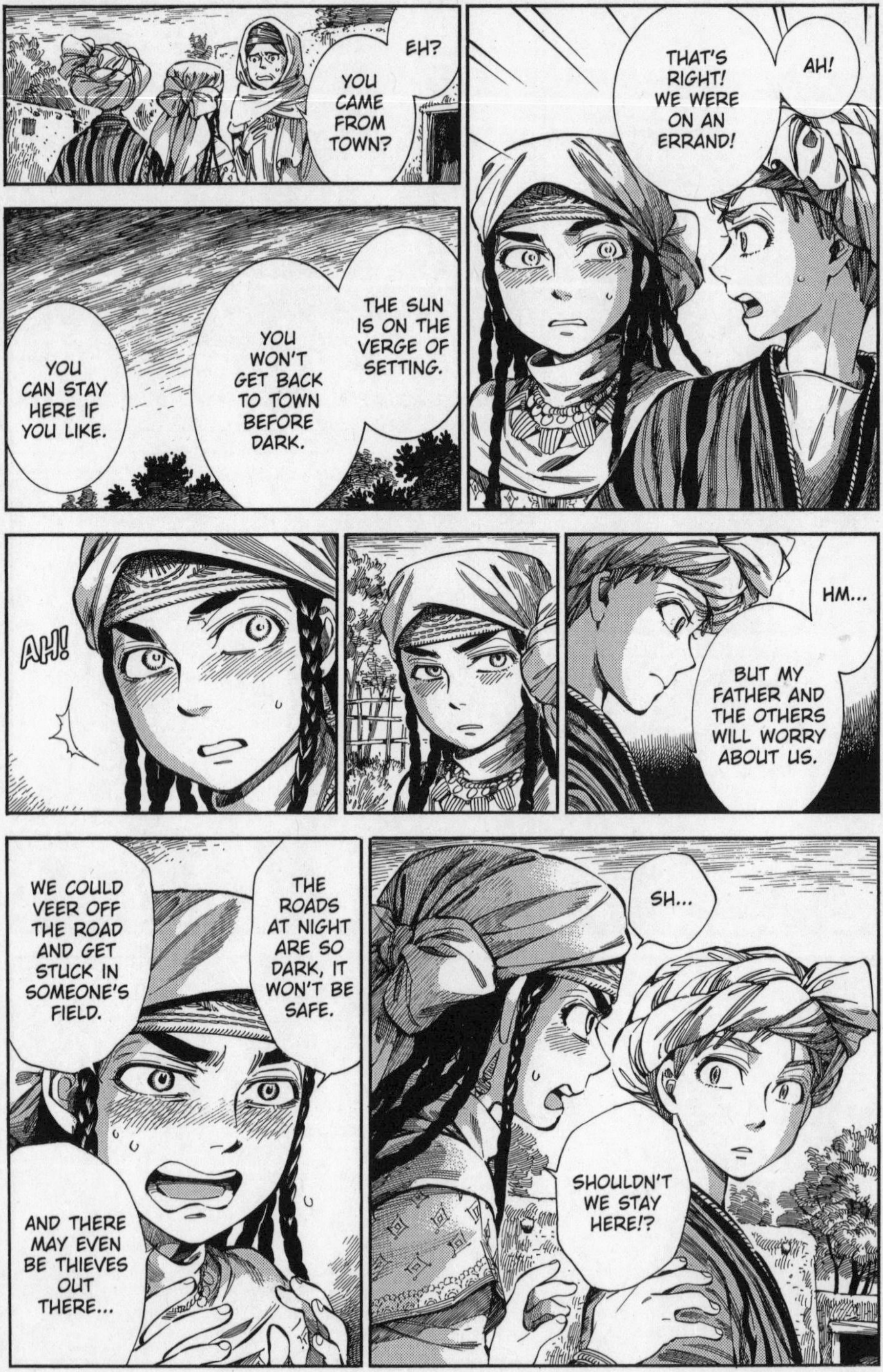
AH!
THAT'S RIGHT! WE WERE ON AN ERRAND!
EH?
YOU CAME FROM TOWN?
THE SUN IS ON THE VERGE OF SETTING.
YOU WON'T GET BACK TO TOWN BEFORE DARK.
YOU CAN STAY HERE IF YOU LIKE.
HM...
BUT MY FATHER AND THE OTHERS WILL WORRY ABOUT US.
AH!
SH...
SHOULDN'T WE STAY HERE!?
THE ROADS AT NIGHT ARE SO DARK, IT WON'T BE SAFE.
WE COULD VEER OFF THE ROAD AND GET STUCK IN SOMEONE'S FIELD.
AND THERE MAY EVEN BE THIEVES OUT THERE...

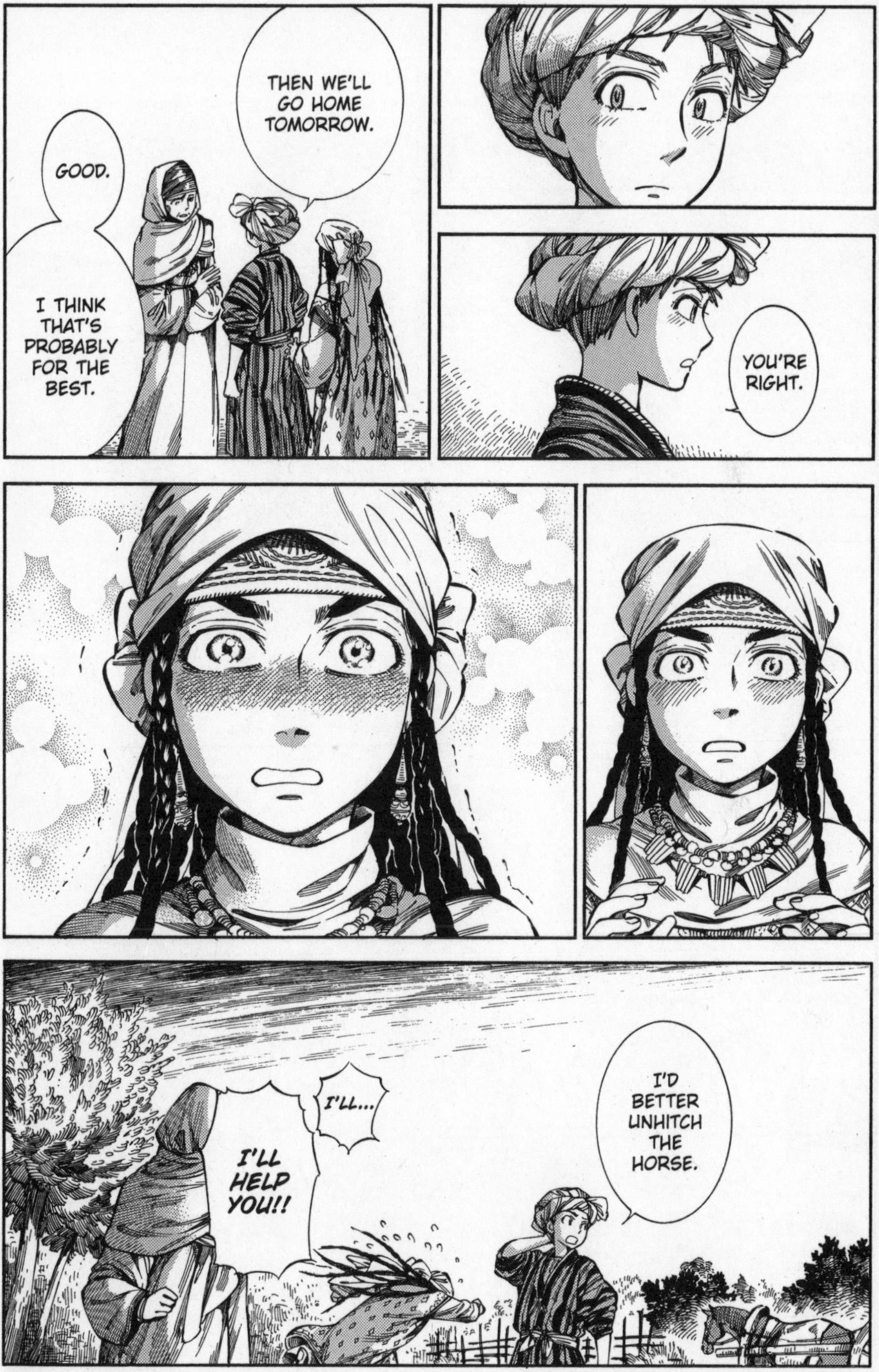
YOU'RE RIGHT.
THEN WE'LL GO HOME TOMORROW.
GOOD.
I THINK THAT'S PROBABLY FOR THE BEST.
I'D BETTER UNHITCH THE HORSE.
I'LL...
I'LL HELP YOU!!

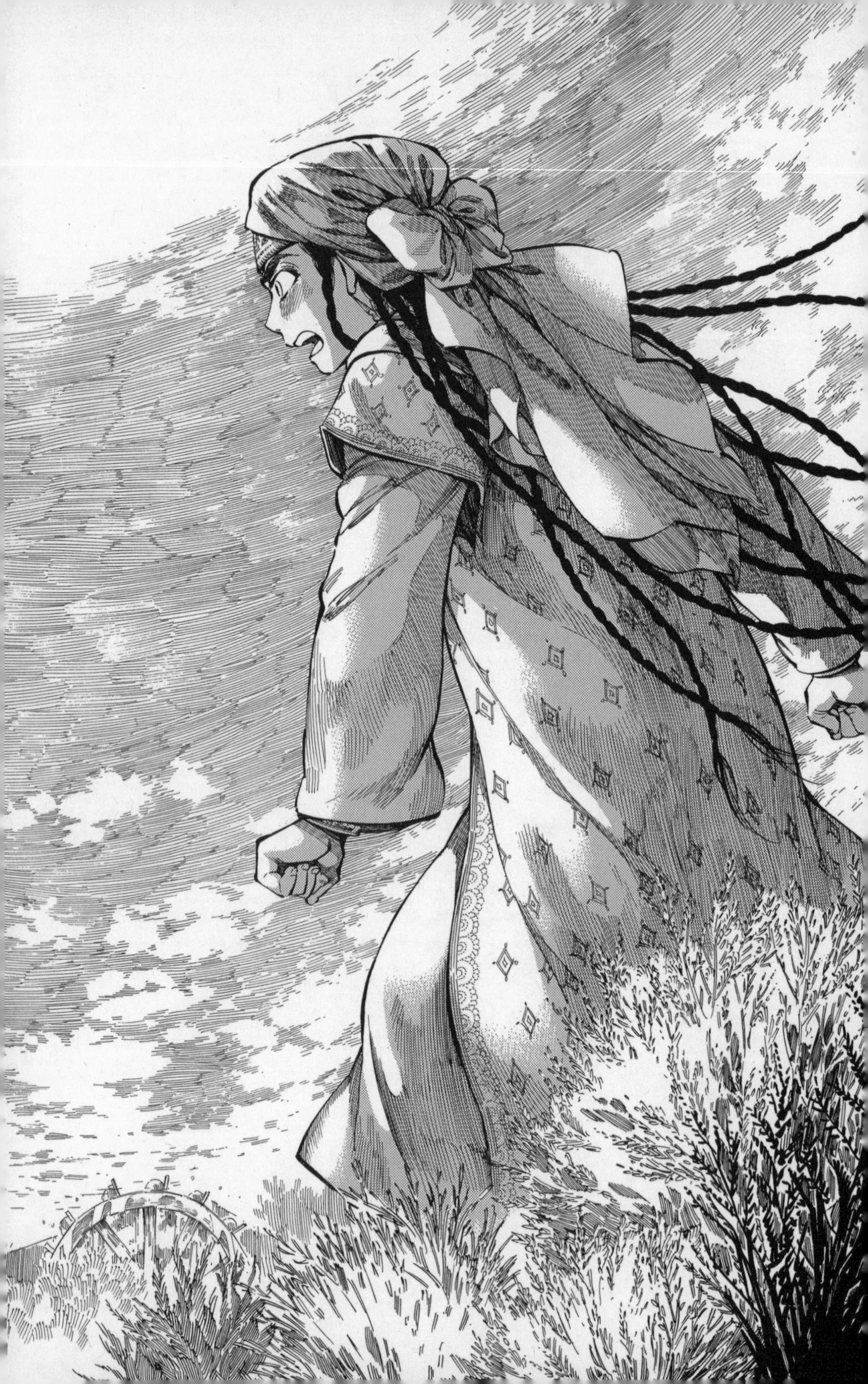

Chapter 57
Stopover

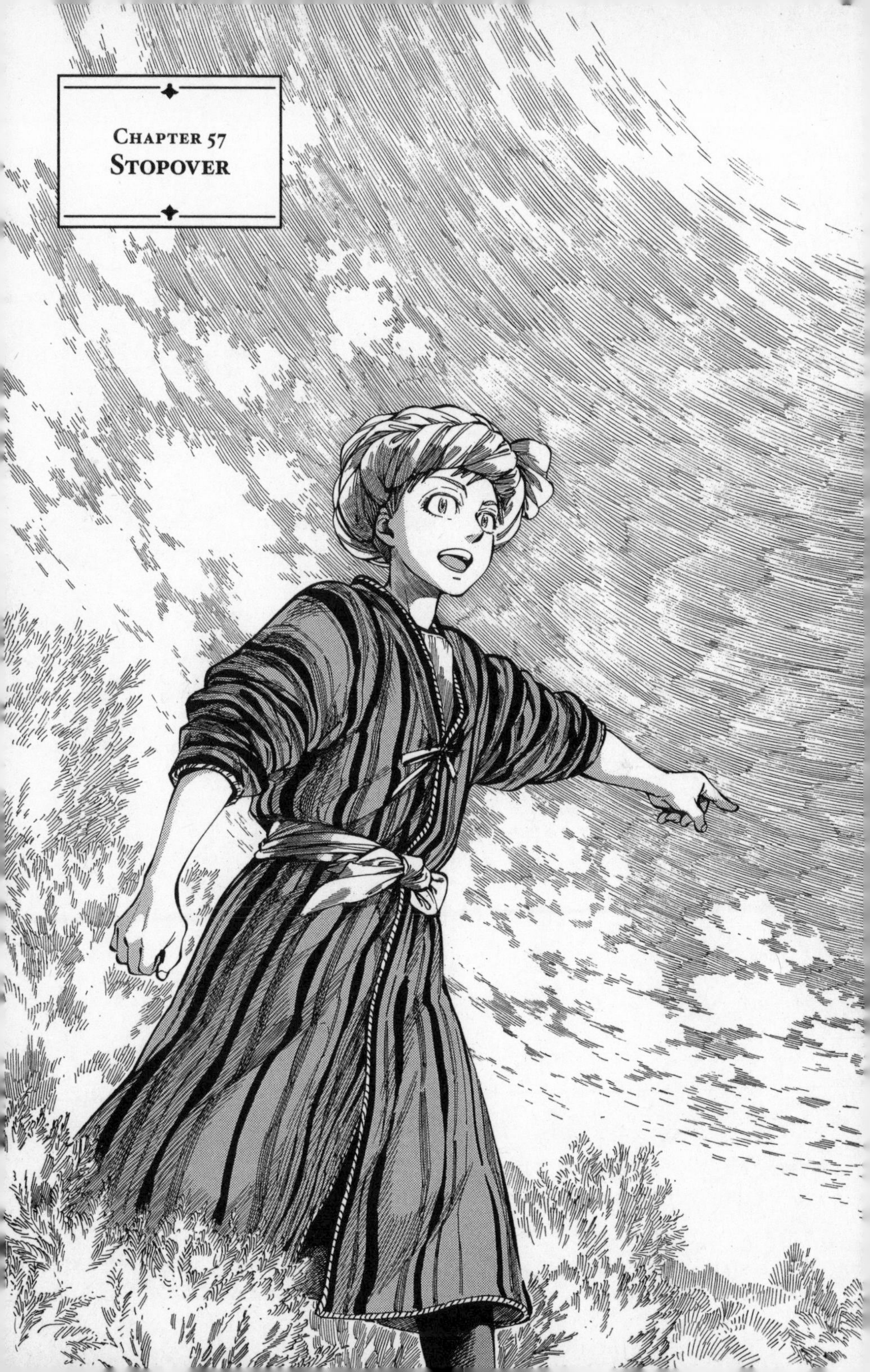

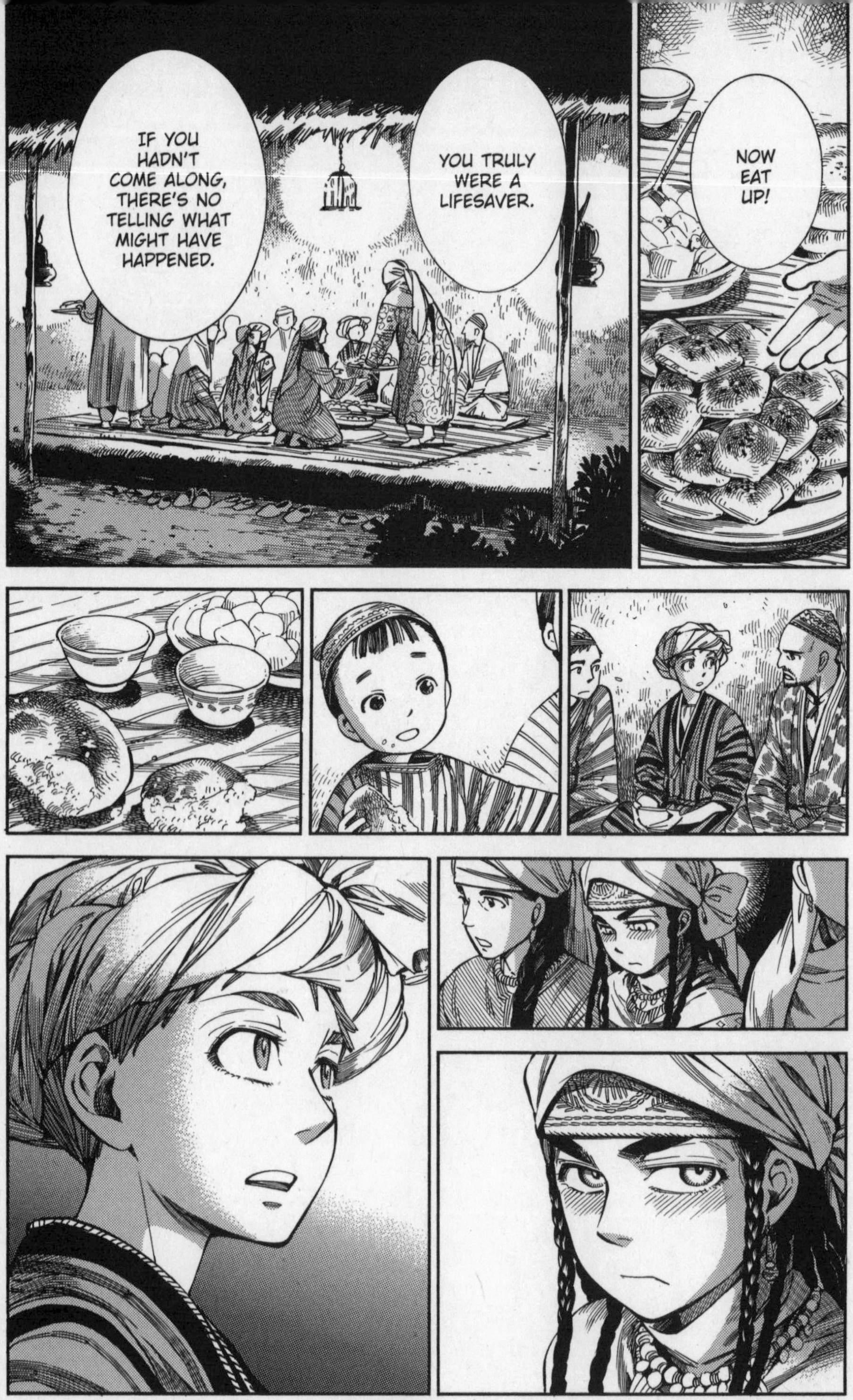
NOW EAT UP!
YOU TRULY WERE A LIFESAVER.
IF YOU HADN'T COME ALONG, THERE'S NO TELLING WHAT MIGHT HAVE HAPPENED.

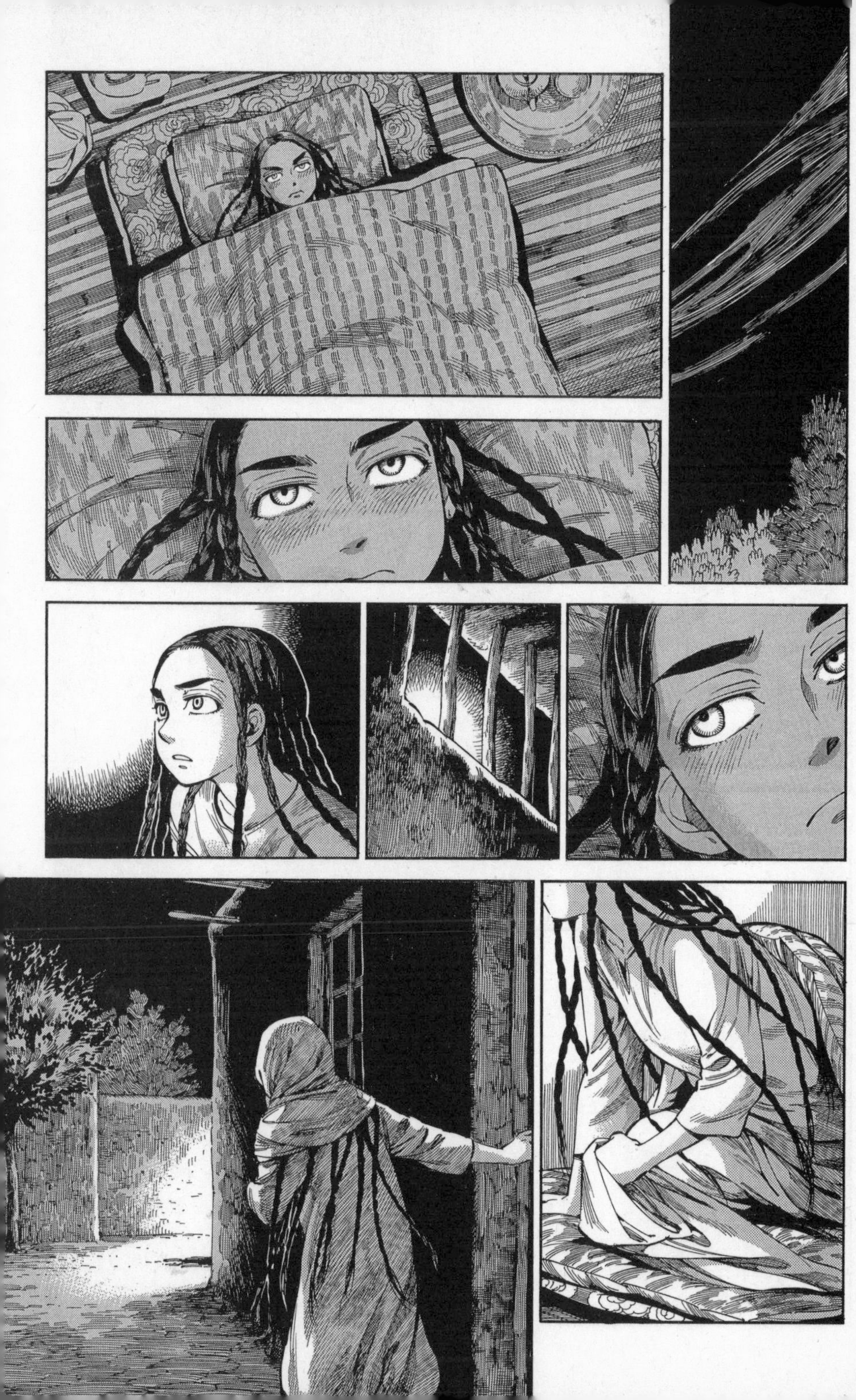

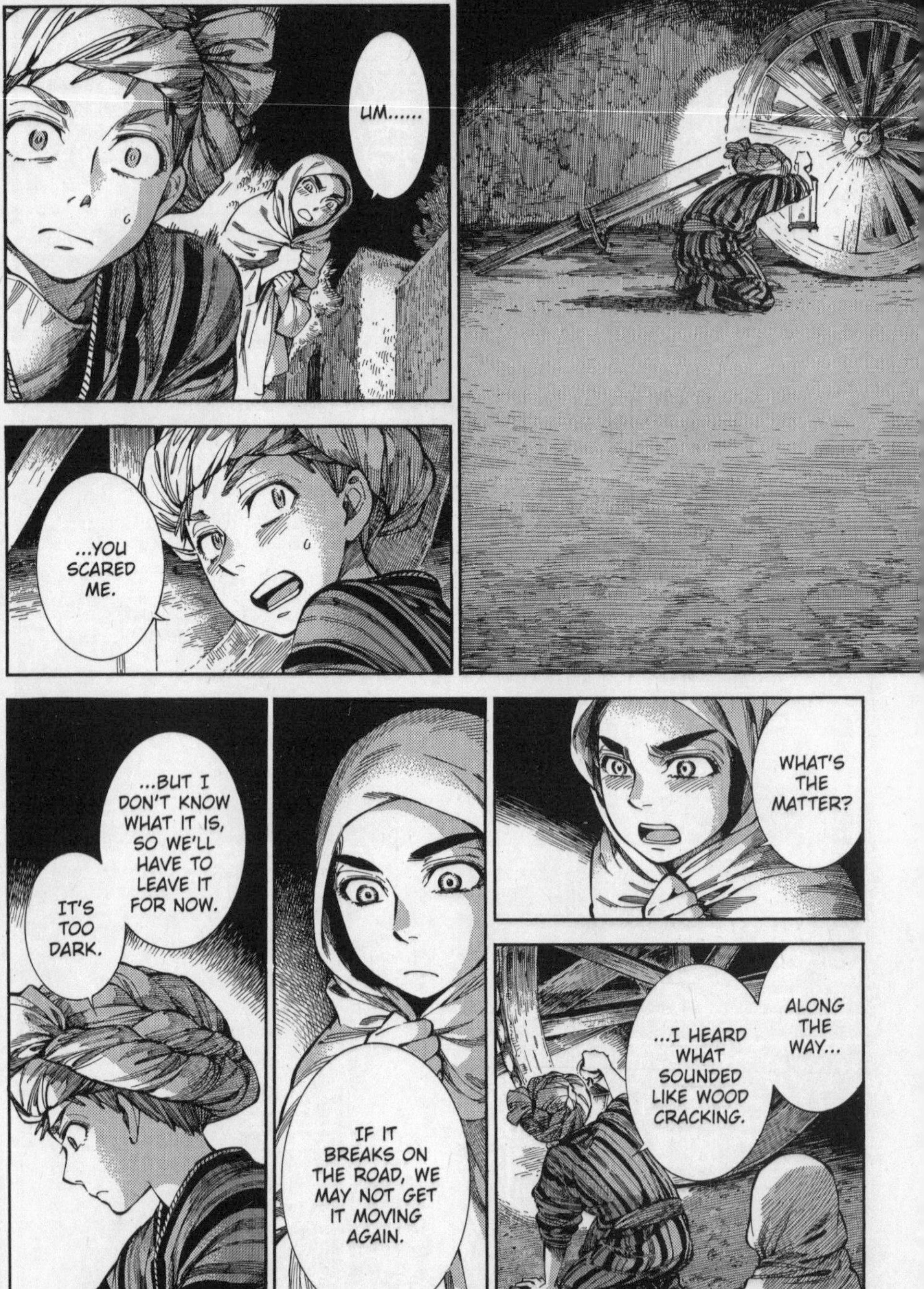
UM......
...YOU SCARED ME.
WHAT'S THE MATTER?
ALONG THE WAY...
...I HEARD WHAT SOUNDED LIKE WOOD CRACKING.
IF IT BREAKS ON THE ROAD, WE MAY NOT GET IT MOVING AGAIN.
...BUT I DON'T KNOW WHAT IT IS, SO WE'LL HAVE TO LEAVE IT FOR NOW.
IT'S TOO DARK.

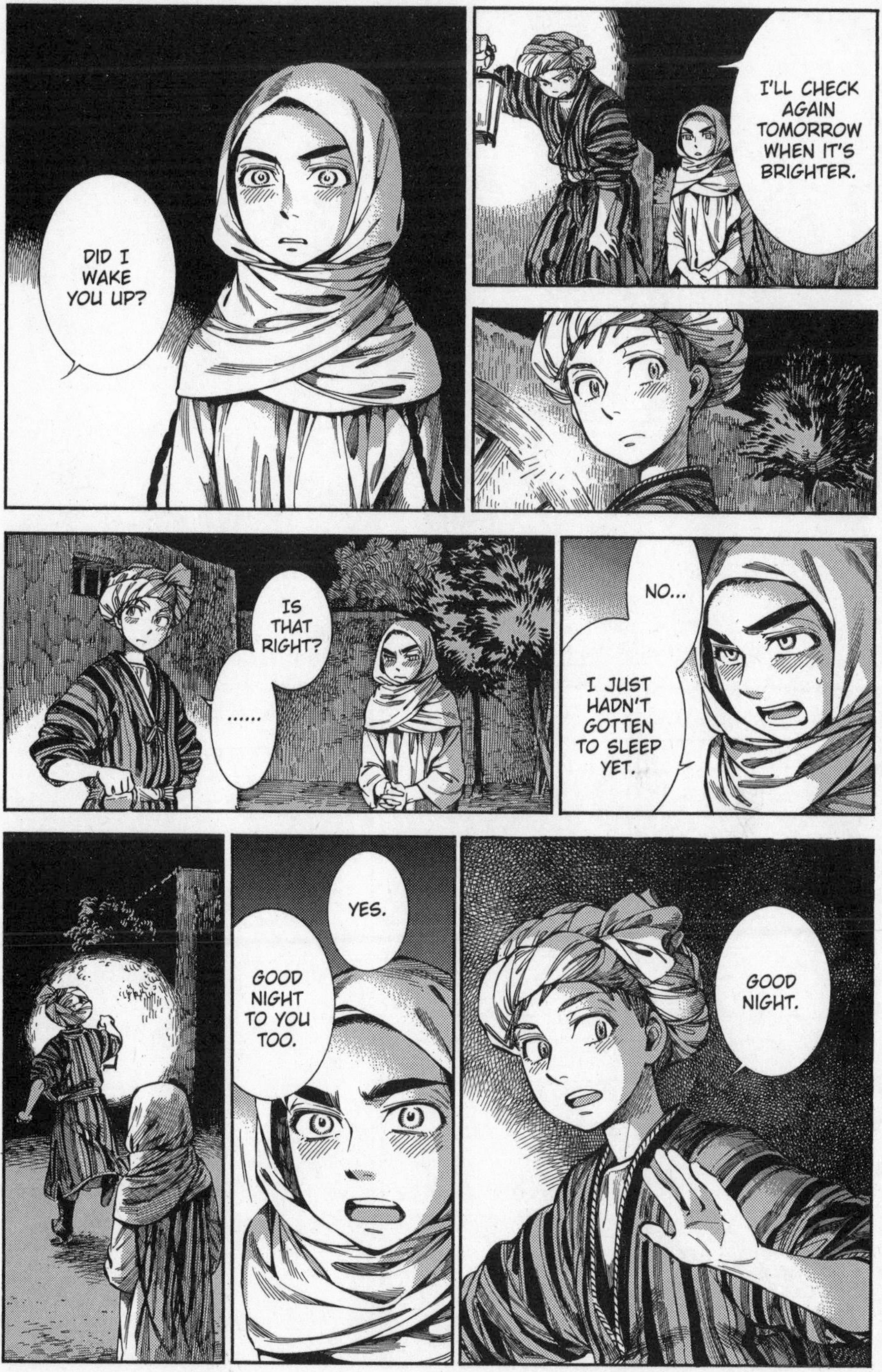
I'LL CHECK AGAIN TOMORROW WHEN IT'S BRIGHTER.
DID I WAKE YOU UP?
NO...
I JUST HADN'T GOTTEN TO SLEEP YET.
IS THAT RIGHT?
......
GOOD NIGHT.
YES.
GOOD NIGHT TO YOU TOO.

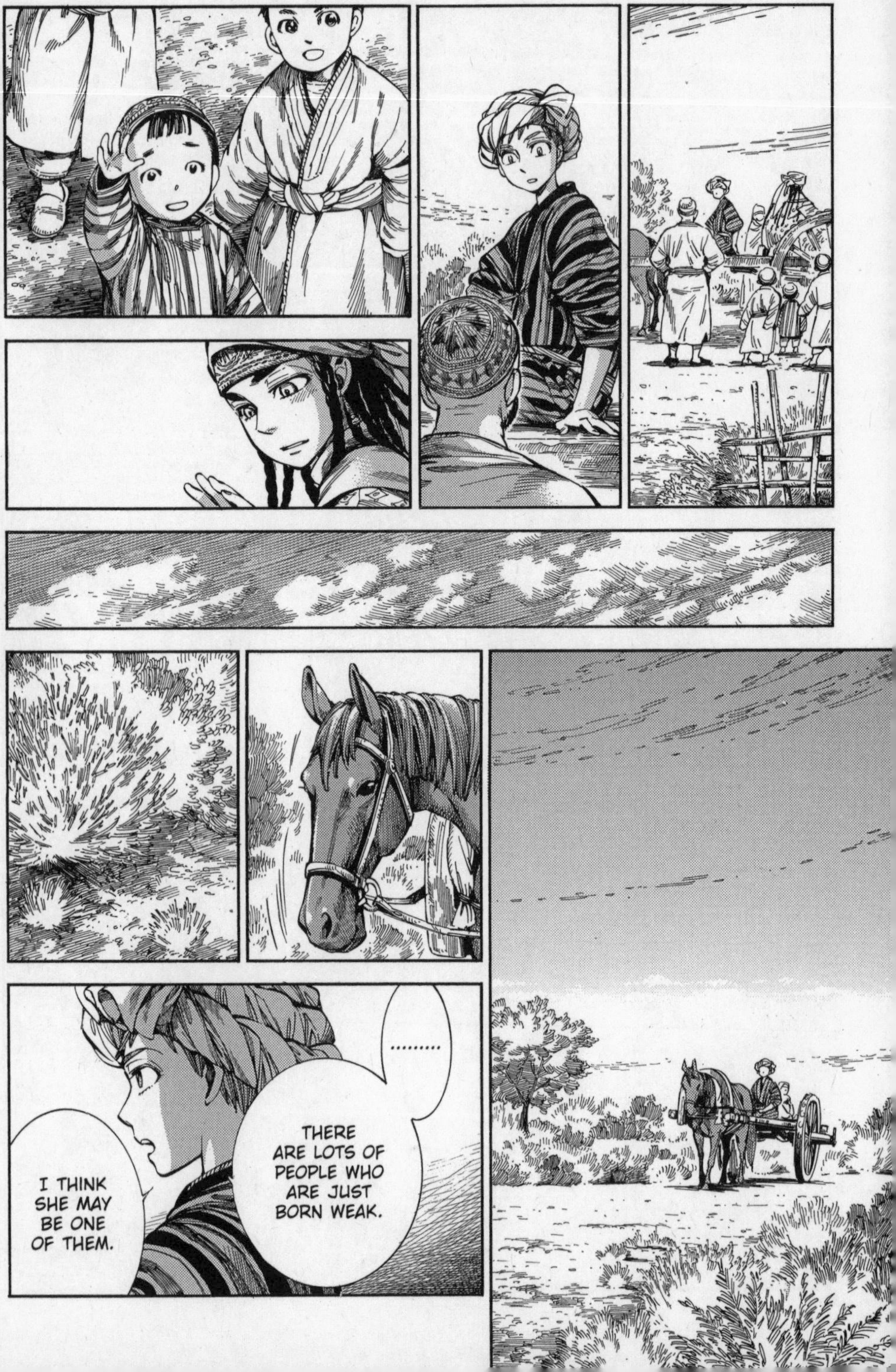
....
THERE ARE LOTS OF PEOPLE WHO ARE JUST BORN WEAK.
I THINK SHE MAY BE ONE OF THEM.

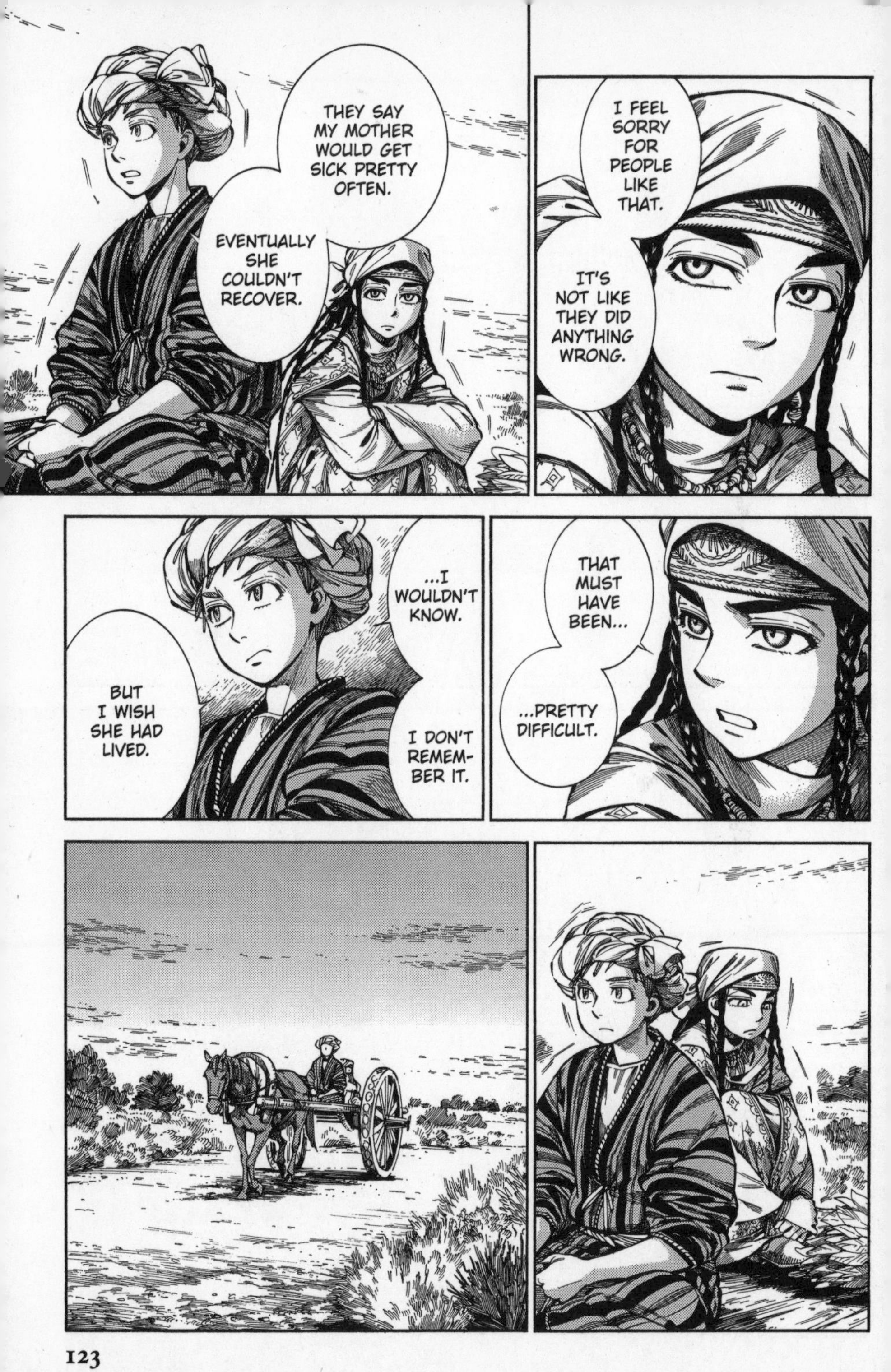
I FEEL SORRY FOR PEOPLE LIKE THAT.
IT'S NOT LIKE THEY DID ANYTHING WRONG.
THEY SAY MY MOTHER WOULD GET SICK PRETTY OFTEN.
EVENTUALLY SHE COULDN'T RECOVER.
THAT MUST HAVE BEEN...
...PRETTY DIFFICULT.
...I WOULDN'T KNOW.
I DON'T REMEMBER IT.
BUT I WISH SHE HAD LIVED.

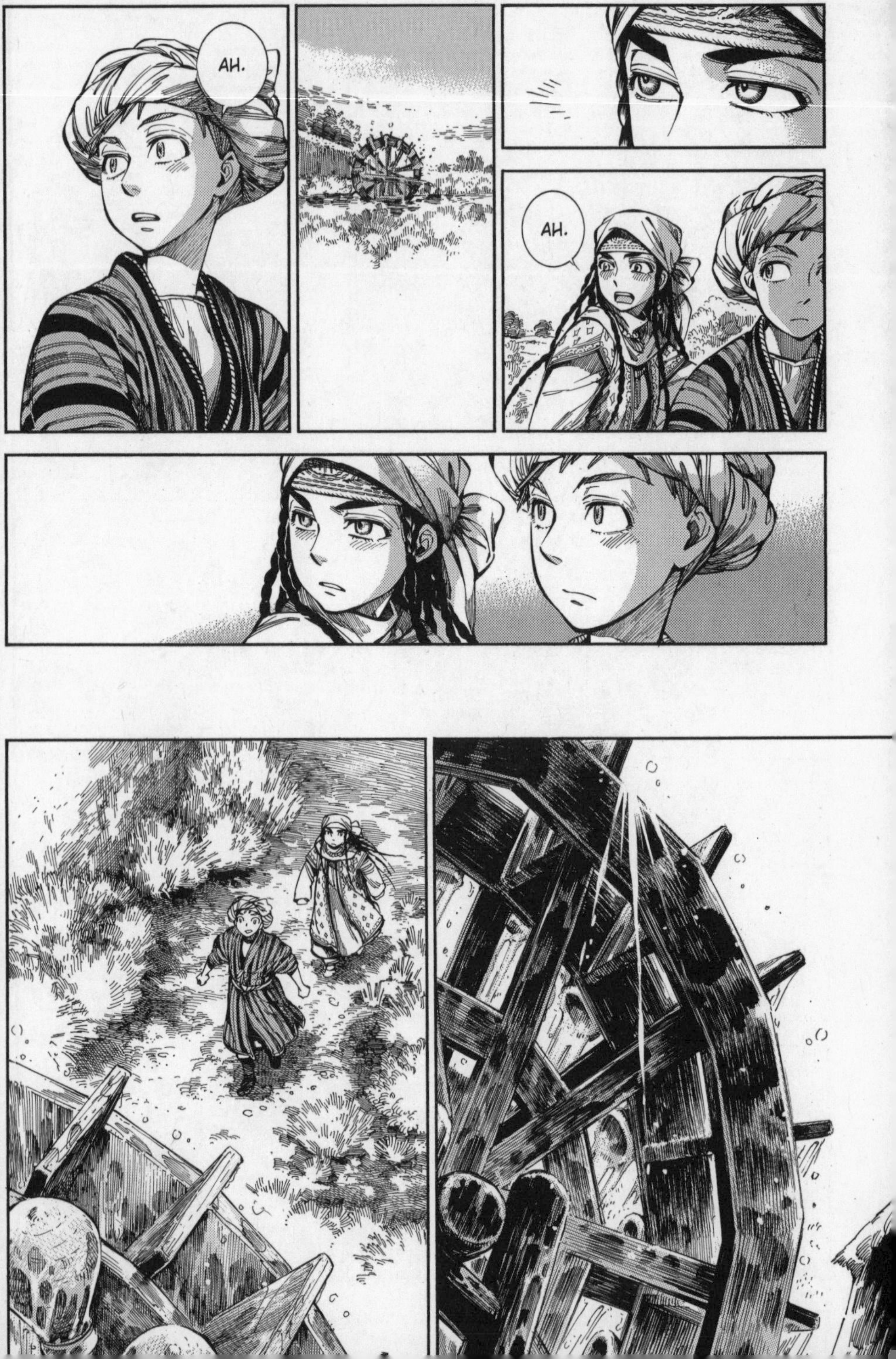
AH.
AH.

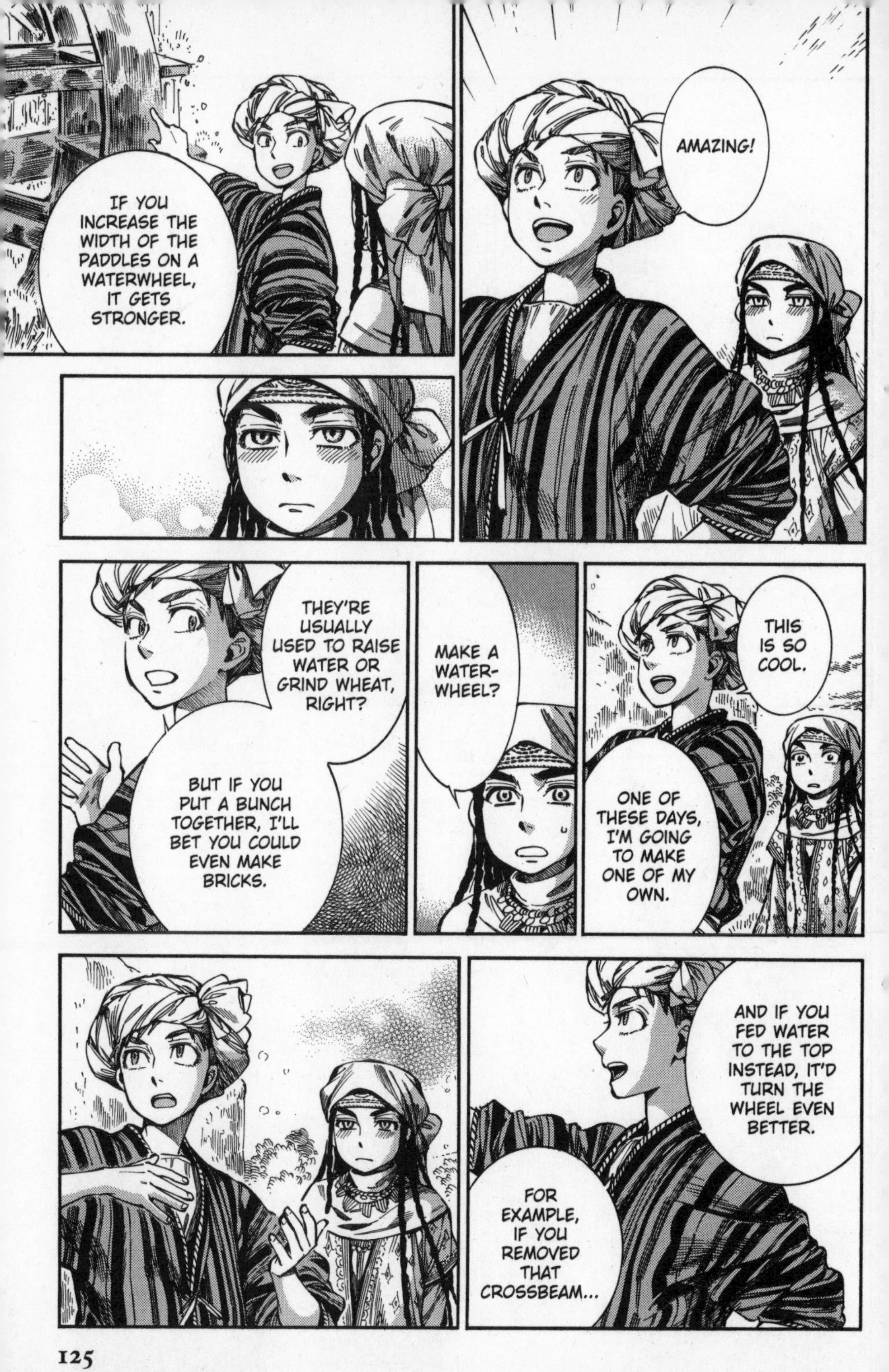
AMAZING!
IF YOU INCREASE THE WIDTH OF THE PADDLES ON A WATERWHEEL, IT GETS STRONGER.
THIS IS SO COOL.
ONE OF THESE DAYS, I'M GOING TO MAKE ONE OF MY OWN.
MAKE A WATER-WHEEL?
THEY'RE USUALLY USED TO RAISE WATER OR GRIND WHEAT, RIGHT?
BUT IF YOU PUT A BUNCH TOGETHER, I'LL BET YOU COULD EVEN MAKE BRICKS.
AND IF YOU FED WATER TO THE TOP INSTEAD, IT'D TURN THE WHEEL EVEN BETTER.
FOR EXAMPLE, IF YOU REMOVED THAT CROSSBEAM...

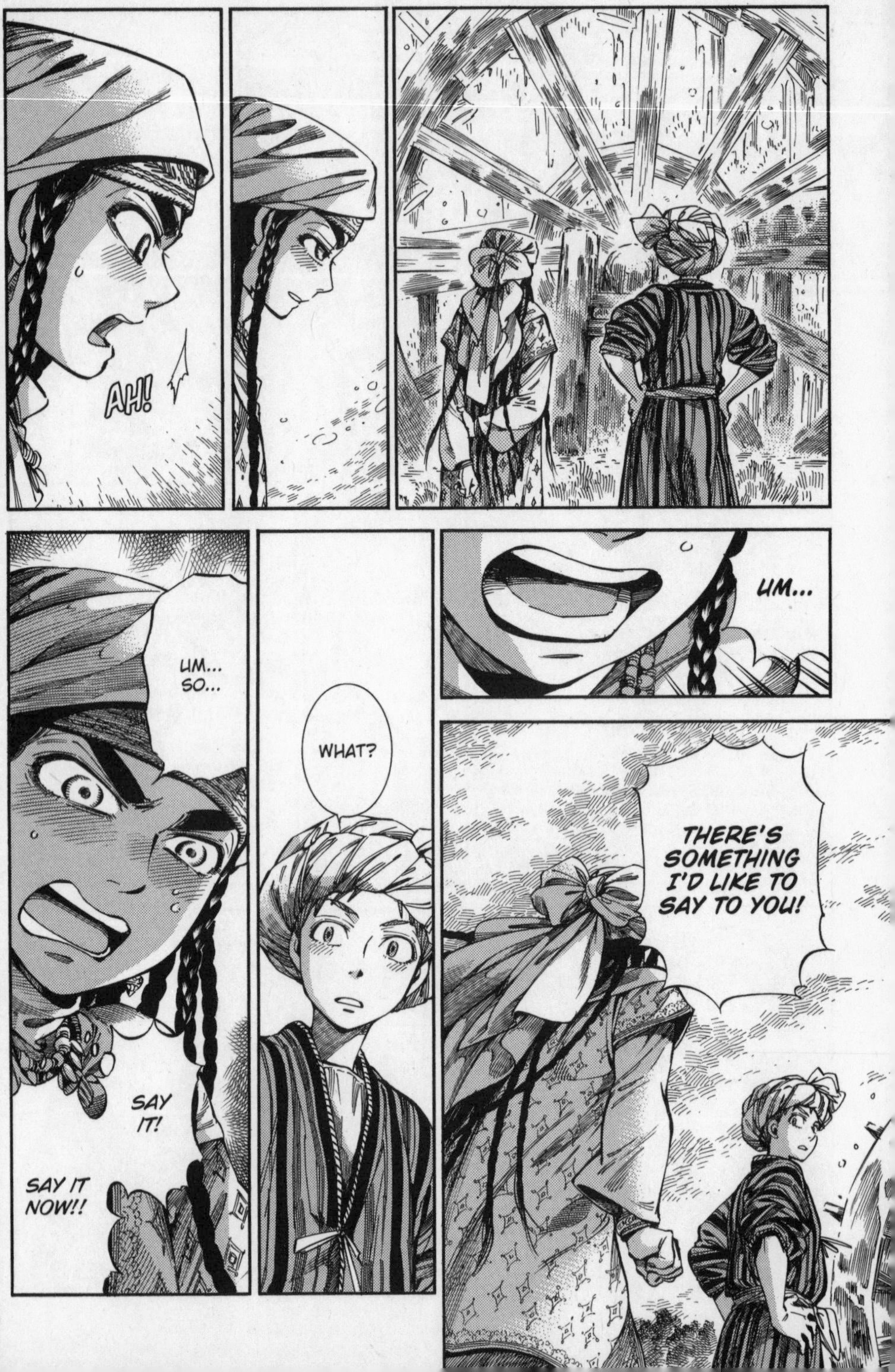
AH!
UM...
THERE'S SOMETHING I'D LIKE TO SAY TO YOU!
WHAT?
UM... SO...
SAY IT!
SAY IT NOW!!

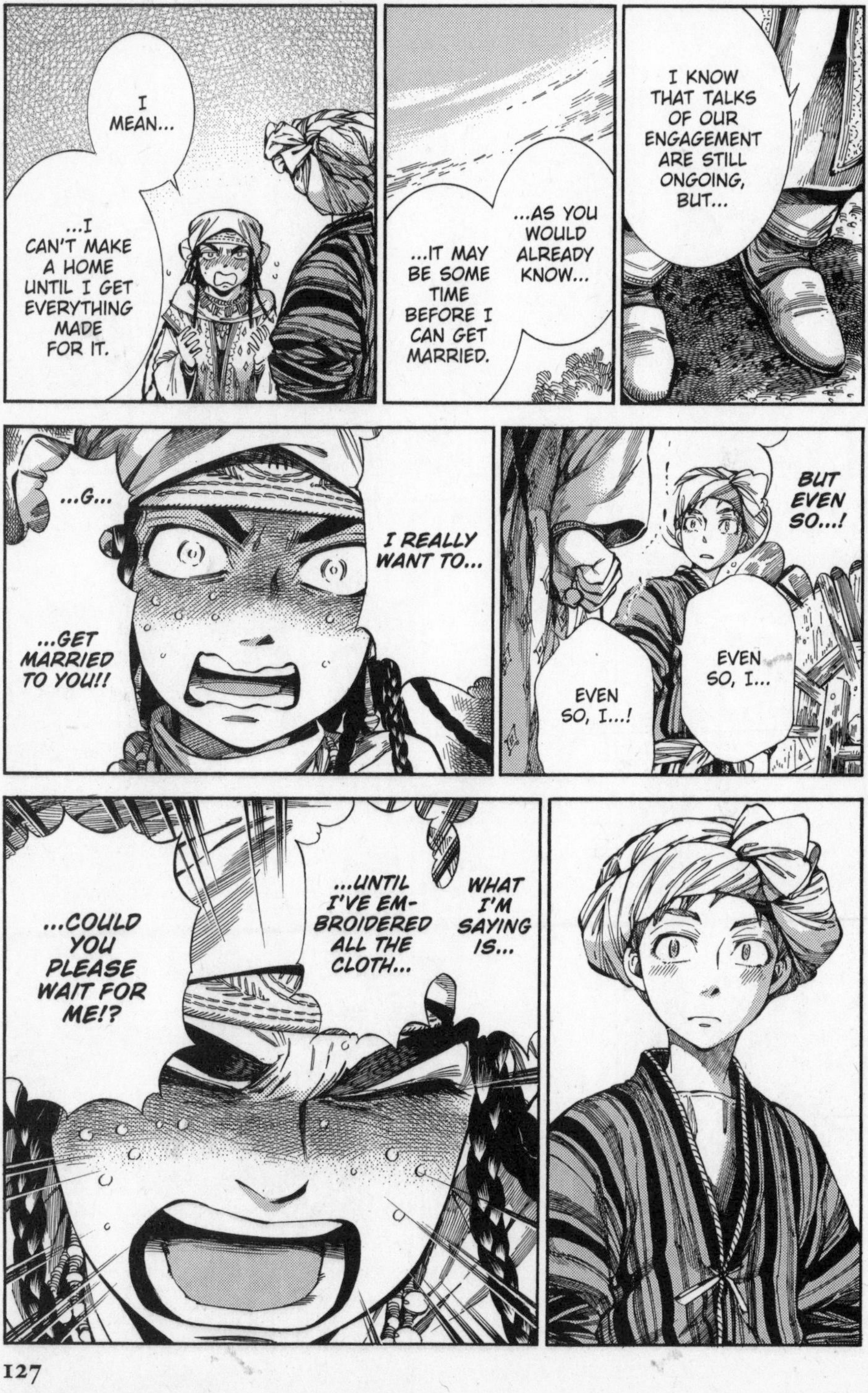

I KNOW THAT TALKS OF OUR ENGAGEMENT ARE STILL ONGOING, BUT...
...AS YOU WOULD ALREADY KNOW...
...IT MAY BE SOME TIME BEFORE I CAN GET MARRIED.
I MEAN...
...I CAN'T MAKE A HOME UNTIL I GET EVERYTHING MADE FOR IT.
BUT EVEN SO...!
EVEN SO, I...
EVEN SO, I...!
I REALLY WANT TO...
...G...
...GET MARRIED TO YOU!!
WHAT I'M SAYING IS...
...UNTIL I'VE EMBROIDERED ALL THE CLOTH...
...COULD YOU PLEASE WAIT FOR ME!?

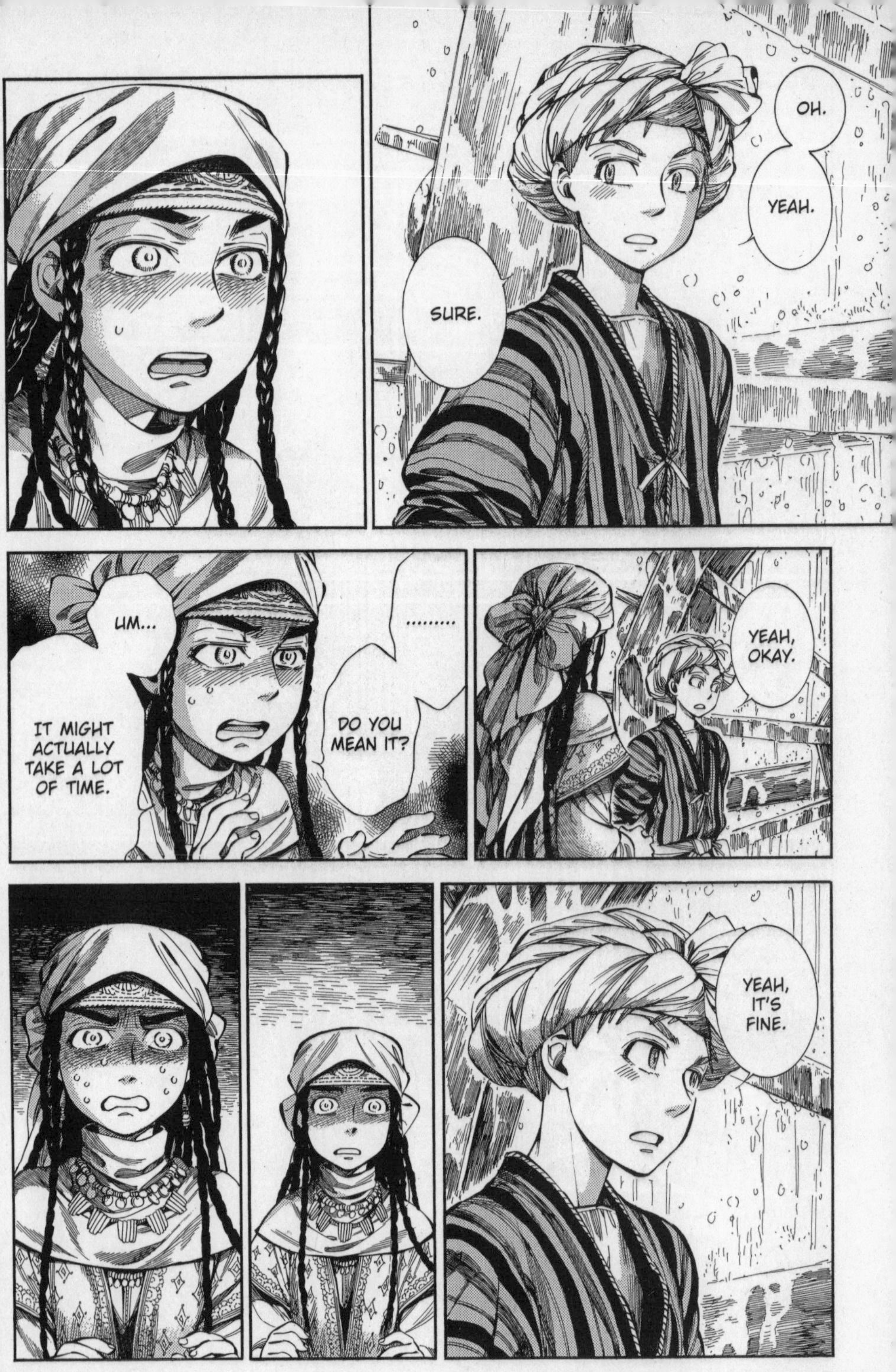
OH.
YEAH.
SURE.
YEAH, OKAY.
.... DO YOU MEAN IT?
UM...
IT MIGHT ACTUALLY TAKE A LOT OF TIME.
YEAH, IT'S FINE.

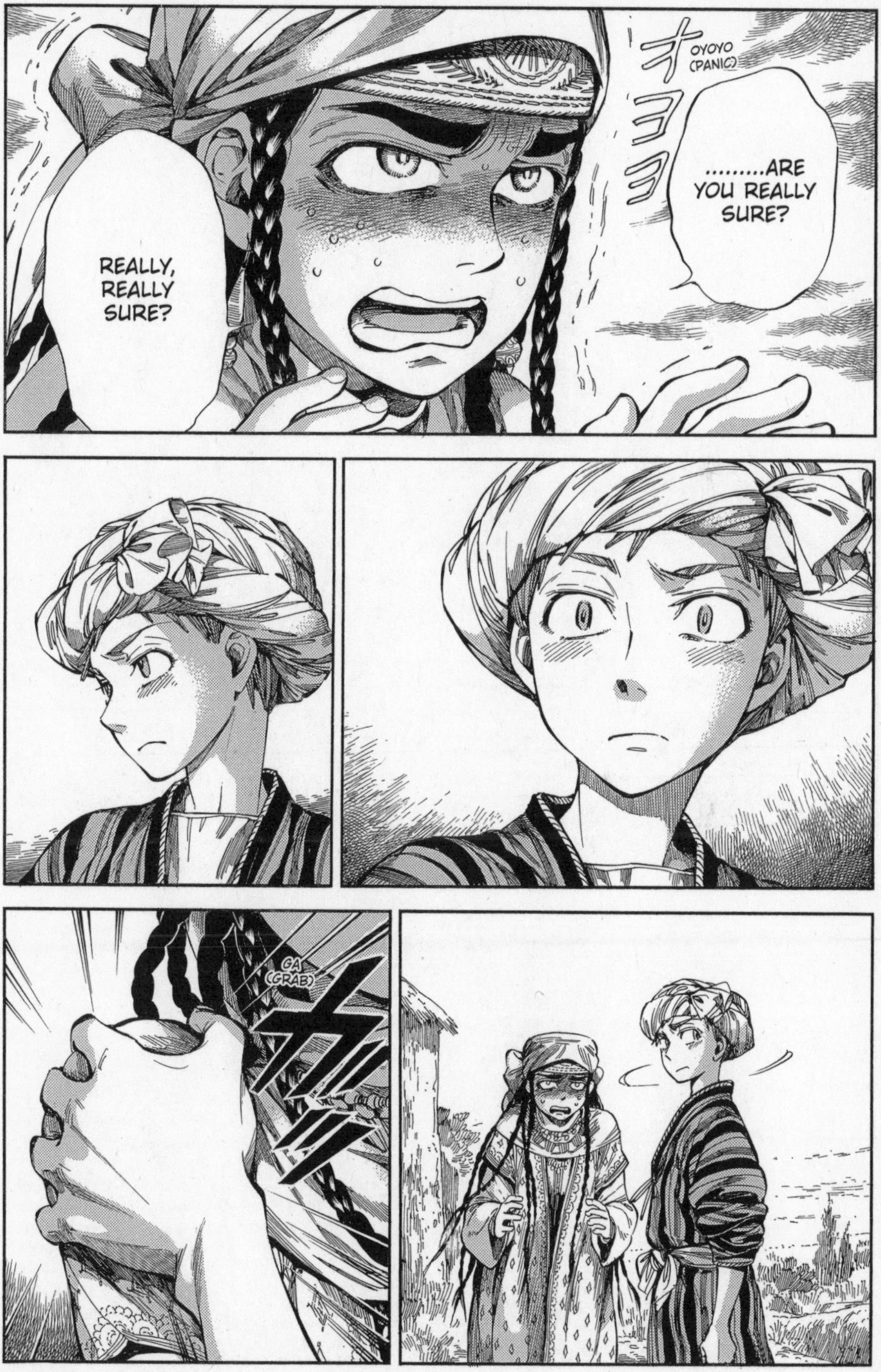
オヨヨ
OYOYO (PANIC)
.........ARE YOU REALLY SURE?
REALLY, REALLY SURE?
ガ
GA (GRAB)

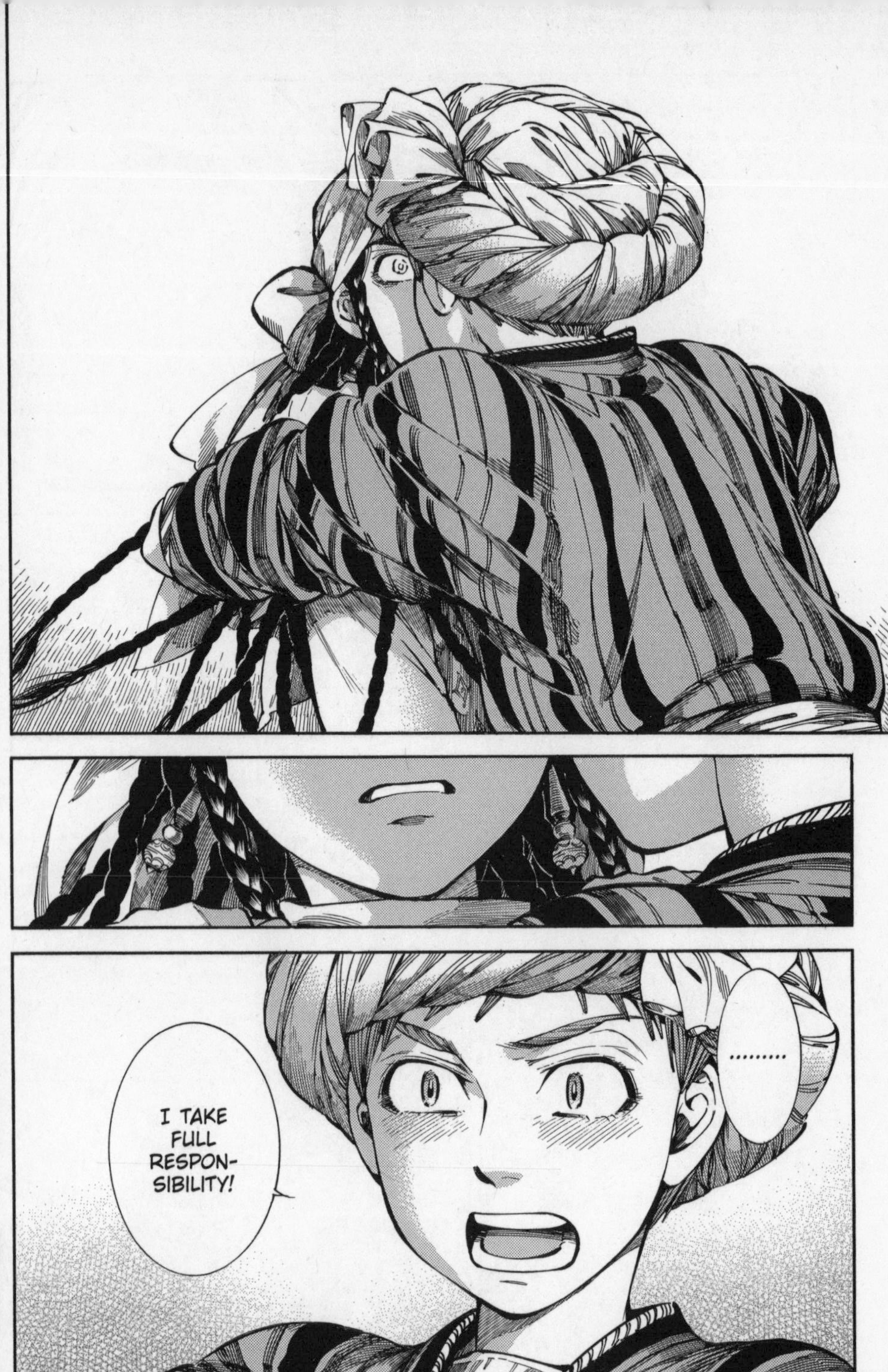
....
I TAKE FULL RESPON-SIBILITY!

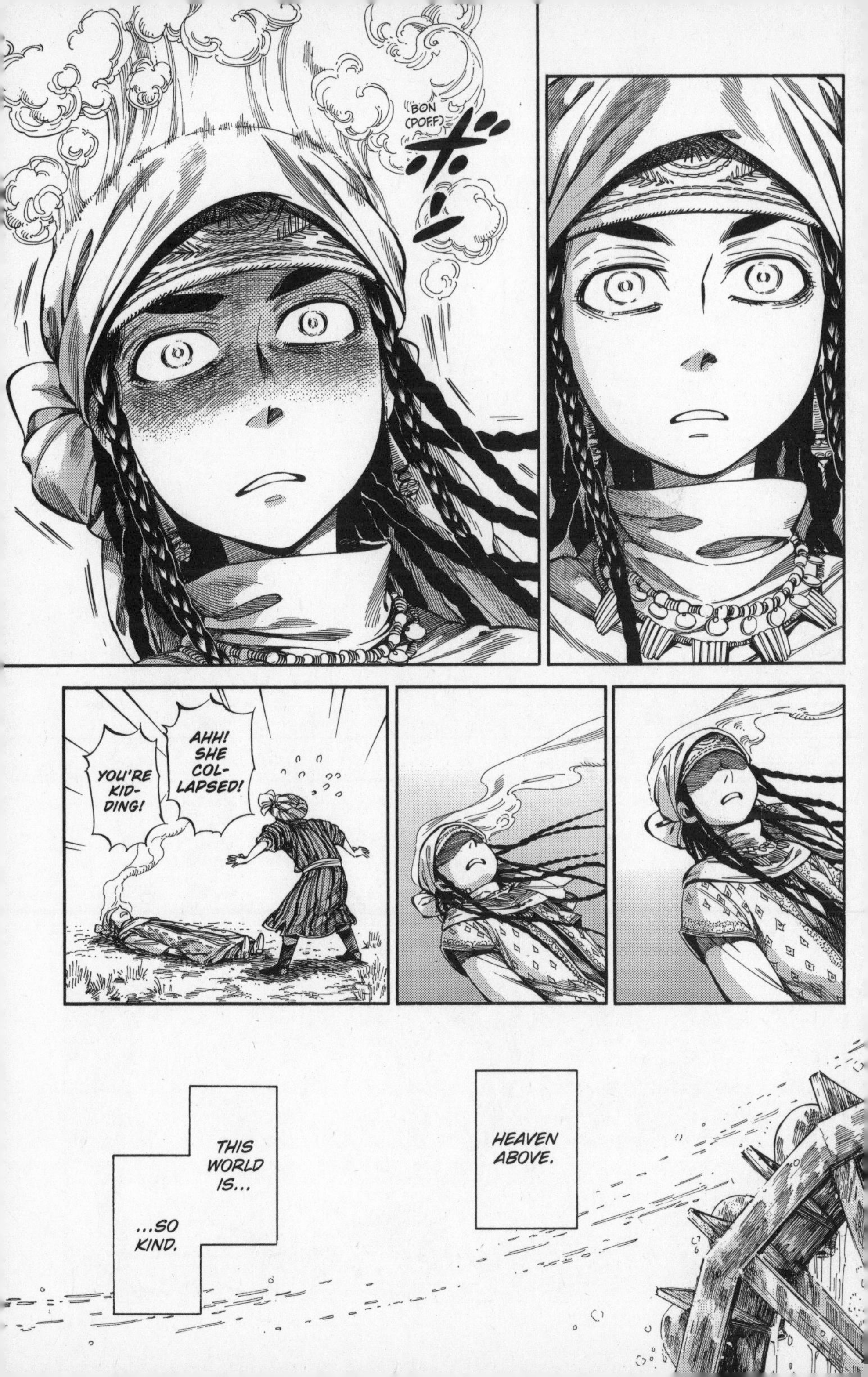
BON (POFF)
AHH! SHE COL-LAPSED!
YOU'RE KID-DING!
HEAVEN ABOVE.
THIS WORLD IS...
...SO KIND.

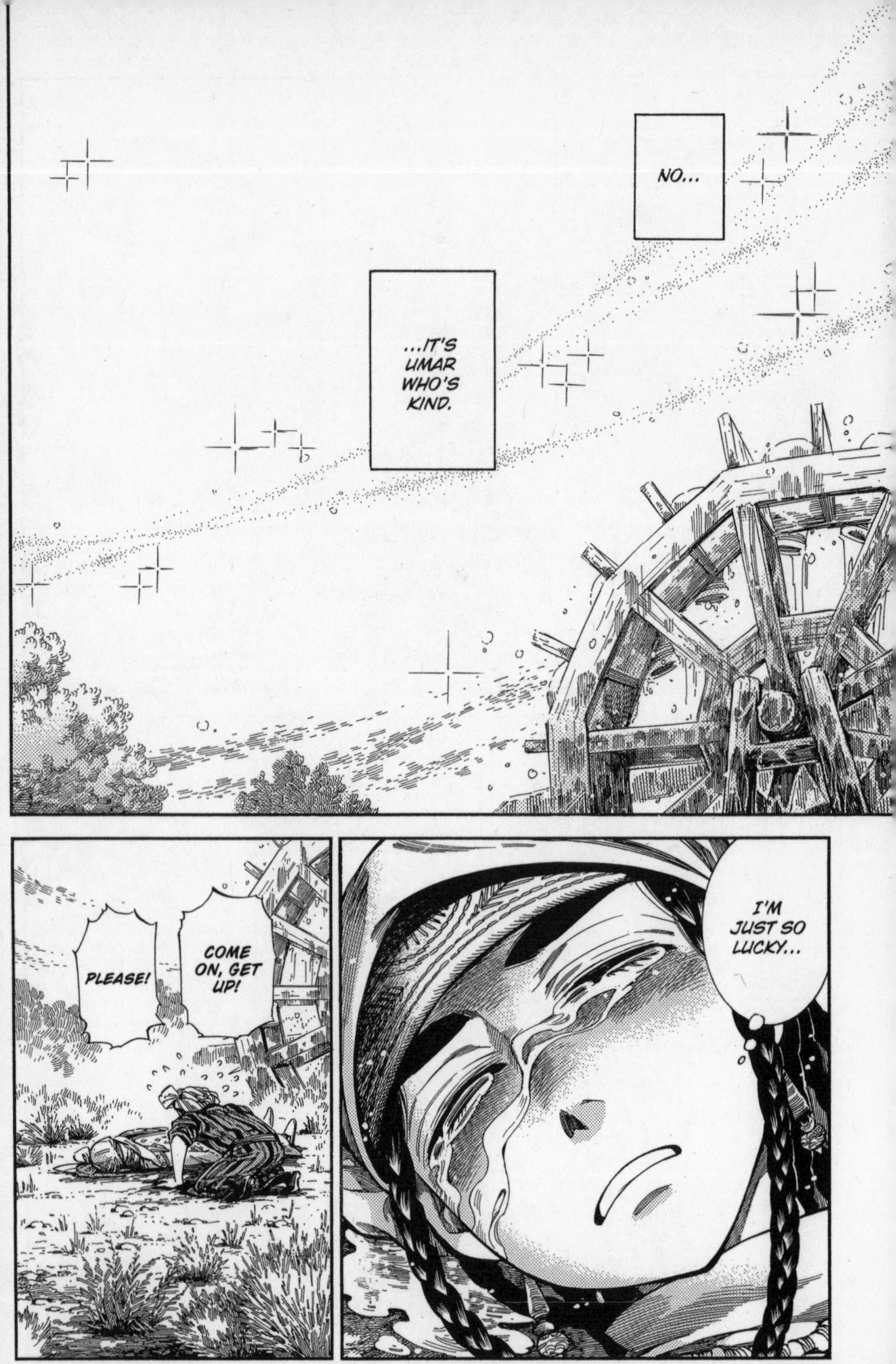
NO...
...IT'S UMAR WHO'S KIND.
I'M JUST SO LUCKY...
COME ON, GET UP!
PLEASE!

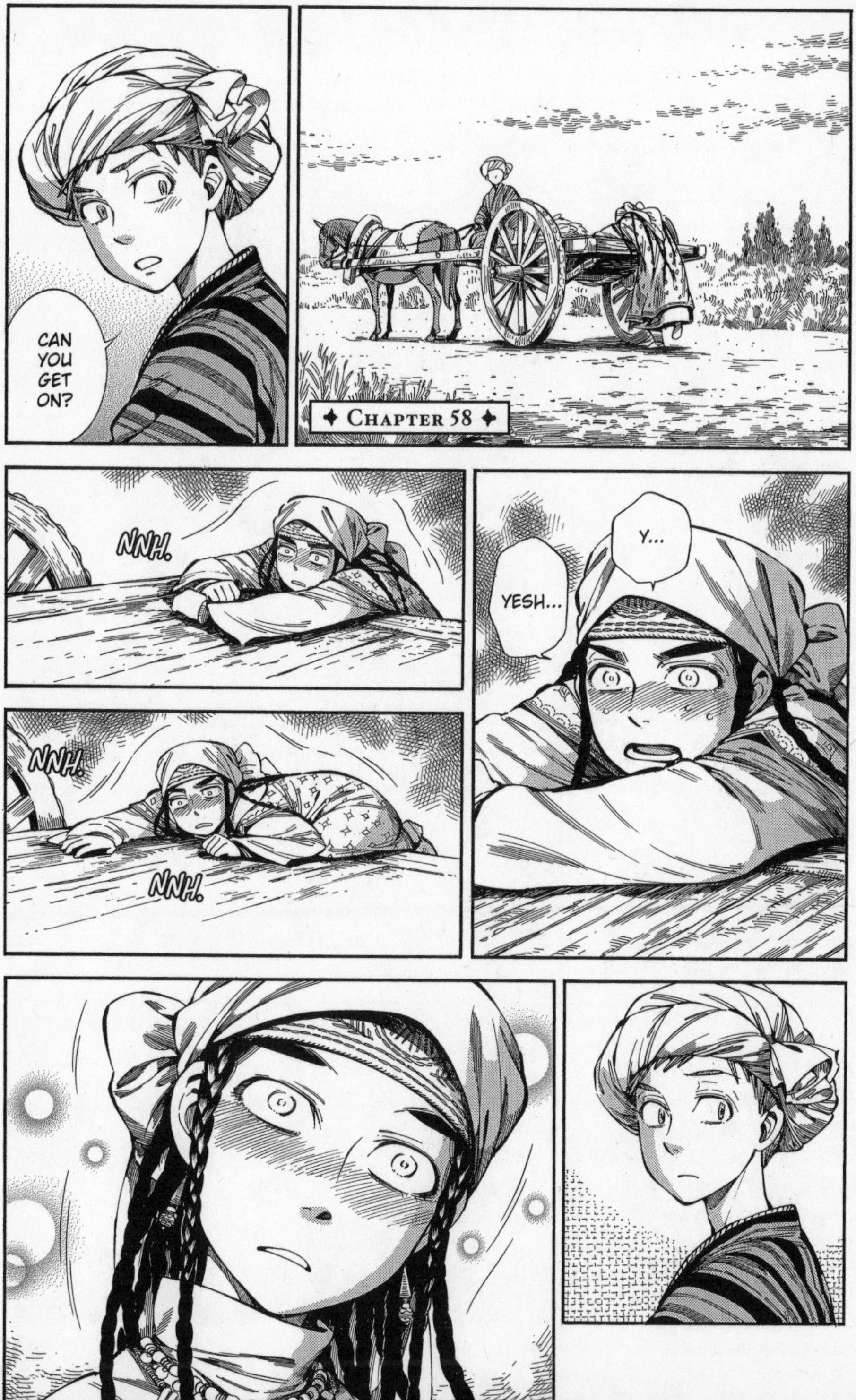

Chapter 58
CAN YOU GET ON?
Y...
YESH...
NNH.
NNH.
NNH.

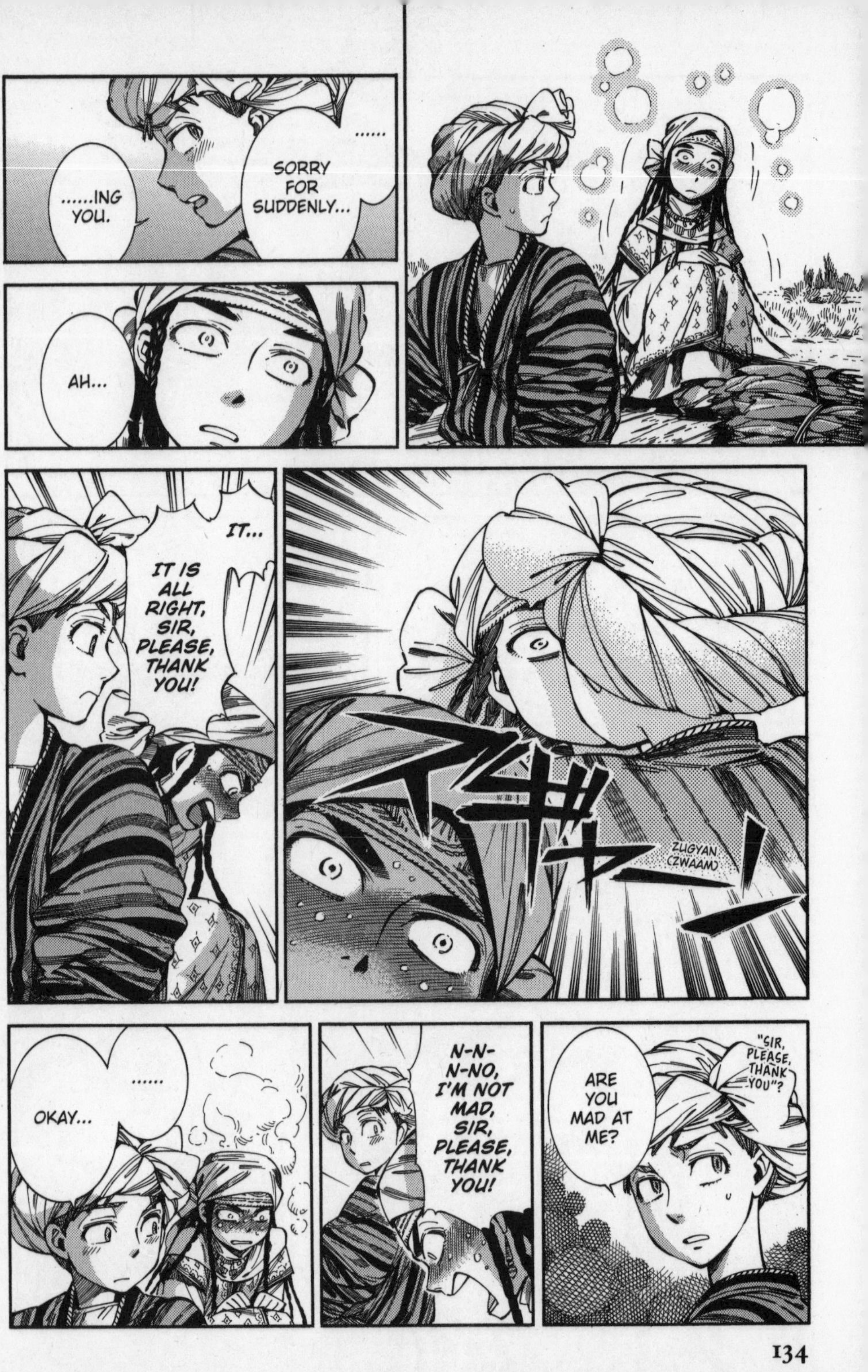
......
SORRY FOR SUDDENLY...
......ING YOU.
AH...
ZUGYAN (ZWAAM)
IT...
IT IS ALL RIGHT, SIR, PLEASE, THANK YOU!
"SIR, PLEASE, THANK YOU"?
ARE YOU MAD AT ME?
N-N-N-NO, I'M NOT MAD, SIR, PLEASE, THANK YOU!
......
OKAY...

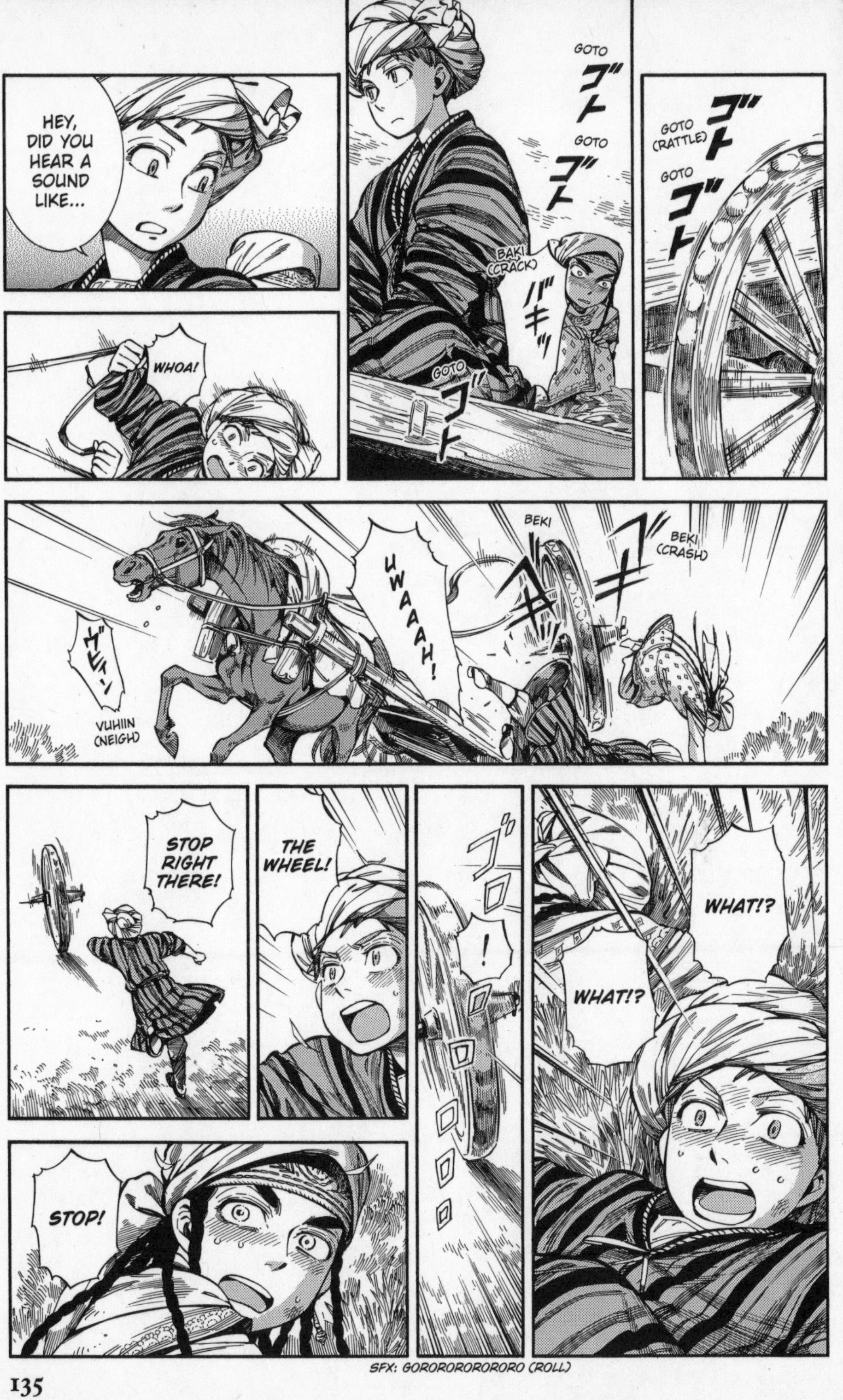
GOTO
(RATTLE)
GOTO
GOTO
GOTO
BAKI
(CRACK)
GOTO
HEY, DID YOU HEAR A SOUND LIKE...
WHOA!
BEKI
BEKI
(CRASH)
UWAAAAH!
VUHIIN
(NEIGH)
WHAT!?
WHAT!?
THE WHEEL!
STOP RIGHT THERE!
STOP!

SFX: GORORORORORORO (ROLL)

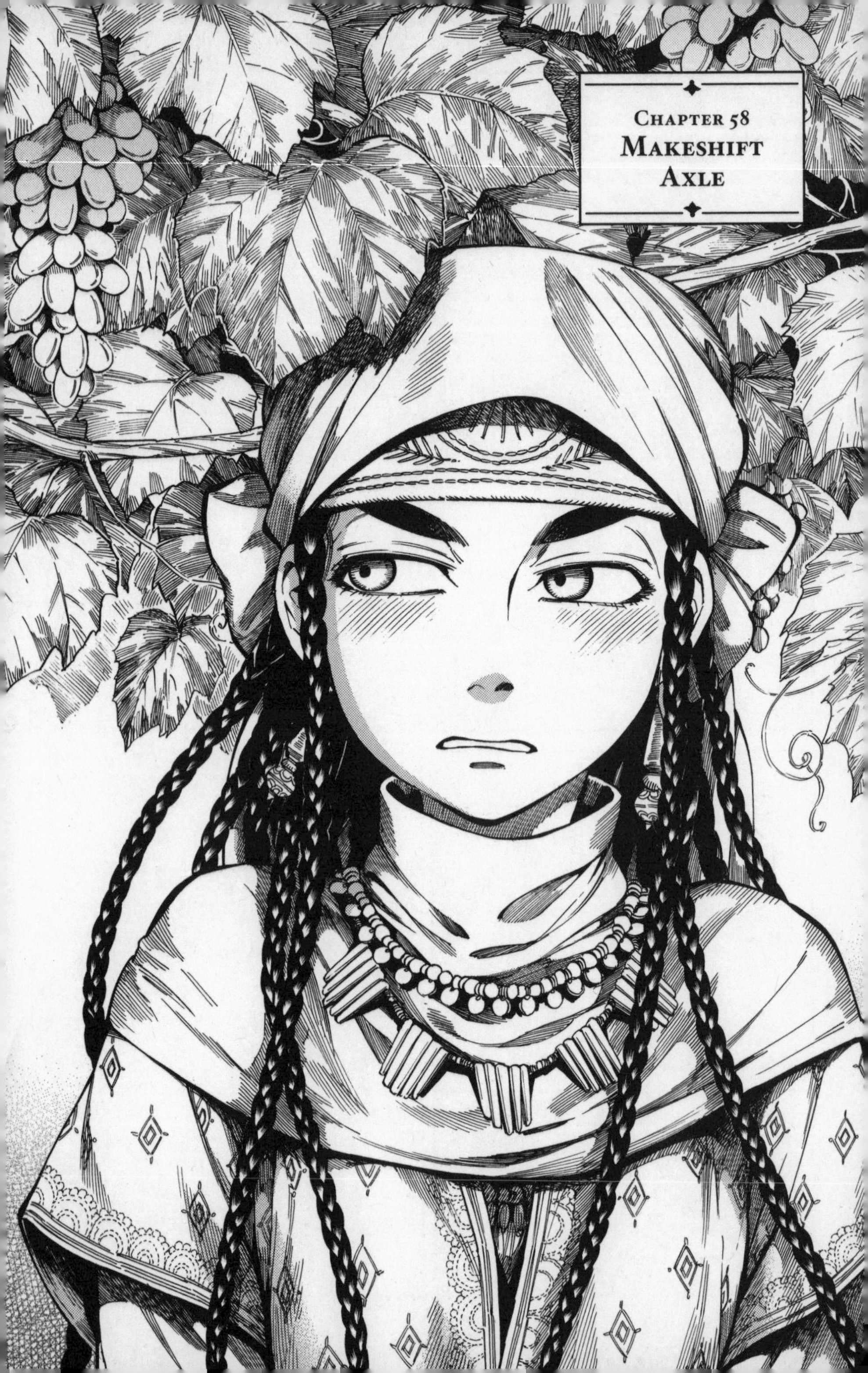
Chapter 58
Makeshift
Axle

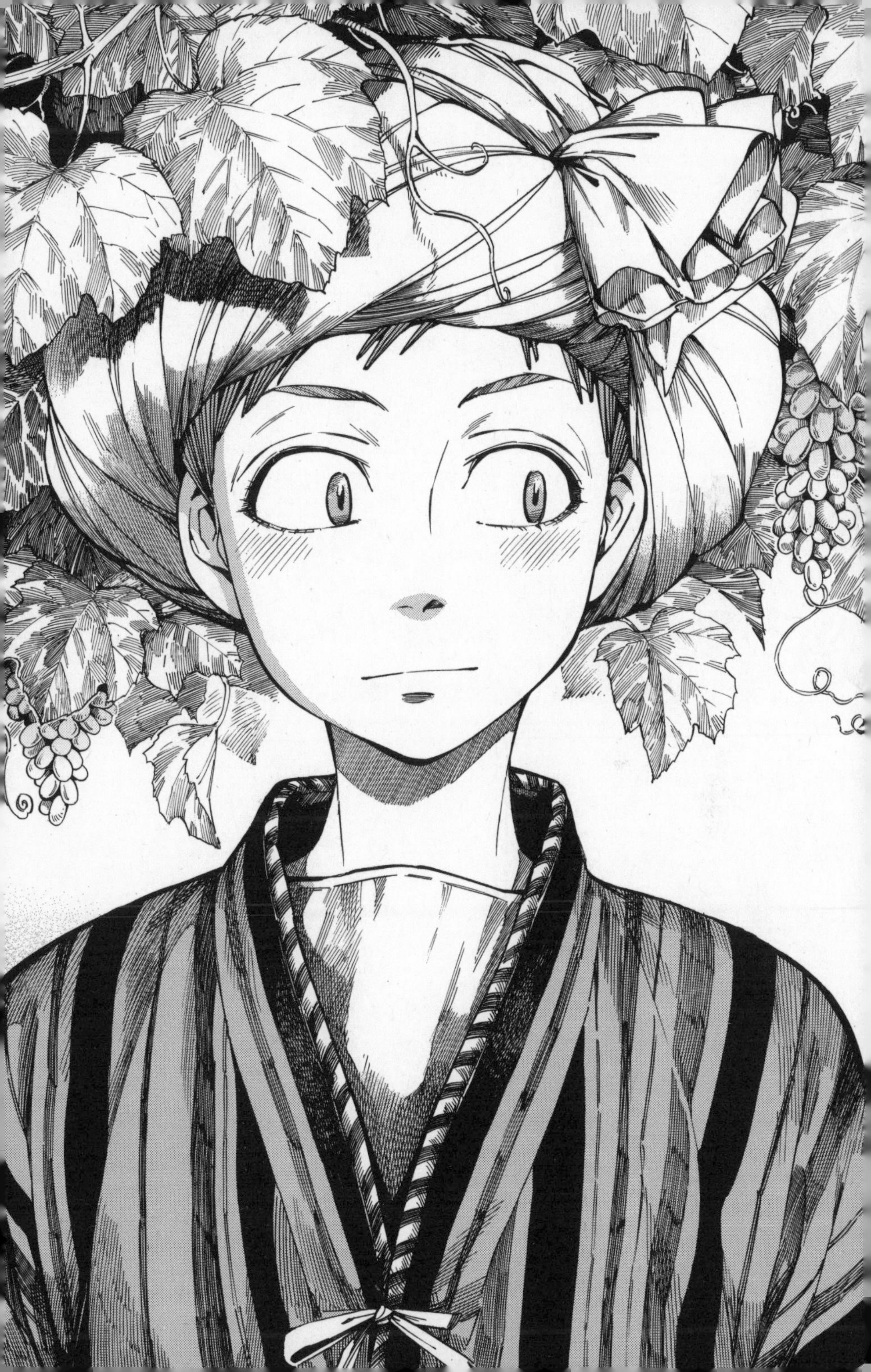

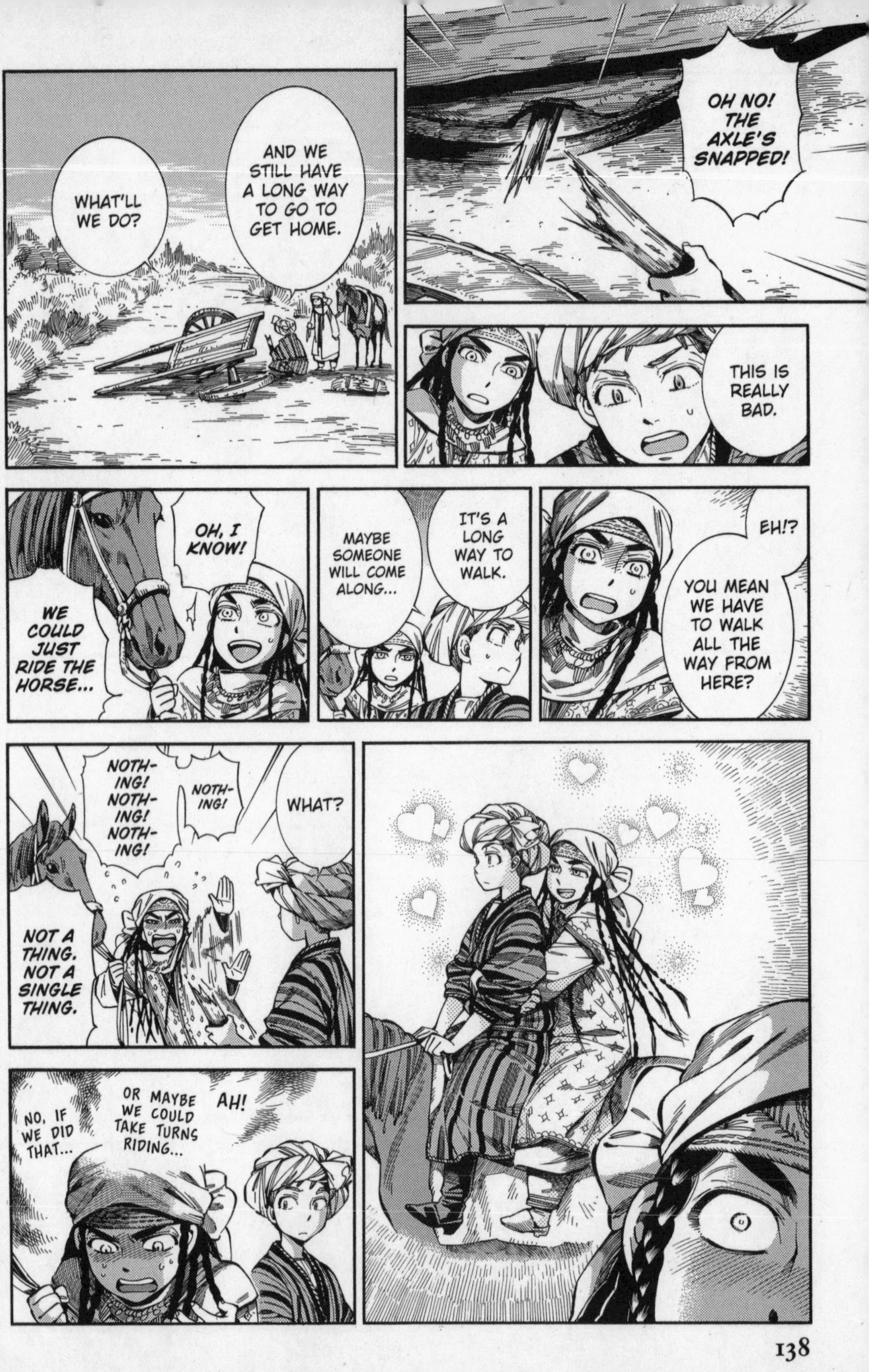
OH NO! THE AXLE'S SNAPPED!
THIS IS REALLY BAD.
AND WE STILL HAVE A LONG WAY TO GO TO GET HOME.
WHAT'LL WE DO?
EH!?
YOU MEAN WE HAVE TO WALK ALL THE WAY FROM HERE?
IT'S A LONG WAY TO WALK.
MAYBE SOMEONE WILL COME ALONG...
OH, I KNOW!
WE COULD JUST RIDE THE HORSE...
WHAT?
NOTH-ING!
NOTH-ING! NOTH-ING! NOTH-ING!
NOT A THING. NOT A SINGLE THING.
AH!
OR MAYBE WE COULD TAKE TURNS RIDING...
NO, IF WE DID THAT...

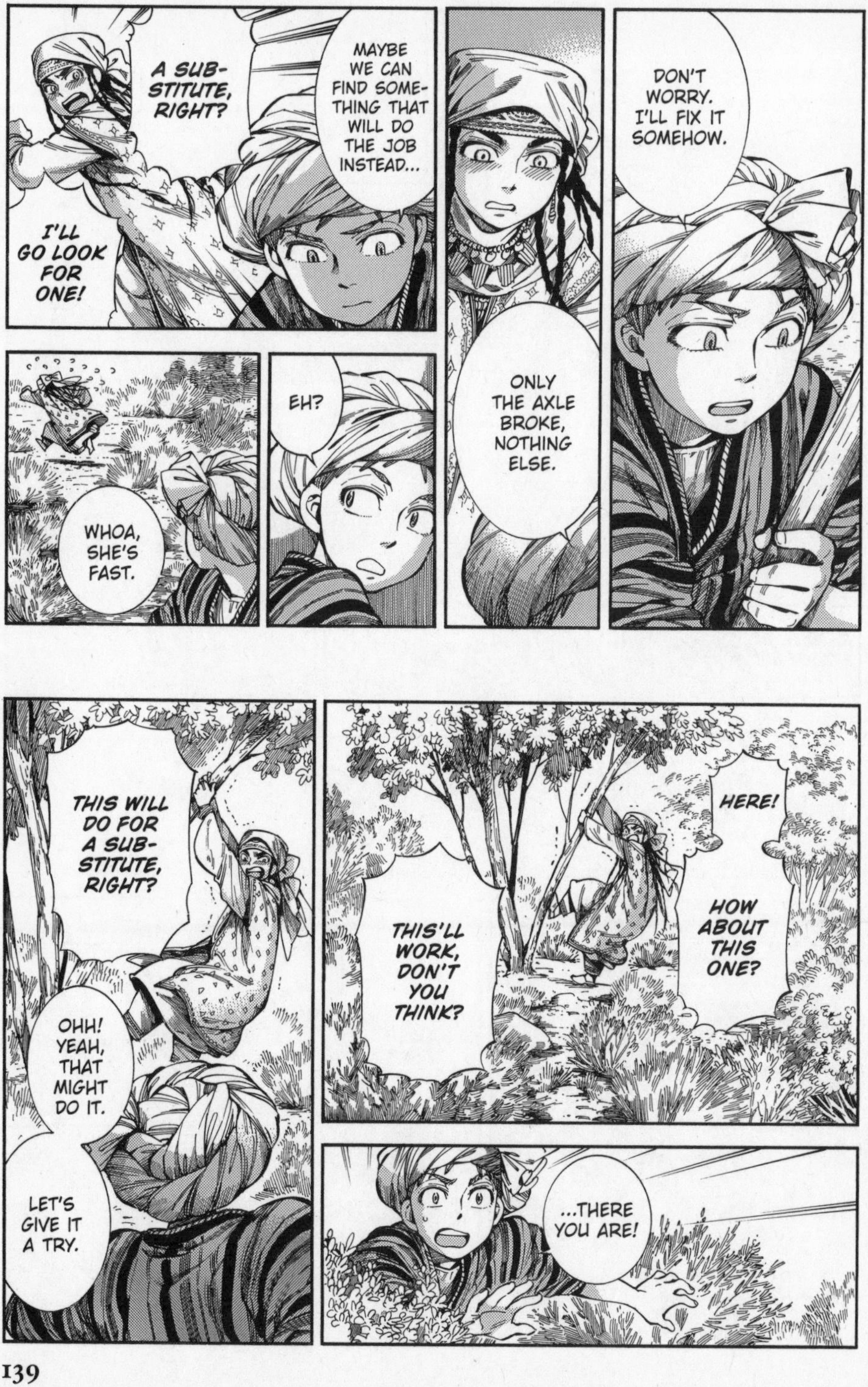
DON'T WORRY. I'LL FIX IT SOMEHOW.
ONLY THE AXLE BROKE, NOTHING ELSE.
MAYBE WE CAN FIND SOME-THING THAT WILL DO THE JOB INSTEAD...
A SUB-STITUTE, RIGHT?
I'LL GO LOOK FOR ONE!
EH?
WHOA, SHE'S FAST.
HERE!
HOW ABOUT THIS ONE?
THIS'LL WORK, DON'T YOU THINK?
...THERE YOU ARE!
THIS WILL DO FOR A SUB-STITUTE, RIGHT?
OHH! YEAH, THAT MIGHT DO IT.
LET'S GIVE IT A TRY.

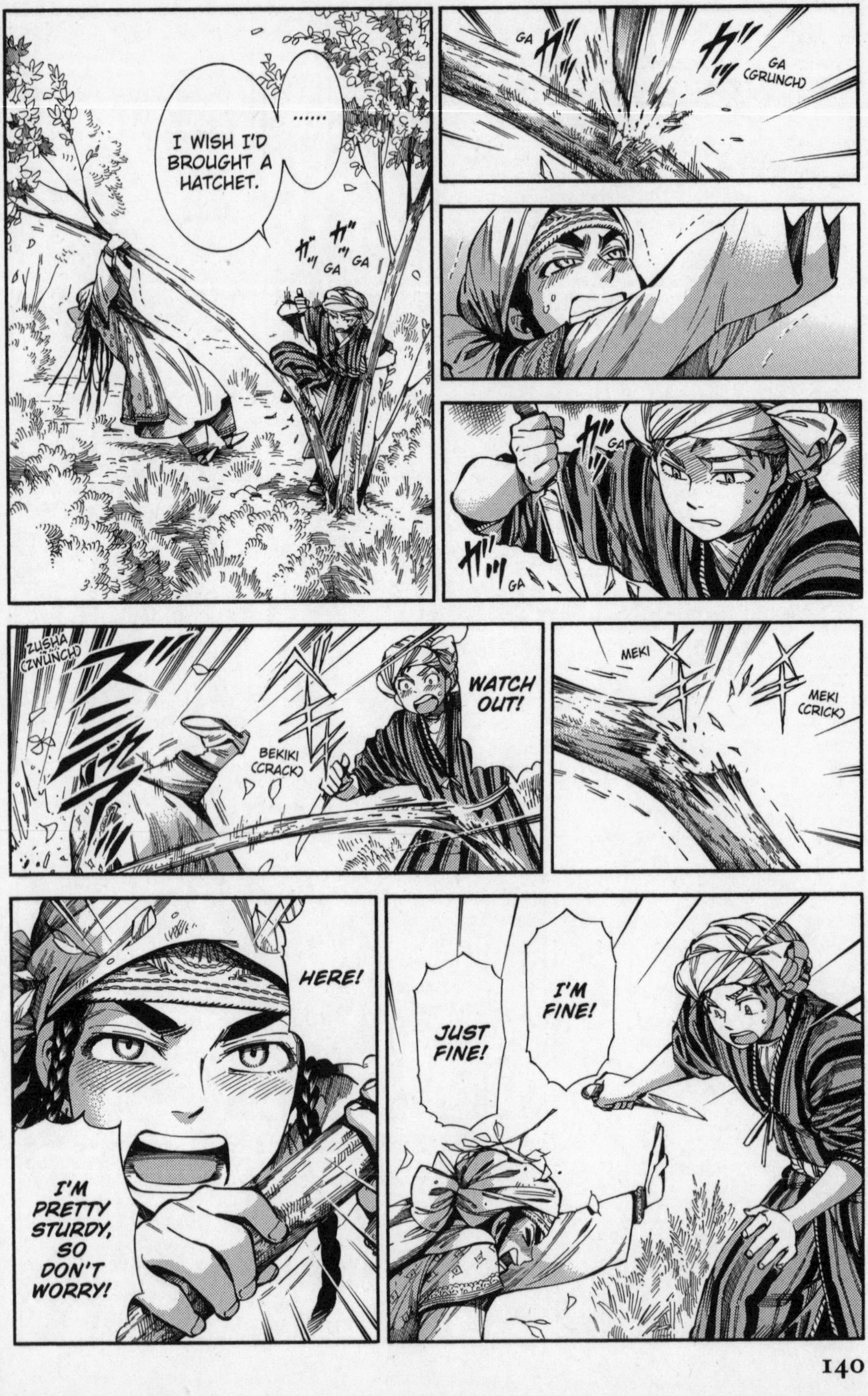
GA
GA (GRUNCH)
GA
GA
......
I WISH I'D BROUGHT A HATCHET.
GA
GA
MEKI
MEKI (CRICK)
WATCH OUT!
BEKIKI (CRACK)
ZUSHA (ZWUNCH)
I'M FINE!
JUST FINE!
HERE!
I'M PRETTY STURDY, SO DON'T WORRY!

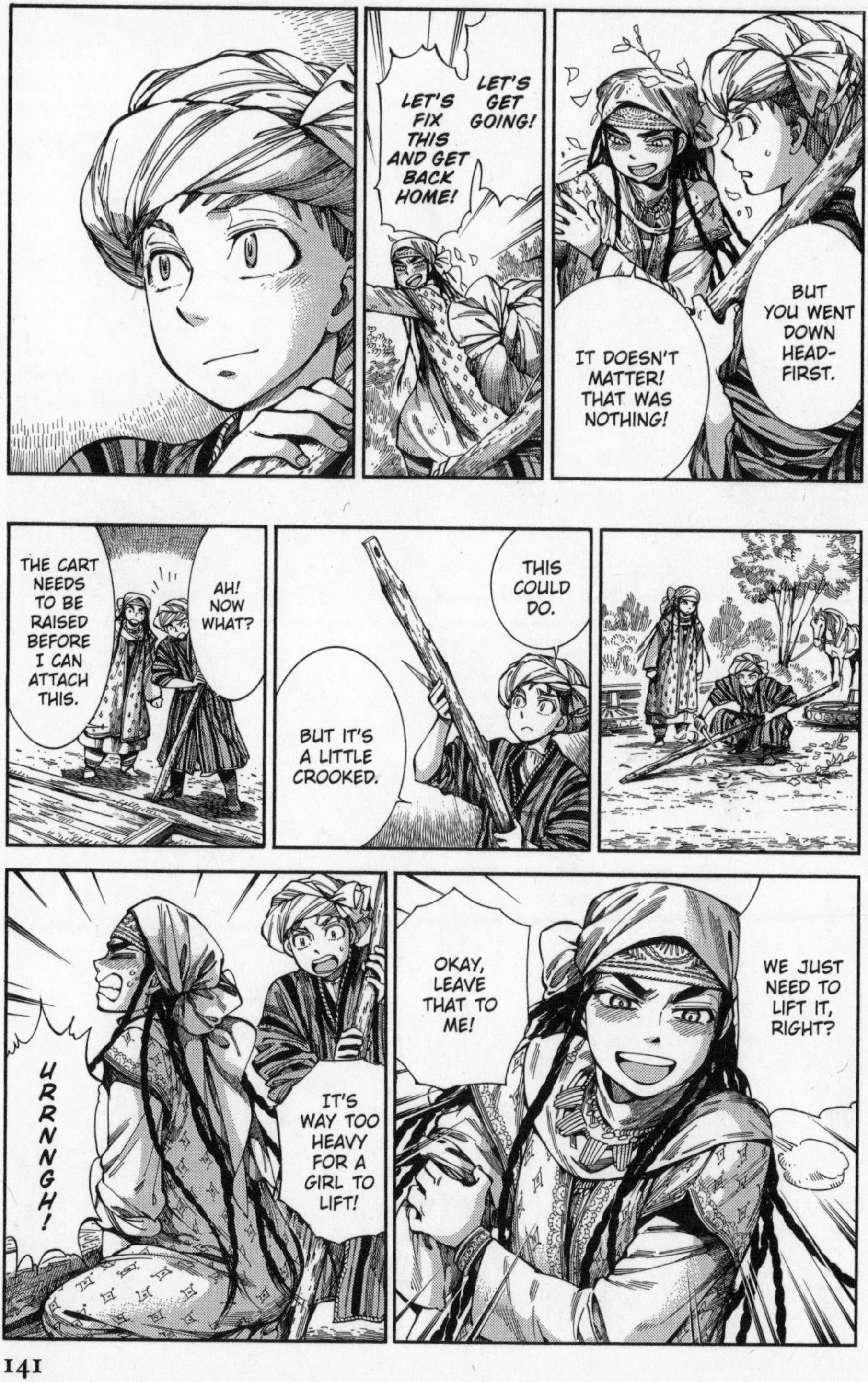
BUT YOU WENT DOWN HEAD-FIRST.
IT DOESN'T MATTER! THAT WAS NOTHING!
LET'S GET GOING!
LET'S FIX THIS AND GET BACK HOME!
THIS COULD DO.
BUT IT'S A LITTLE CROOKED.
AH! NOW WHAT?
THE CART NEEDS TO BE RAISED BEFORE I CAN ATTACH THIS.
WE JUST NEED TO LIFT IT, RIGHT?
OKAY, LEAVE THAT TO ME!
IT'S WAY TOO HEAVY FOR A GIRL TO LIFT!
URRNNGH!

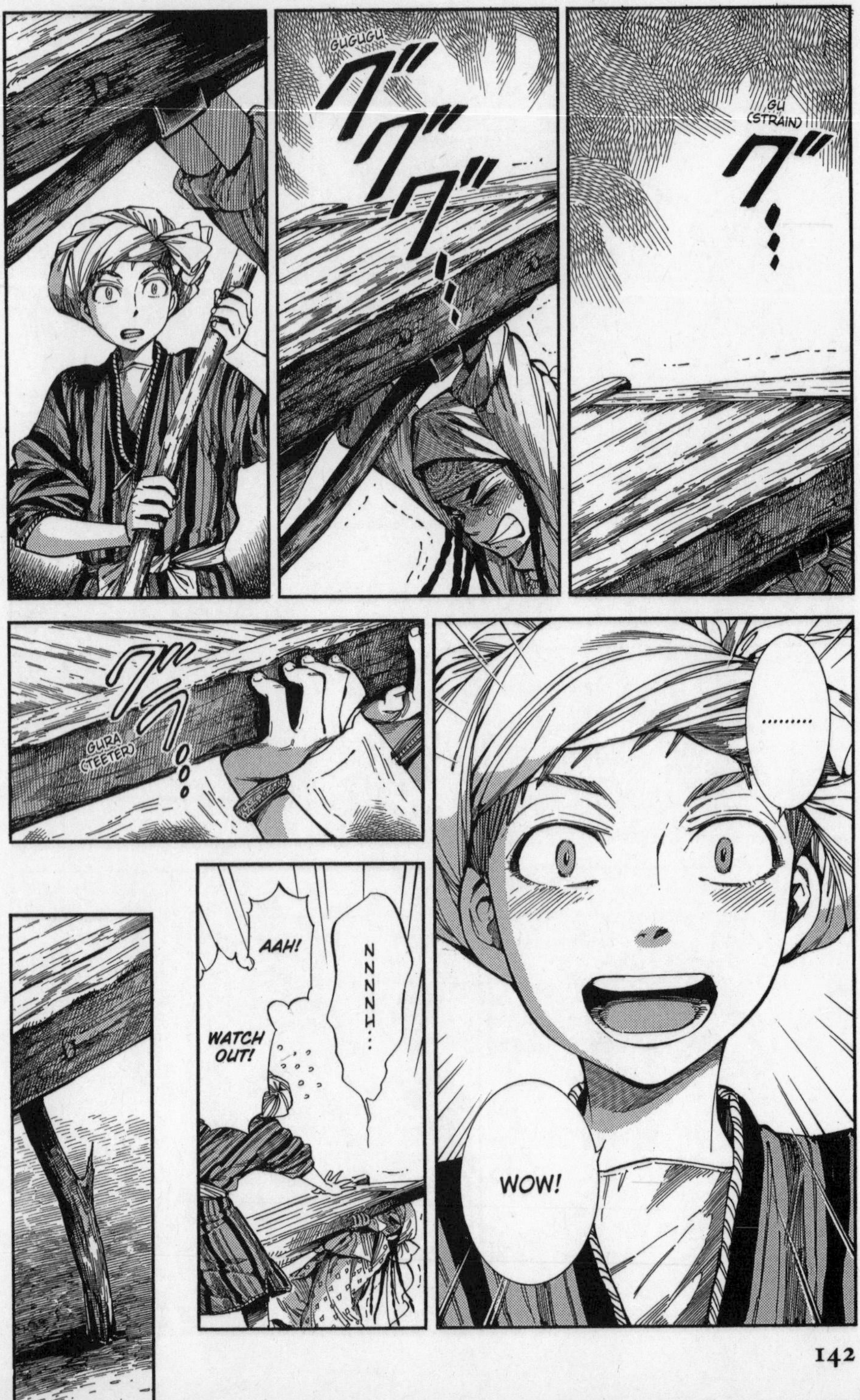
GU
(STRAIN)
GUGUGU
....
WOW!
GURA
(TEETER)
NNNNH...
AAH!
WATCH OUT!

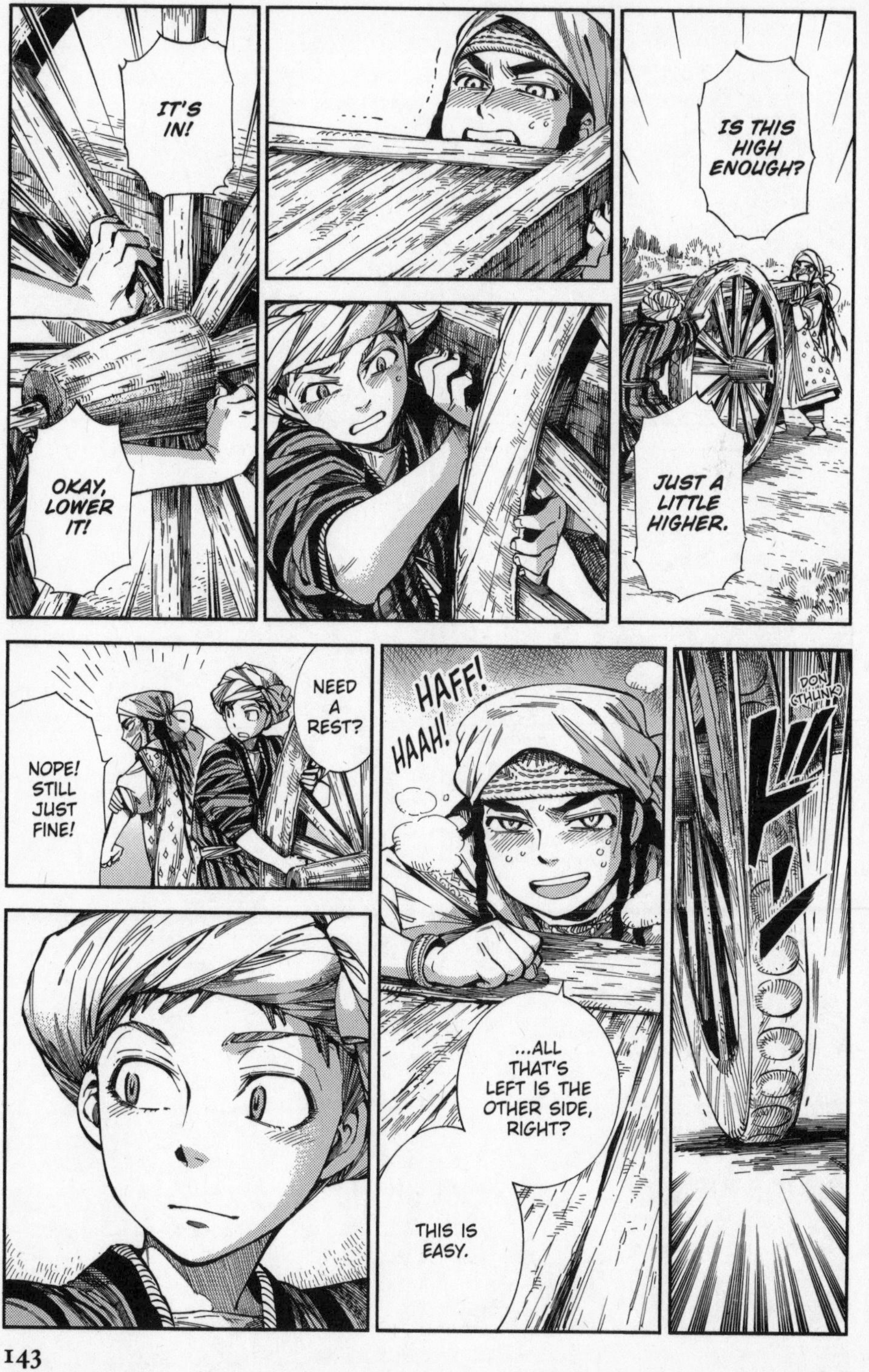
IS THIS HIGH ENOUGH?
JUST A LITTLE HIGHER.
IT'S IN!
OKAY, LOWER IT!
DON (THUNK)
HAFF!
HAAH!
...ALL THAT'S LEFT IS THE OTHER SIDE, RIGHT?
THIS IS EASY.
NEED A REST?
NOPE! STILL JUST FINE!

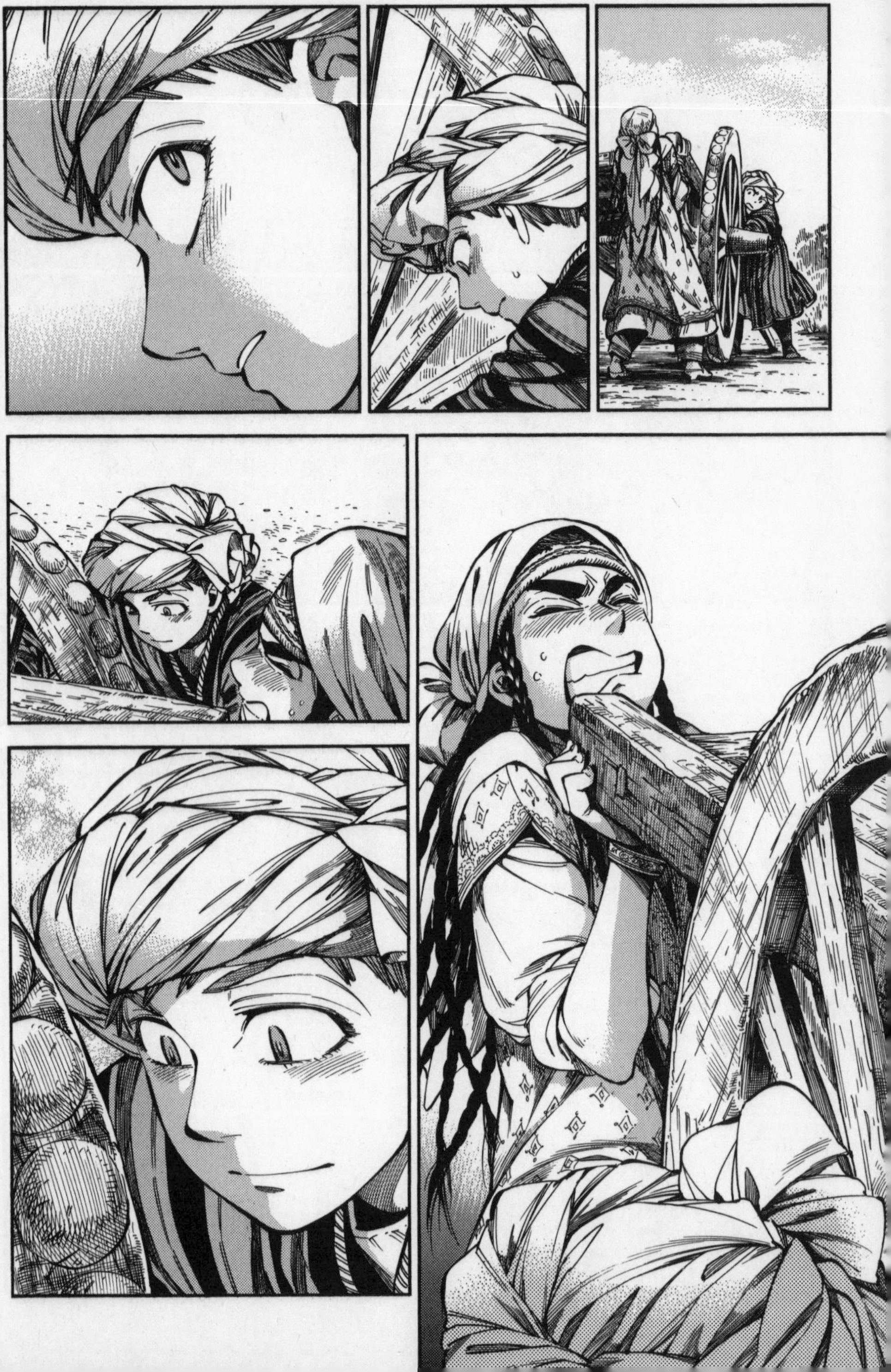

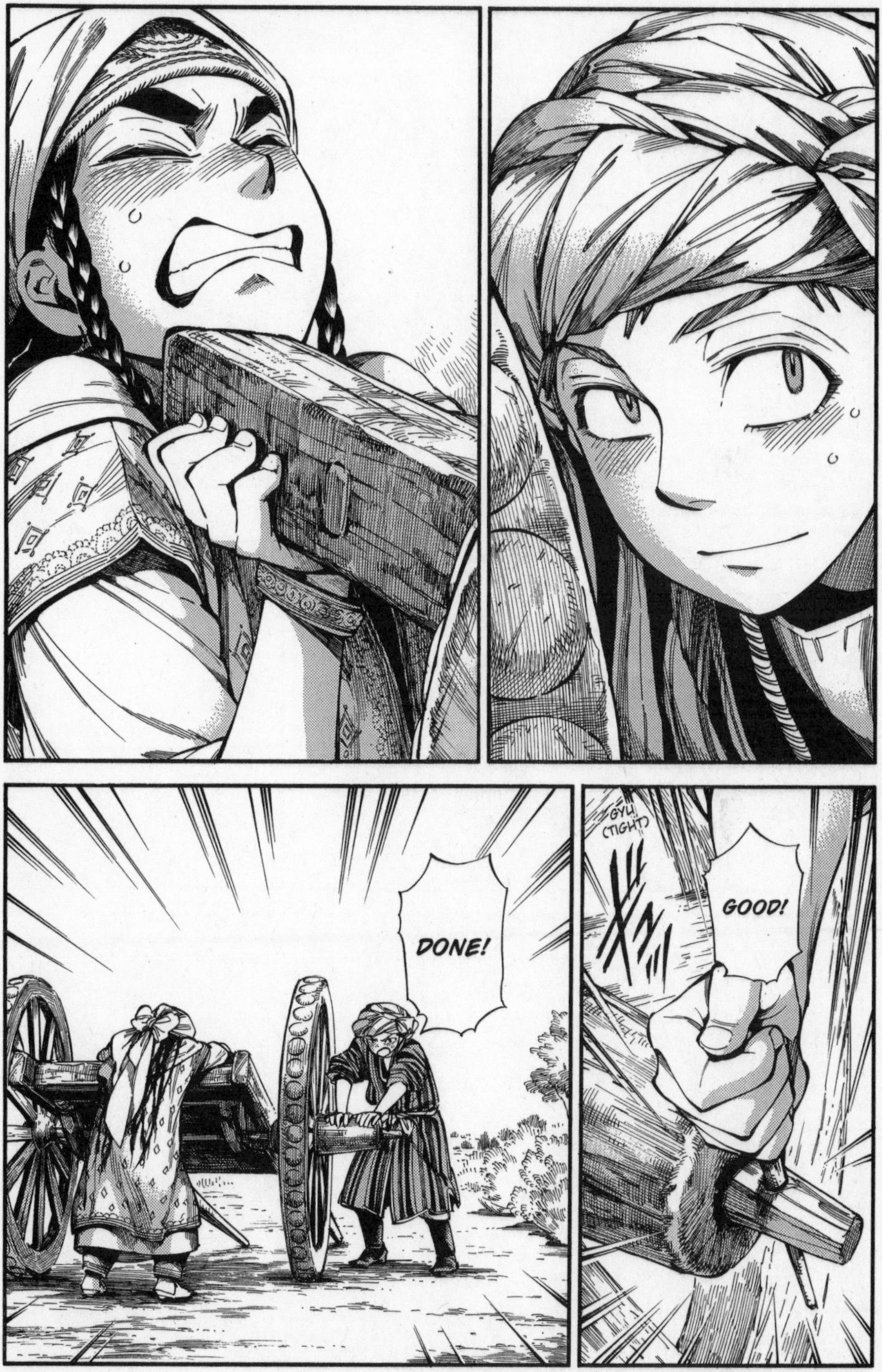
GYU (TIGHT)
GOOD!
DONE!

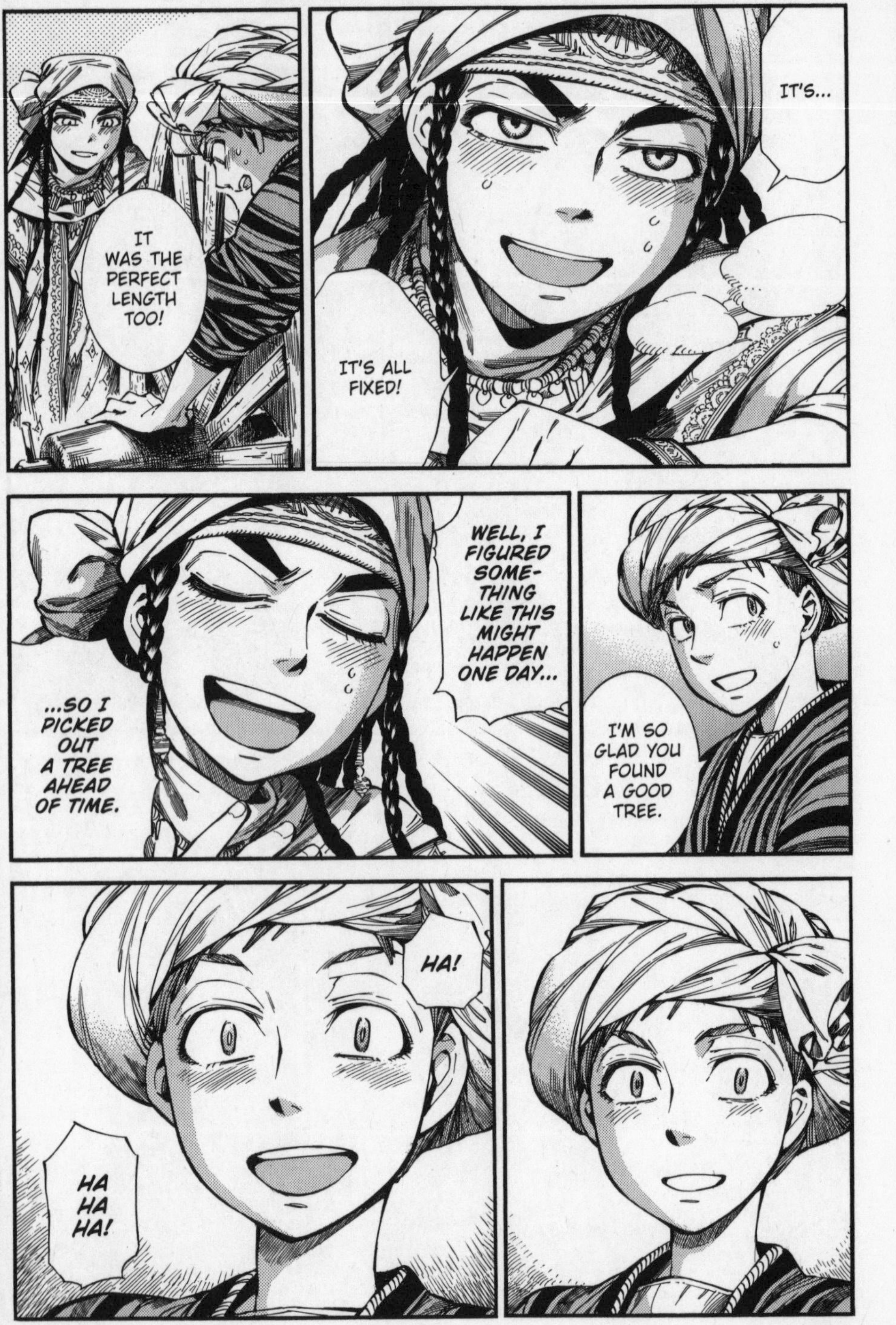
IT'S...
IT'S ALL FIXED!
IT WAS THE PERFECT LENGTH TOO!
I'M SO GLAD YOU FOUND A GOOD TREE.
WELL, I FIGURED SOMETHING LIKE THIS MIGHT HAPPEN ONE DAY...
...SO I PICKED OUT A TREE AHEAD OF TIME.
HA!
HA HA HA!

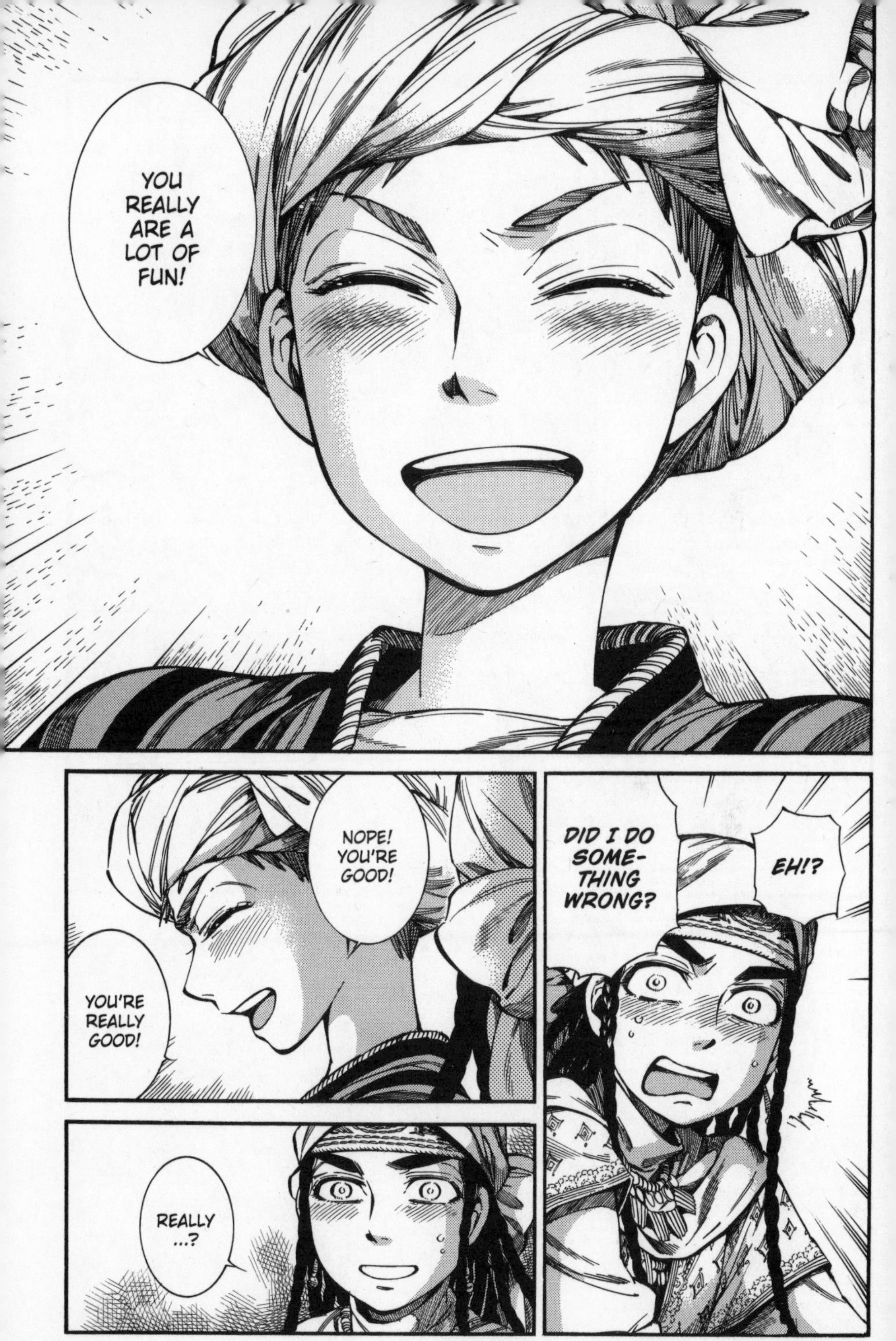
YOU REALLY ARE A LOT OF FUN!
EH!?
DID I DO SOME-THING WRONG?
NOPE! YOU'RE GOOD!
YOU'RE REALLY GOOD!
REALLY ...?

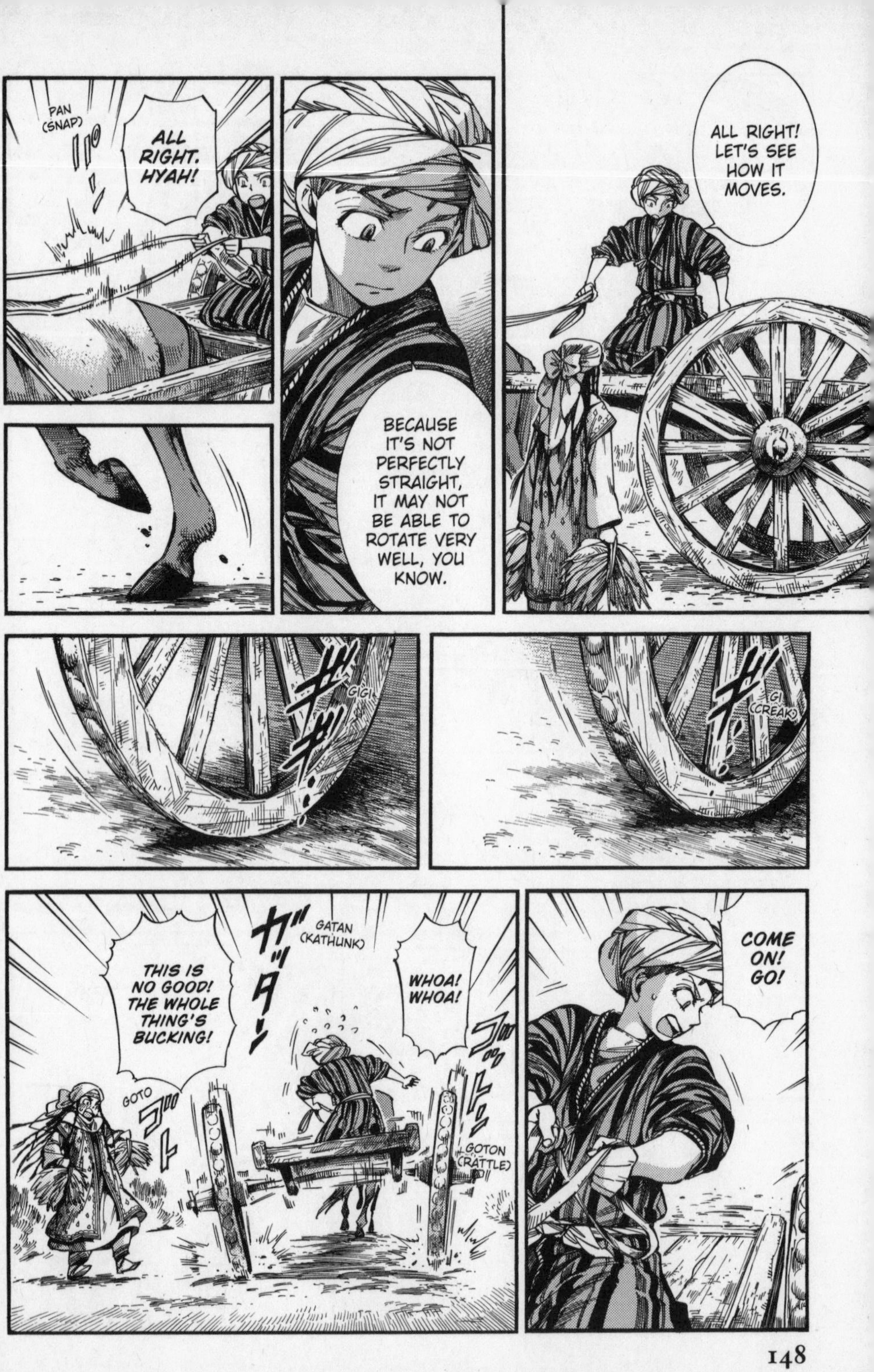
ALL RIGHT! LET'S SEE HOW IT MOVES.
BECAUSE IT'S NOT PERFECTLY STRAIGHT, IT MAY NOT BE ABLE TO ROTATE VERY WELL, YOU KNOW.
PAN (SNAP)
ALL RIGHT. HYAH!
GI (CREAK)
GIGI
COME ON! GO!
GOTON (RATTLE)
GATAN (KATHUNK)
WHOA! WHOA!
GOTO
THIS IS NO GOOD! THE WHOLE THING'S BUCKING!

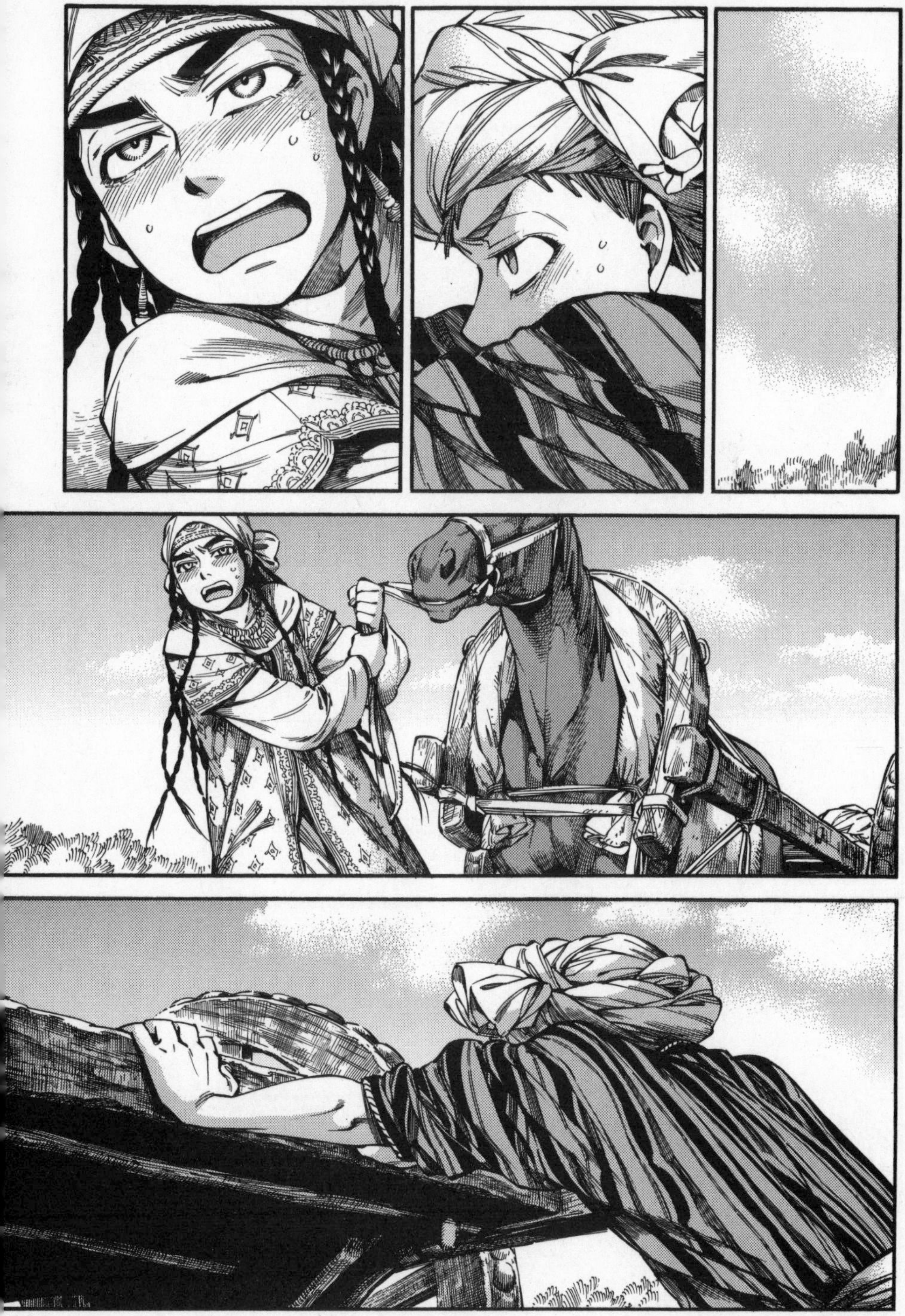

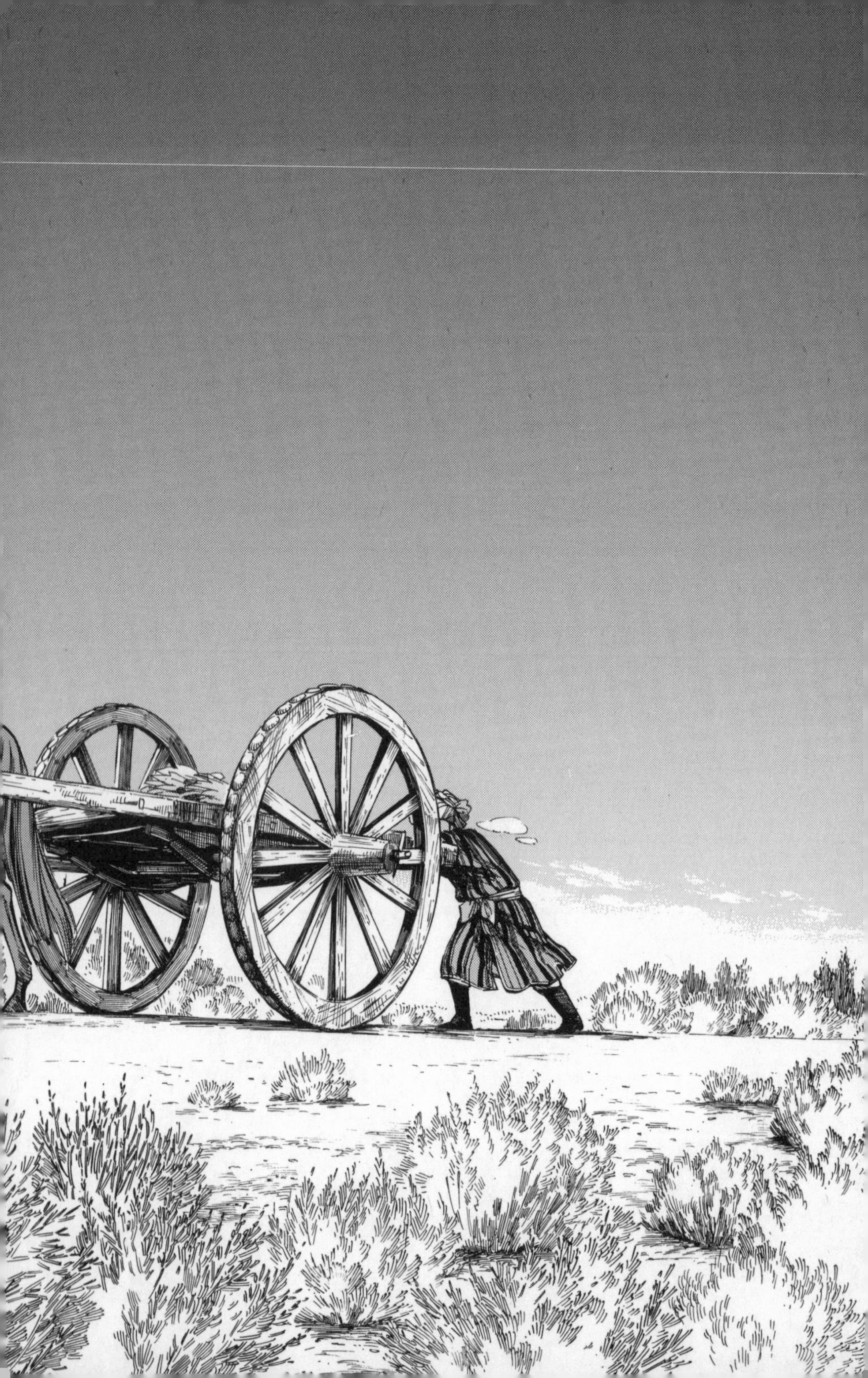

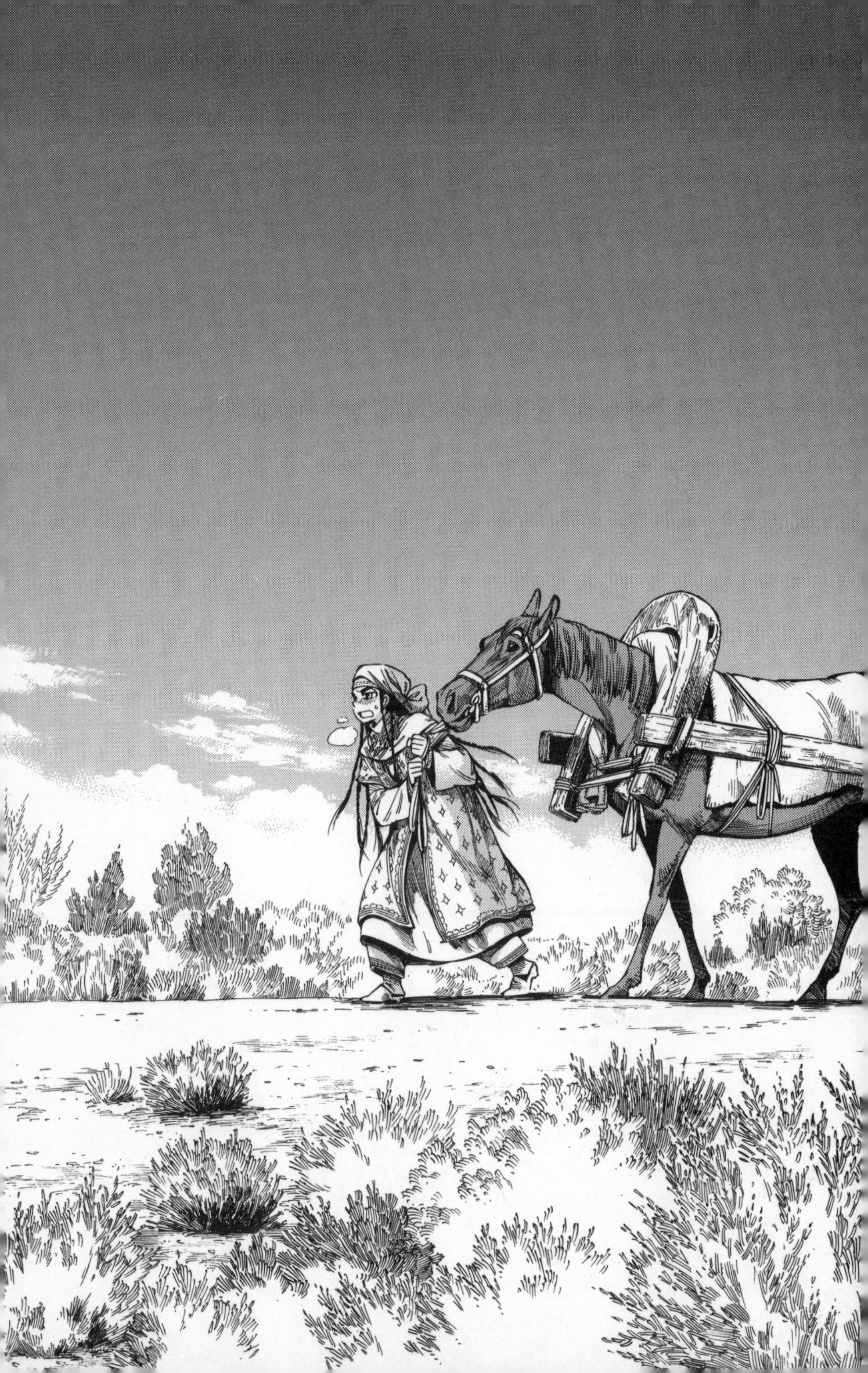

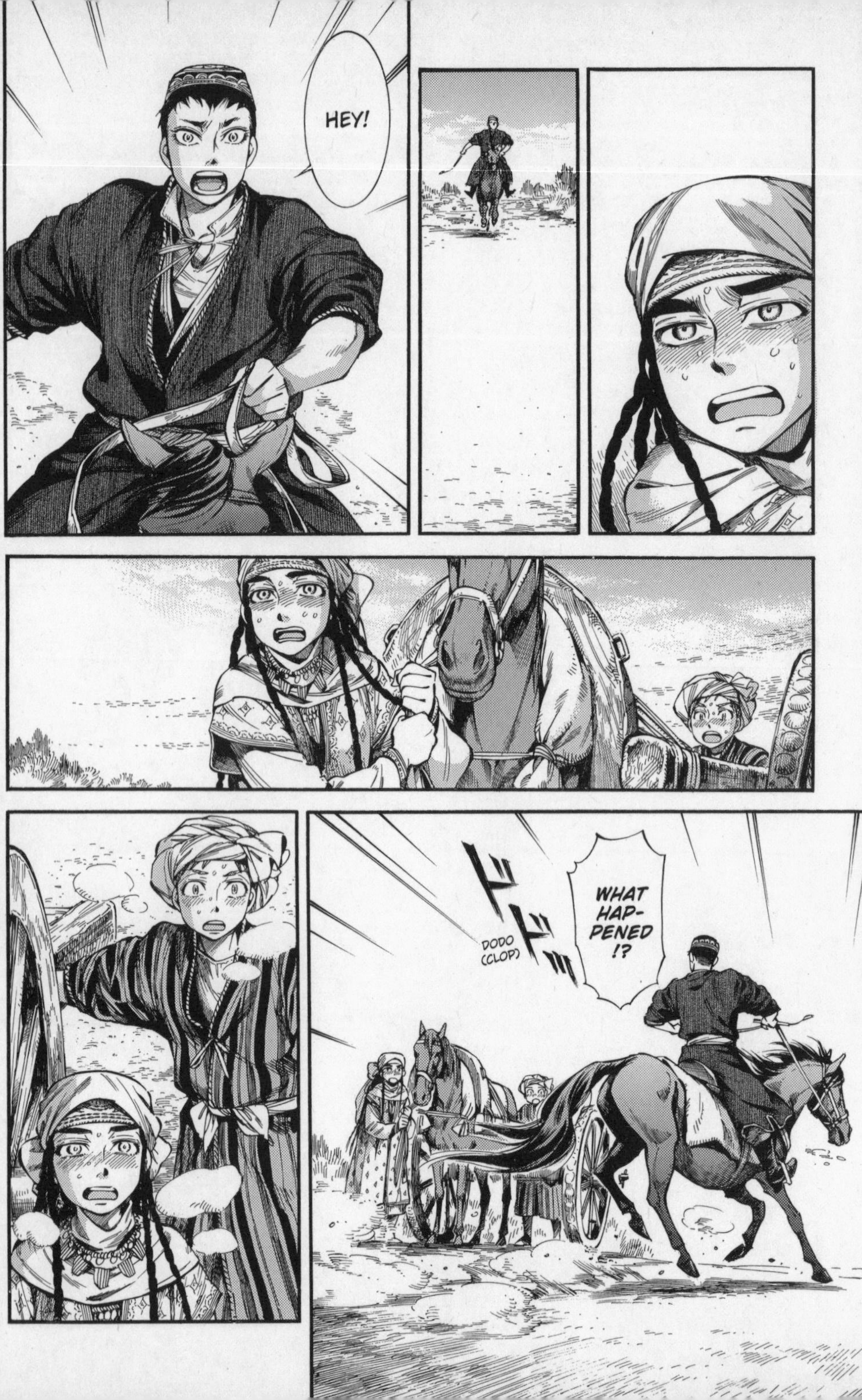
HEY!
WHAT HAP-PENED !?
ドドッ
DODO (CLOP)

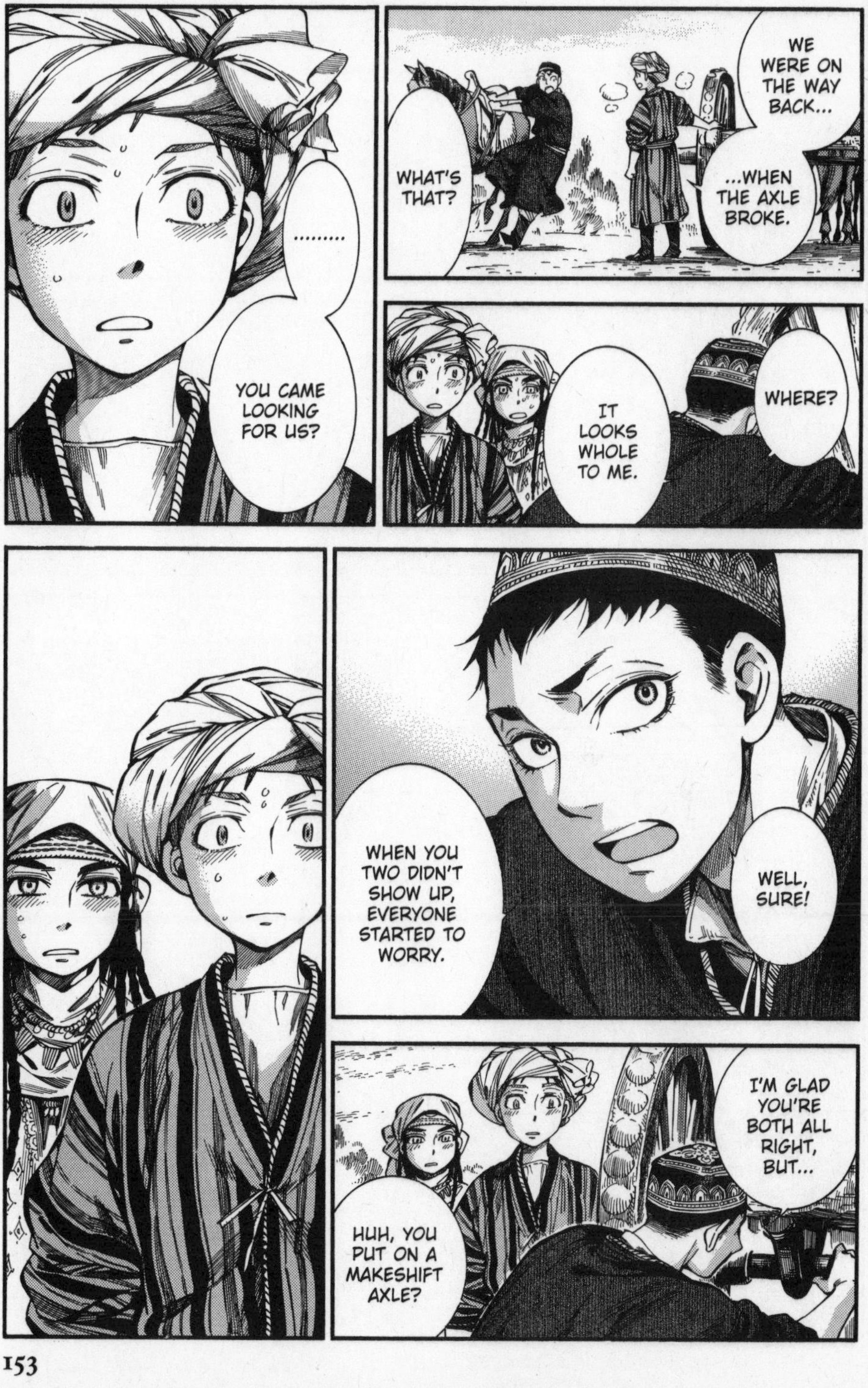
WE WERE ON THE WAY BACK...
...WHEN THE AXLE BROKE.
WHAT'S THAT?
WHERE?
IT LOOKS WHOLE TO ME.
....
YOU CAME LOOKING FOR US?
WELL, SURE!
WHEN YOU TWO DIDN'T SHOW UP, EVERYONE STARTED TO WORRY.
I'M GLAD YOU'RE BOTH ALL RIGHT, BUT...
HUH, YOU PUT ON A MAKESHIFT AXLE?

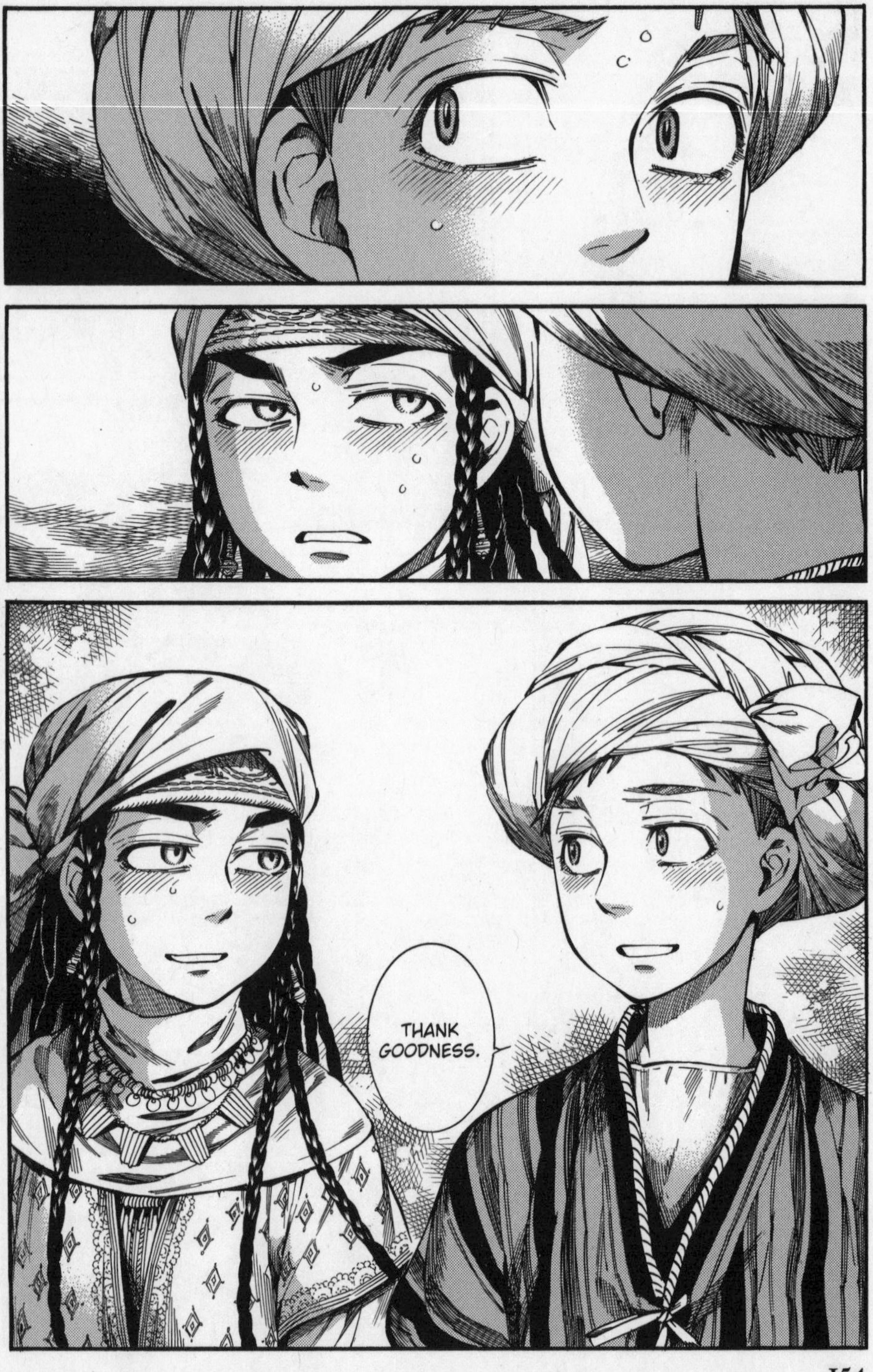
THANK GOODNESS.

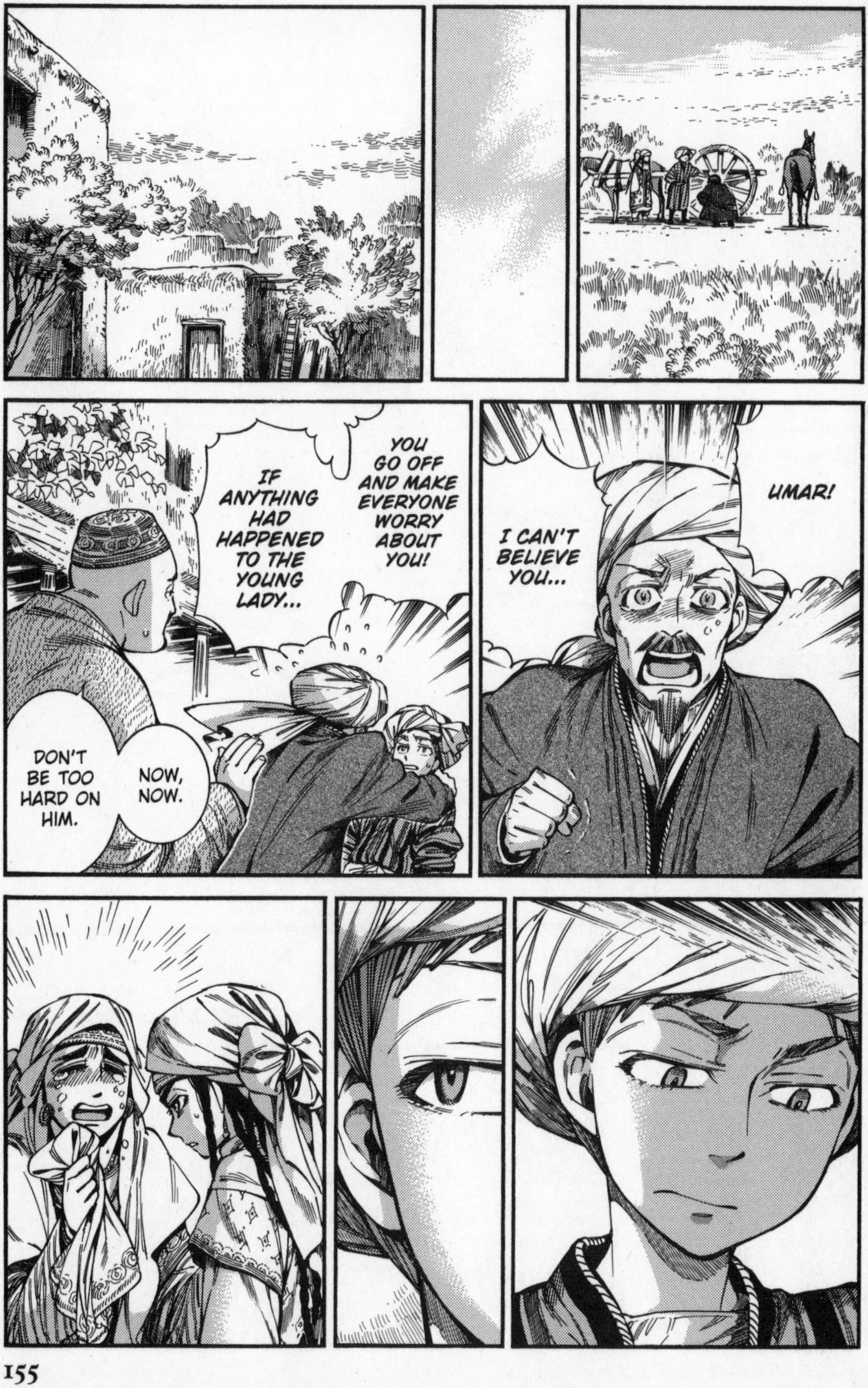
UMAR!
I CAN'T BELIEVE YOU...
YOU GO OFF AND MAKE EVERYONE WORRY ABOUT YOU!
IF ANYTHING HAD HAPPENED TO THE YOUNG LADY...
NOW, NOW.
DON'T BE TOO HARD ON HIM.

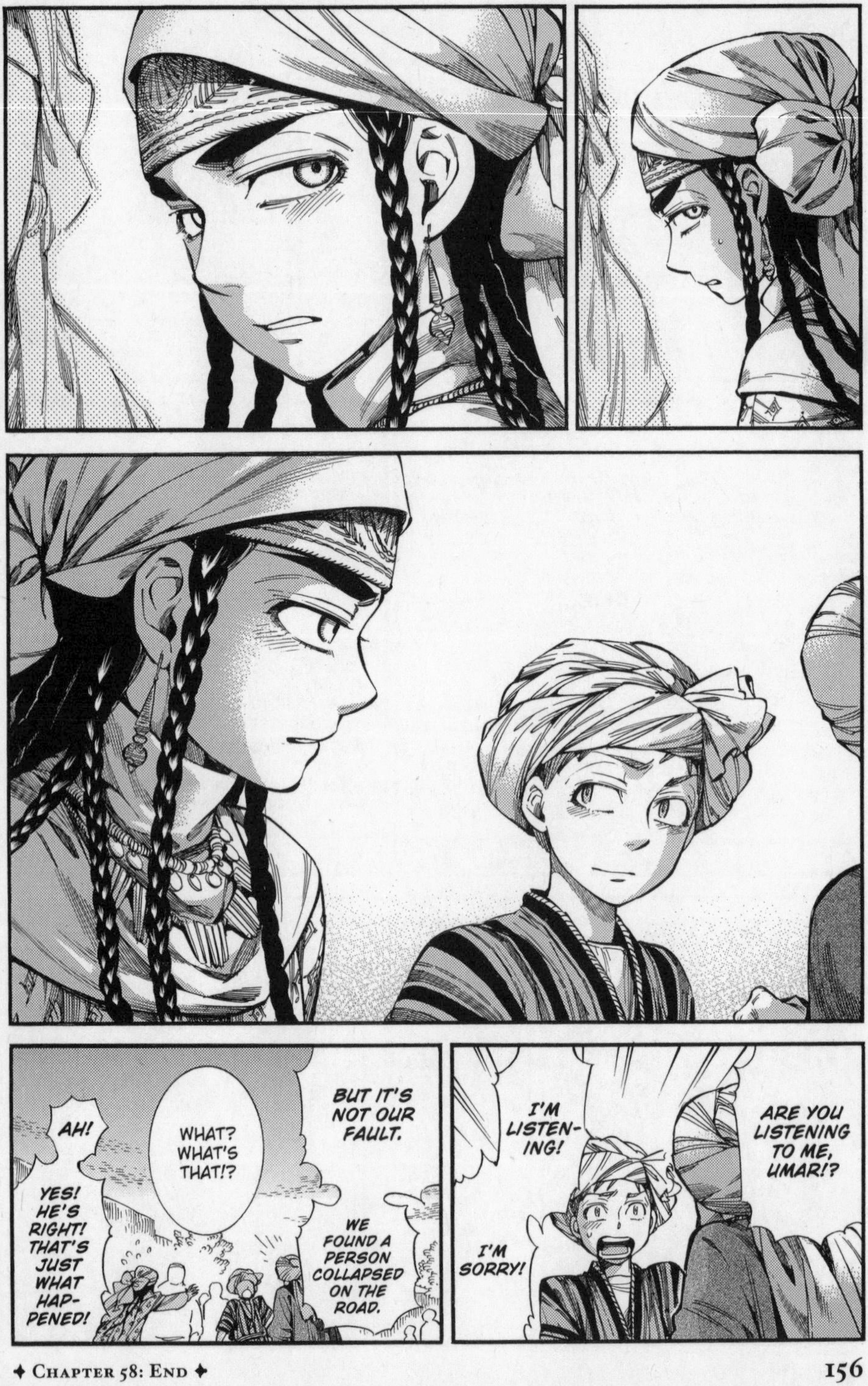
ARE YOU LISTENING TO ME, UMAR!?
I'M LISTEN-ING!
I'M SORRY!
BUT IT'S NOT OUR FAULT.
WE FOUND A PERSON COLLAPSED ON THE ROAD.
WHAT? WHAT'S THAT!?
AH!
YES! HE'S RIGHT! THAT'S JUST WHAT HAP-PENED!

✦ Chapter 58: End ✦

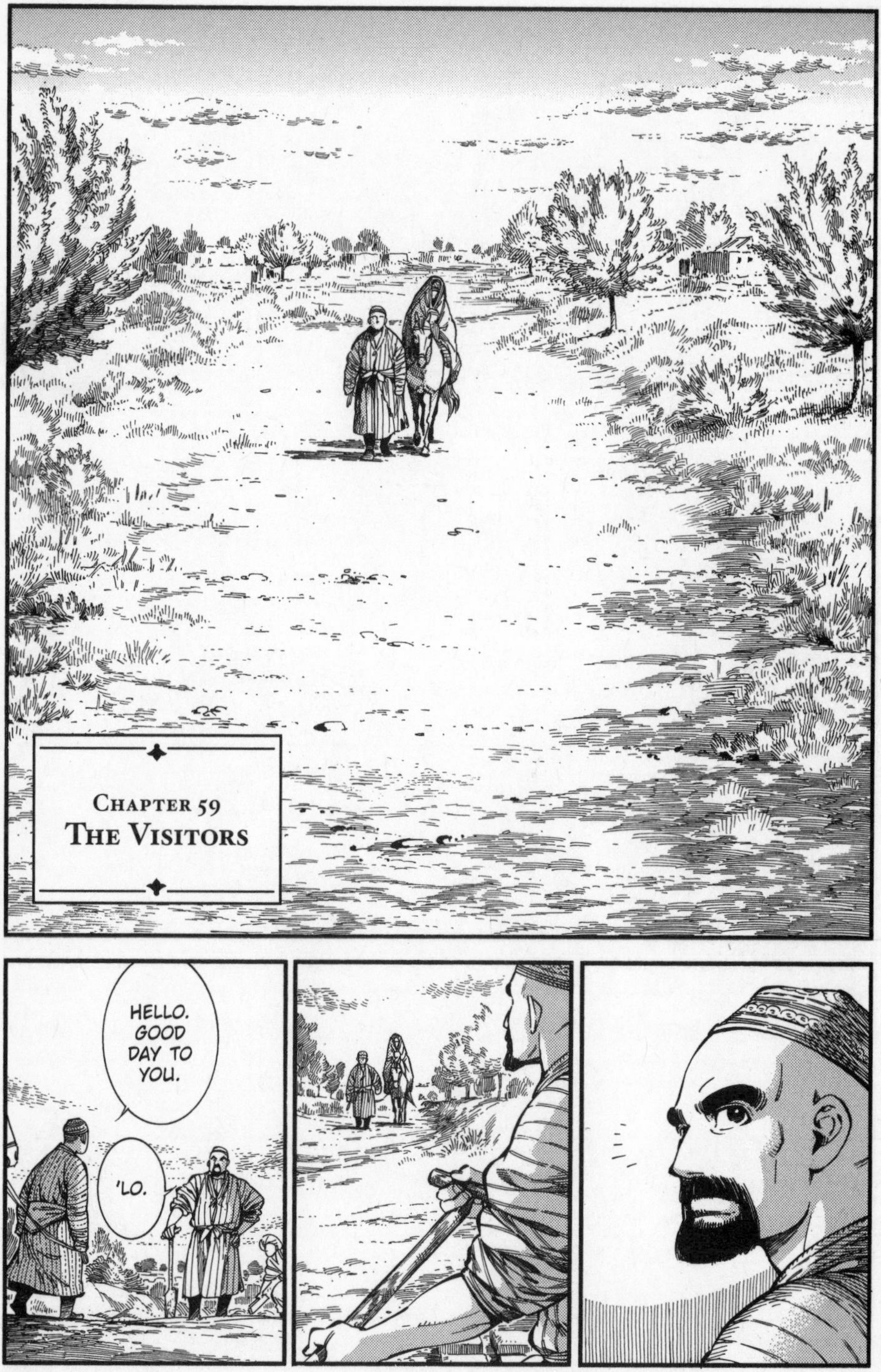
Chapter 59
The Visitors
HELLO. GOOD DAY TO YOU.
'LO.

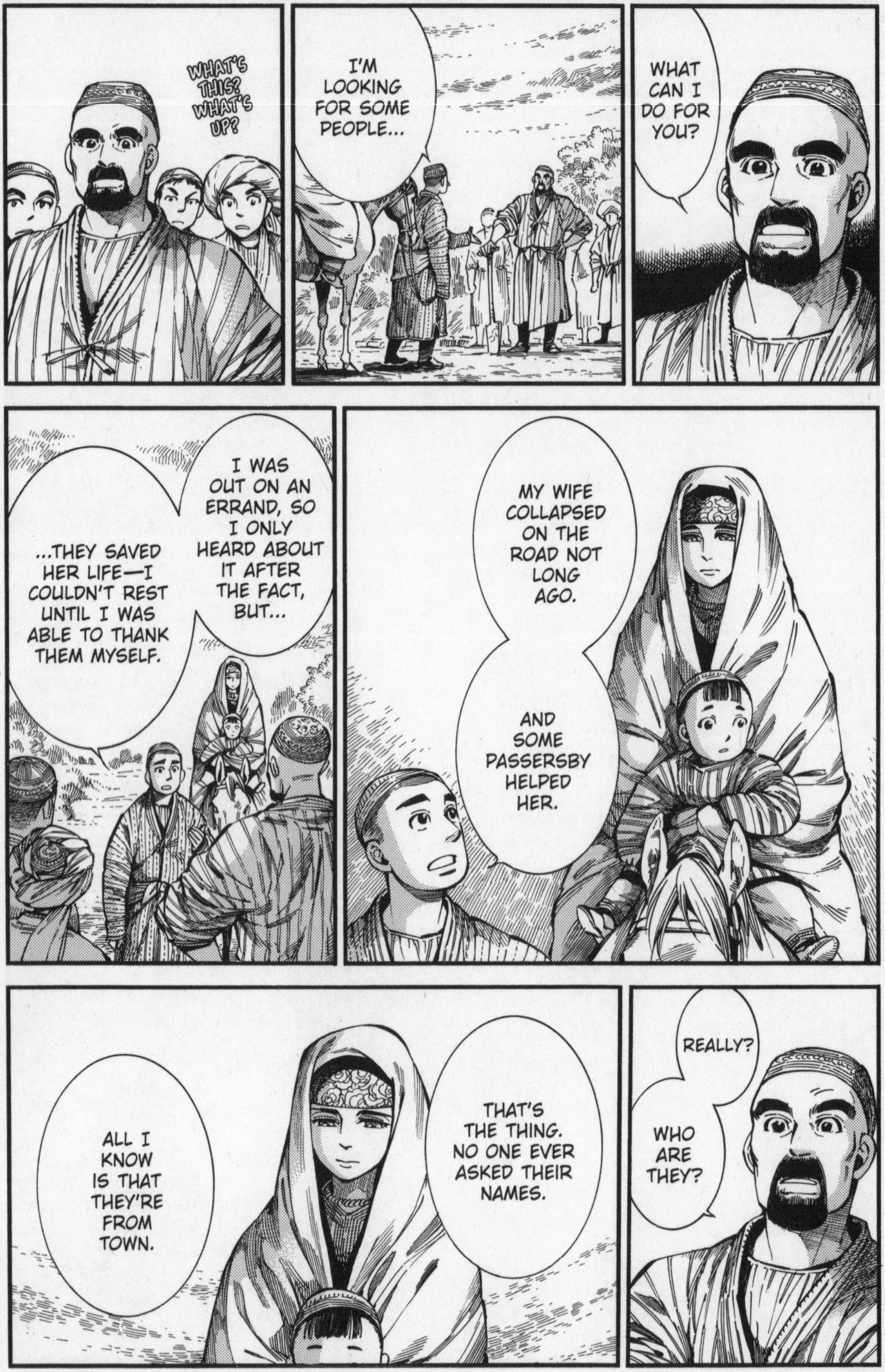
WHAT CAN I DO FOR YOU?
I'M LOOKING FOR SOME PEOPLE...
WHAT'S THIS? WHAT'S UP?
MY WIFE COLLAPSED ON THE ROAD NOT LONG AGO.
AND SOME PASSERSBY HELPED HER.
I WAS OUT ON AN ERRAND, SO I ONLY HEARD ABOUT IT AFTER THE FACT, BUT...
...THEY SAVED HER LIFE—I COULDN'T REST UNTIL I WAS ABLE TO THANK THEM MYSELF.
REALLY?
WHO ARE THEY?
THAT'S THE THING. NO ONE EVER ASKED THEIR NAMES.
ALL I KNOW IS THAT THEY'RE FROM TOWN.

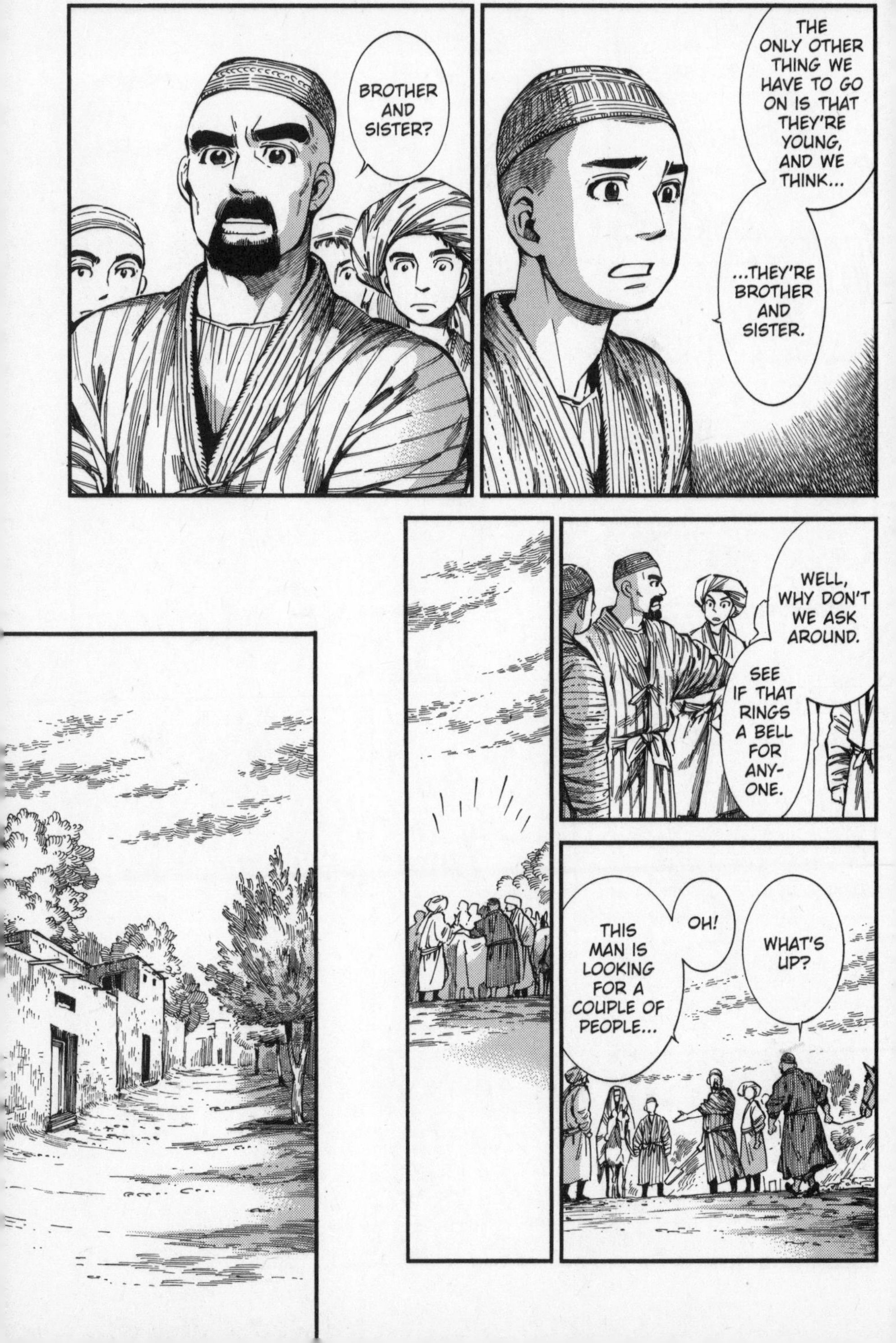
THE ONLY OTHER THING WE HAVE TO GO ON IS THAT THEY'RE YOUNG, AND WE THINK...
...THEY'RE BROTHER AND SISTER.
BROTHER AND SISTER?
WELL, WHY DON'T WE ASK AROUND.
SEE IF THAT RINGS A BELL FOR ANY-ONE.
WHAT'S UP?
OH!
THIS MAN IS LOOKING FOR A COUPLE OF PEOPLE...

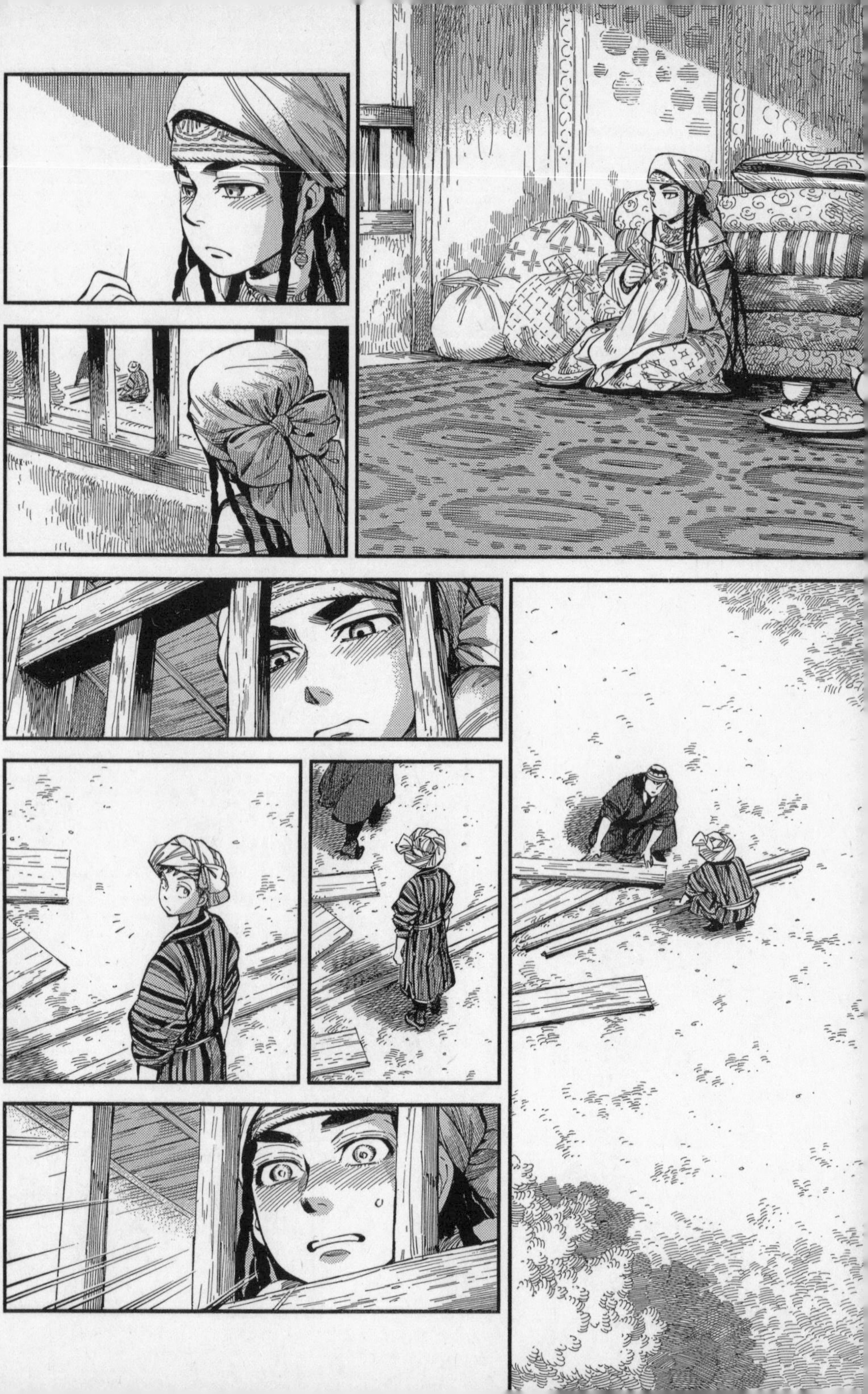

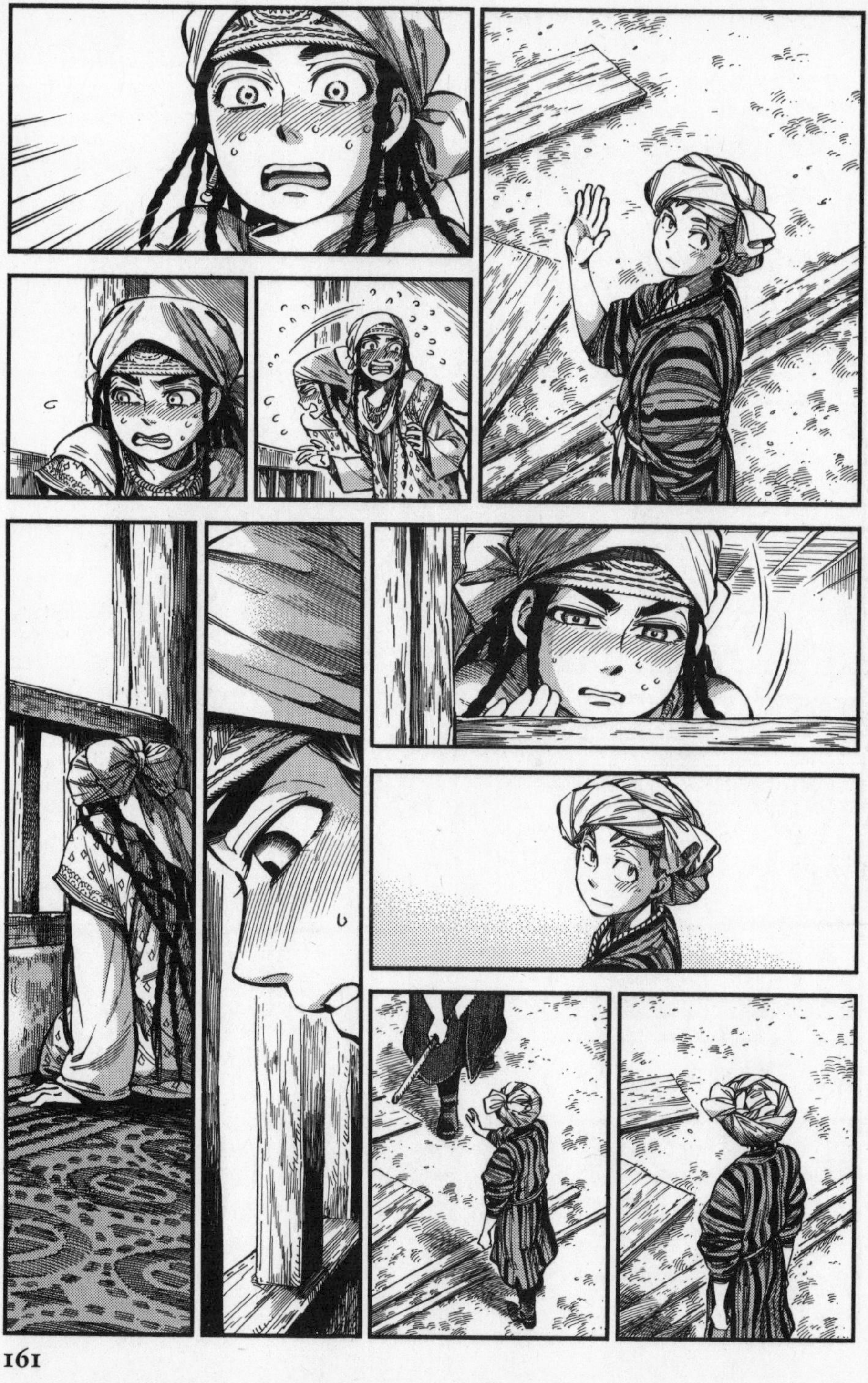

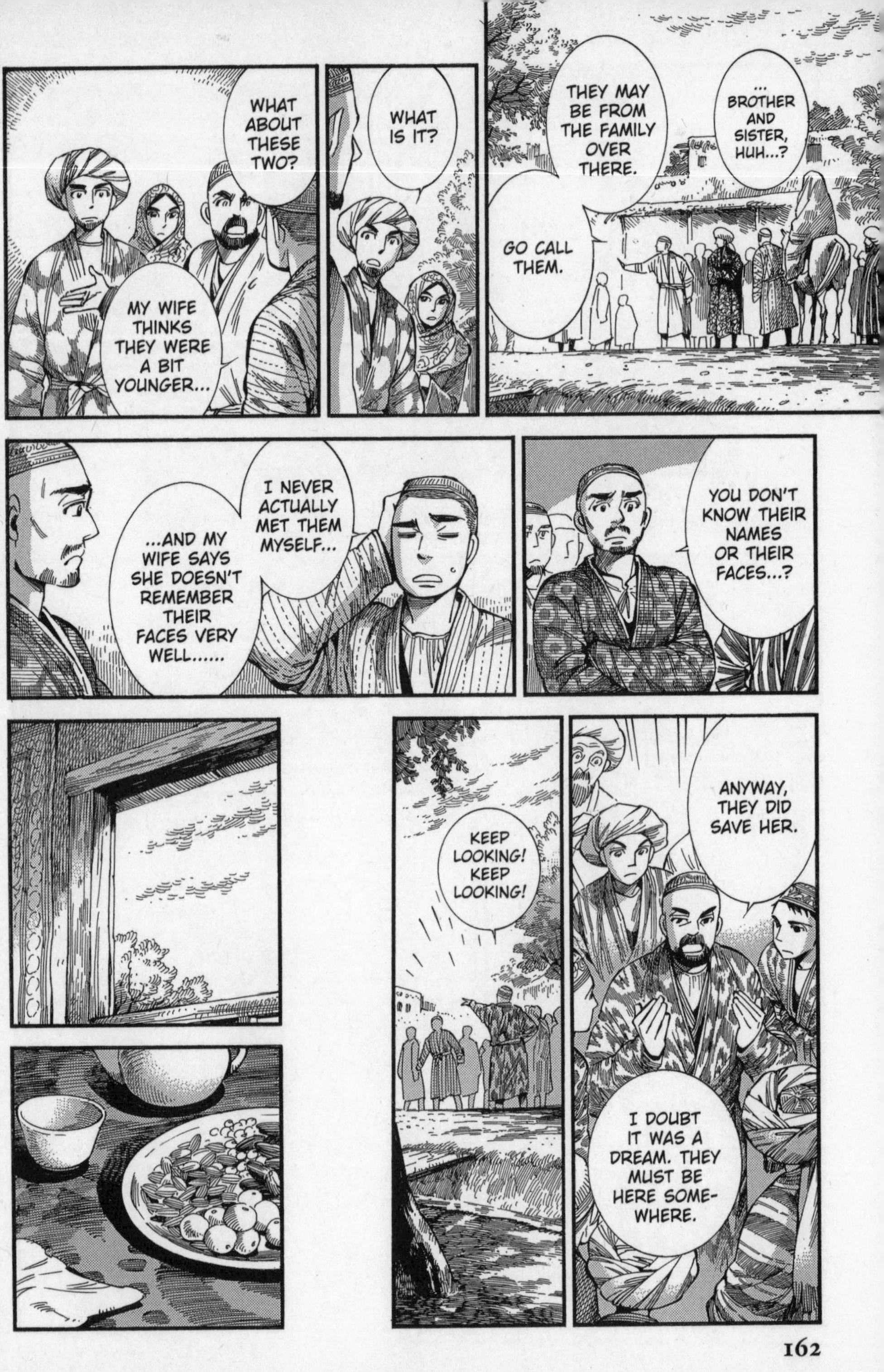
...BROTHER AND SISTER, HUH...?
THEY MAY BE FROM THE FAMILY OVER THERE.
GO CALL THEM.
WHAT IS IT?
WHAT ABOUT THESE TWO?
MY WIFE THINKS THEY WERE A BIT YOUNGER...
YOU DON'T KNOW THEIR NAMES OR THEIR FACES...?
I NEVER ACTUALLY MET THEM MYSELF...
...AND MY WIFE SAYS SHE DOESN'T REMEMBER THEIR FACES VERY WELL......
ANYWAY, THEY DID SAVE HER.
I DOUBT IT WAS A DREAM. THEY MUST BE HERE SOME-WHERE.
KEEP LOOKING! KEEP LOOKING!

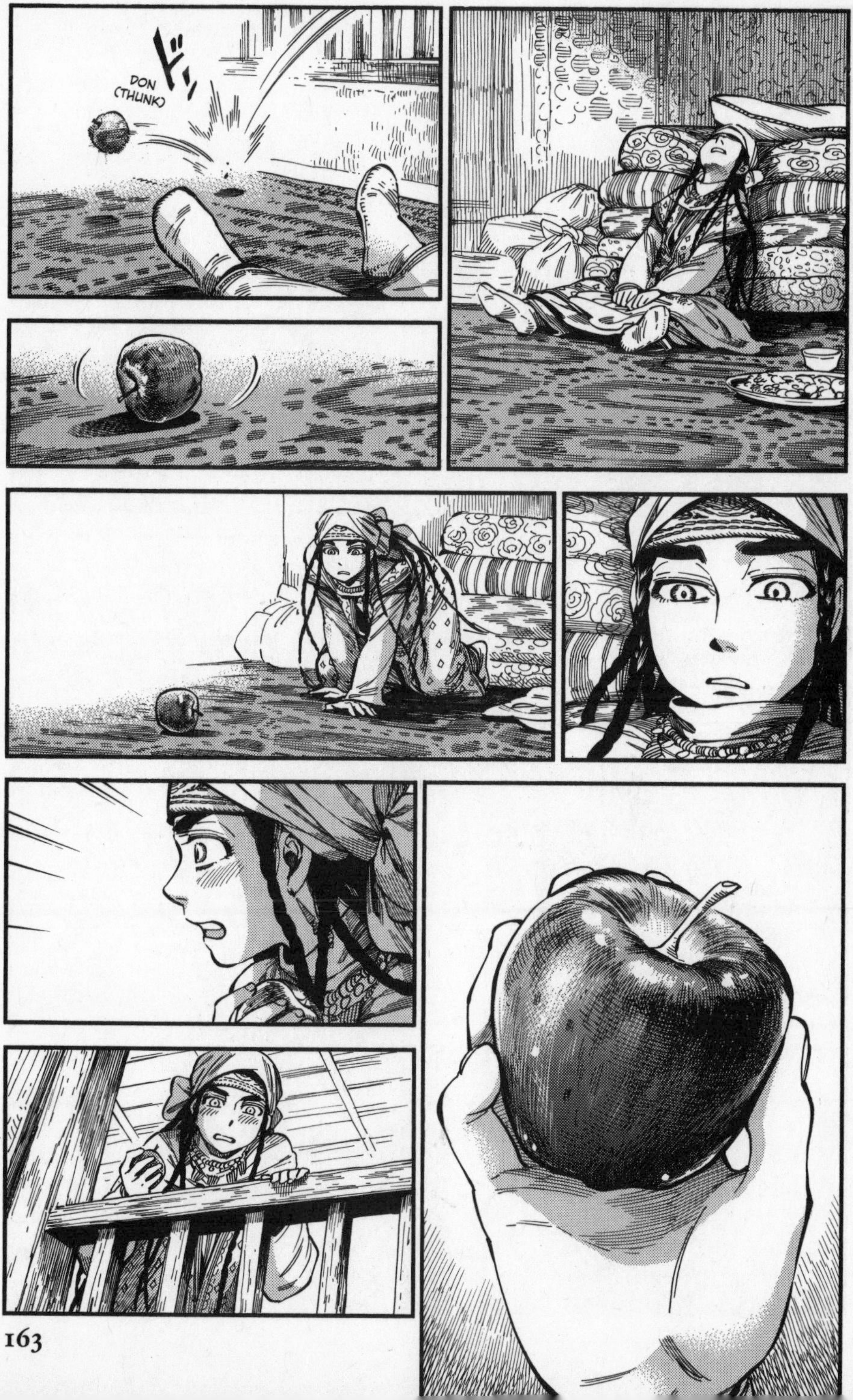
ドッ
DON (THUNK)

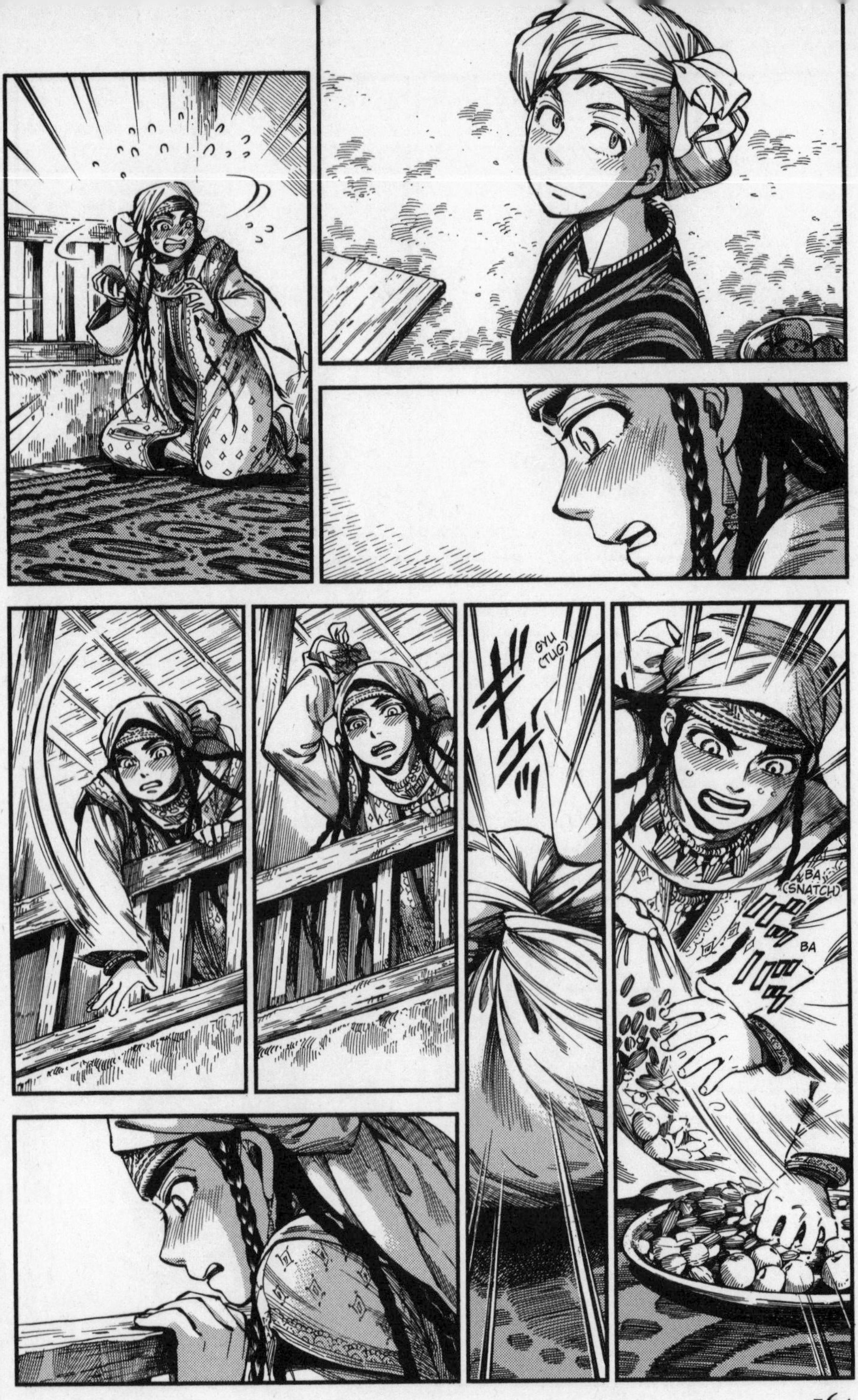
GYU (TUG)
BA (SNATCH)
BA

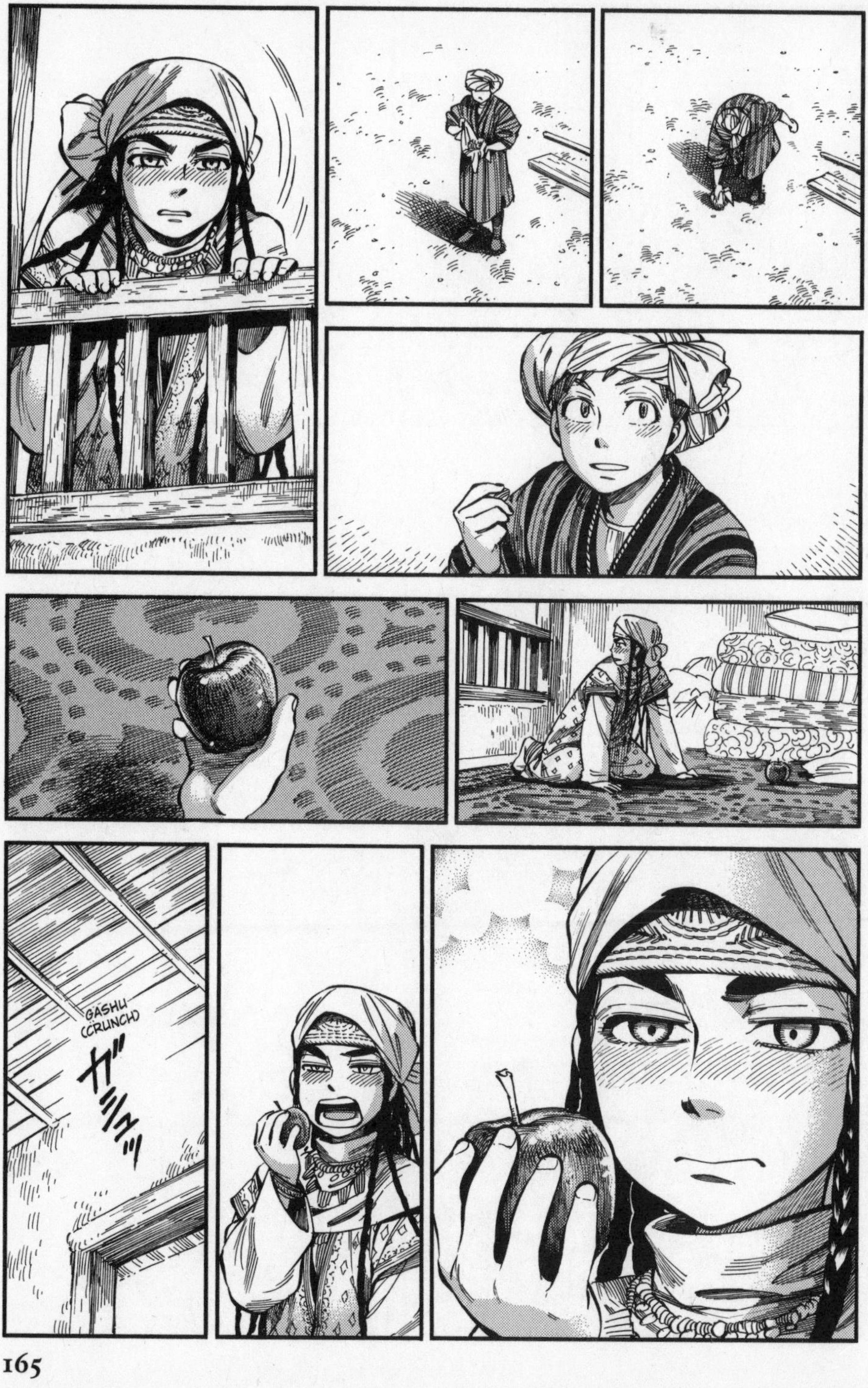
GASHU (CRUNCH)
ガシッ

SHAKU
SHAKU

SHAKU
SHAKU

GASHU
(CRUNCH)

SHAKU
(MUNCH)

SHAKU
SHAKU

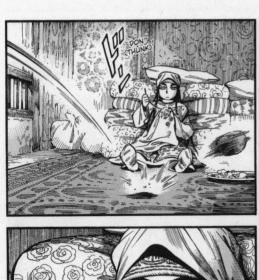

DON
(THUNK)

PARA
(LAZE)

PARA

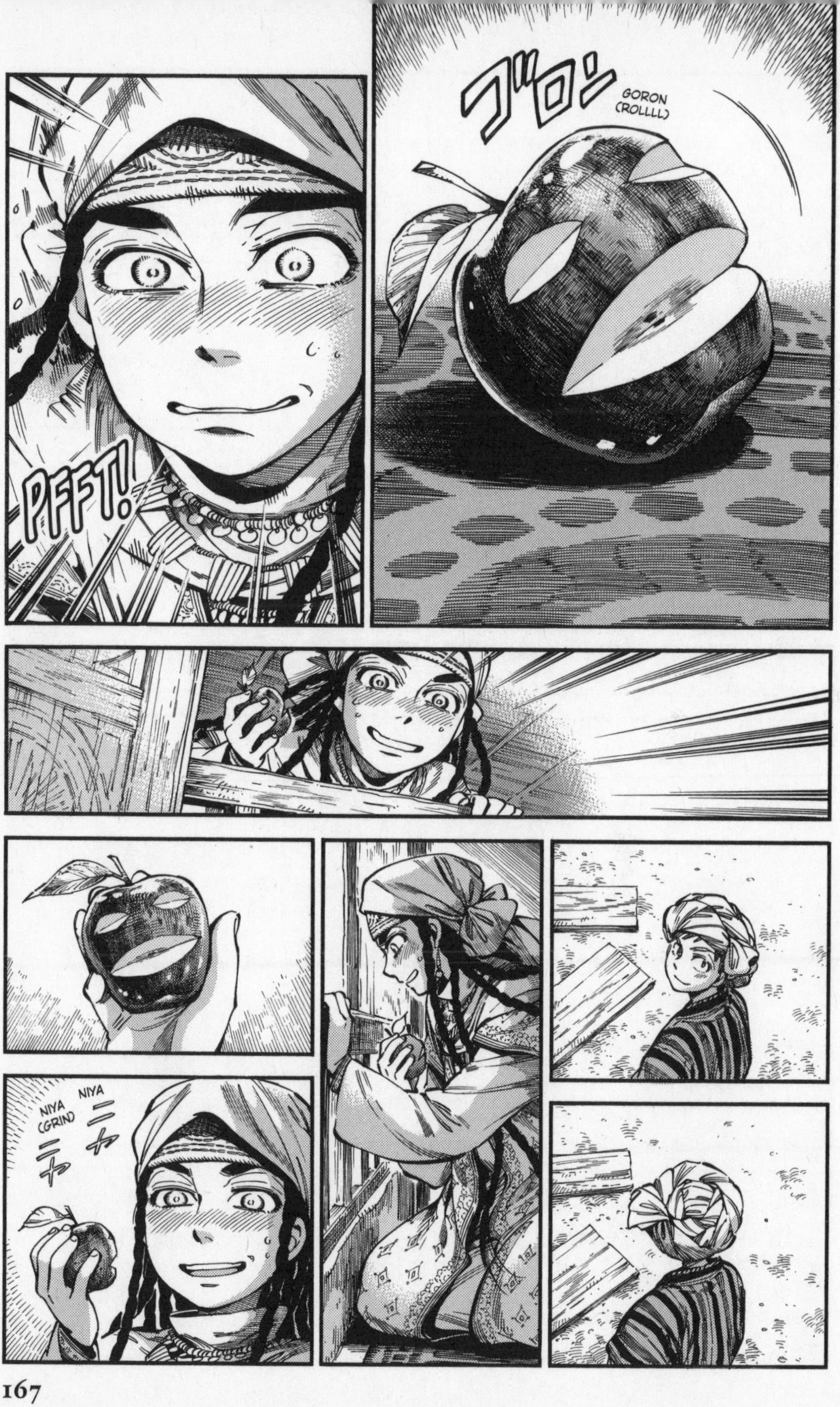
ゴロン
GORON (ROLLLL)
PFFT!
ニヤ ニヤ
NIYA NIYA (GRIND

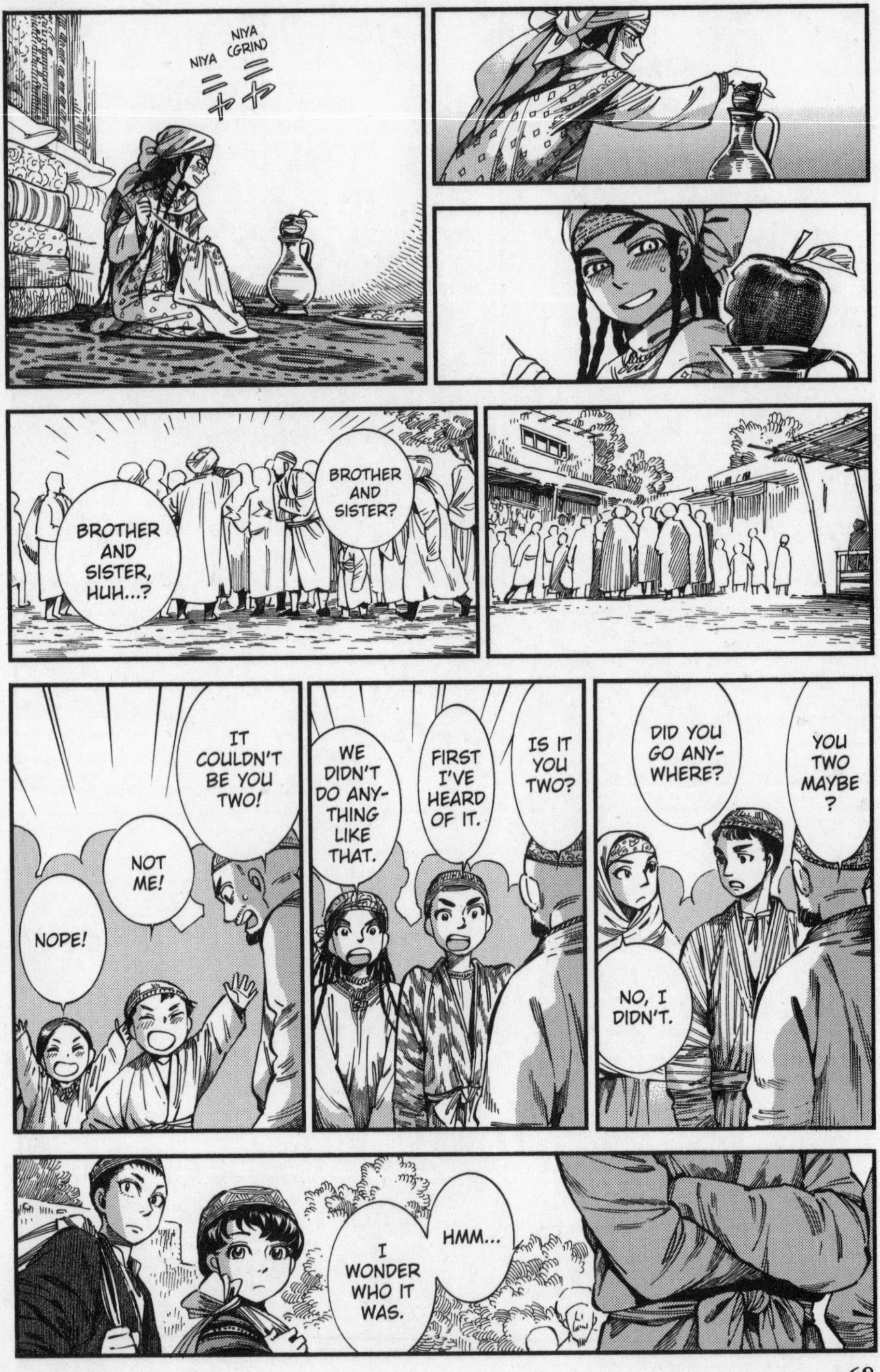
NIYA NIYA (GRIN)
ニヤニヤ
BROTHER AND SISTER?
BROTHER AND SISTER, HUH...?
YOU TWO MAYBE?
DID YOU GO ANYWHERE?
NO, I DIDN'T.
IS IT YOU TWO?
FIRST I'VE HEARD OF IT.
WE DIDN'T DO ANYTHING LIKE THAT.
IT COULDN'T BE YOU TWO!
NOT ME!
NOPE!
HMM...
I WONDER WHO IT WAS.

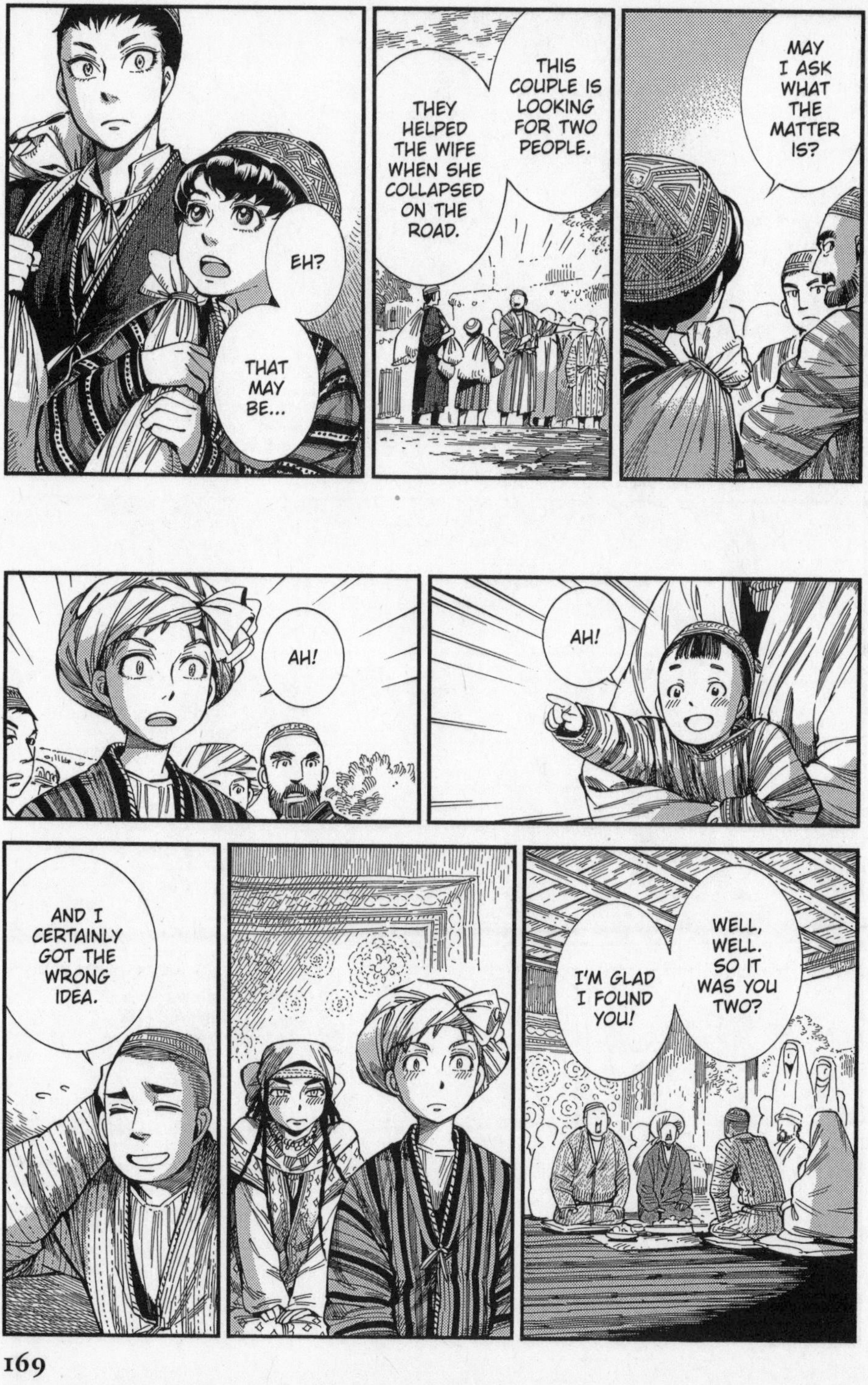
MAY I ASK WHAT THE MATTER IS?
THIS COUPLE IS LOOKING FOR TWO PEOPLE.
THEY HELPED THE WIFE WHEN SHE COLLAPSED ON THE ROAD.
EH?
THAT MAY BE...
AH!
AH!
WELL, WELL. SO IT WAS YOU TWO?
I'M GLAD I FOUND YOU!
AND I CERTAINLY GOT THE WRONG IDEA.

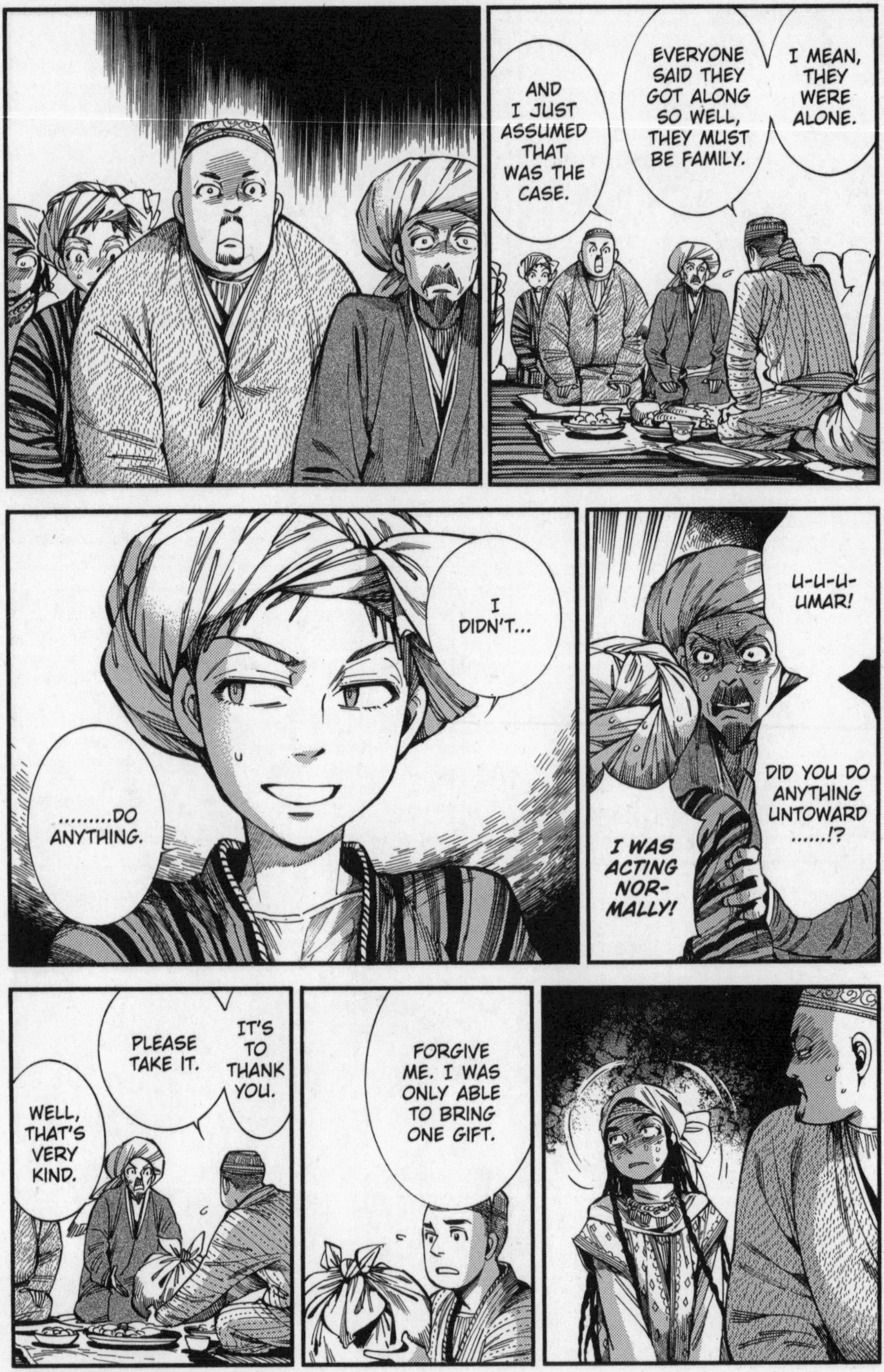
I MEAN, THEY WERE ALONE.
EVERYONE SAID THEY GOT ALONG SO WELL, THEY MUST BE FAMILY.
AND I JUST ASSUMED THAT WAS THE CASE.
U-U-U-UMAR!
DID YOU DO ANYTHING UNTOWARD ......!?
I WAS ACTING NOR-MALLY!
I DIDN'T...
.........DO ANYTHING.
FORGIVE ME. I WAS ONLY ABLE TO BRING ONE GIFT.
IT'S TO THANK YOU.
PLEASE TAKE IT.
WELL, THAT'S VERY KIND.

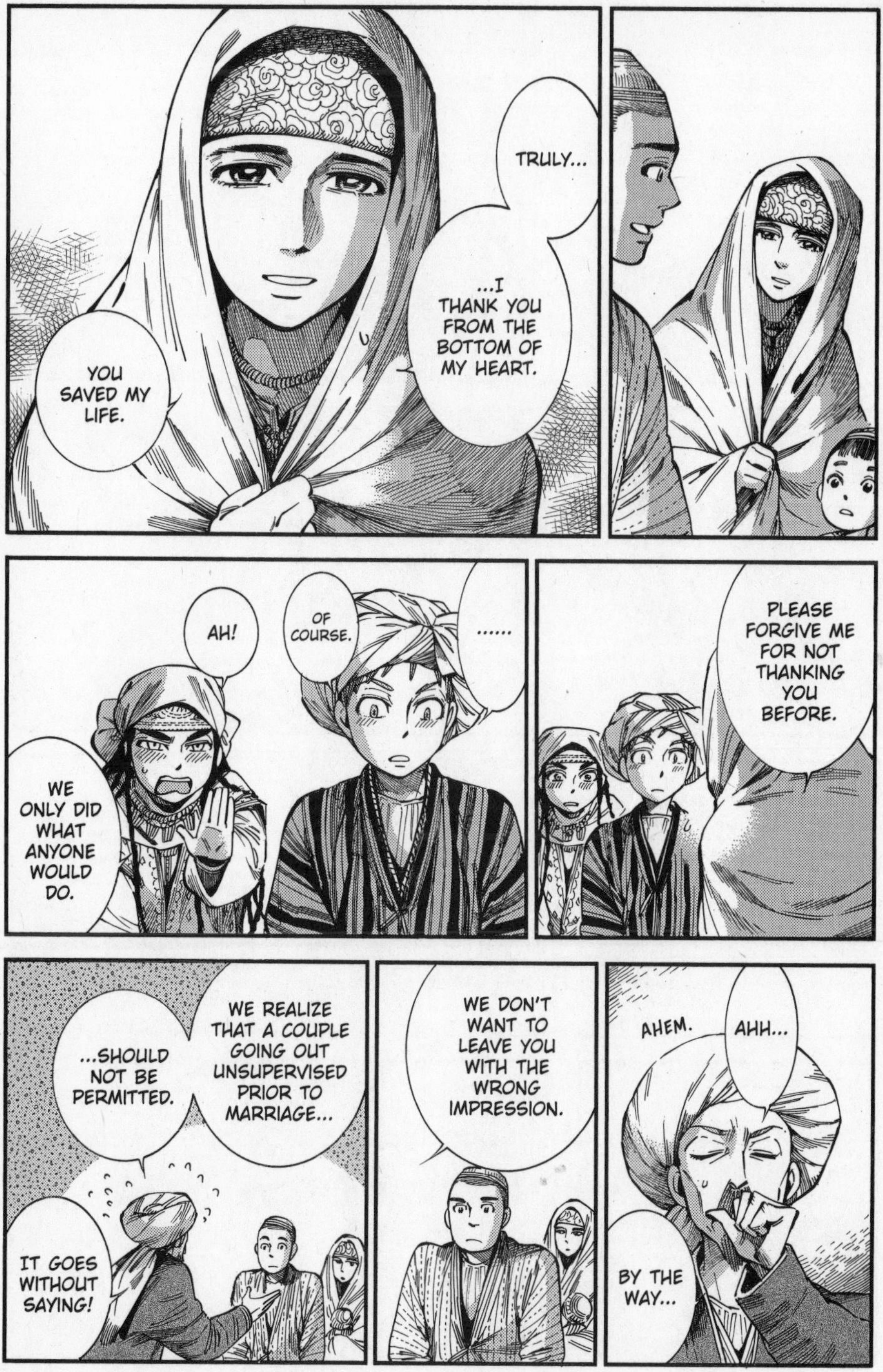
TRULY...
...I THANK YOU FROM THE BOTTOM OF MY HEART.
YOU SAVED MY LIFE.
PLEASE FORGIVE ME FOR NOT THANKING YOU BEFORE.
......
OF COURSE.
AH!
WE ONLY DID WHAT ANYONE WOULD DO.
AHH...
AHEM.
BY THE WAY...
WE DON'T WANT TO LEAVE YOU WITH THE WRONG IMPRESSION.
WE REALIZE THAT A COUPLE GOING OUT UNSUPERVISED PRIOR TO MARRIAGE...
...SHOULD NOT BE PERMITTED.
IT GOES WITHOUT SAYING!

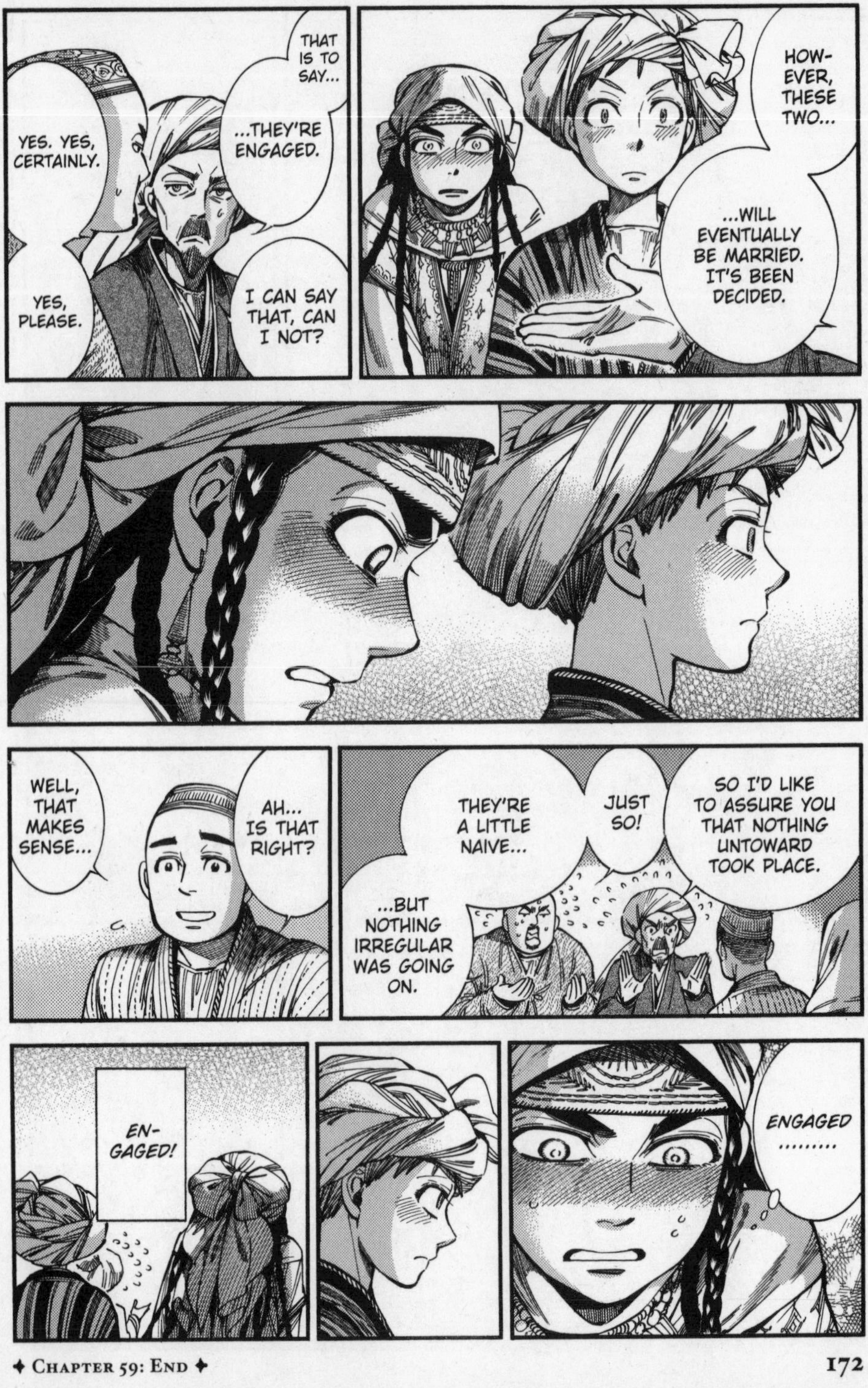
HOW-EVER, THESE TWO...
...WILL EVENTUALLY BE MARRIED. IT'S BEEN DECIDED.
THAT IS TO SAY...
...THEY'RE ENGAGED.
YES. YES, CERTAINLY.
I CAN SAY THAT, CAN I NOT?
YES, PLEASE.
SO I'D LIKE TO ASSURE YOU THAT NOTHING UNTOWARD TOOK PLACE.
JUST SO!
THEY'RE A LITTLE NAIVE...
...BUT NOTHING IRREGULAR WAS GOING ON.
AH... IS THAT RIGHT?
WELL, THAT MAKES SENSE...
ENGAGED ....
EN-GAGED!

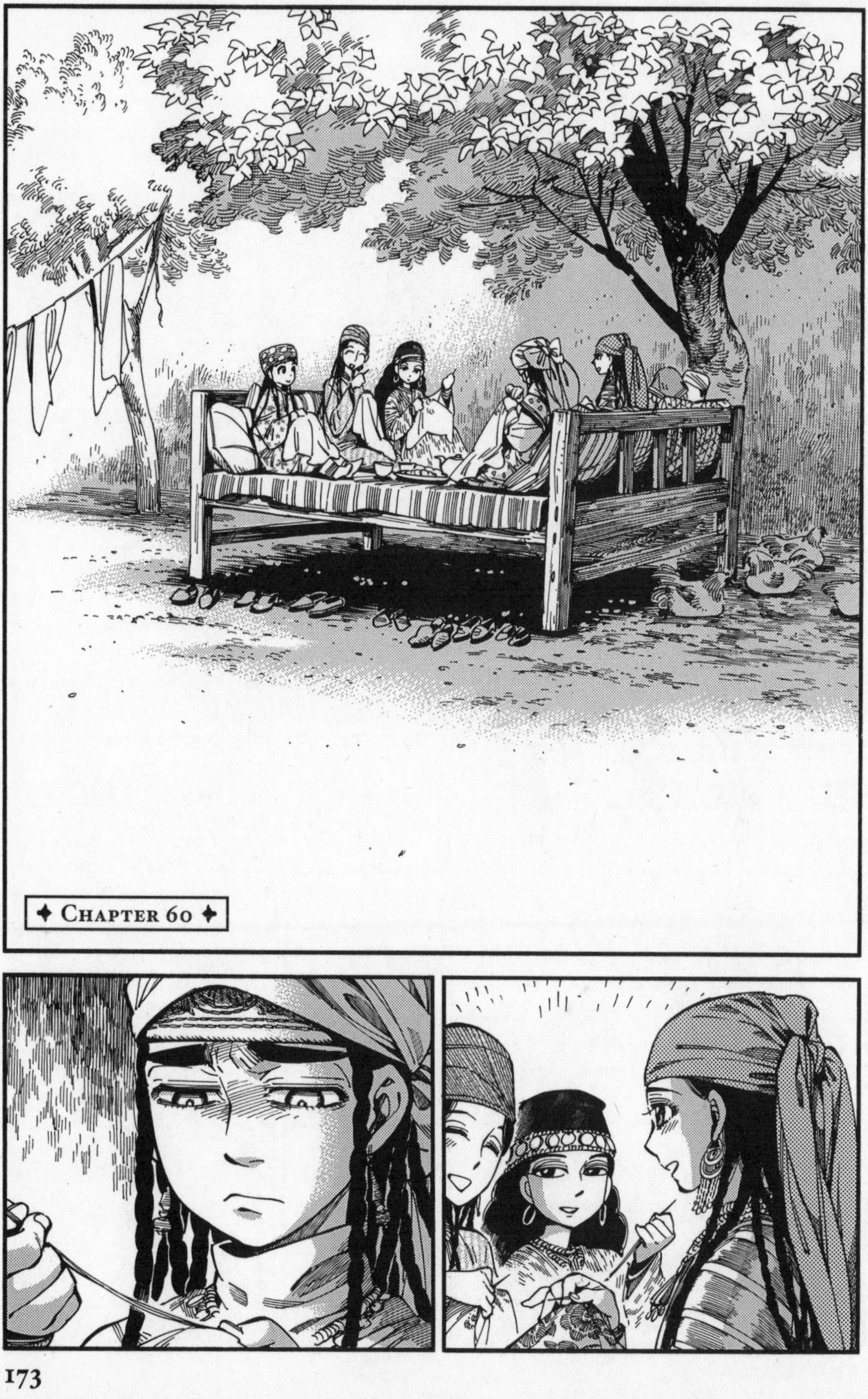
✦ Chapter 60 ✦

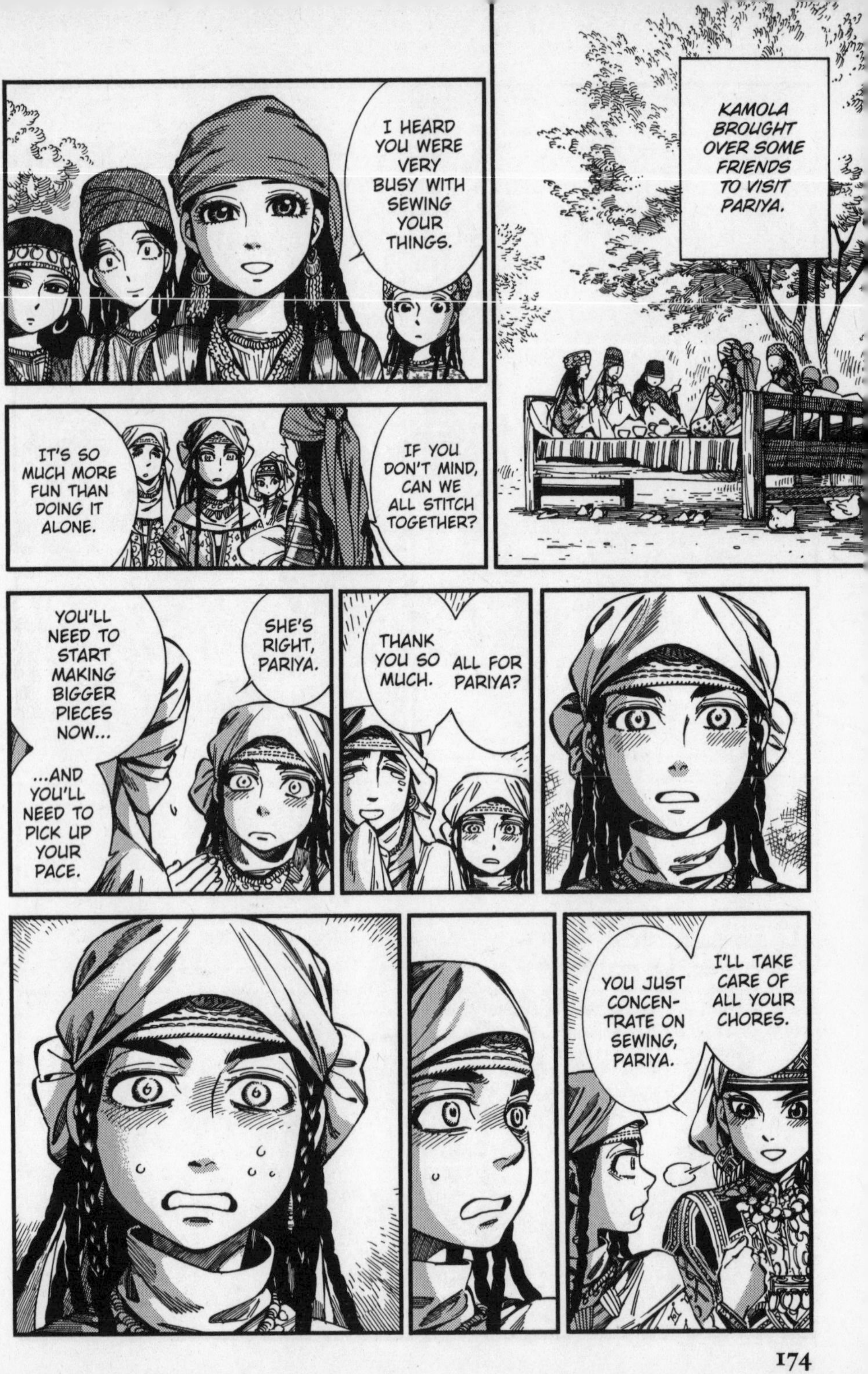
KAMOLA BROUGHT OVER SOME FRIENDS TO VISIT PARIYA.
I HEARD YOU WERE VERY BUSY WITH SEWING YOUR THINGS.
IF YOU DON'T MIND, CAN WE ALL STITCH TOGETHER?
IT'S SO MUCH MORE FUN THAN DOING IT ALONE.
ALL FOR PARIYA?
THANK YOU SO MUCH.
SHE'S RIGHT, PARIYA.
YOU'LL NEED TO START MAKING BIGGER PIECES NOW...
...AND YOU'LL NEED TO PICK UP YOUR PACE.
I'LL TAKE CARE OF ALL YOUR CHORES.
YOU JUST CONCENTRATE ON SEWING, PARIYA.

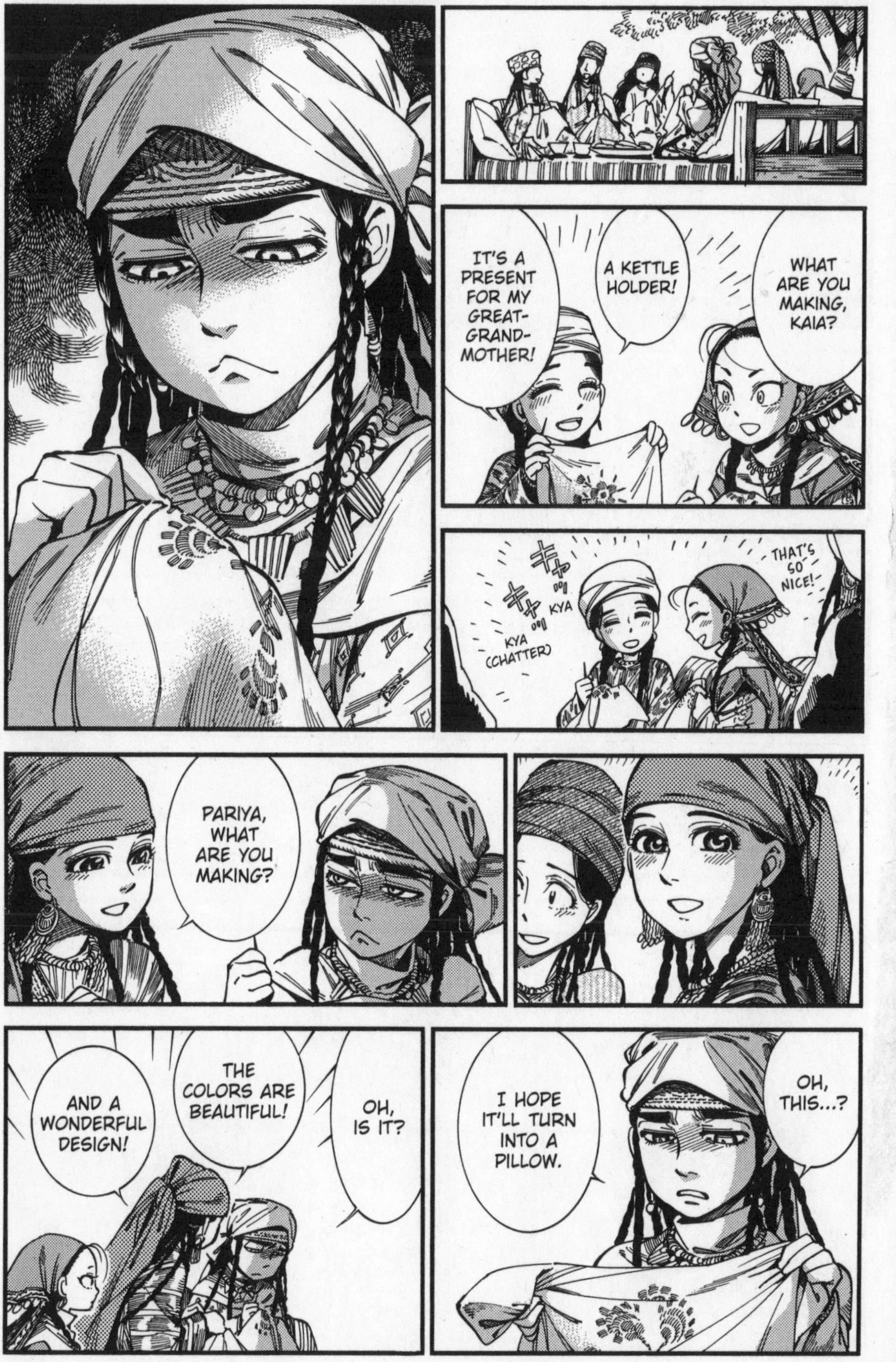
WHAT ARE YOU MAKING, KAIA?
A KETTLE HOLDER!
IT'S A PRESENT FOR MY GREAT-GRANDMOTHER!
THAT'S SO NICE!
KYA
KYA (CHATTER)
PARIYA, WHAT ARE YOU MAKING?
OH, THIS...?
I HOPE IT'LL TURN INTO A PILLOW.
OH, IS IT?
THE COLORS ARE BEAUTIFUL!
AND A WONDERFUL DESIGN!

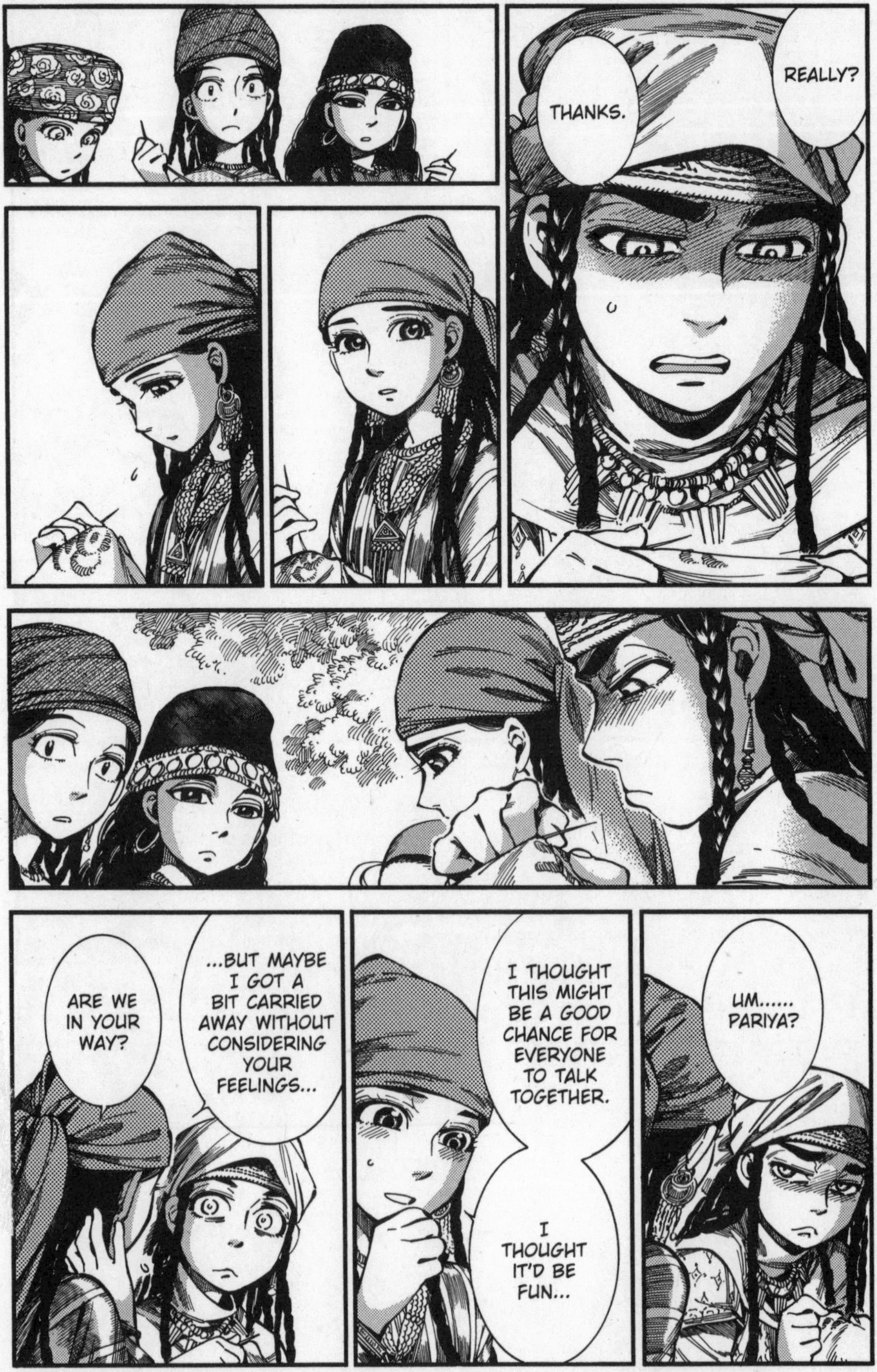
REALLY?
THANKS.
UM...... PARIYA?
I THOUGHT THIS MIGHT BE A GOOD CHANCE FOR EVERYONE TO TALK TOGETHER.
I THOUGHT IT'D BE FUN...
...BUT MAYBE I GOT A BIT CARRIED AWAY WITHOUT CONSIDERING YOUR FEELINGS...
ARE WE IN YOUR WAY?

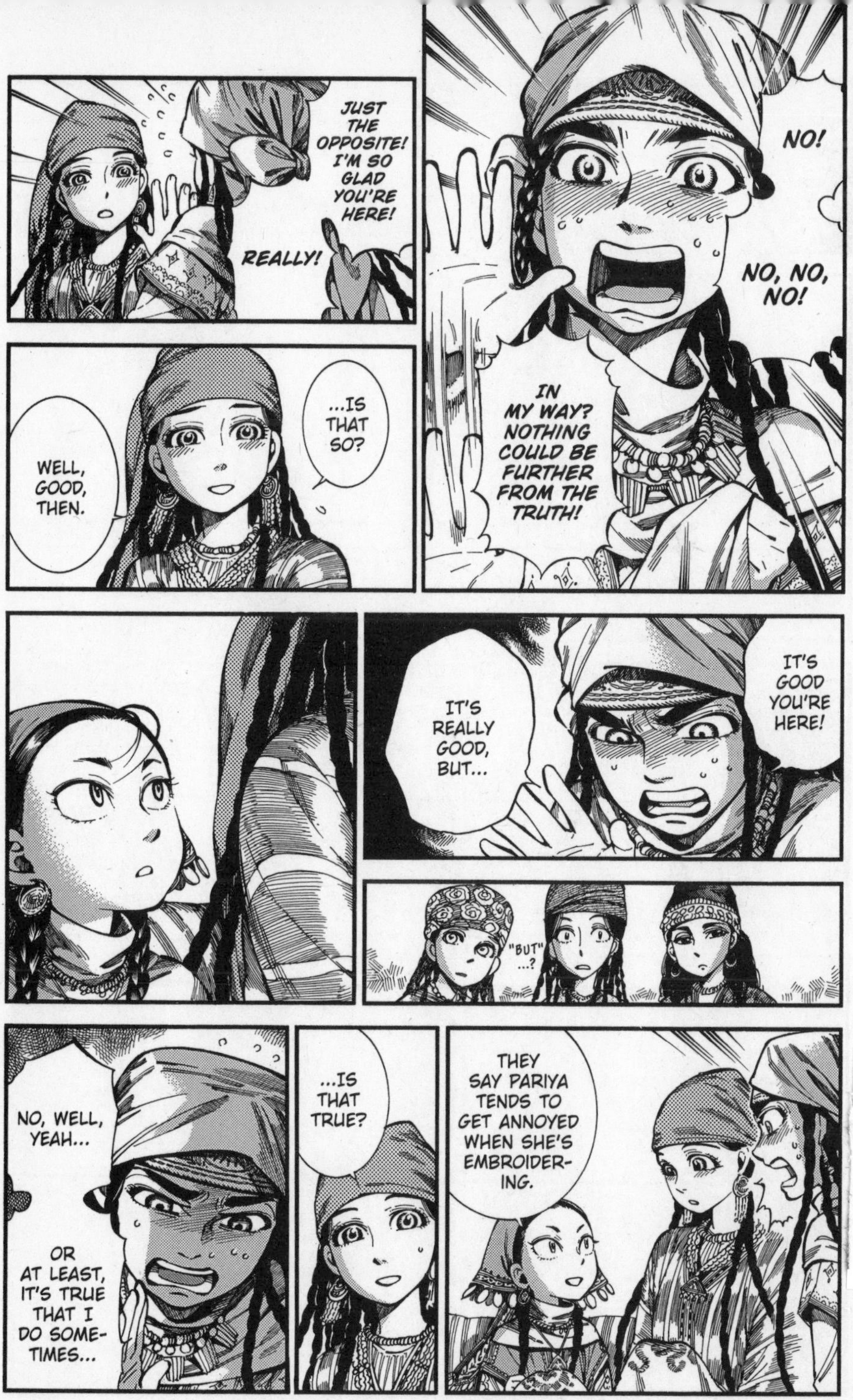
NO!
NO, NO, NO!
IN MY WAY? NOTHING COULD BE FURTHER FROM THE TRUTH!
JUST THE OPPOSITE! I'M SO GLAD YOU'RE HERE!
REALLY!
...IS THAT SO?
WELL, GOOD, THEN.
IT'S GOOD YOU'RE HERE!
IT'S REALLY GOOD, BUT...
"BUT" ...?
THEY SAY PARIYA TENDS TO GET ANNOYED WHEN SHE'S EMBROIDER-ING.
...IS THAT TRUE?
NO, WELL, YEAH...
OR AT LEAST, IT'S TRUE THAT I DO SOME-TIMES...

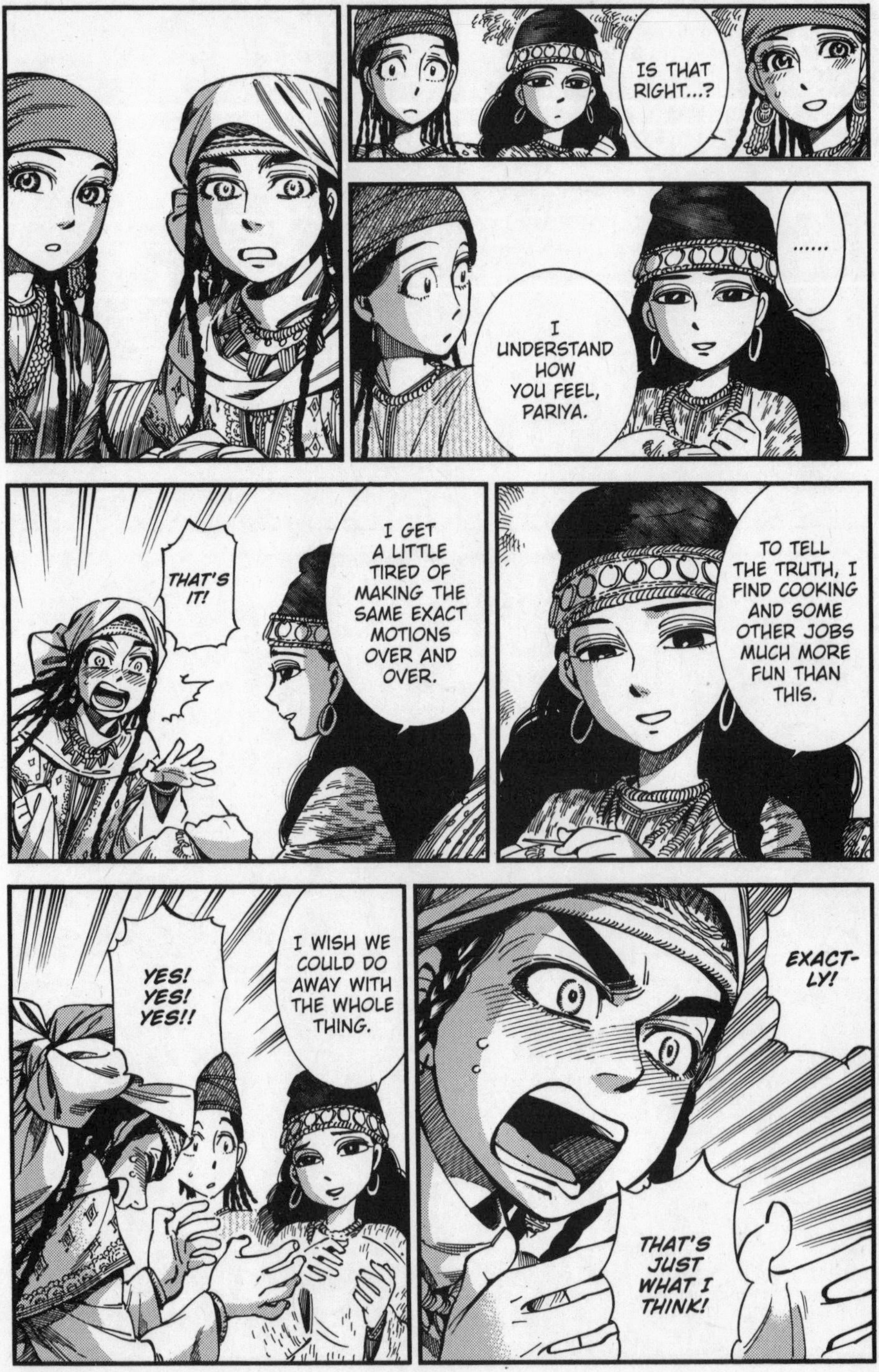
IS THAT RIGHT...?
......
I UNDERSTAND HOW YOU FEEL, PARIYA.
TO TELL THE TRUTH, I FIND COOKING AND SOME OTHER JOBS MUCH MORE FUN THAN THIS.
I GET A LITTLE TIRED OF MAKING THE SAME EXACT MOTIONS OVER AND OVER.
THAT'S IT!
EXACT-LY!
THAT'S JUST WHAT I THINK!
I WISH WE COULD DO AWAY WITH THE WHOLE THING.
YES! YES! YES!!

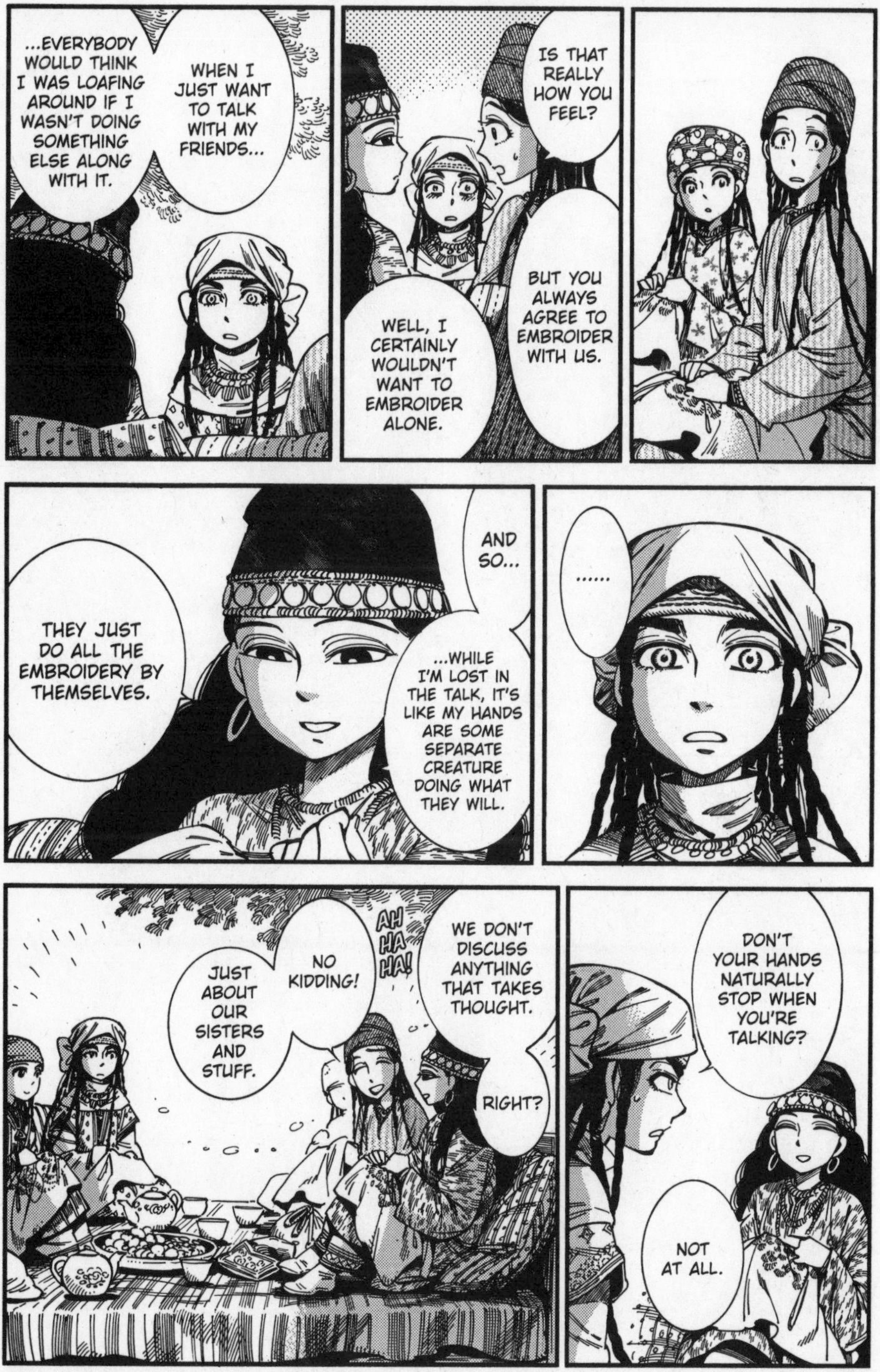
IS THAT REALLY HOW YOU FEEL?
BUT YOU ALWAYS AGREE TO EMBROIDER WITH US.
WELL, I CERTAINLY WOULDN'T WANT TO EMBROIDER ALONE.
WHEN I JUST WANT TO TALK WITH MY FRIENDS...
...EVERYBODY WOULD THINK I WAS LOAFING AROUND IF I WASN'T DOING SOMETHING ELSE ALONG WITH IT.
......
AND SO...
...WHILE I'M LOST IN THE TALK, IT'S LIKE MY HANDS ARE SOME SEPARATE CREATURE DOING WHAT THEY WILL.
THEY JUST DO ALL THE EMBROIDERY BY THEMSELVES.
DON'T YOUR HANDS NATURALLY STOP WHEN YOU'RE TALKING?
NOT AT ALL.
WE DON'T DISCUSS ANYTHING THAT TAKES THOUGHT.
RIGHT?
AH HA HA!
NO KIDDING!
JUST ABOUT OUR SISTERS AND STUFF.

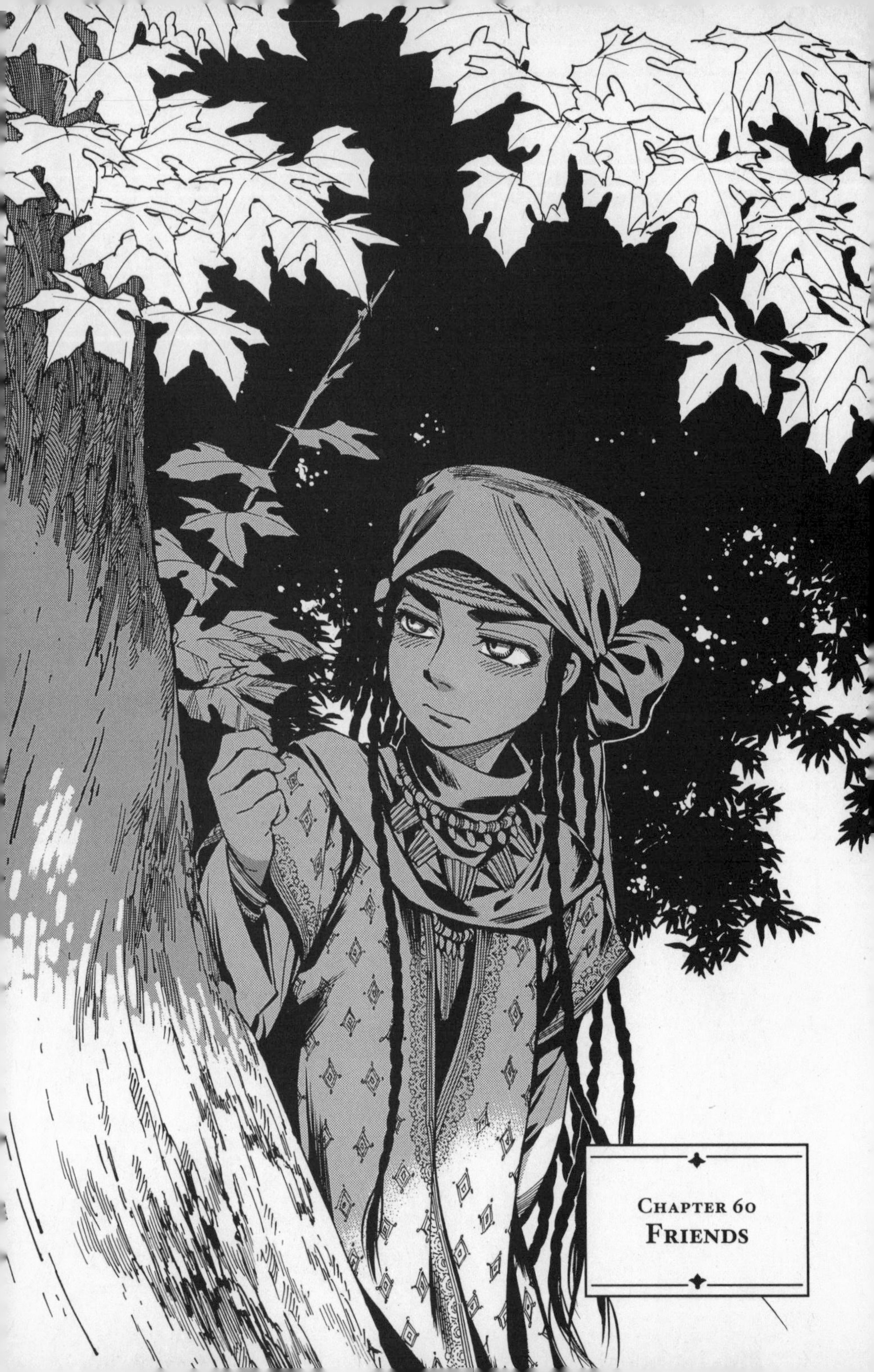
Chapter 60
Friends

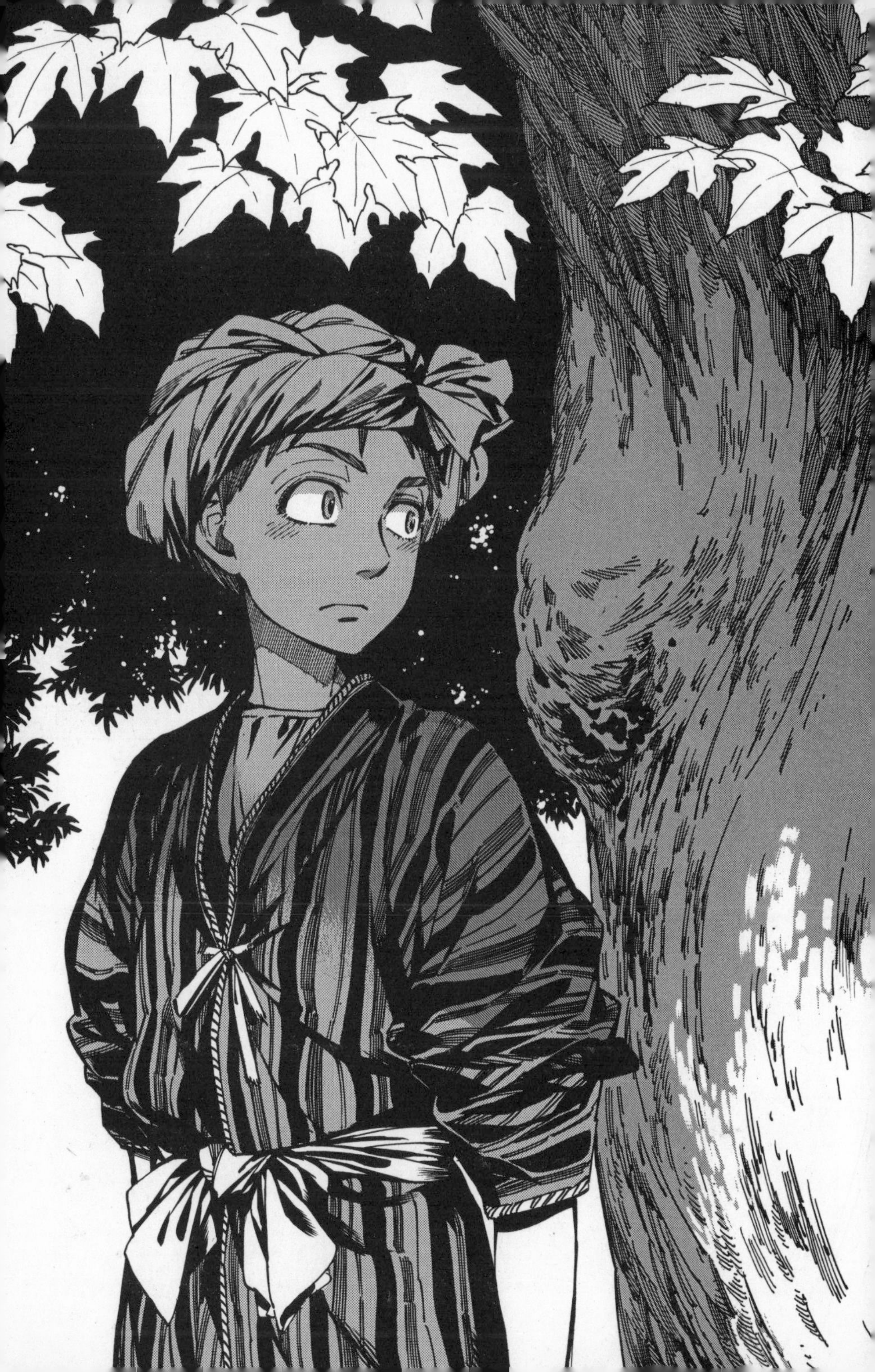

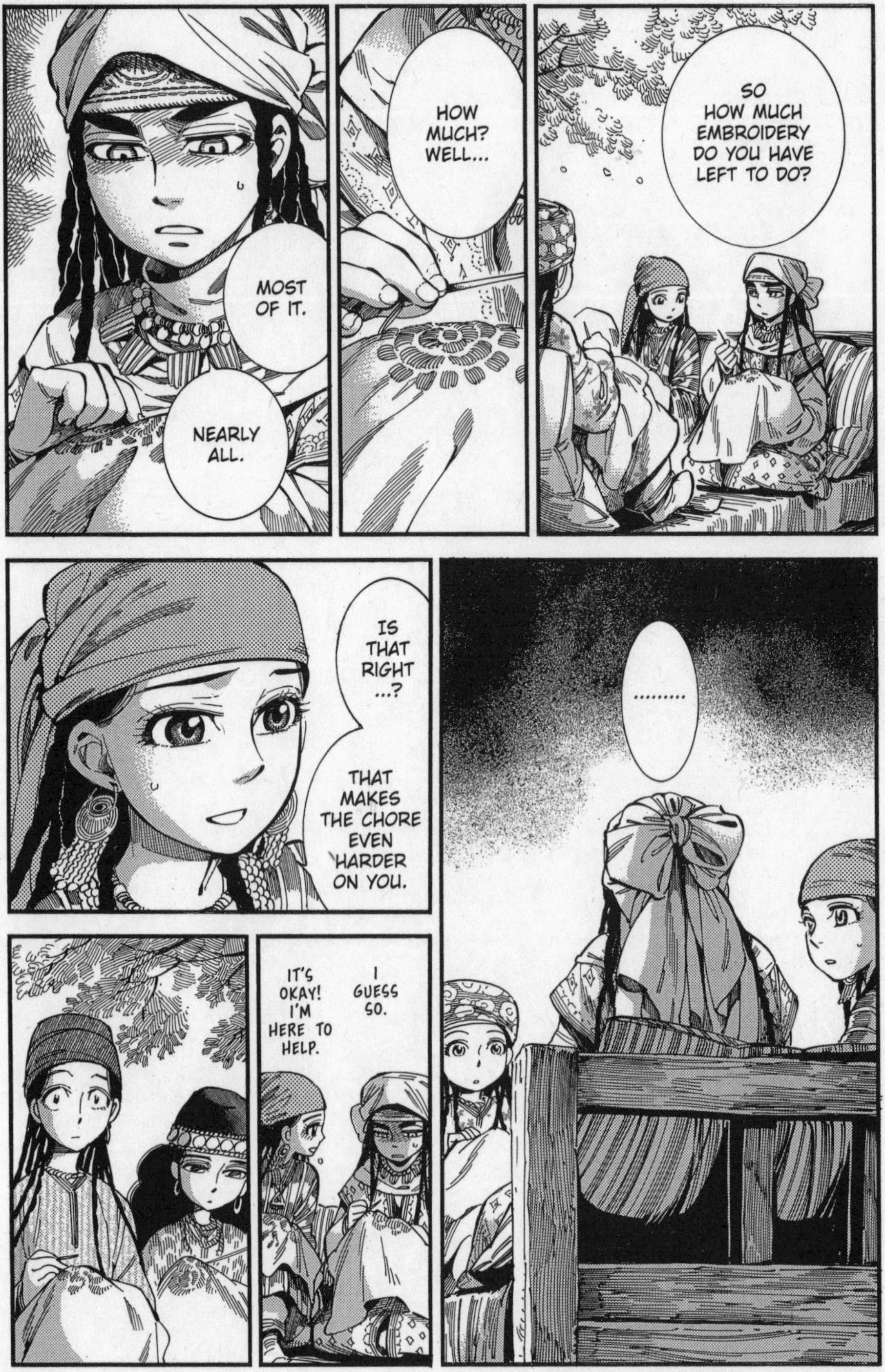
SO HOW MUCH EMBROIDERY DO YOU HAVE LEFT TO DO?
HOW MUCH? WELL...
MOST OF IT.
NEARLY ALL.
....
IS THAT RIGHT ...?
THAT MAKES THE CHORE EVEN HARDER ON YOU.
I GUESS SO.
IT'S OKAY! I'M HERE TO HELP.

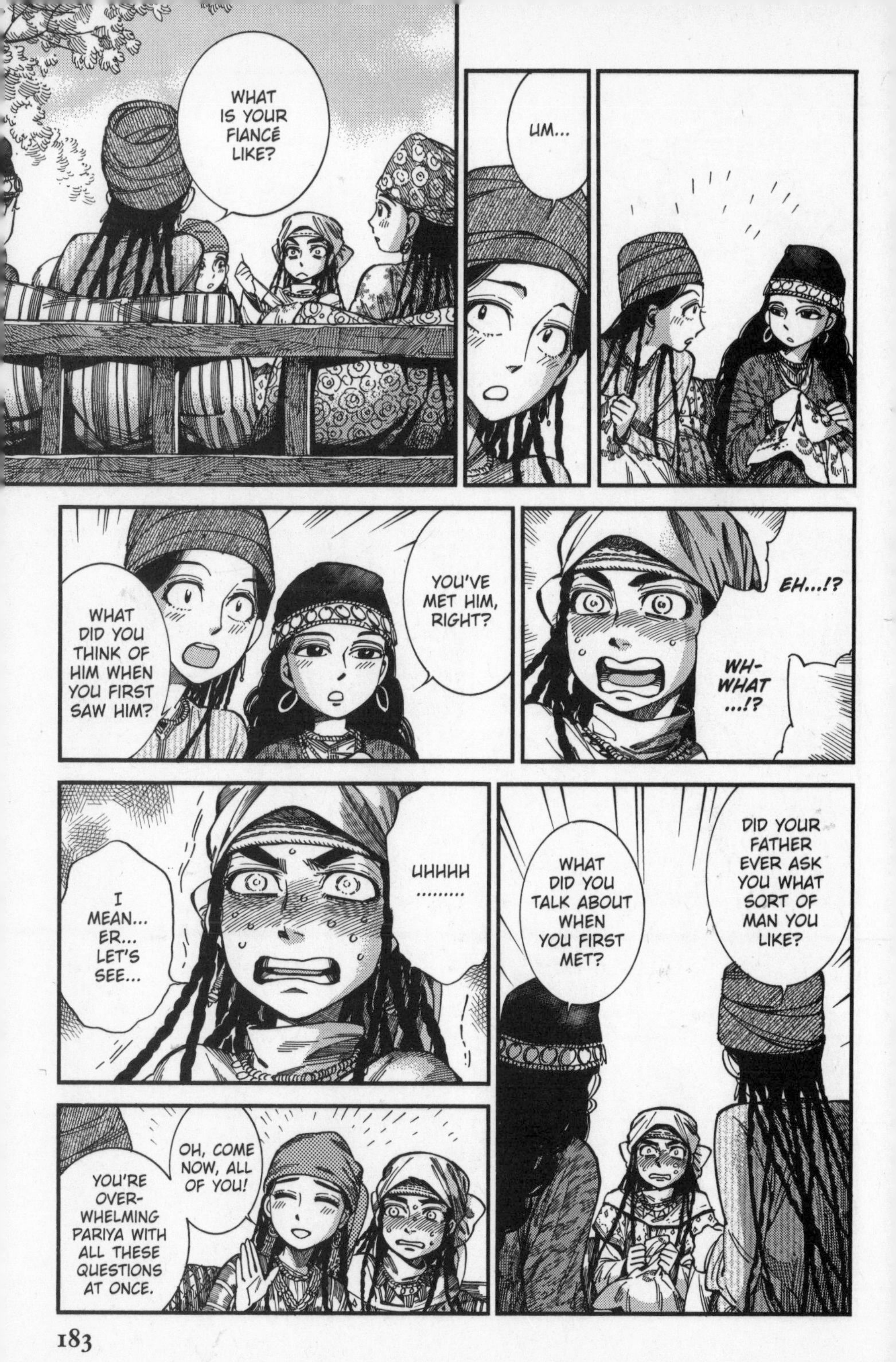
UM...
WHAT IS YOUR FIANCÉ LIKE?
EH...!?
WH-WHAT ...!?
YOU'VE MET HIM, RIGHT?
WHAT DID YOU THINK OF HIM WHEN YOU FIRST SAW HIM?
DID YOUR FATHER EVER ASK YOU WHAT SORT OF MAN YOU LIKE?
WHAT DID YOU TALK ABOUT WHEN YOU FIRST MET?
UHHHH ....
I MEAN... ER... LET'S SEE...
OH, COME NOW, ALL OF YOU!
YOU'RE OVER-WHELMING PARIYA WITH ALL THESE QUESTIONS AT ONCE.

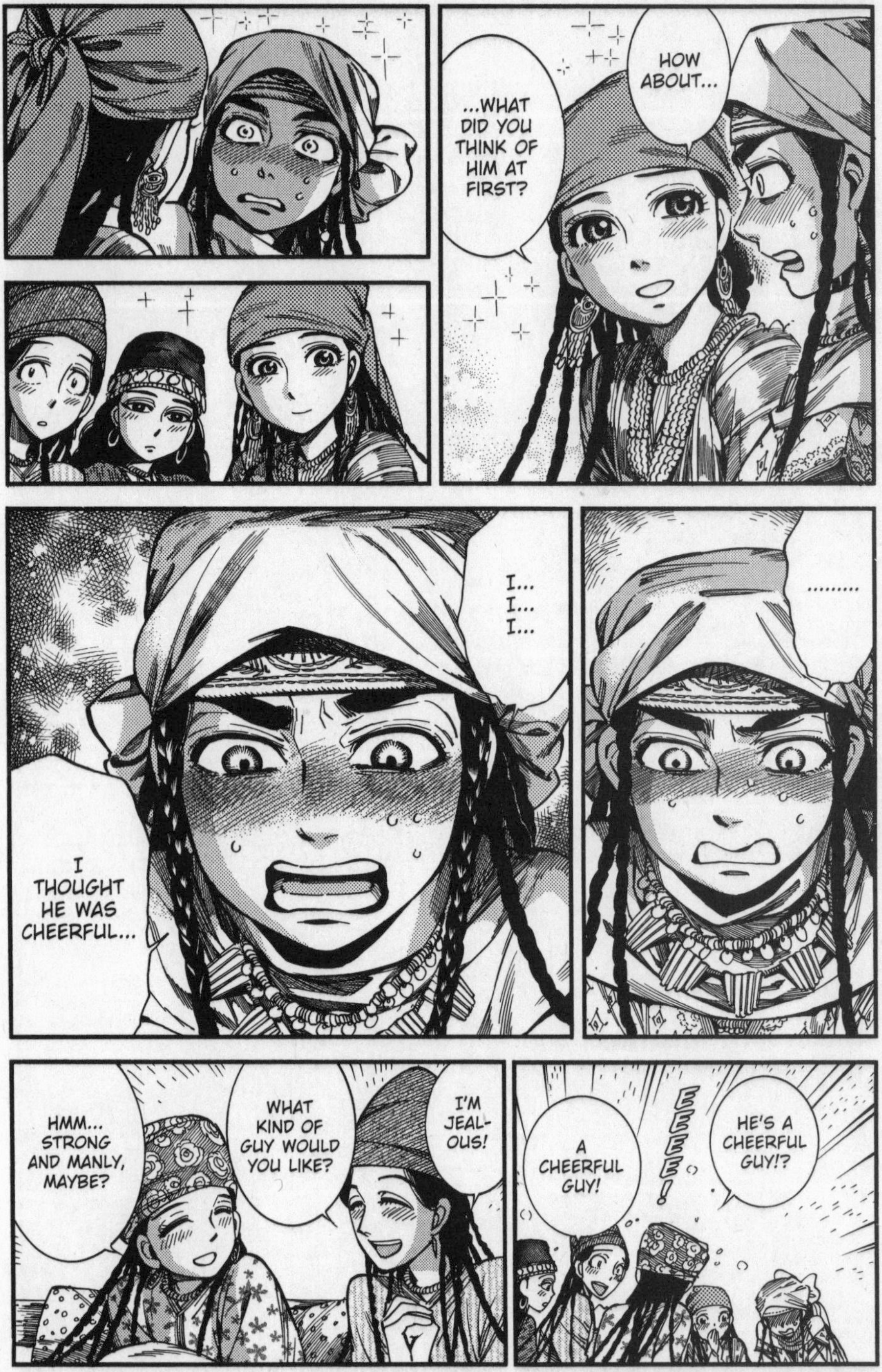
HOW ABOUT...
...WHAT DID YOU THINK OF HIM AT FIRST?
....
I... I... I...
I THOUGHT HE WAS CHEERFUL...
HE'S A CHEERFUL GUY!?
EEEEE!
A CHEERFUL GUY!
I'M JEAL-OUS!
WHAT KIND OF GUY WOULD YOU LIKE?
HMM... STRONG AND MANLY, MAYBE?

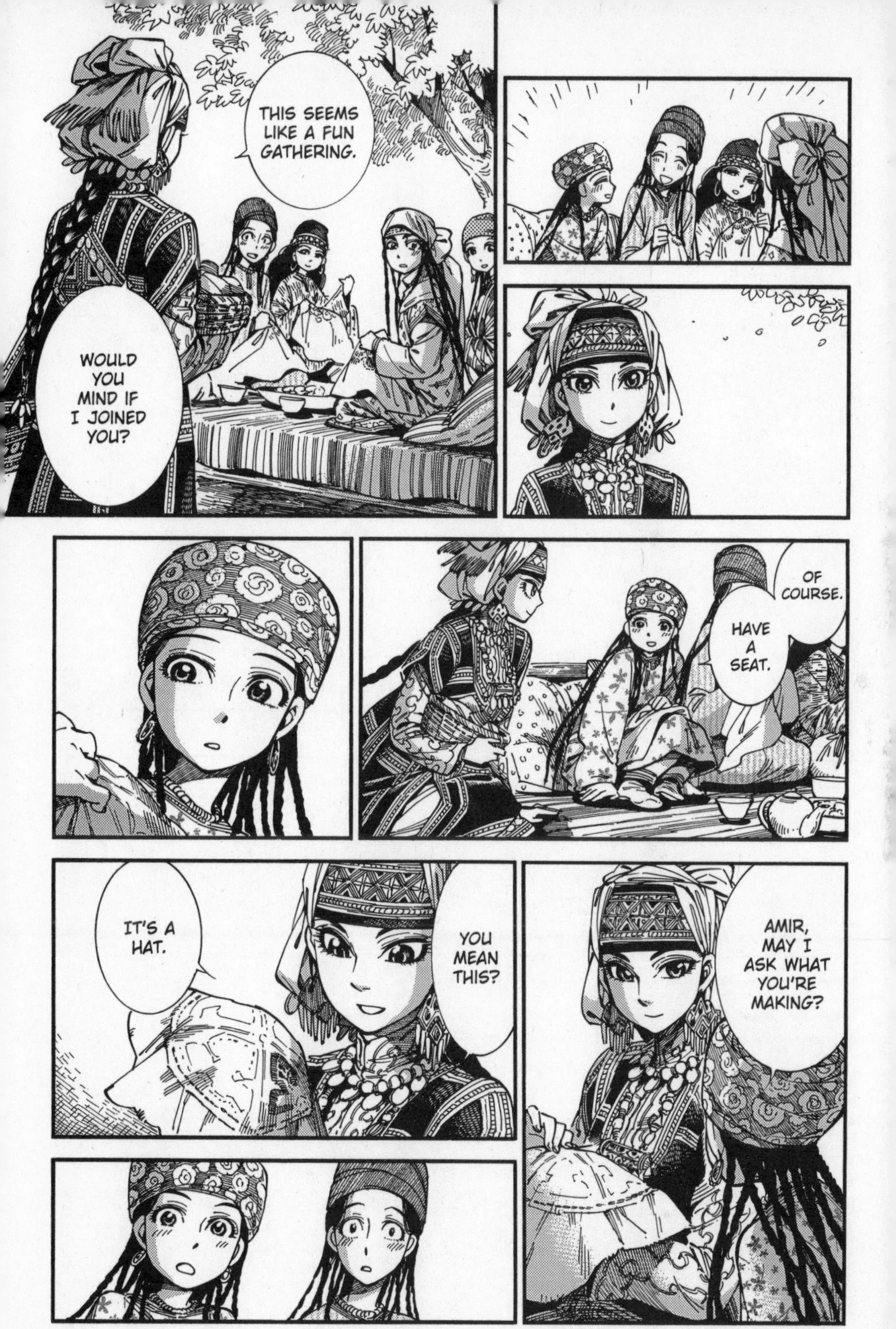
THIS SEEMS LIKE A FUN GATHERING.
WOULD YOU MIND IF I JOINED YOU?
OF COURSE.
HAVE A SEAT.
AMIR, MAY I ASK WHAT YOU'RE MAKING?
YOU MEAN THIS?
IT'S A HAT.

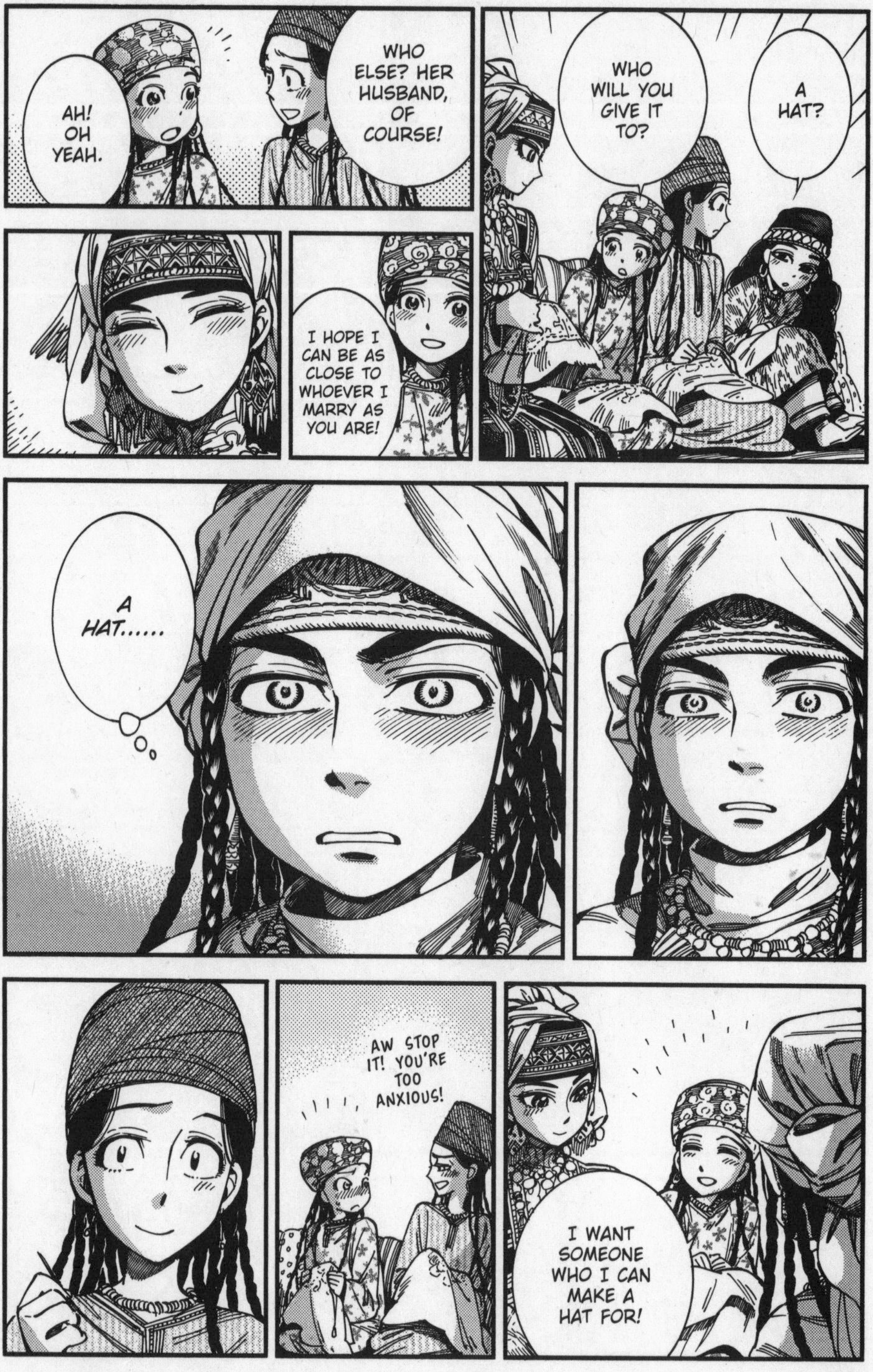
A HAT?
WHO WILL YOU GIVE IT TO?
WHO ELSE? HER HUSBAND, OF COURSE!
AH! OH YEAH.
I HOPE I CAN BE AS CLOSE TO WHOEVER I MARRY AS YOU ARE!
A HAT......
I WANT SOMEONE WHO I CAN MAKE A HAT FOR!
AW STOP IT! YOU'RE TOO ANXIOUS!

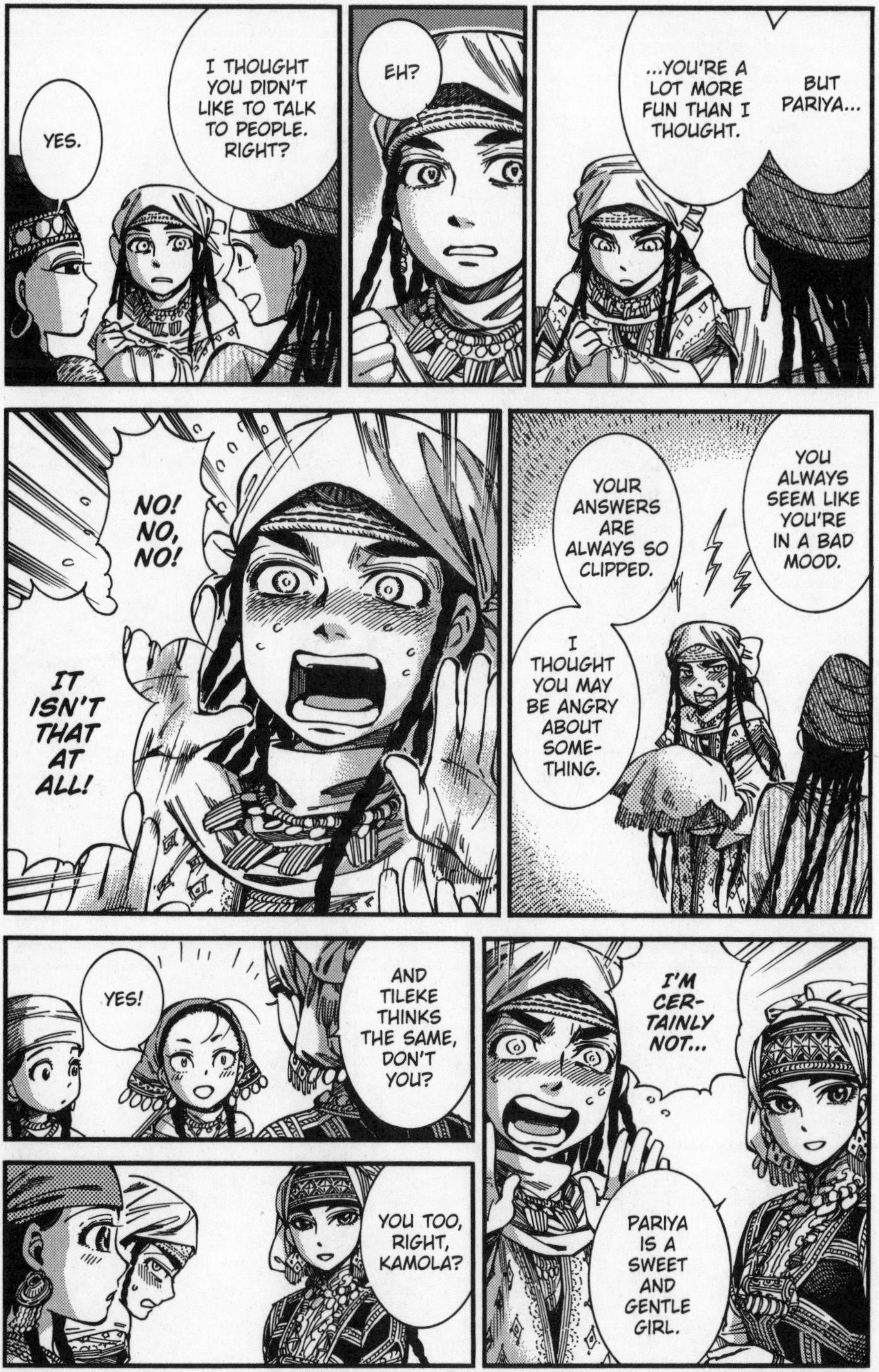
BUT PARIYA...
...YOU'RE A LOT MORE FUN THAN I THOUGHT.
EH?
I THOUGHT YOU DIDN'T LIKE TO TALK TO PEOPLE. RIGHT?
YES.
YOU ALWAYS SEEM LIKE YOU'RE IN A BAD MOOD.
YOUR ANSWERS ARE ALWAYS SO CLIPPED.
I THOUGHT YOU MAY BE ANGRY ABOUT SOME-THING.
NO! NO, NO!
IT ISN'T THAT AT ALL!
I'M CER-TAINLY NOT...
PARIYA IS A SWEET AND GENTLE GIRL.
AND TILEKE THINKS THE SAME, DON'T YOU?
YES!
YOU TOO, RIGHT, KAMOLA?

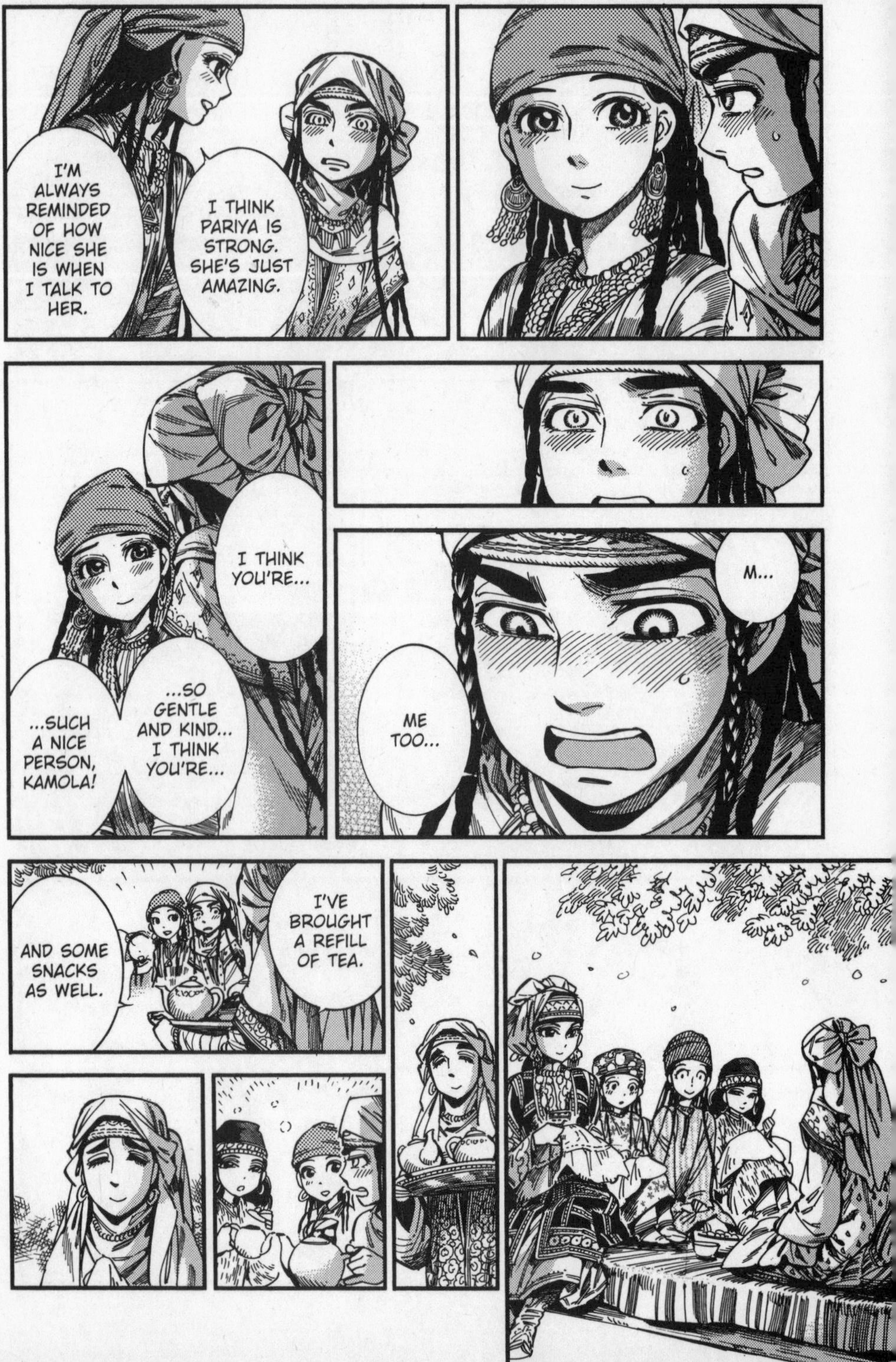
I THINK PARIYA IS STRONG. SHE'S JUST AMAZING.
I'M ALWAYS REMINDED OF HOW NICE SHE IS WHEN I TALK TO HER.
M...
ME TOO...
I THINK YOU'RE...
...SO GENTLE AND KIND... I THINK YOU'RE...
...SUCH A NICE PERSON, KAMOLA!
I'VE BROUGHT A REFILL OF TEA.
AND SOME SNACKS AS WELL.

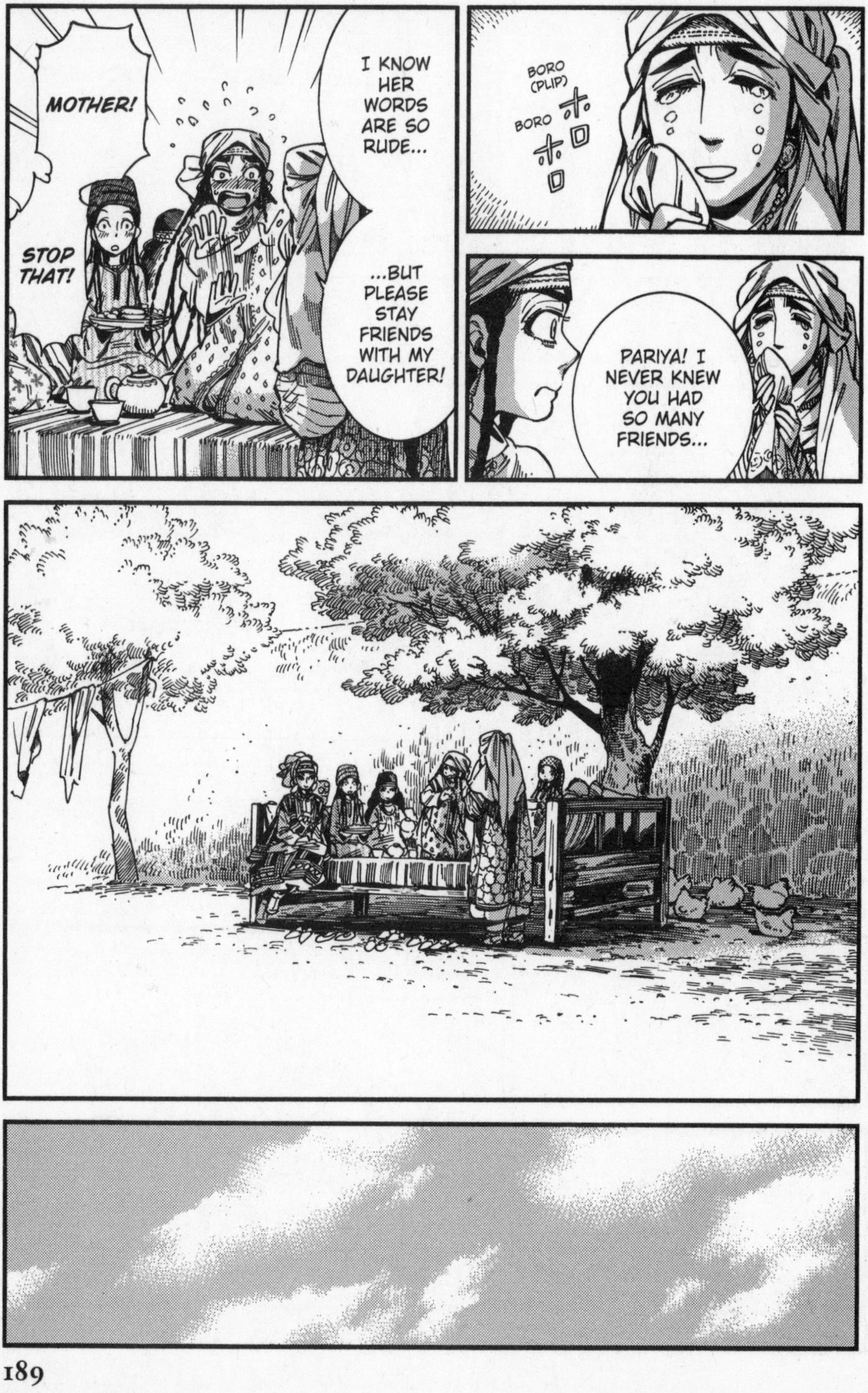
BORO (PLIP)
BORO
PARIYA! I NEVER KNEW YOU HAD SO MANY FRIENDS...
I KNOW HER WORDS ARE SO RUDE...
...BUT PLEASE STAY FRIENDS WITH MY DAUGHTER!
MOTHER!
STOP THAT!

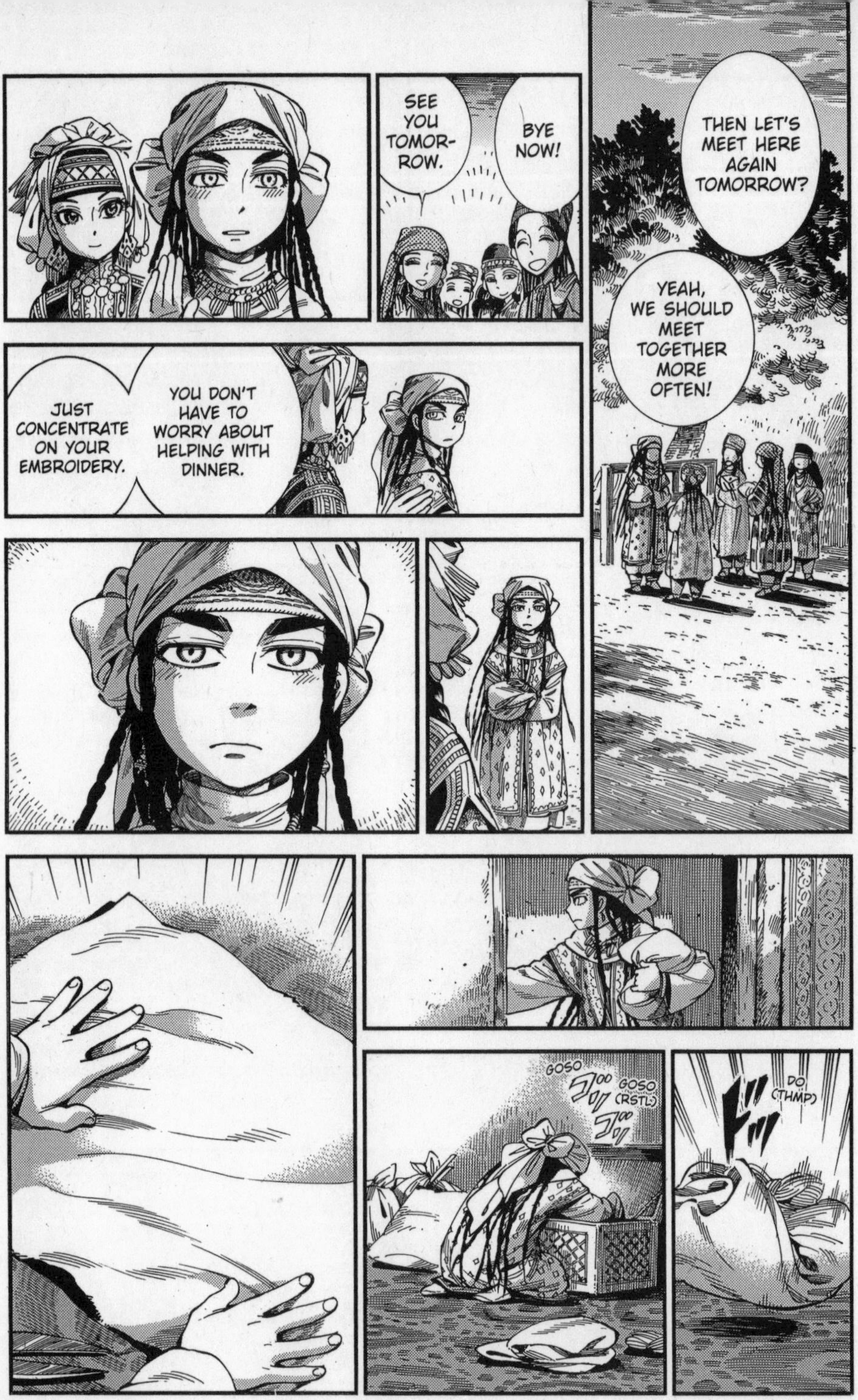
THEN LET'S MEET HERE AGAIN TOMORROW?
YEAH, WE SHOULD MEET TOGETHER MORE OFTEN!
BYE NOW!
SEE YOU TOMOR-ROW.
YOU DON'T HAVE TO WORRY ABOUT HELPING WITH DINNER.
JUST CONCENTRATE ON YOUR EMBROIDERY.
DO (THMP)
GOSO GOSO (RSTL)

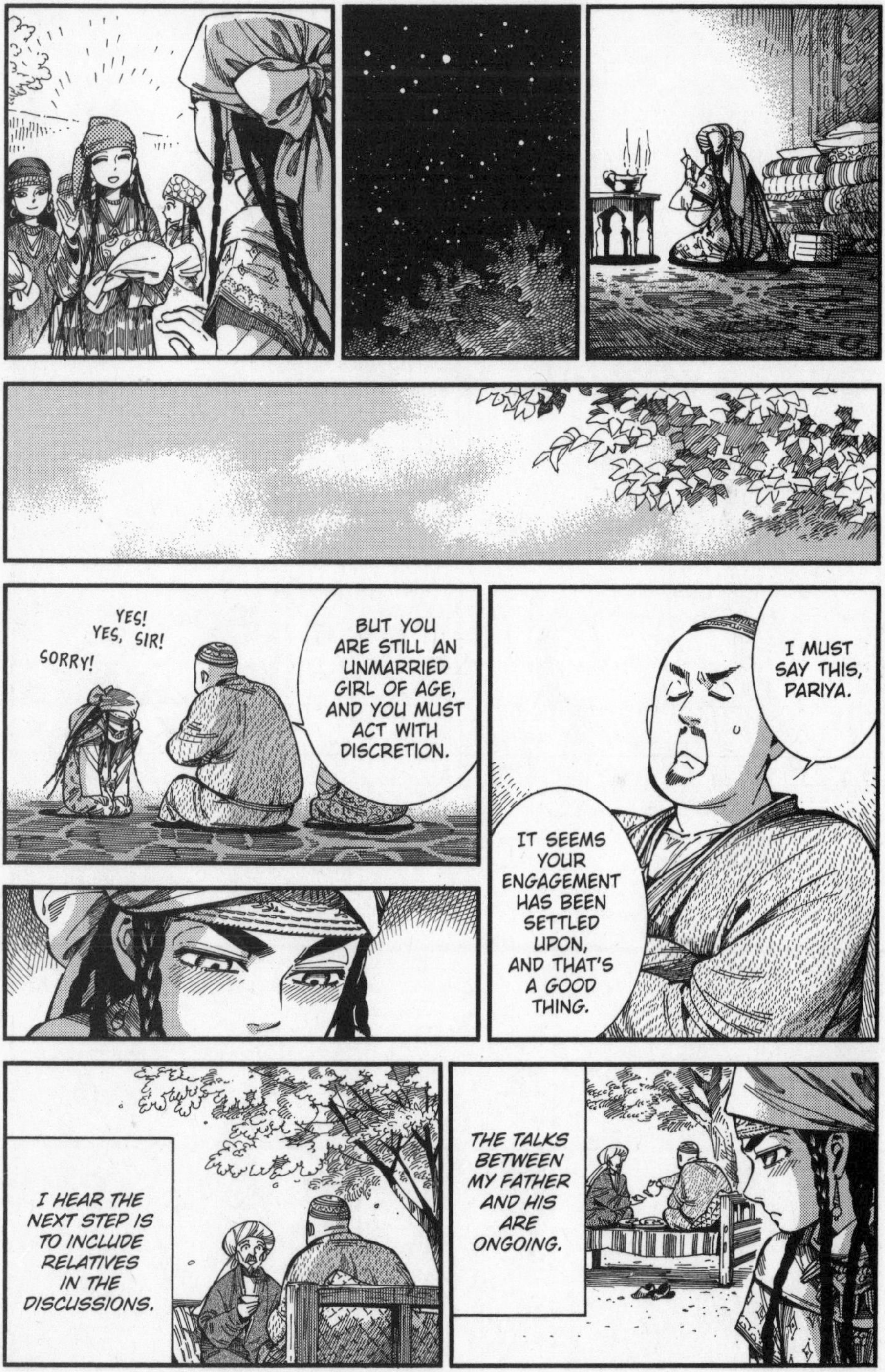
I MUST SAY THIS, PARIYA.
IT SEEMS YOUR ENGAGEMENT HAS BEEN SETTLED UPON, AND THAT'S A GOOD THING.
BUT YOU ARE STILL AN UNMARRIED GIRL OF AGE, AND YOU MUST ACT WITH DISCRETION.
YES! YES, SIR!
SORRY!
THE TALKS BETWEEN MY FATHER AND HIS ARE ONGOING.
I HEAR THE NEXT STEP IS TO INCLUDE RELATIVES IN THE DISCUSSIONS.

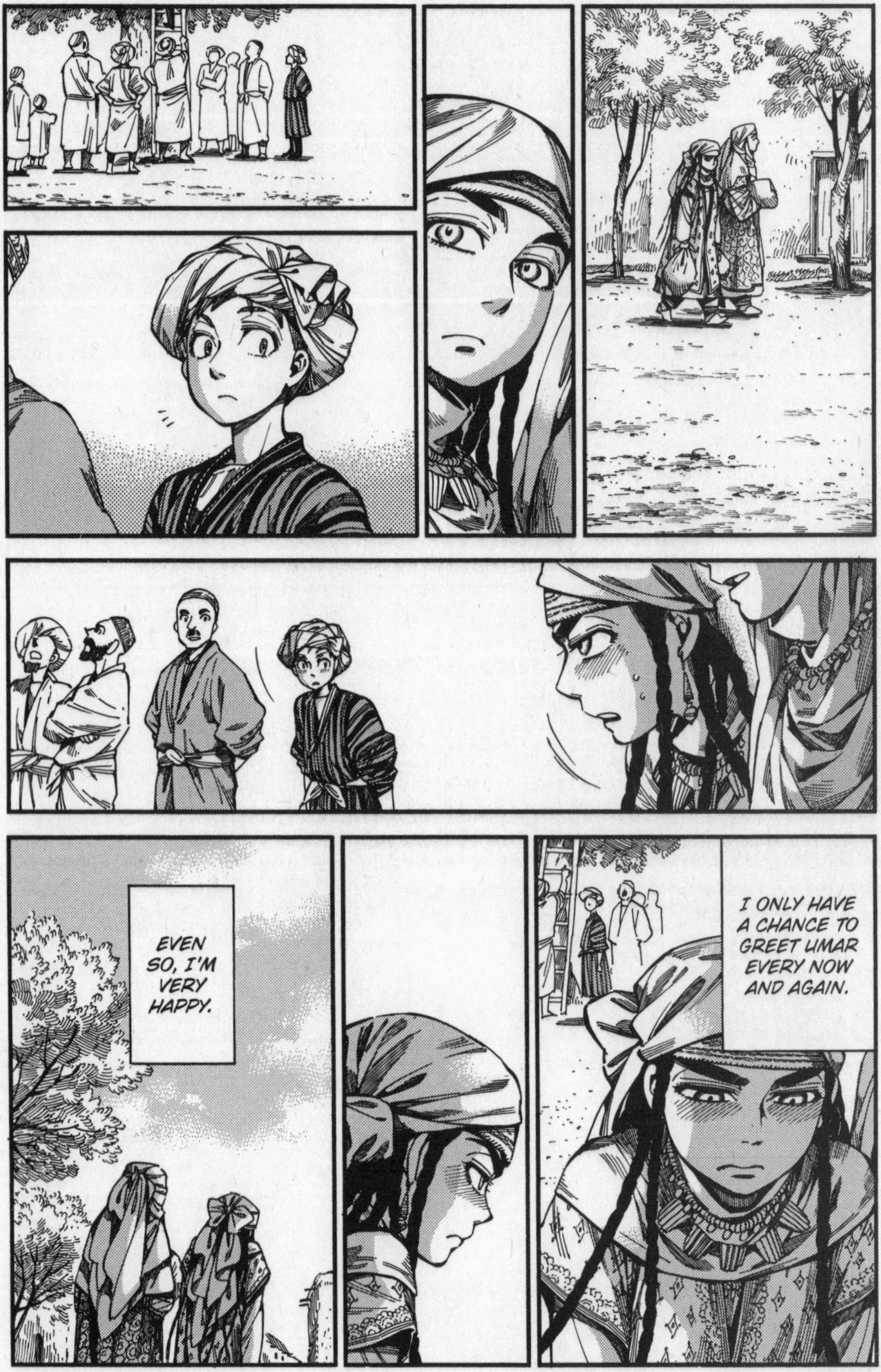
I ONLY HAVE A CHANCE TO GREET UMAR EVERY NOW AND AGAIN.
EVEN SO, I'M VERY HAPPY.

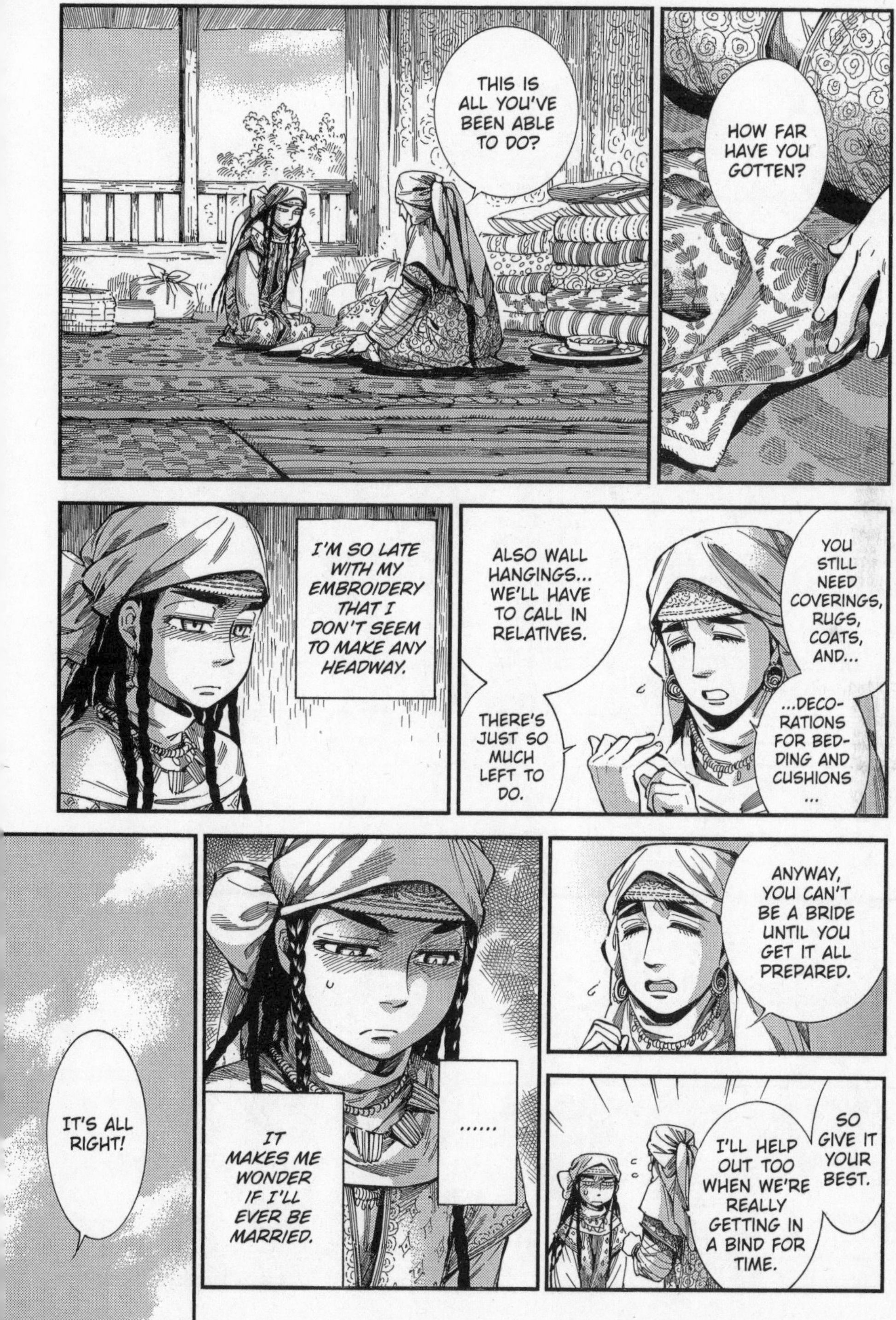
HOW FAR HAVE YOU GOTTEN?
THIS IS ALL YOU'VE BEEN ABLE TO DO?
YOU STILL NEED COVERINGS, RUGS, COATS, AND...
...DECORATIONS FOR BEDDING AND CUSHIONS...
ALSO WALL HANGINGS... WE'LL HAVE TO CALL IN RELATIVES.
THERE'S JUST SO MUCH LEFT TO DO.
I'M SO LATE WITH MY EMBROIDERY THAT I DON'T SEEM TO MAKE ANY HEADWAY.
ANYWAY, YOU CAN'T BE A BRIDE UNTIL YOU GET IT ALL PREPARED.
SO GIVE IT YOUR BEST.
I'LL HELP OUT TOO WHEN WE'RE REALLY GETTING IN A BIND FOR TIME.
......
IT MAKES ME WONDER IF I'LL EVER BE MARRIED.
IT'S ALL RIGHT!

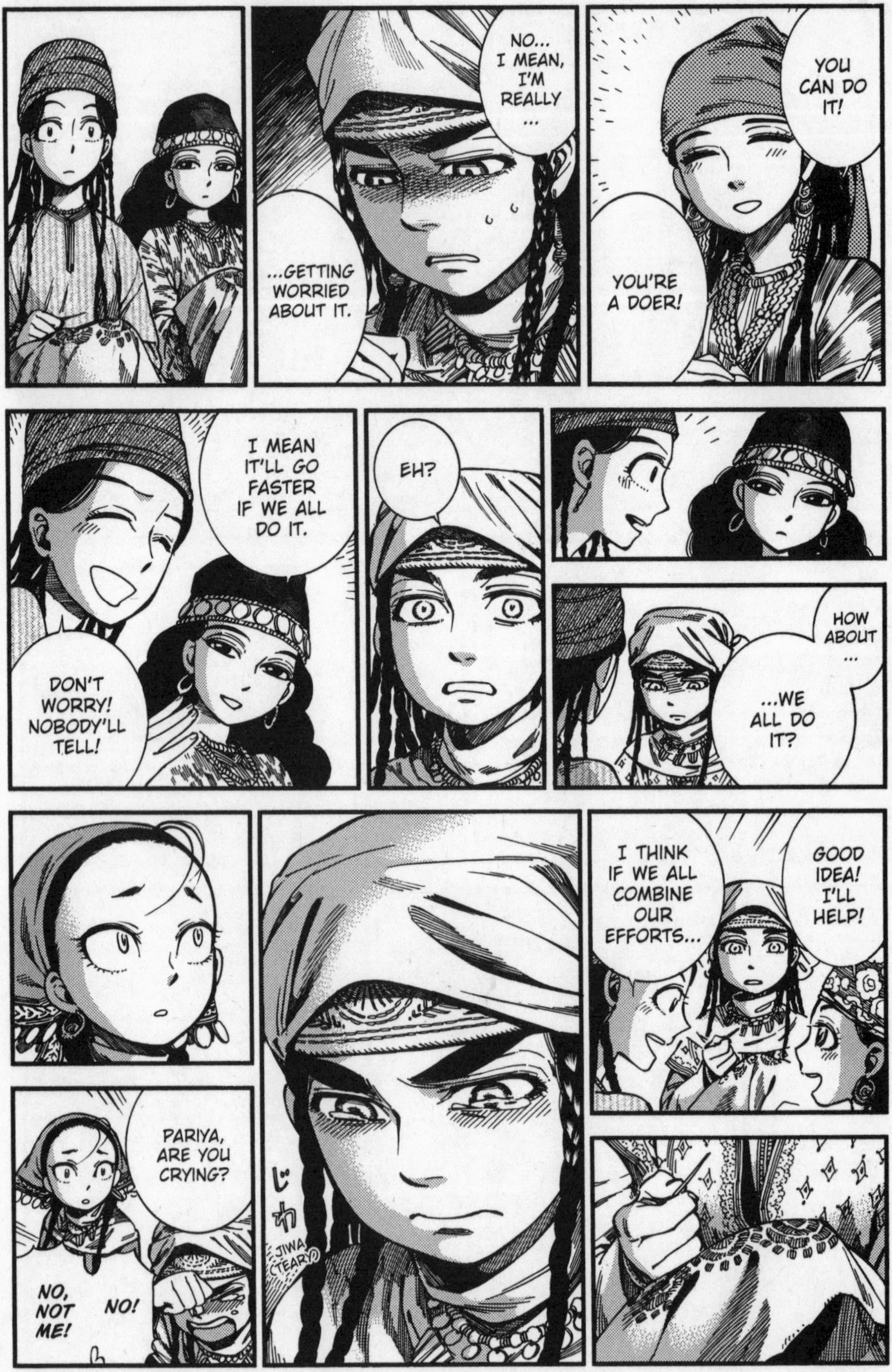
YOU CAN DO IT!
YOU'RE A DOER!
NO... I MEAN, I'M REALLY ...
...GETTING WORRIED ABOUT IT.
HOW ABOUT ...
...WE ALL DO IT?
EH?
I MEAN IT'LL GO FASTER IF WE ALL DO IT.
DON'T WORRY! NOBODY'LL TELL!
GOOD IDEA! I'LL HELP!
I THINK IF WE ALL COMBINE OUR EFFORTS...
じわ
JIWA (TEARY)
PARIYA, ARE YOU CRYING?
NO!
NO, NOT ME!

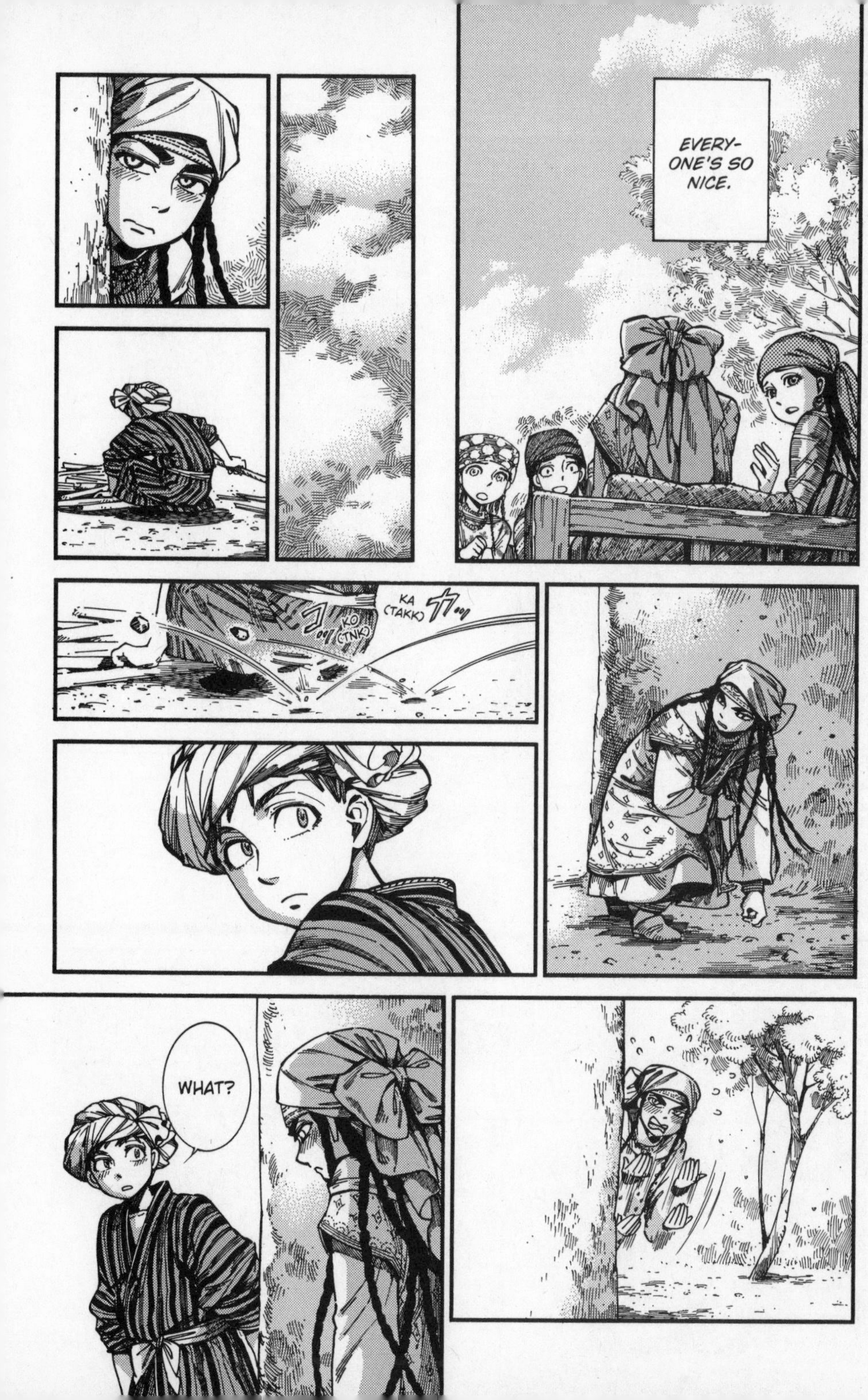
EVERY-ONE'S SO NICE.
KA (TAKK)
KO (TNK)
WHAT?

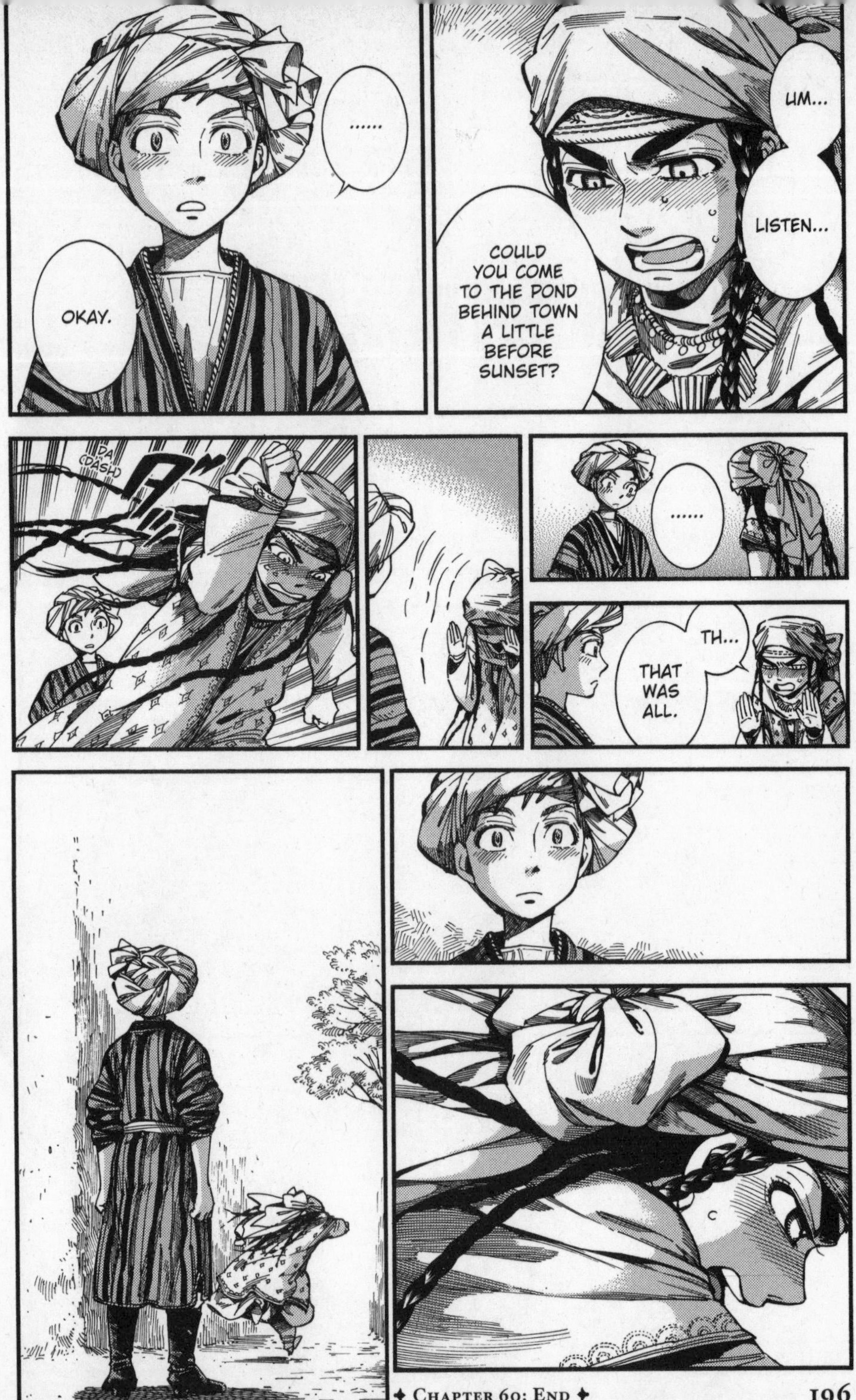
UM...
LISTEN...
COULD YOU COME TO THE POND BEHIND TOWN A LITTLE BEFORE SUNSET?
......
OKAY.
......
TH...
THAT WAS ALL.
DA (DASH)

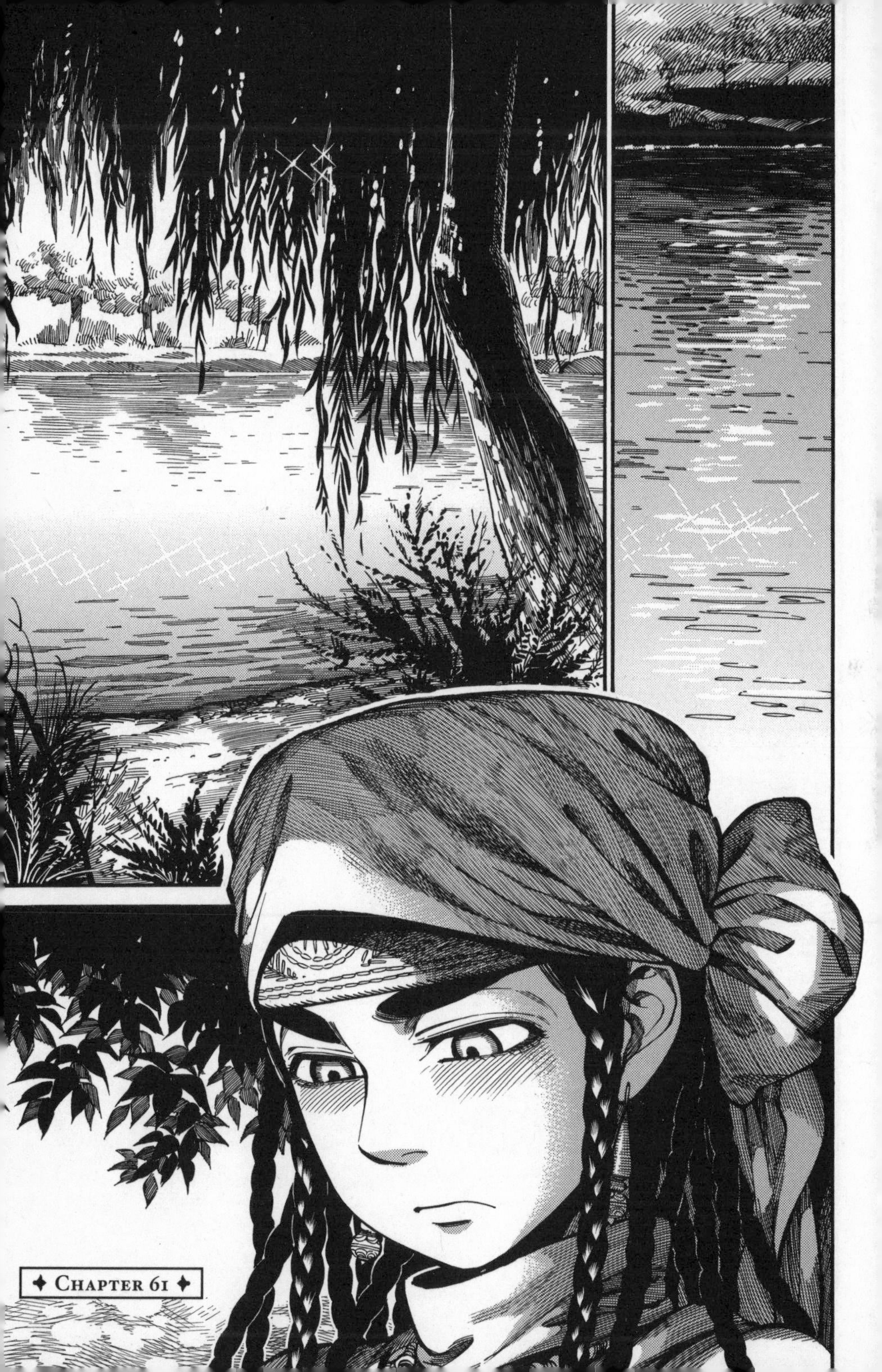
✦ Chapter 61 ✦

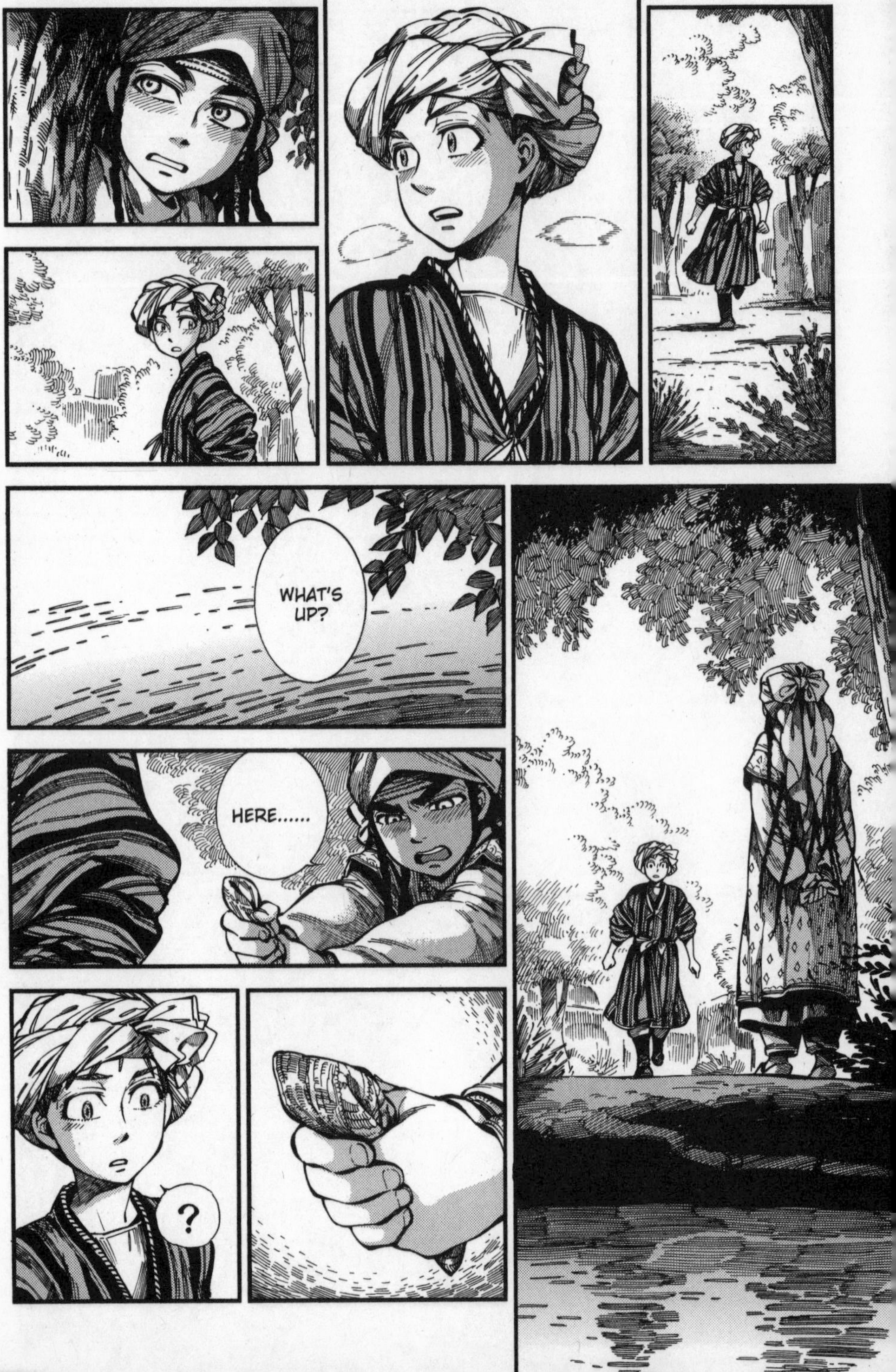
WHAT'S UP?
HERE......
?

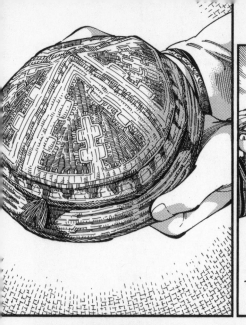

HERE.

IF YOU WANT, PLEASE TAKE IT!

ポフッ
BOFU
(POFF)

OH!

AH...

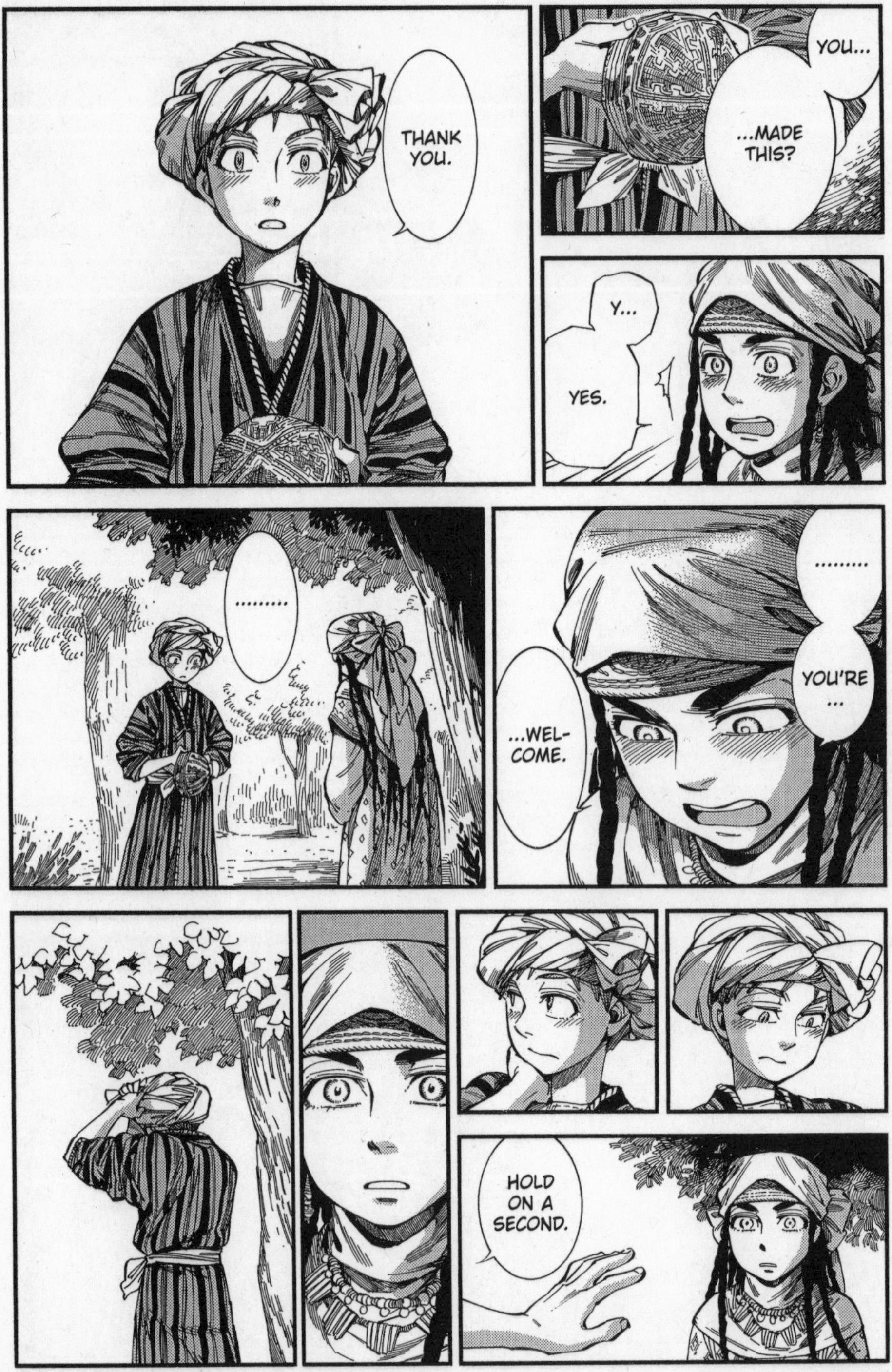
YOU...
...MADE THIS?
Y...
YES.
THANK YOU.
....
YOU'RE ...
...WEL- COME.
....
HOLD ON A SECOND.

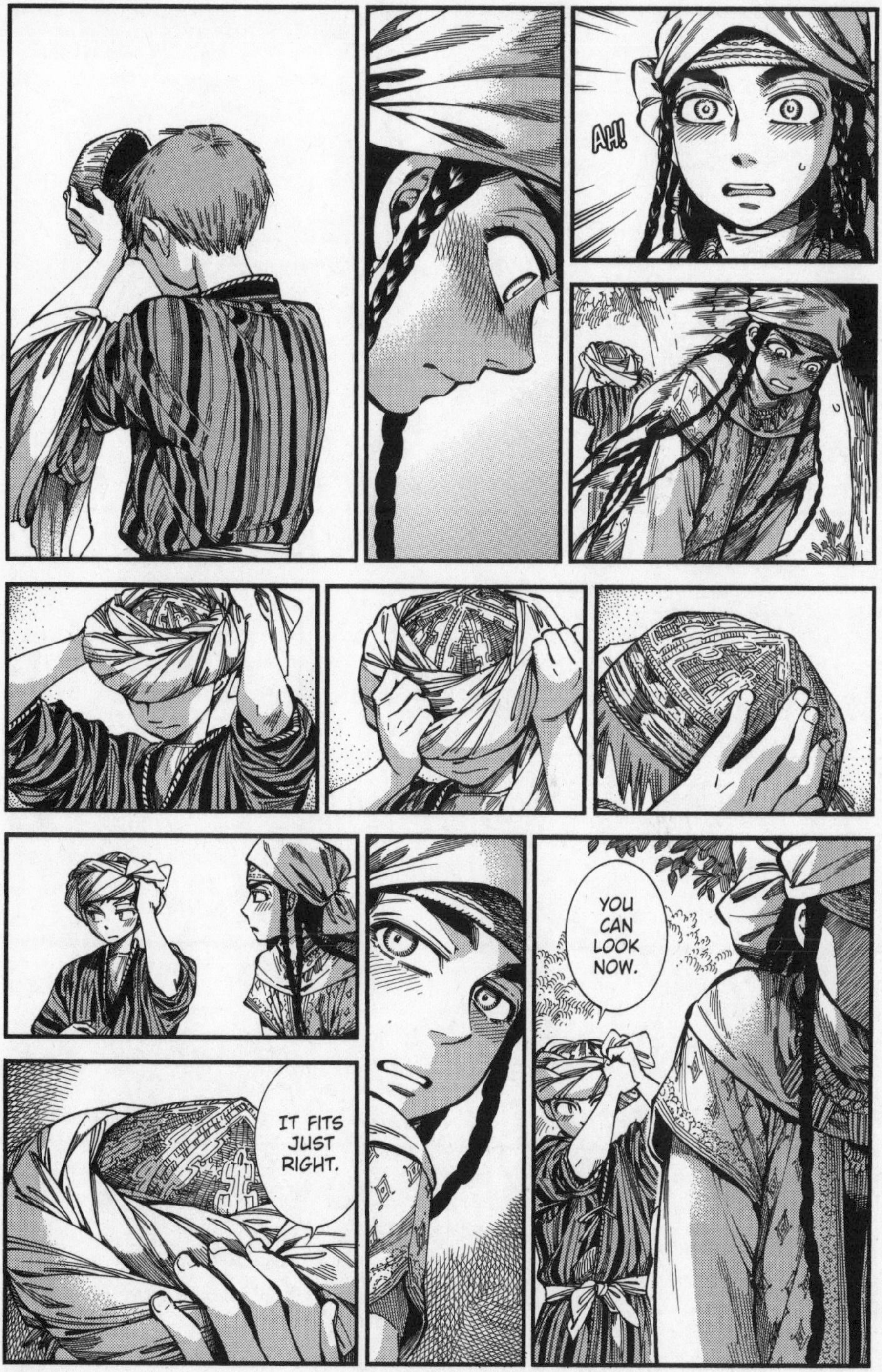
AH!
YOU CAN LOOK NOW.
IT FITS JUST RIGHT.

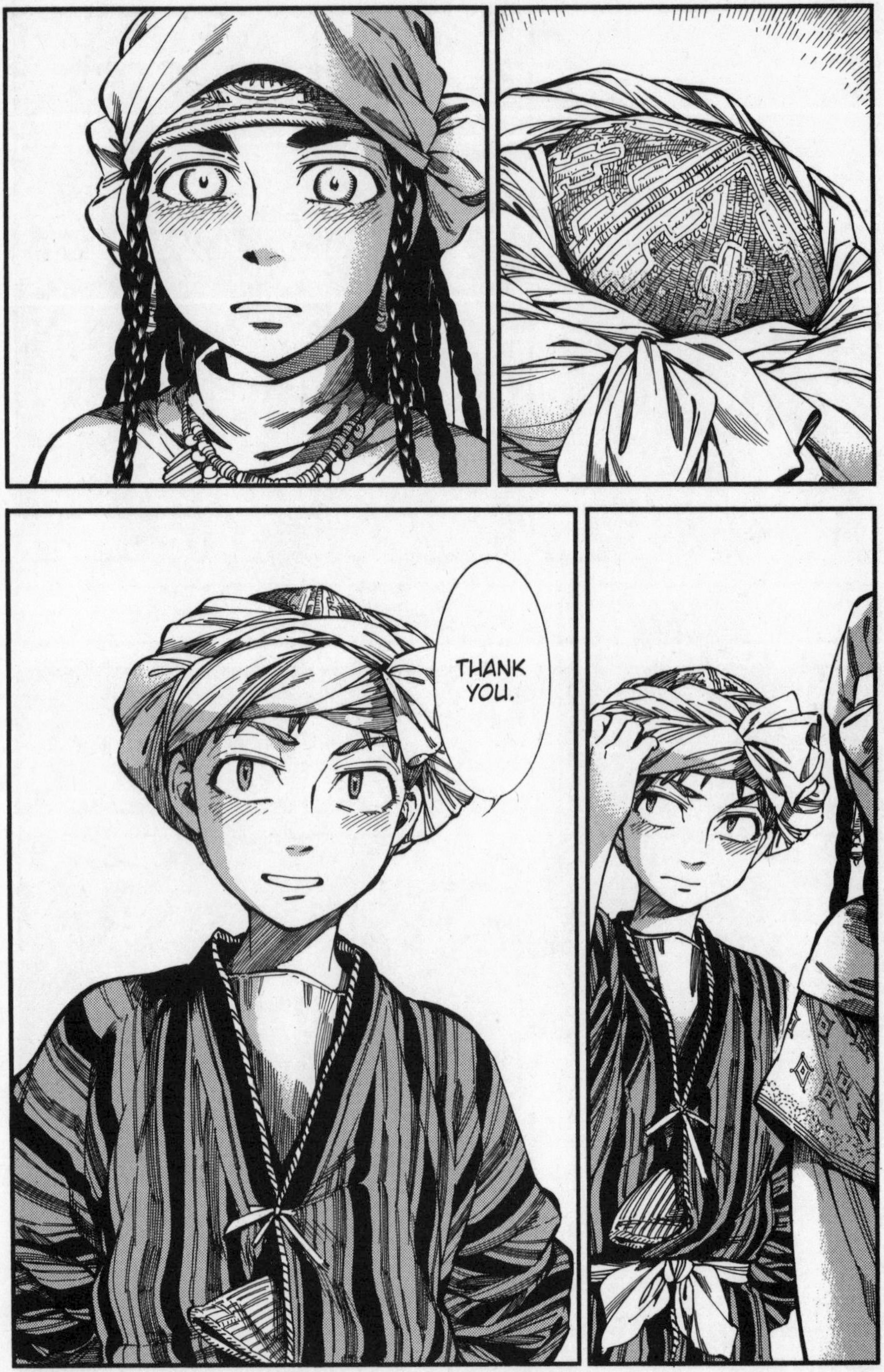
THANK YOU.

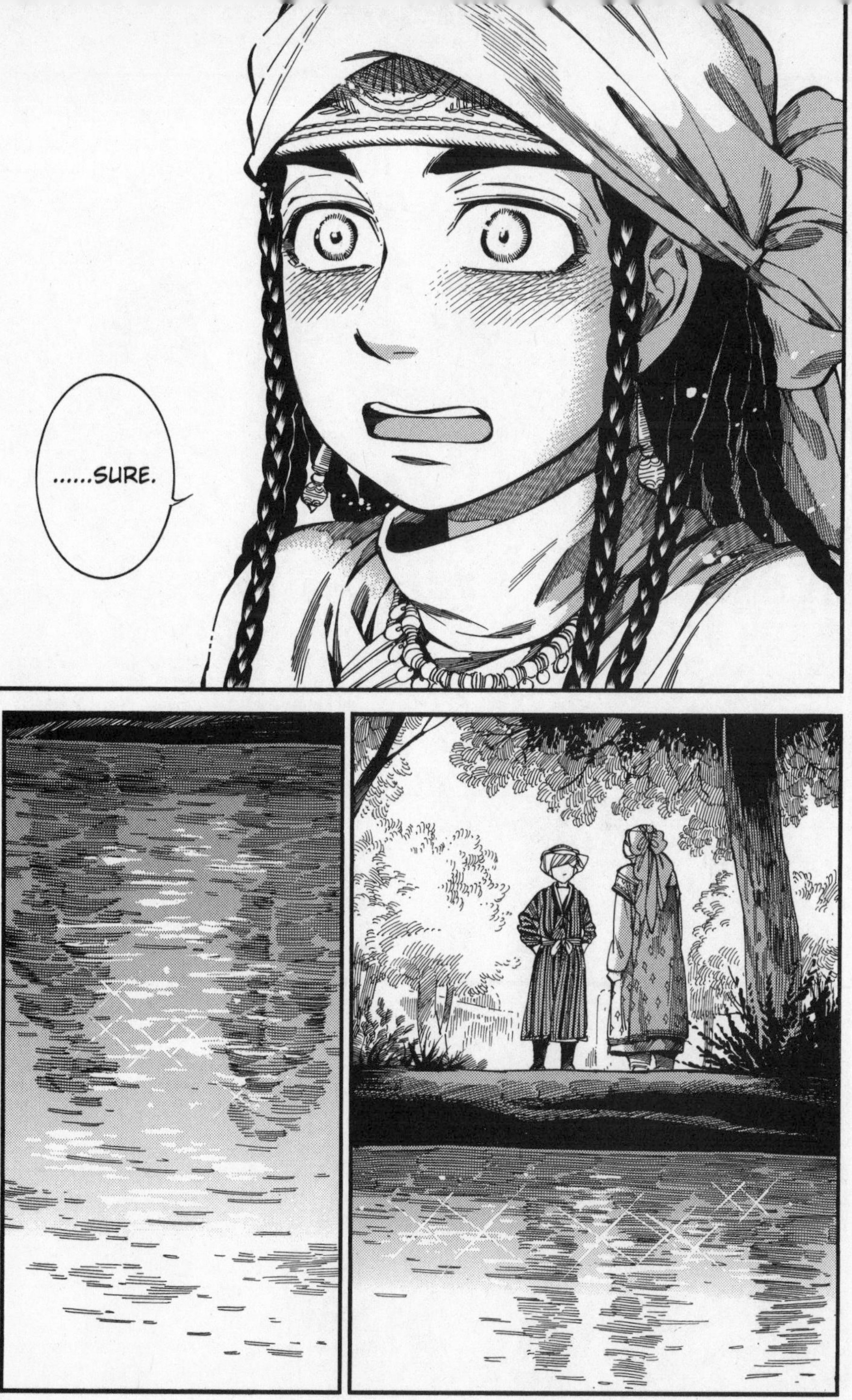
......SURE.

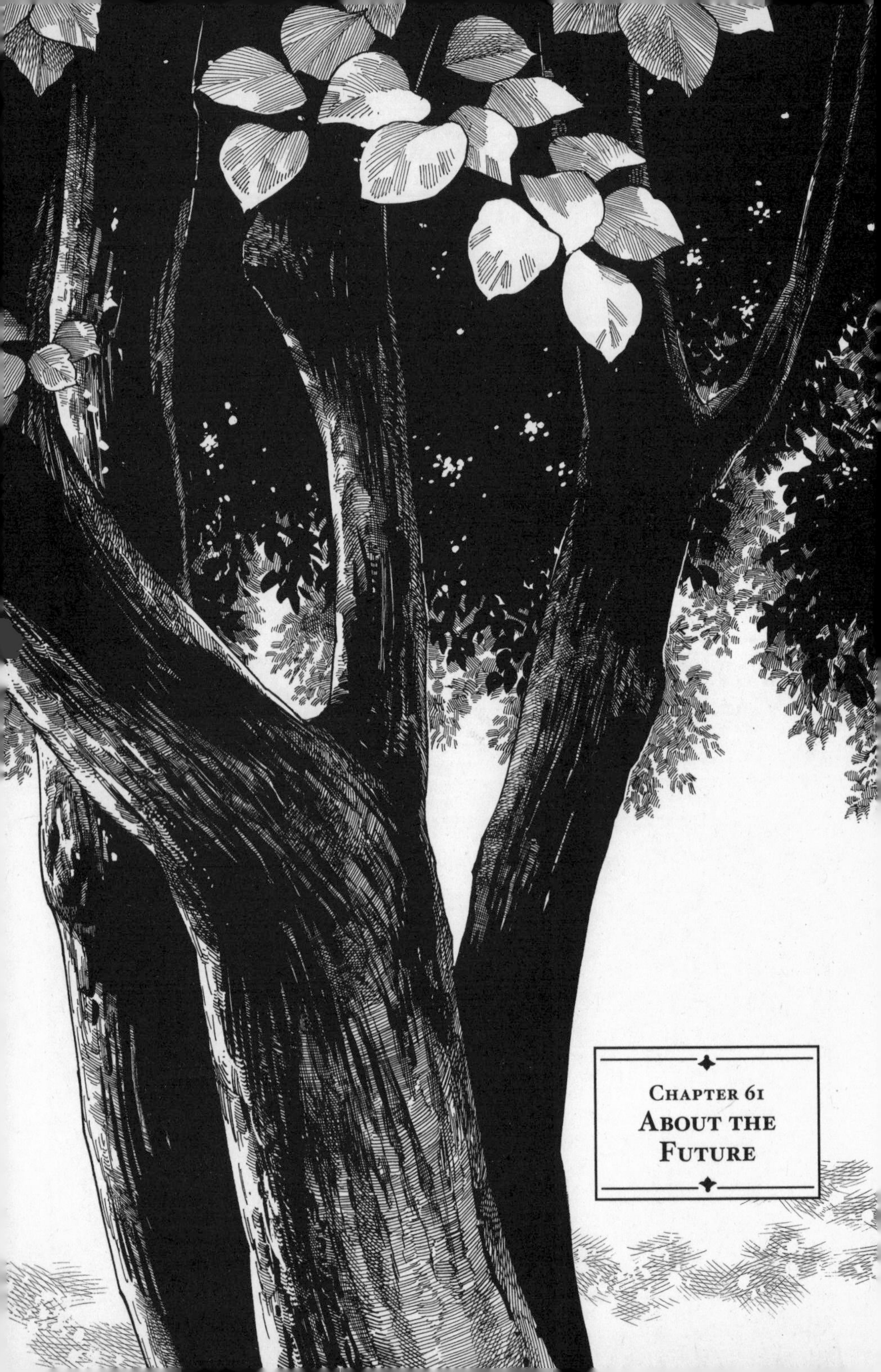

Chapter 61
About the Future

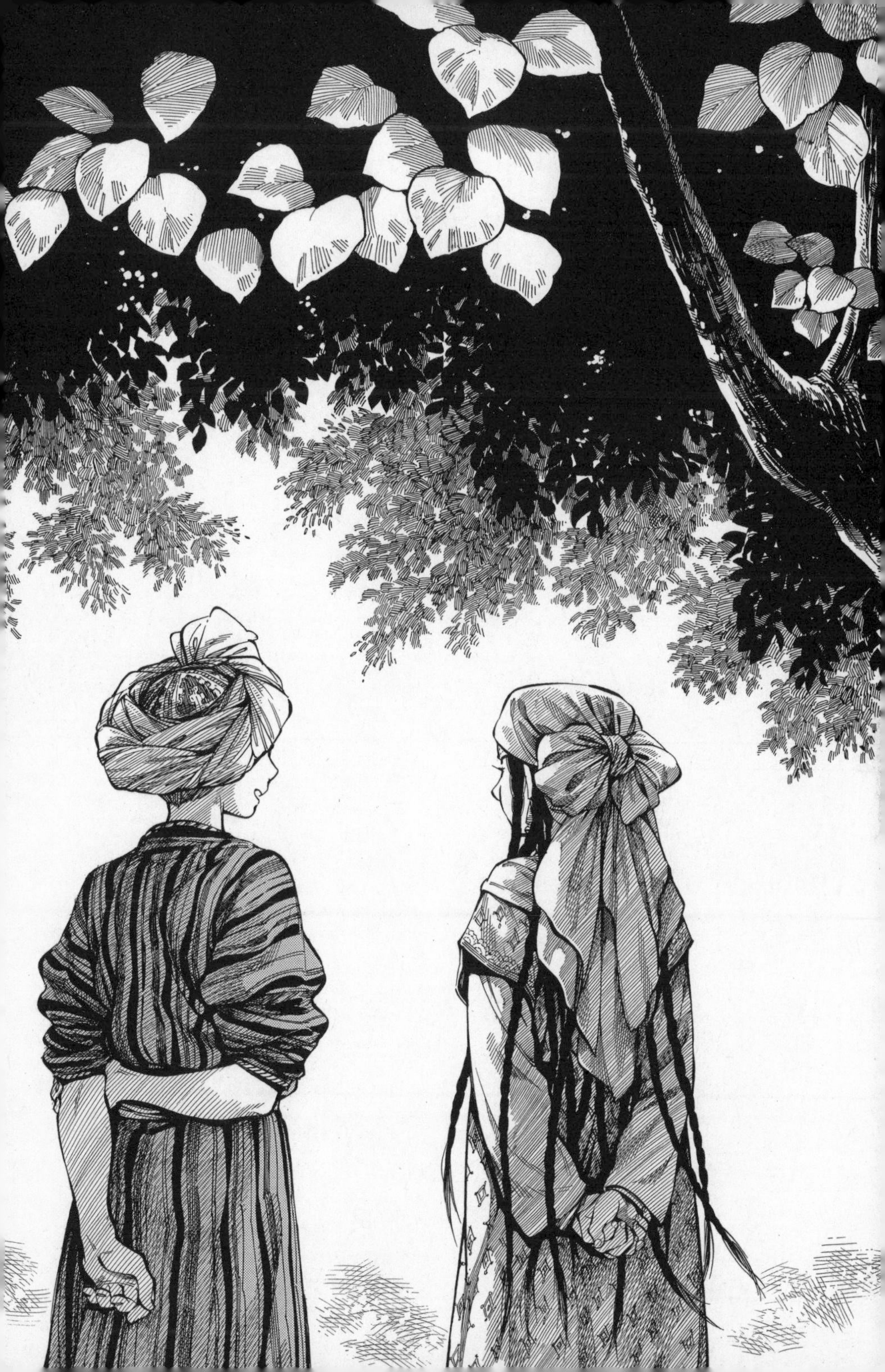

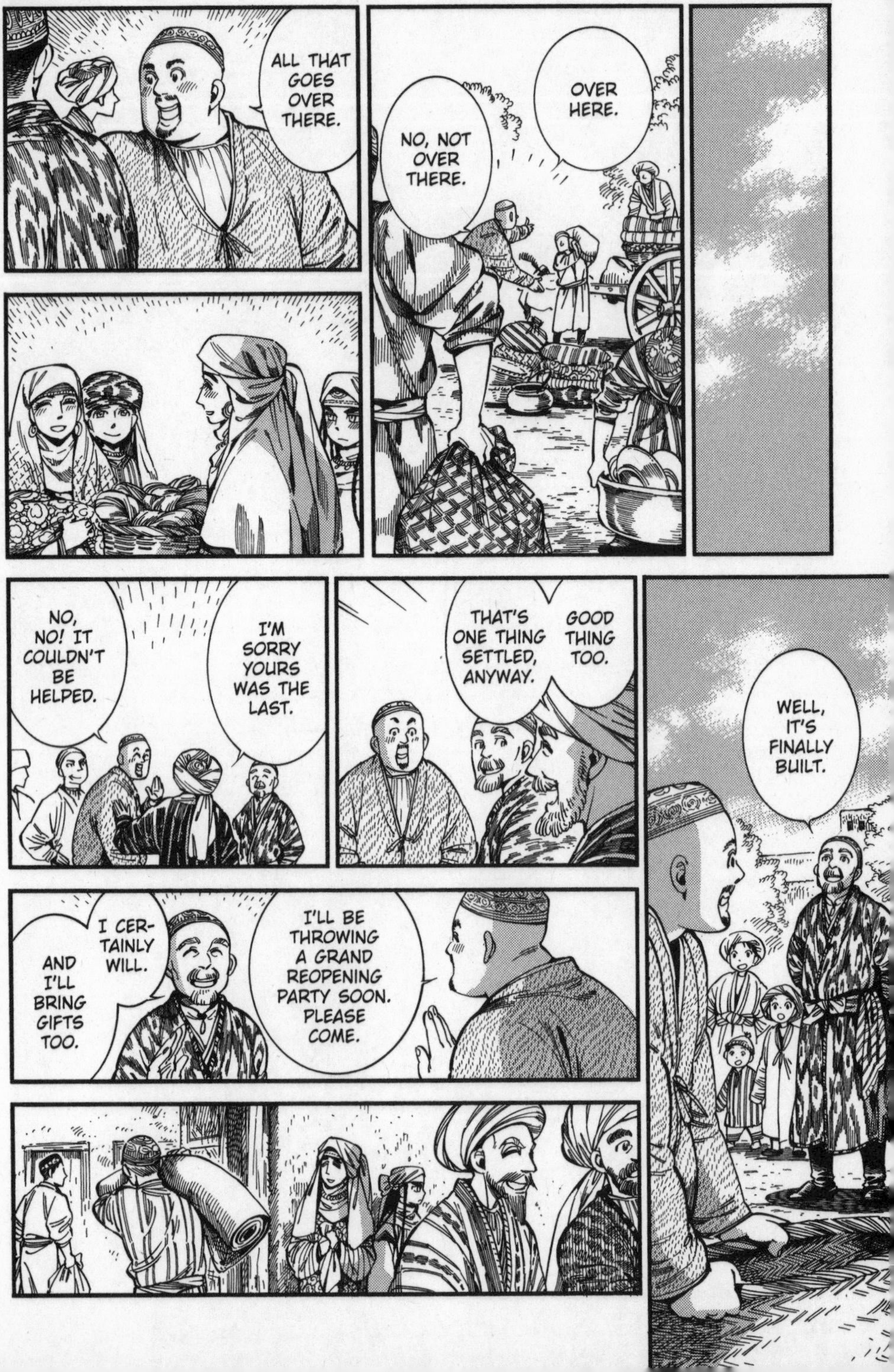
OVER HERE.
NO, NOT OVER THERE.
ALL THAT GOES OVER THERE.
WELL, IT'S FINALLY BUILT.
GOOD THING TOO.
THAT'S ONE THING SETTLED, ANYWAY.
I'M SORRY YOURS WAS THE LAST.
NO, NO! IT COULDN'T BE HELPED.
I'LL BE THROWING A GRAND REOPENING PARTY SOON. PLEASE COME.
I CER-TAINLY WILL.
AND I'LL BRING GIFTS TOO.

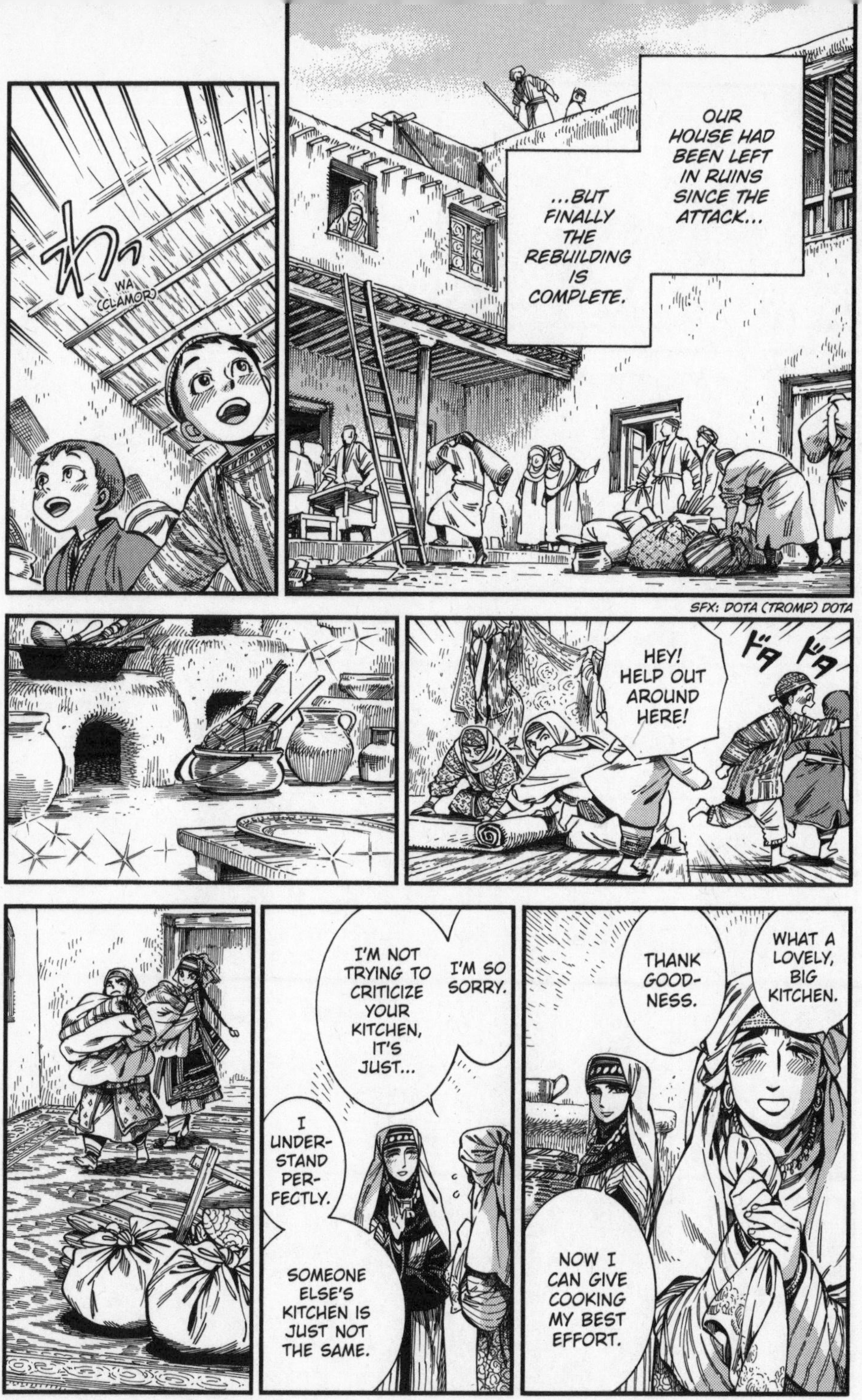

OUR HOUSE HAD BEEN LEFT IN RUINS SINCE THE ATTACK...
...BUT FINALLY THE REBUILDING IS COMPLETE.
わっ
WA (CLAMOR)
SFX: DOTA (TROMP) DOTA
ドタ ドタ
HEY! HELP OUT AROUND HERE!
WHAT A LOVELY, BIG KITCHEN.
THANK GOODNESS.
NOW I CAN GIVE COOKING MY BEST EFFORT.
I'M SO SORRY.
I'M NOT TRYING TO CRITICIZE YOUR KITCHEN, IT'S JUST...
I UNDERSTAND PERFECTLY.
SOMEONE ELSE'S KITCHEN IS JUST NOT THE SAME.

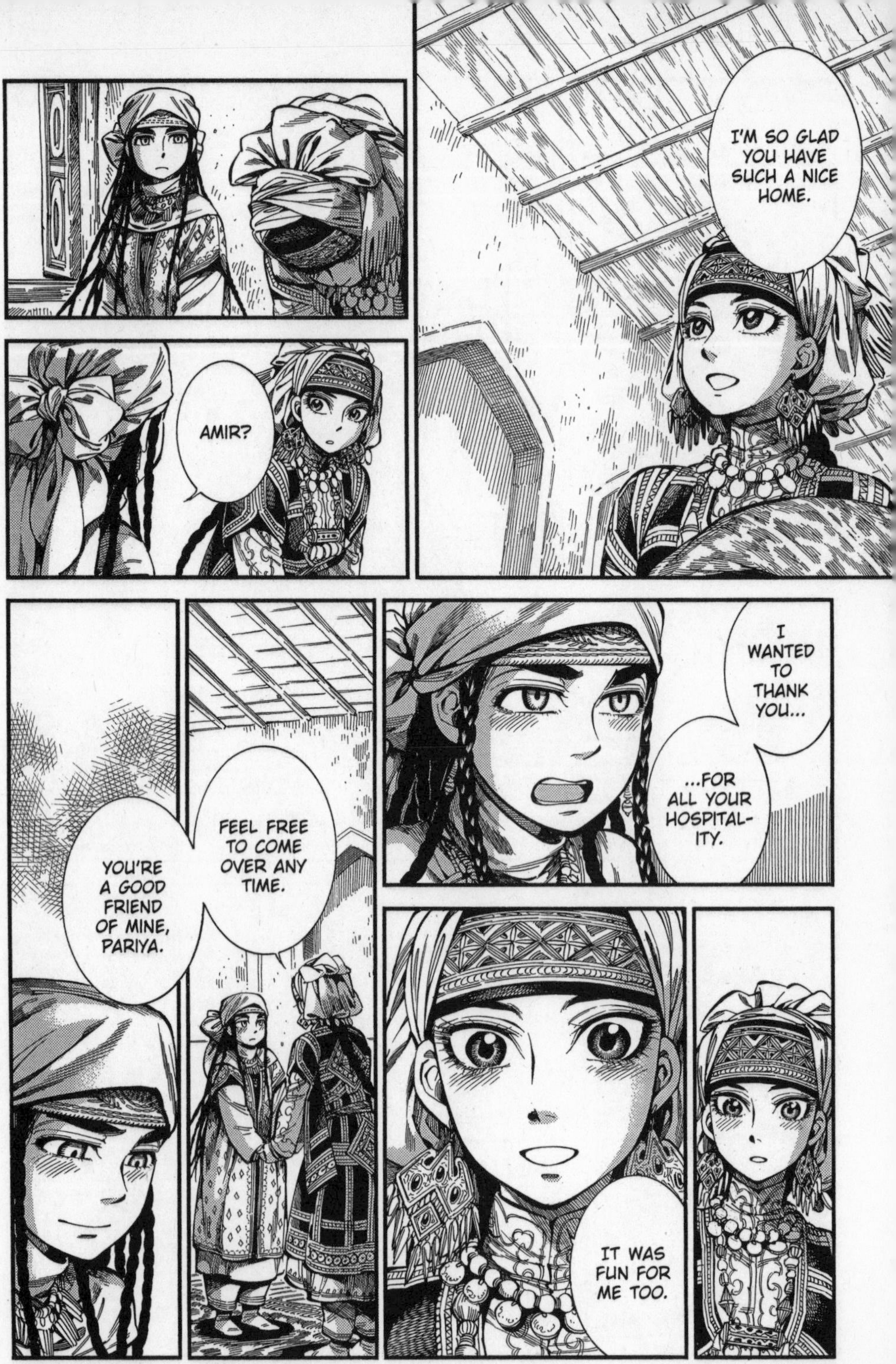
I'M SO GLAD YOU HAVE SUCH A NICE HOME.
AMIR?
I WANTED TO THANK YOU...
...FOR ALL YOUR HOSPITAL-ITY.
IT WAS FUN FOR ME TOO.
FEEL FREE TO COME OVER ANY TIME.
YOU'RE A GOOD FRIEND OF MINE, PARIYA.

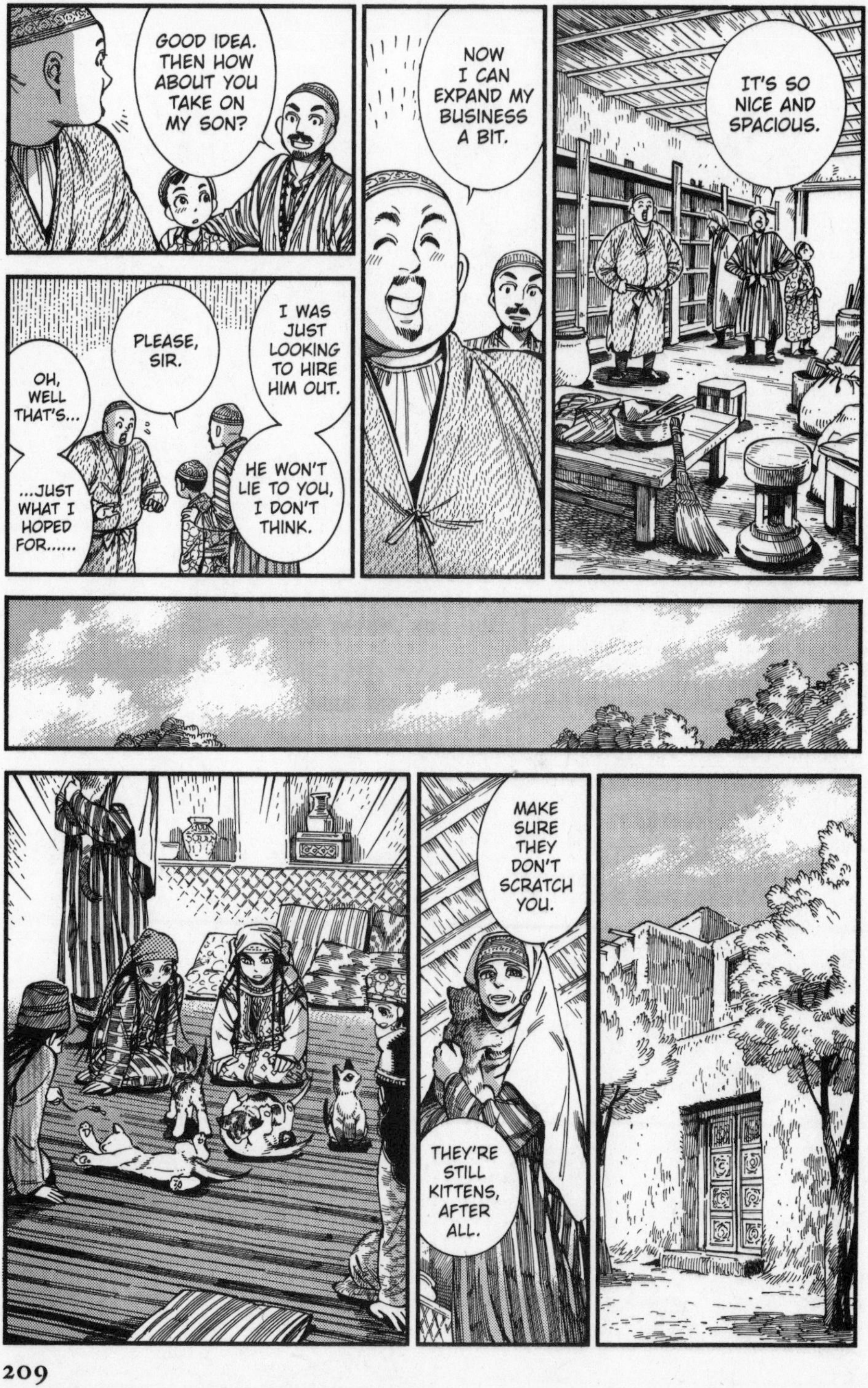
IT'S SO NICE AND SPACIOUS.
NOW I CAN EXPAND MY BUSINESS A BIT.
GOOD IDEA. THEN HOW ABOUT YOU TAKE ON MY SON?
I WAS JUST LOOKING TO HIRE HIM OUT.
HE WON'T LIE TO YOU, I DON'T THINK.
PLEASE, SIR.
OH, WELL THAT'S...
...JUST WHAT I HOPED FOR......
MAKE SURE THEY DON'T SCRATCH YOU.
THEY'RE STILL KITTENS, AFTER ALL.

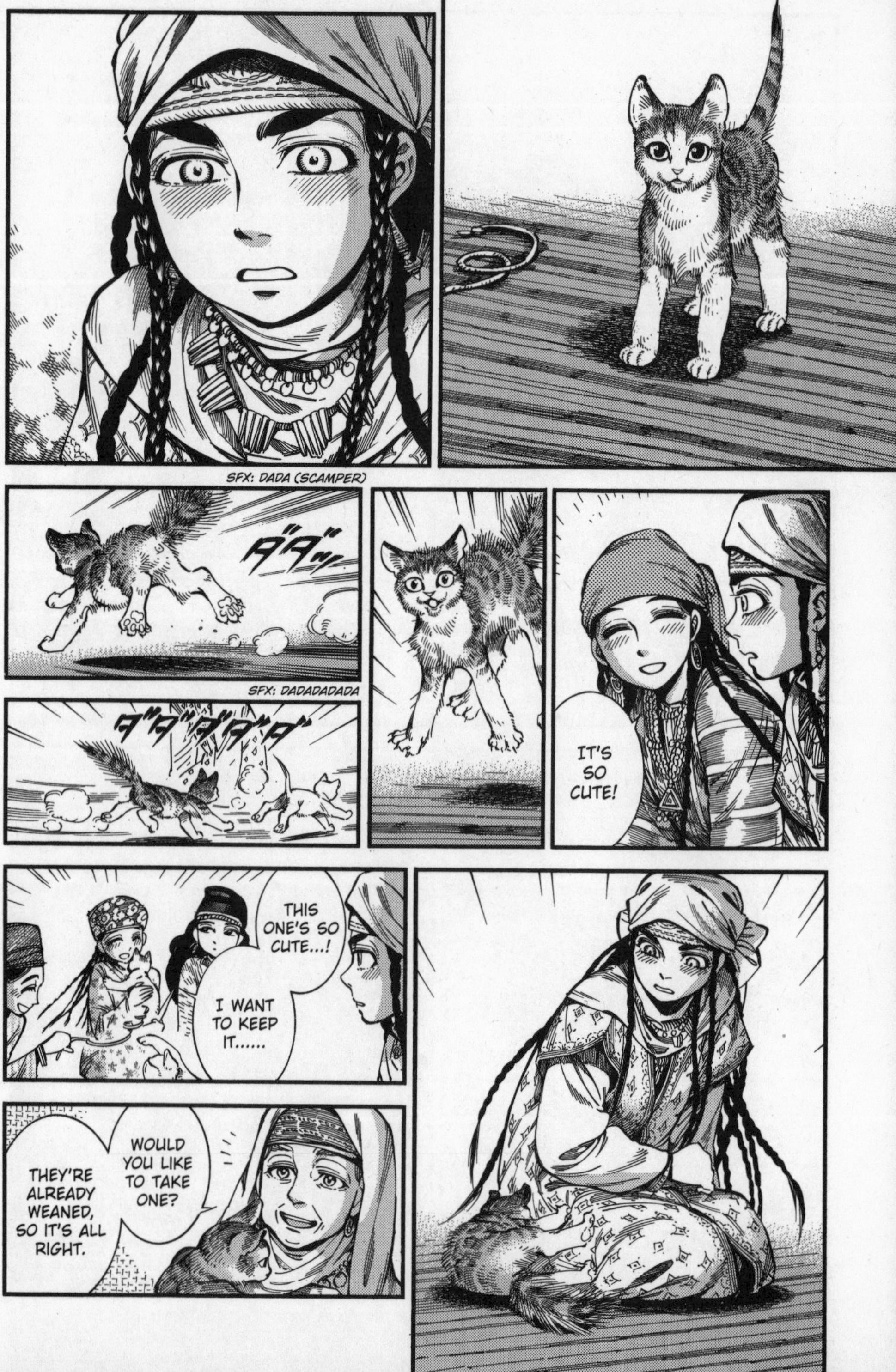
IT'S SO CUTE!
SFX: DADA (SCAMPER)
SFX: DADADADADA
THIS ONE'S SO CUTE...!
I WANT TO KEEP IT......
WOULD YOU LIKE TO TAKE ONE?
THEY'RE ALREADY WEANED, SO IT'S ALL RIGHT.

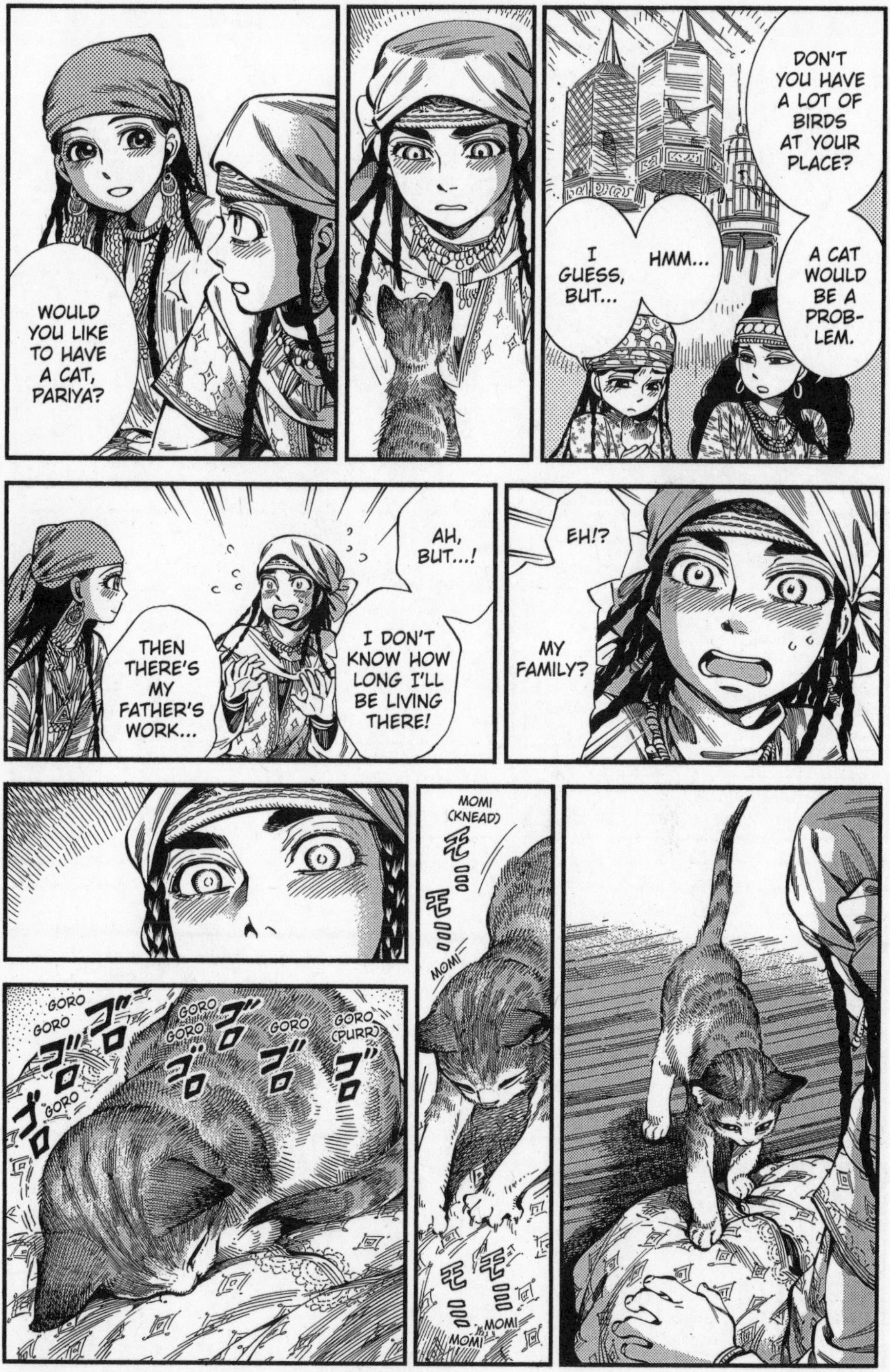
DON'T YOU HAVE A LOT OF BIRDS AT YOUR PLACE?
A CAT WOULD BE A PROBLEM.
HMM...
I GUESS, BUT...
WOULD YOU LIKE TO HAVE A CAT, PARIYA?
EH!?
MY FAMILY?
AH, BUT...!
I DON'T KNOW HOW LONG I'LL BE LIVING THERE!
THEN THERE'S MY FATHER'S WORK...
MOMI (KNEAD)
モミ
モミ
MOMI
モミ
モミ
MOMI
MOMI
GORO (PURR)
ゴロ
GORO
ゴロ
GORO
GORO
ゴロ
ゴロ
GORO
GORO
ゴロ
ゴロ
GORO
ゴロ

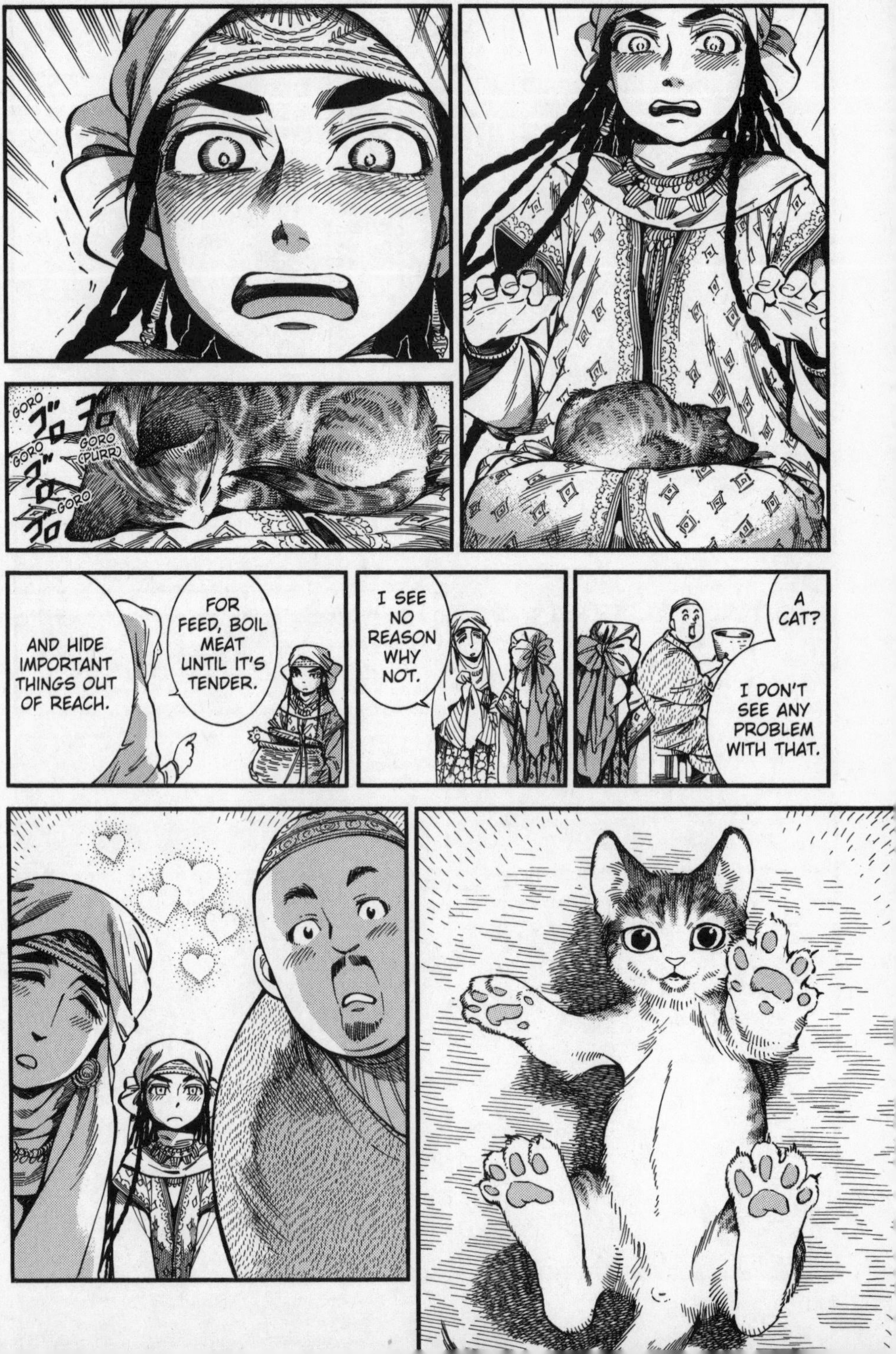
GORO
ゴロ
GORO (PURR)
ゴロ
GORO
ゴロ
GORO
ゴロ
A CAT?
I DON'T SEE ANY PROBLEM WITH THAT.
I SEE NO REASON WHY NOT.
FOR FEED, BOIL MEAT UNTIL IT'S TENDER.
AND HIDE IMPORTANT THINGS OUT OF REACH.

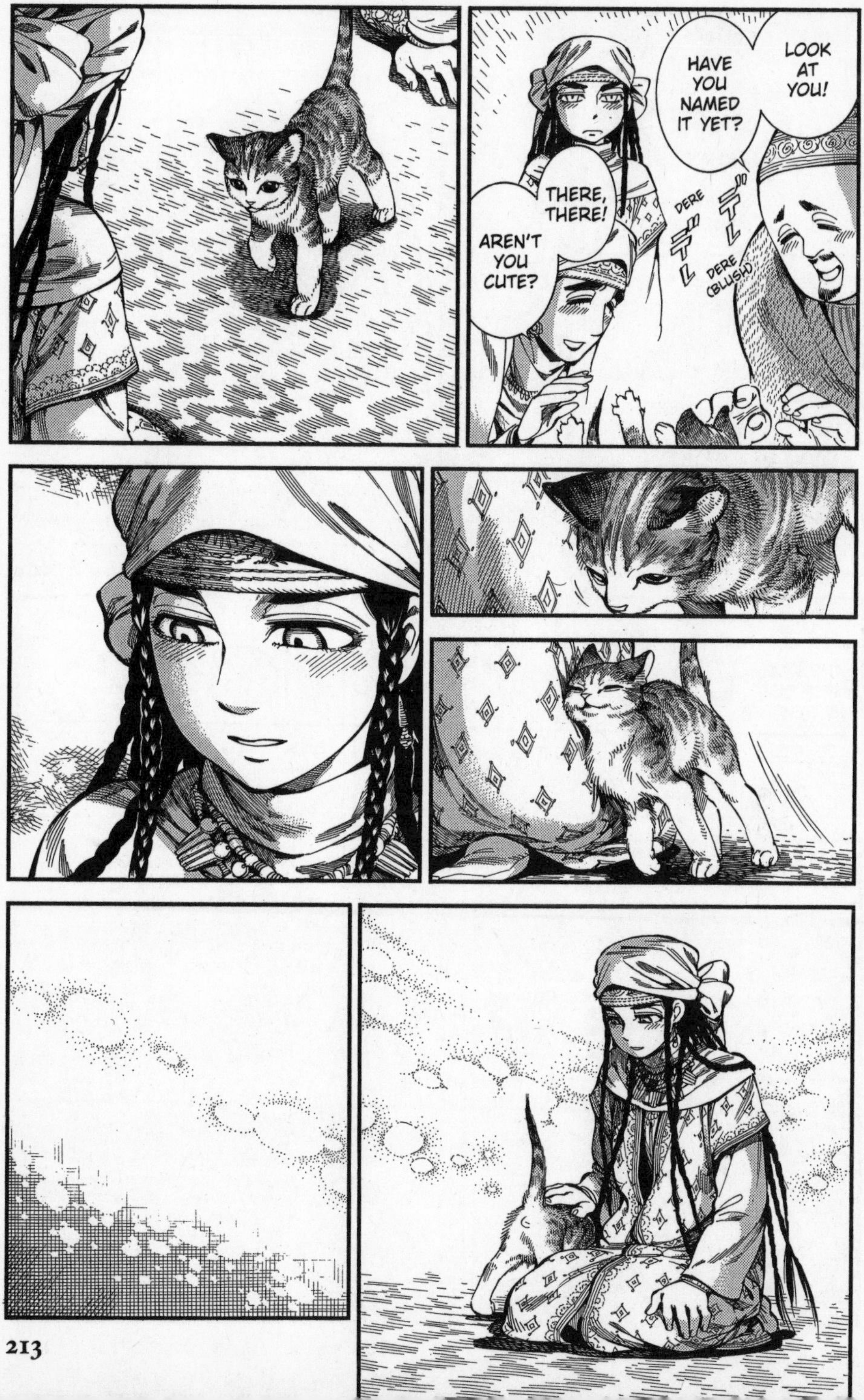
LOOK AT YOU!
HAVE YOU NAMED IT YET?
DERE DERE (BLUSH)
THERE, THERE!
AREN'T YOU CUTE?

THE GANG'S ALL HERE.

I'M SORRY I'M LATE.

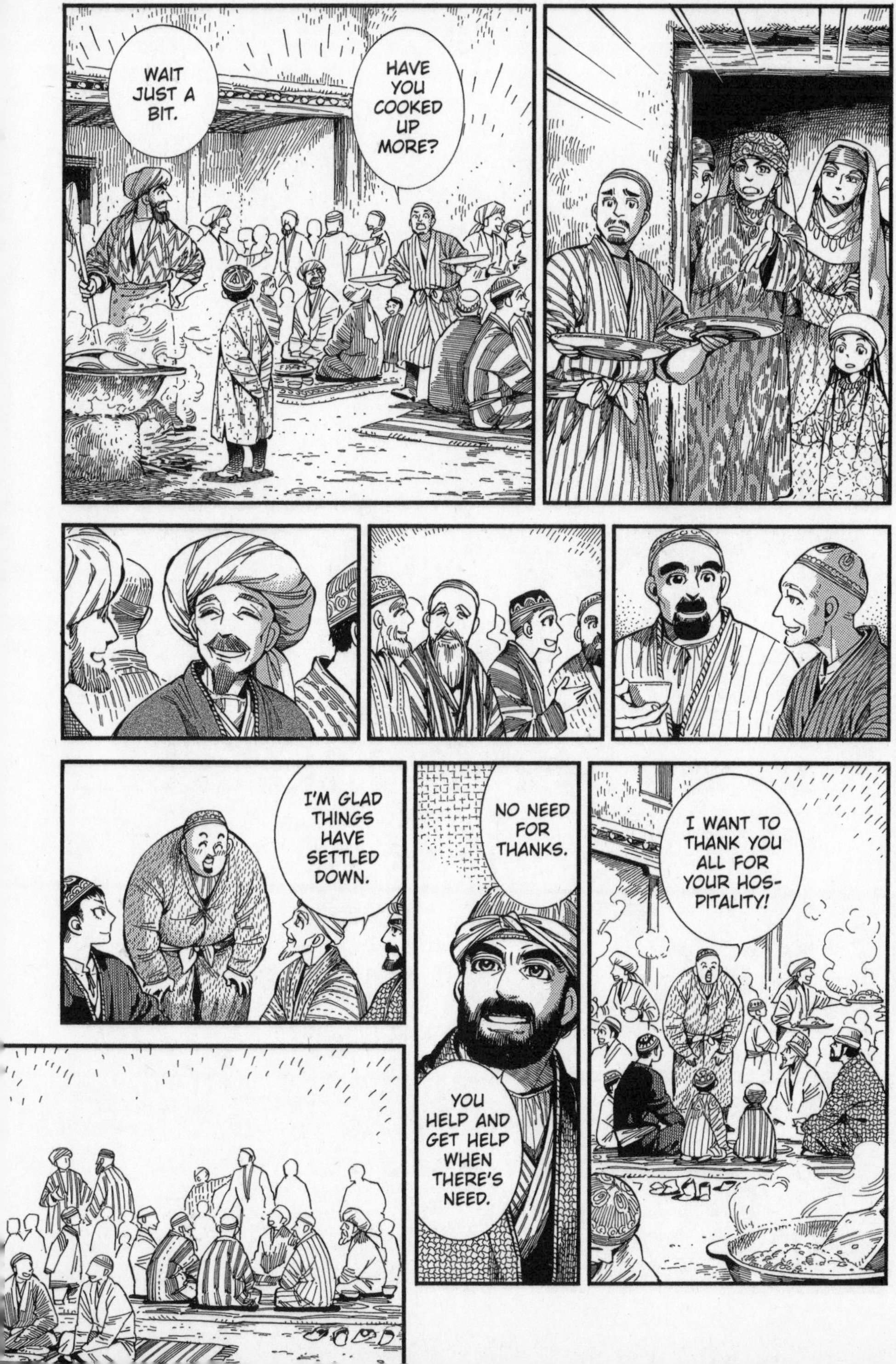
HAVE YOU COOKED UP MORE?
WAIT JUST A BIT.
I WANT TO THANK YOU ALL FOR YOUR HOS-PITALITY!
NO NEED FOR THANKS.
YOU HELP AND GET HELP WHEN THERE'S NEED.
I'M GLAD THINGS HAVE SETTLED DOWN.

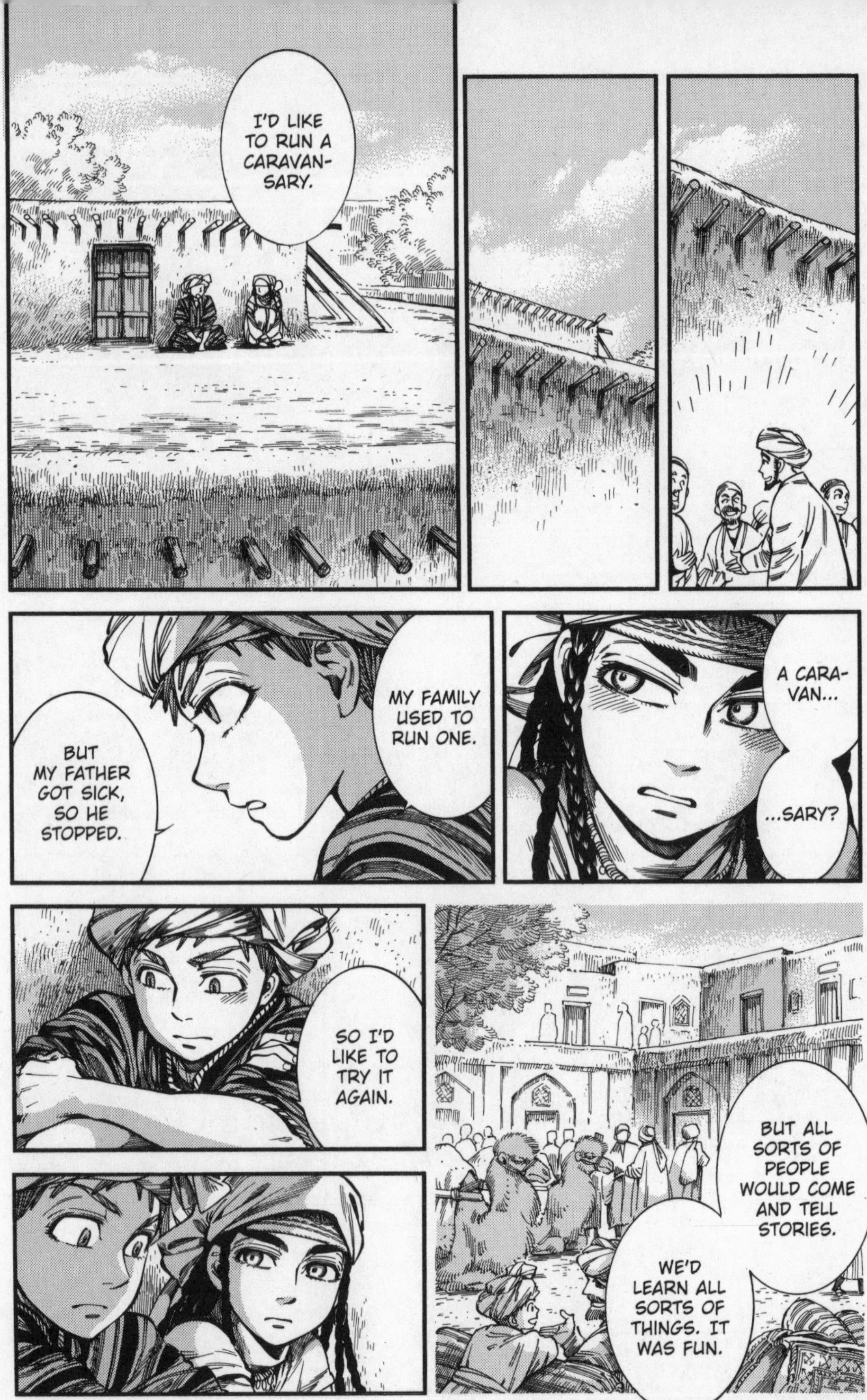
I'D LIKE TO RUN A CARAVAN-SARY.
A CARA-VAN...
...SARY?
MY FAMILY USED TO RUN ONE.
BUT MY FATHER GOT SICK, SO HE STOPPED.
BUT ALL SORTS OF PEOPLE WOULD COME AND TELL STORIES.
WE'D LEARN ALL SORTS OF THINGS. IT WAS FUN.
SO I'D LIKE TO TRY IT AGAIN.

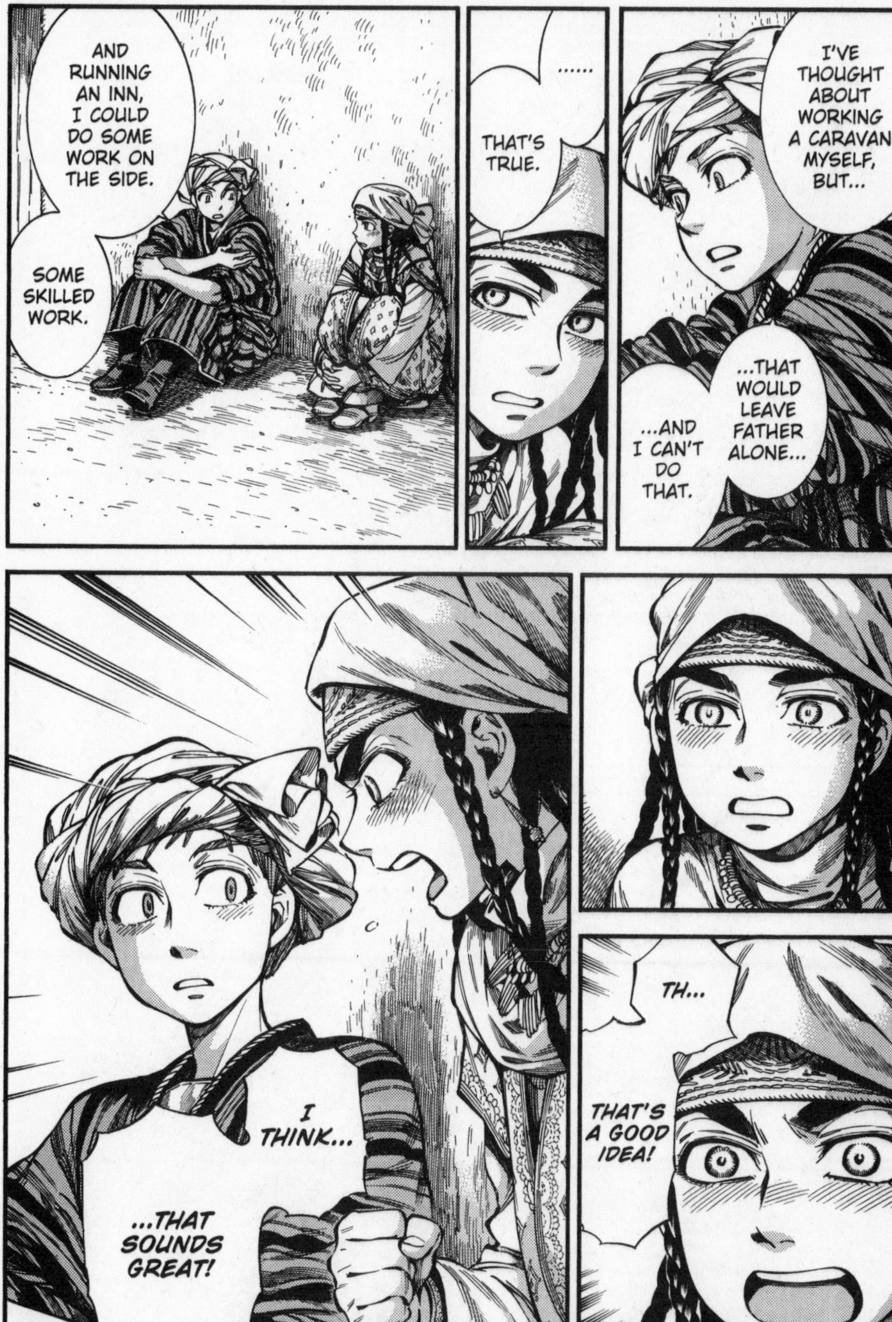
I'VE THOUGHT ABOUT WORKING A CARAVAN MYSELF, BUT...
...THAT WOULD LEAVE FATHER ALONE...
...AND I CAN'T DO THAT.
......
THAT'S TRUE.
AND RUNNING AN INN, I COULD DO SOME WORK ON THE SIDE.
SOME SKILLED WORK.
TH...
THAT'S A GOOD IDEA!
I THINK...
...THAT SOUNDS GREAT!

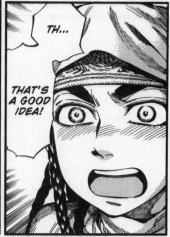

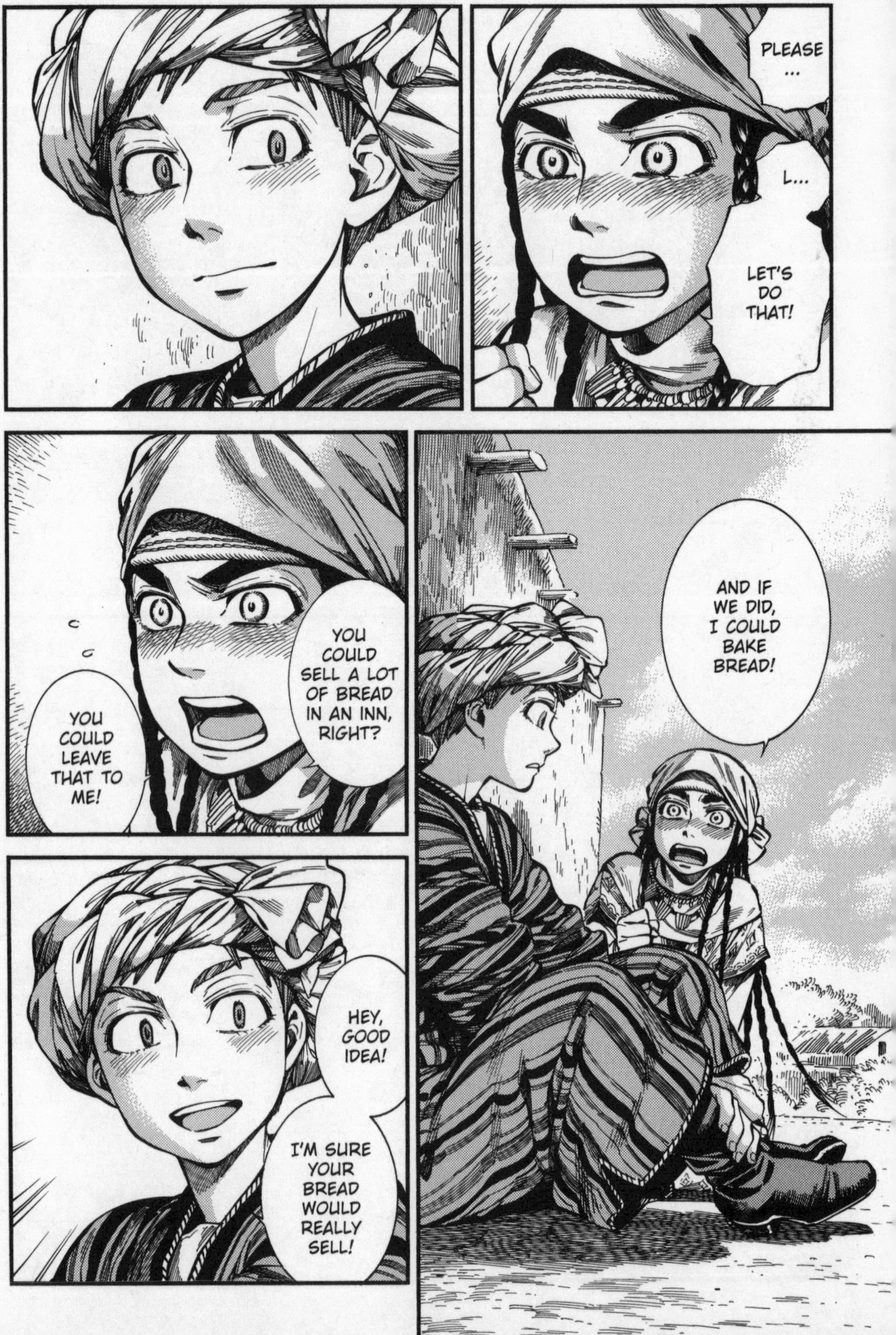
PLEASE ...
I...
LET'S DO THAT!
AND IF WE DID, I COULD BAKE BREAD!
YOU COULD SELL A LOT OF BREAD IN AN INN, RIGHT?
YOU COULD LEAVE THAT TO ME!
HEY, GOOD IDEA!
I'M SURE YOUR BREAD WOULD REALLY SELL!

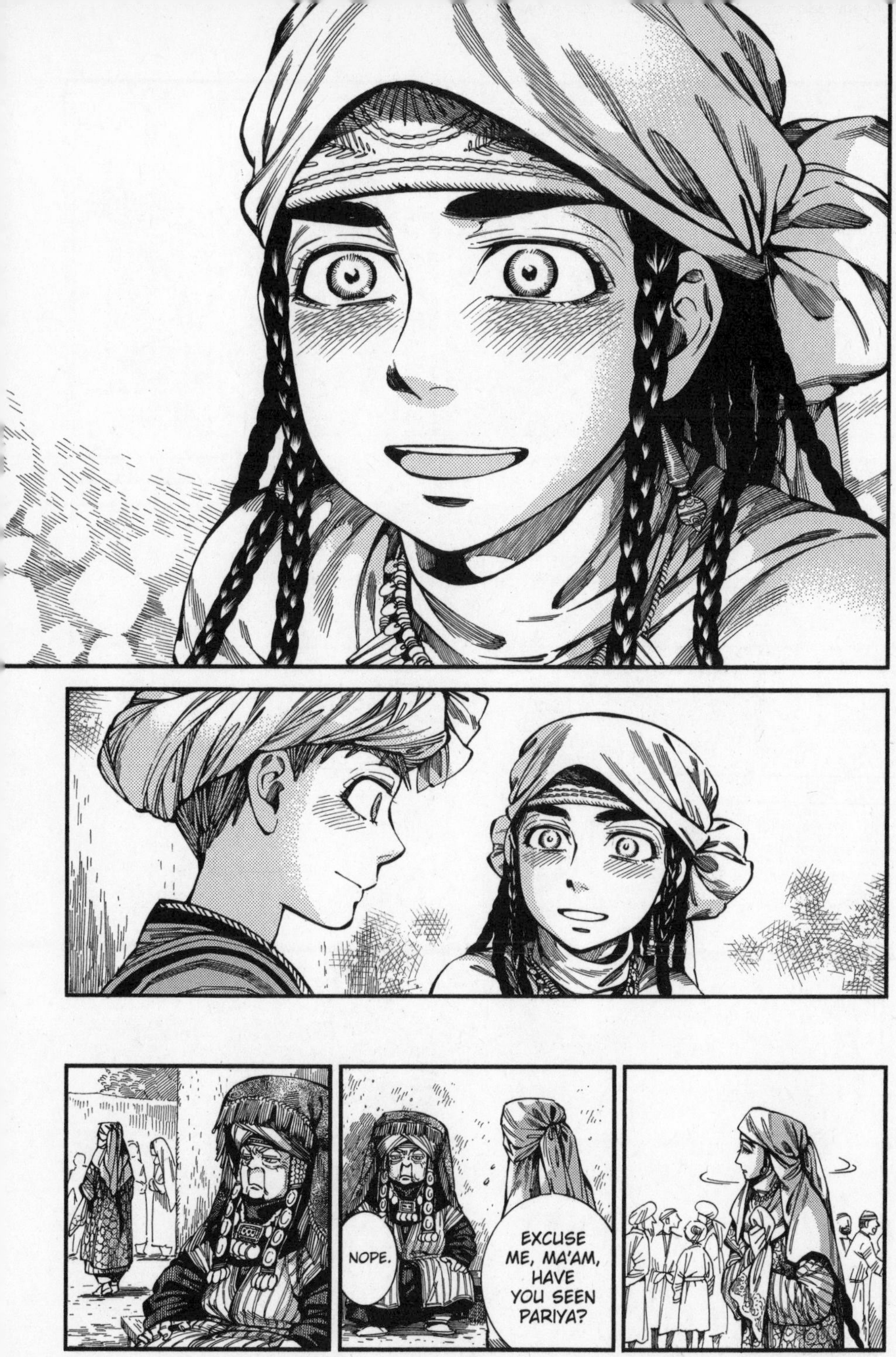
EXCUSE ME, MA'AM, HAVE YOU SEEN PARIYA?
NOPE.

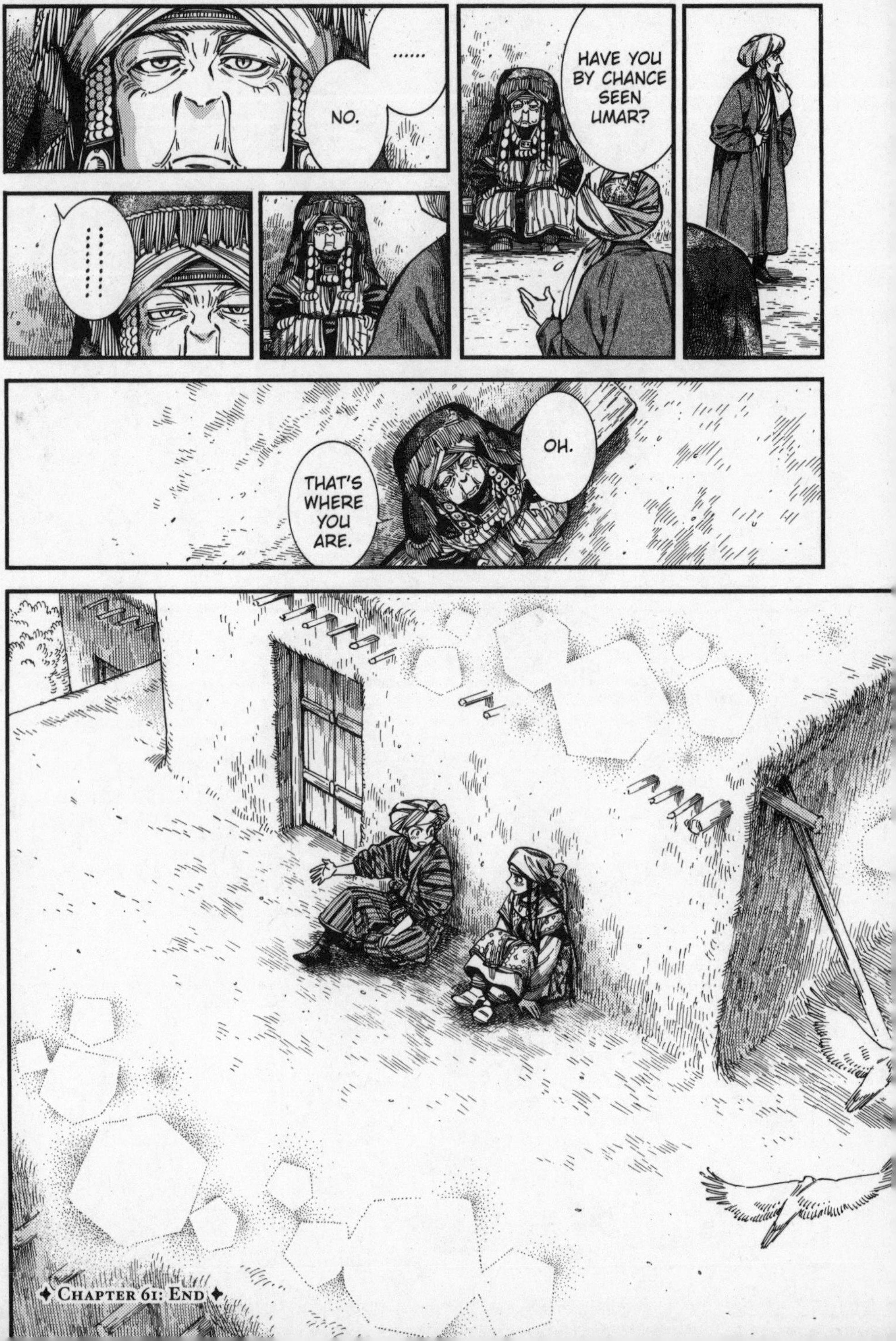
HAVE YOU BY CHANCE SEEN UMAR?
......
NO.
......
OH.
THAT'S WHERE YOU ARE.
✦Chapter 61: End✦